Theoloop

A. SCOTT HOWE

Fourth Revision 2024
Plug-in Creations, Beaverton, Oregon, USA

ISBN: 0-9850765-7-7
ISBN-13: 978-0-9850765-7-3

DEDICATION

Unfortunately, the predictions in *50-year Window to Establish a Space Faring Civilization* are coming true. Pandemics have struck, concerns about energy and climate change are beginning to sap the enthusiasm and priorities of space exploration, and new generations would rather live in worlds of make-believe rather than build a real future. But there is hope! Therefore, this book is dedicated to the few who will heed the warnings and get us safely into a new millennium.

ACKNOWLEDGMENTS

Special thanks go to Ingping Howe, Jerry Jorgenson, and Karen Young for valuable feedback and proofreading. Thanks to Lincoln Hale for his expert views on Coptic Egyptian.

PROLOGUE

It was in the news. 32-year-old Teruo Ninomiya, a local unemployed drifter from Misaki had gotten up before dawn to go fishing. He drove his scooter along remote Route 256 on Sadamisaki Peninsula and rode down to the waterfront at Kushi Port, where a few buildings clustered near a sheltered anchorage.

After parking the scooter on the gravel lot across from Kikuchi liquor store, Teruo walked over to the water's edge and stood on the concrete wall. There was a heavy fog overlaying the smooth, dark liquid so that he could hardly make out the cement wave break looming to his right. Most of the fishing boats had already gone out to sea and would be returning in a few hours with their catches. The salty air smelled of decaying kelp, with a hint of dead fish. He could see no one around.

Retrieving a pole, tackle box, and bucket, Teruo walked past the dark fisheries co-op building and reached the sea wall. Someone was under the flat-roofed, open air market area banging around with a small portable lantern, probably getting one of the stalls ready for the return of the fishing boats. Every coastal town in Japan had a fish market, and the little villages of Ehime Prefecture were no exception.

Teruo turned to the right and switched on a small flashlight to help him find his way down to the beach. Large concrete tetrapods had been piled up to slow down coastal erosion, and he could have hopped along the tops of the massive structures down to the sand but elected to descend the stairway at the end of the sea wall instead. No use taking a chance in the dark.

Teruo longed to light up a cigarette like he used to as a teenager, when he would sit in the dark for hours watching his pole by the light of the moon, listening to the soothing sound of waves crashing on the rocks. But the pandemics from years before had taken many of his friends who had succumbed to respiratory infections and taught him the only way to survive was to have strong lungs. The brief craving passed, and instead Teruo pulled out a tsumayoji, or wooden toothpick, and began chewing on it as he walked.

At the bottom of the stairs was a small beach where tendrils of fog obscured parts of the sandy ground ahead of him. The sand turned to pebbles and small stones that crunched loudly. The water was very calm, almost like that of a lake. Teruo liked this coastline, which was exposed to the Pacific Ocean, but being 'around the corner' from the Seto Inland Sea sometimes meant the sea could be surprisingly calm. The beauty of Kushi was that if stormy waves pounded the coast on the ocean side, all one had to do was to walk a few blocks across the peninsula and the Seto waters were usually a lot calmer.

The pebbles were hard to walk on — every step he took crunched and lost traction, and sometimes uneven larger rounded stones caused him to twist his ankles in unintended ways. Fortunately, the pebbles gave way to rocky outcroppings that afforded a much smoother path. Thousands of fishermen had passed this way over the decades and centuries, but the hard-beaten path still caused one to scramble over uneven jagged formations and slip through undergrowth.

Teruo made his way around the base of a sea cliff, at times having to tenaciously cling to narrow ledges to avoid falling into dark swirling cauldrons below. One stretch of wave-blasted rockface continued on for dozens of meters and would have caused him to turn back had it not been for the uncountable times he had come this way before. Teruo put the small flashlight in his mouth, hooked the bucket in his belt, and tucked the equipment under his arm as he slowly went from foothold to foothold. He felt like the ninja Kirigakure Saizō stealthily climbing a castle wall in the mist. Or Saizō's pal Sarutobi Sasuke. Teruo's mind wandered and was briefly flooded with images of a different Sasuke in the *Naruto* manga series that he loved so much.

Finally, the way opened up a bit and he flashed the light along an uneven expanse of broken tidal rocks. His destination would have been in view then, except for the fog that drifted in off the ocean. Teruo looked out to his left and tried to see the lights of Usuki or Tsukimi towns across the channel in Kyushu, but it was hopeless. Suddenly he thought he saw ghostly shapes drifting out there on the quiet surf, but the impression slipped away, and he turned his attention back to his feet where he had to cross another deep slot in the rock. A cold gust of wind came up and caused him to shiver.

The large boulder that had become his favorite fishing spot was high above waterline over deep water and had a sheltered notch that he could crouch in away from the wind. Sometimes in the past he had built small fires there and roasted fish on a stick. Teruo paused and chewed on the tsumayoji for a while before setting down the bucket and tackle box.

The flashlight briefly shined down into the clear waters and captured movement. Teruo leaned over to get a closer look and almost tumbled in with surprise. Large spidery shapes clung to the growths and rocks underwater and seemed to boil out of a crevice deep below. He got down on his belly and illuminated one of the large spindly creatures moving about near the surface. It had four long legs and what appeared to be several other smaller appendages attached to a round body. Teruo watched as the crustacean worked its way along the seaweed growths and suddenly tipped itself giving him a full view of its backside. The pattern on the body momentarily startled the fisherman. The face of an ancient warrior seemed etched on the shell with deep grooves and bulges — it was a Heikegani! Teruo was surprised that the long-legged bottom-dweller crab would be in such shallow waters.

The Heikegani crustaceans had gotten their name from the historical Battle of Dan-no-ura fought between the Genji and the Heike clans in the year 1185. Again, one of Teruo's favorite manga comic series *Dan-no-ura* came to mind with the famous samurai Minamoto Yoshitsune defeating the Heike warriors and sending them to their death at the bottom of the sea. It was said that the Heikegani crabs were reincarnations of the Heike warriors whose faces were depicted on their shells. For centuries out of reverence, fishermen who accidentally caught one of the creatures would throw them back with a silent prayer for the unfortunate soul.

Teruo got up to set his pole. He wasn't sure if the Heikegani infestation filled this whole area or not — crabs tended to steal fish bait. He set a float with only a couple meters of line to make sure the hook would not drag on the bottom and cast it out into the fog. He spent a few minutes vainly peering into the mist. About this time the calming cigarette would have helped him pass the time, but now he had a different addiction — he pulled out a smartphone and started playing a game.

Minutes later something caught on his line and pulled him back to the real world. Startled, he grabbed the pole and looked up — were those dark shapes looming in the mist? A spooky feeling came over him as he thought about the *Dan-no-ura* manga episode with arrow-riddled ghost ships drifting to shore, their Heike crews missing. Teruo slowly reeled in the line without resistance.

Momentarily the fog parted a little, exposing the placid surface of dark liquid. There was something there! Numerous items like flotsam and jetsam bobbed about and drifted toward his rock. Teruo watched the debris as he tied off the line and carefully set down the pole. There would be no fishing around here with junk in the water that could catch a hook. Most of the items he could identify: a crushed Styrofoam ice chest; plastic bottles; bits of lumber or tree branches, etc. The tides, he thought, must have brought these around the point from the Seto side. Teruo's favorite fishing rock bordered on a crescent-shaped beach that made a good fishing area, but unfortunately caught storm trash if the tides and winds lined up right.

Something else caught his eye just at the edge of visibility. It was a mesh diver's bag, barely keeping buoyancy above the surface. Something was moving there, as if it were alive. Curiously, Teruo dropped down from the rock onto the beach and looked around for something to snag the diver's bag to pull it ashore. It didn't take long to find a length of frayed, weathered nylon rope and a piece of wood with several broken-off branches spiking out in all directions. He untangled the rope, tied it around the wood, and tossed it out past the floating diver's bag. He was a good shot — as he pulled in the rope, the spiky branches caught on and pulled the bag in his direction.

There was more movement around the bag which he couldn't make out, even when he shone his flashlight down from a higher angle. Suddenly his pulling motions became more labored, as if the bag were caught on something, or — something pulling the other way? The fisherman in Teruo pulled even harder, refusing to give up a good catch. The bag grew closer and gradually another line, presumably tied to the bag, emerged from the water, and stretched out taut into the dark fog. There was something much larger out there that the bag was attached to!

As the bag got closer Teruo could see what had flickered in motion — several Heikegani crabs were holding on and seemed to be swarming all over it. What could have attracted the creatures to cause them to behave so — was there bait inside? Suddenly a dark shape loomed out of the mist and caused Teruo to look up. The diver's bag was apparently tied to a small dinghy, and his efforts had brought it closer to shore as well. No one appeared to be on board — it was like a ghost ship, and Teruo imagined ancient arrows protruding from wooden gunwales and decks.

The diver's bag came within reach between two taller stones which Teruo stepped on for better access. As he reached down, it seemed to him that the crustaceans were still reluctant to give up their prize, but finally he was able to shoo them away. Teruo held onto the dinghy rope and lifted the diver's bag out of the water. He half expected to see rotting fish inside but felt several hard objects instead. He quickly opened up the bag to look inside. Four barnacle-crusted misshapen lumps spilled out onto the stone.

Two of the pieces were unknown, but the others he recognized immediately. The detailed historical descriptions meticulously drawn in the *Dan-no-ura* manga pages jumped out at him in real life. They were arrowheads of apparent ancient origin, metallic and partially corroded, but well-preserved as if they had been covered in mud since the day they were made. One was a bulbous kabura-ya, or 'whistling arrow' which was shaped like a turnip (and indeed kabura meant 'turnip-headed' in Japanese). The samurai Yoshitsune would have shot these whistling arrows at the beginning of the battle, to strike fear in the hearts of the Heike warriors. The second piece was a karimata arrowhead, shaped like an inverted vee with the legs pointing forward and the vertex of the vee fitted with 'nakago' tangs meant to bind the arrowhead to a now-missing shaft. The warriors in the Dan-no-ura battle would have mostly used the karimata for hunting large game, but some could have been used to exchange fire with the enemy if the warrior were short of regular narrow arrowheads — a very rare find indeed!

The ancient-looking artifacts and Heikegani crabs gave him the creepy feeling that perhaps the old stories were true — maybe these creatures were reincarnated Heike clansmen loathe to give up their weapons of war. What were these pieces doing out here? The actual location Dan-no-ura wasn't too far away. It was conceivable to Teruo that floating objects from Shimonoseki city, or the Dan-no-ura Bay could have drifted for days and perhaps blown into this cove.

Teruo looked up at the empty dinghy out on the end of the rope. That shouldn't be drifting out in open waters, he thought — it could pose a nautical hazard especially in the fog. He proceeded to pull the little vessel into the shore, intending to pull it up on the beach above high tide line. But the boat never made it that far.

Teruo almost passed out as he saw the bloodied corpse laying prone in the bottom of the skiff. The partially decomposed body was fully clad in scuba gear, its head severed from the body. Teruo cried out as he ran back to the Kushi port area to find the authorities.

A. SCOTT HOWE

CHAPTER 1

A small skiff rested in the sand high above the waterline. The boys rushed over to it and stared transfixed as I slowly walked up. Why would an old, sunbaked boat hold their interest? The mound it sat on was slightly higher than the rest of the beach, so one had to get up next to it in order to see inside. My gaze shifted from my sons' faces as I reached out to grab hold of the bow to steady myself, and I peered over the edge. A set of oars and a tangle of old hemp rope were pushed up against one side, but otherwise the wood plank floor was bare.

"Dad, can we take it out?" Heebs asked.

Hibiki 'Heebs' was the older of the two. The name meant 'echo' and certainly fit the persistent way he would keep nagging for something he wanted. Back in the States, Heebs had access to all sorts of adrenaline toys, including a motorcycle, uncle's jet skis, and grandpa's snowmobiles. It was not an environment where one would foster patience. The sixteen-year-old must have had his eye on the little vessel ever since we arrived at the inn across the street the previous evening. I looked at his face and could see water play written all over it. Entertaining two bored teenagers is not easy. Heebs and Gilly had come with me on a research trip to Japan and I never realized how much time I would spend keeping them out of trouble.

"We have no idea whose boat that is. And besides, breakfast will be ready soon," I said.

Heebs protested and tried to tug at the boat, "Come on Dad, nobody has moved it in years! Look at all the weeds growing up around it."

I knew he was right, but today we didn't have time to go play in the water. We had already loaded our bags into the rental car, with just a few minutes to take a stroll in the sand before the proprietor called us in to eat. It was just a small strip of beach alongside the Keihama Highway on the Satsumasendai River.

"Maybe you could pretend that it floats." I pointed out a gaping hole in the stern that might have rotted through years ago. "Won't go as fast as a jet ski."

"Dad, you promised we could do something fun." Heebs complained, "All we do is drive around and look in dusty old caves."

That was my research, mapping and cataloging artificial tunnels and excavations that might be of historical interest. Classes were out for the summer, so I had taken leave from the Oklahoma State University Department of Surveying Technologies to follow my passion in cave surveying. Unfortunately, it didn't matter how interesting dad's job was, because the teenaged son will always think anything you do is uncool.

"I just have a few more and we can play. I promise we'll go boating later." I apologized.

Gilly had even less attention span than his older brother. The thirteen-year-old ran over to where a concrete wall ended the beach and a landfill parking area had been constructed near a boat anchorage. Minato-cho village supported a small fishing population that caught fresh fish for the local Kagoshima markets. A couple of old men sat on folding chairs, casting right into the river. Something swimming in a large bucket between them flipped around and splashed water onto the cement. Gilly could not resist finding out what sort of creature they had caught.

Guilherme was my only child that went by his Portuguese name, and we called him 'Gilly' from birth. Since my wife was Brazilian Japanese, all of our children had both Japanese and Portuguese names. Gilly was less an adrenaline junkie than he was an explorer. He had no qualms about exploring caves and usually asked to come with me on my travels. If there was some critter, Gilly would figure out a way to catch it and make it into a pet.

Heebs gave up on the boat and watched his brother head toward the men. There was another person near them that could have been a granddaughter. She was cute, perhaps late middle school-age or early high school. I watched the aura about Heebs change into an awkward girl-hungry look, half wolf and half swagger. The excited boyish curiosity that had him running around earlier gave in to more of a macho gait as he wordlessly made his way over to where Gilly poked around at the swimming thing in the bucket.

Until he tripped, that is.

Heebs staggered after stubbing his toe on a large stone and got a horrified expression on his face. He looked up at the girl on the dock and showed relief that she had not seen his embarrassing mistake. Recovering his posture, he continued to cautiously peek around in case someone else had seen him. His eyes focused on me as I grinned at his teenage antics. Heebs pouted and turned away.

Suddenly a voice from behind us called out, "O-kyakusan — dekimashita yo!"

I turned to see the inn proprietor, a sixty something Japanese woman, call out to us from across the road. I didn't know much Japanese, but I knew that meant breakfast was ready.

"Heebs! Gilly! Let's go!" I called out.

Heebs had heard the proprietor too, and reluctantly turned back with a scowl on his face — no romance today. Gilly also started walking over. The girl looked up as well, and seemed to notice Heebs for the first time but the boy already had his back to her. I think I was more entertained than anyone, smiling inside at all the subtle teenage drama.

The breakfast was wonderful, everything you would expect in a small Japanese fishing village. It included pickled vegetables, various sashimi and other raw snails, octopus, and shellfish, but my favorite was the salted broiled fish. My teenagers were picky eaters, so they left all the raw things untouched (or rather passed them along to me). Fortunately, we had plenty of snacks in the car or they would have starved to death.

I paid the bill and the three of us piled into the rental car. Heebs longingly looked out the back window at the girl who was still standing there on the dock. *Oh, my love* — his eyes seemed to say. We followed the Sendai River inland, driving on Keihama Highway 44 along the north bank and worked our way through Satsumasendai Town. Our destination was Kumanojo-cho, a small neighborhood just south of the downtown area. There was a raised bypass road constructed overhead, with dozens of residences nestled around the concrete pilasters. The last time I had been there was over 20 years before, so it took a while to figure out how to get down off the bypass and find a way onto the lower surface streets in the neighborhood. The houses pushed against the side of a mountain, with individual streets snaking around the contours.

"Dad, what are we looking for?" Gilly asked as I backed out of a dead-end street.

What had I seen so long ago? Was it really in this neighborhood? Or was it in neighboring Hiyamizu-cho? I remembered pulling out a lighter and holding that small flame ahead of me as I entered that dark hole.

"There's a complex of tunnels up here somewhere, dating from World War II. It's like a grid underground." I answered.

Gilly's eyes lit up. If there was anything more interesting than a cave, it was a cave used in WWII. "Is this where Nazis hid their gold?" He asked.

Heebs grumpily derided his younger brother, "The Nazis weren't in Japan, dummy!"

"Hahaha — no, the Nazis were in Europe. These tunnels were used by civilians during air raids." I found a stretch of ground wide enough for the car and pulled over to park.

Where Gilly was excited and jumped right out, Heebs moved like molasses. I retrieved the case with the LIDAR drone and strapped it on my back.

"Grab your water bottles — it's hot and we may be walking around a bit till we find the bunkers. Flashlights too!" I didn't bother locking the car and began heading up the road.

Hot indeed! We had only gotten ten meters away before our clothes were drenched with sweat. The cicadas screamed all around us giving a psychological impression of blazing summer heat added to the humidity. We walked up several streets until they ran into the mountain and followed some trails where the roads ended. I looked for telltale signs that I had seen many times before. Underground Japanese military bunkers could be found along the coast, usually at strategic locations like peninsulas or entrances to bays and harbors. The entry was never obvious. An earthen tunnel would go in a few meters and look like a dead end, but just before the termination a second tunnel led off to the side. That too only went in a few meters, and again just before the end a third tunnel would drive deeper into the mountain. In my mind's eye I could see myself exploring the military bunkers on Jogashima at the end of Miura Peninsula, sloshing through knee-deep water in the pitch blackness. The zigzag in the tunnel entrance was to prevent ricochet bullets from penetrating the interior, and also to hide dim lantern and candlelight from anyone passing by outside.

On the other hand, civilian air raid shelters were easy to find. They usually consisted of tunnels dug into a cliff face, such as a vertical earthen wall left over from excavating a road cut through a hill, or steep banks bordering stepped residential lots or rice paddies. The civilian tunnels were almost always near groups of houses where residents could rush to and hide inside quickly. They were so common that I read once someone had catalogued over 119 of them in Satsumasendai town alone and 620 in Kagoshima Prefecture. I could only hope to map a small representative sampling of that before they were blocked off, filled in, or excavated out of existence for the sake of new construction.

I had to keep the boys from running off too far ahead. Even in the humidity they seemed to possess boundless energy. Heebs' lethargic attitude didn't leave him much patience with his old man who trudged up every little rise. Thank goodness we were all wearing shorts, or our pants would be clinging miserably to our legs.

Finally, I came across a flat area surrounded by raised ground. By long experience something told me the thick bushes and jungle along the rear hid more than tall bamboo grass.

"Gilly," I called, "see if you can get through that thicket. What's behind there?"

Gilly rushed in followed by his older brother who didn't want to be outdone. I could hear their progress as dry grass and thin bamboo cracked and snapped under the weight of their footsteps. Having a hunch, I headed sideways to see if I could find an easier trail — farmers often used old bunkers as storerooms so they would have maintained a beaten path to their entrances.

"There's a cave here!" Heebs yelled from somewhere deep behind the foliage.

Gilly's voice called out too, from farther along "I found one!"

Just then I stumbled on a well-worn trail. It was a single track, just barely wide enough for a person to ride a small stand-up tractor carrying a load. I turned in and walked in the direction Heebs and Gilly had called from. Underfoot there were very few patches of raw, exposed dirt, but instead new tufts of grass and weeds partially clogged the path, meaning it was unlikely that it had been used yet this season.

I rounded a patch of thick bamboo grass nearly double my height and there they were — multiple arched openings penetrating the moss-covered earthen wall. Oftentimes the civilian shelters (and even military) were barely high enough to allow one to enter crouched over. A common floor plan had a single entrance that branched off in a Tee junction, with twin tunnels opening up tall enough to stand erect penetrating the mountain 10-20 meters deep. But these were large enough to drive in with a 'Keijidosha', the tiny automobiles found on Japanese streets. As I approached the gaping mouth of the closest tunnel, I imagined one of those little 'kei' toy trucks, with a motorcycle-sized motor, backing in and still giving enough room for the driver to squeeze past and unload the cargo. There were no Tee intersections here, but the tunnel went straight back into the darkness.

The boys could not be seen, meaning they had probably switched on their flashlights and gone inside to explore. As I suspected, the first tunnel was mostly clogged with stacks of old equipment, furniture, and piles of used lumber. Some local farmer had adopted the cave as a free overhead roof to store things. I shuffled past the pile, switched on my light, and saw that the tunnel opened up wide only 4-5 meters in. I could hear footfalls and muffled voices from the dark cavern as the boys moved around inside. Just a few more steps told me that this set of tunnels was a rare find, probably consisting of enough volume to house the entire neighborhood population during wartime bombing raids.

Some twenty or thirty meters on and the tunnel ran into a transverse corridor. The entire complex appeared to consist of multiple parallel tunnels penetrating the cliff face and connected together at the back end by the cross-passage. How many parallel tunnels were there? Two swaying points of light approached from the side as Heebs and Gilly came back from their quick exploration.

"I counted at least five tunnels, but some of them were flooded so we didn't go there." Heebs offered.

Gilly added, "Yeah most of them are blocked so we couldn't get out from another hole."

"Okay great. See I told you — aren't we having fun now?" I searched Heebs' face and saw excitement registered there.

It was time to break out the LIDAR mapper drone. I walked just a few meters along the rear passage to the second parallel tunnel and could see a small circle of light where the arched opening let in natural illumination from the dense jungle outside. As I moved toward that exit, Gilly excitedly rushed past and shone his light on a section of wall. Hundreds of small dark patches could be seen dotting the surface.

"Look Dad, what kind of bug is this?" He asked.

As I got closer, I could see oval bodies with dozens of legs. They weren't centipedes, but almost appeared to be large sowbug 'rolly-polly' insects crossed with daddy long-leg spiders. It was sort of creepy, and the presence of such might have discouraged the faint of heart from entering.

I explained, "That's a form of 'funamushi' that lives in caves."

There was a short pause as Gilly reflected for a bit, then he said, "But these don't look like funamushi. The ones I know scurry into hiding on the rocks down on the seashore when someone gets close."

"Well, maybe these are mesmerized by your light," I began, "remember the ones by the seashore have smaller legs. Maybe these long-leg versions can't run very fast."

Heebs walked up and the boys started gently poking at the bugs to prod them into scurrying away. I was thinking *no thanks* — the insects covered the ceiling, and it was not hard to imagine them dropping down on you en masse. They were harmless but it was a creepy thought. I continued to the cave entrance and removed the drone case from my shoulders while looking for a smooth, flat section of tunnel floor to set up the laptop. The drone was easy to deploy just by unfolding rotor arms and locking them in place. The unit was turnkey, all set up to fly as soon as the power was switched on. However, it took a few minutes to make sure the various imagers and spectrometers were feeding into the live telemetry stream.

"Okay boys, I'm ready to fly!" I called out.

Heebs and Gilly emerged from the tunnel and watched the little aircraft rise up and hover. My laptop control panel had several screens to track the data, including a point cloud visualizer that painted an accurate three-dimensional model of the tunnel geometry as the data came in. I let the six-rotor flying instrument platform enter the cave in autonomous mode, meaning all I had to do was to sit back and wait for the little machine to come back out and tell me it was finished. The autonomous navigation worked on the right-hand rule, which was to follow the right wall wherever it led, unless the wall looped back on itself, whereupon it would automatically switch walls. The little aircraft also knew when it approached a tunnel mouth and was smart enough not to go outside and try to map the whole world.

I watched the 3D point cloud tunnel model slowly materialize on the screen — back and forth the machine went painting the walls with LIDAR laser beams, capturing parallel tunnels and cross-passages. The beams bounced back to a range finder, which registered the distance, angle of elevation, and bearing of the little dot, becoming part of a mosaic of information that together mapped a 3D tunnel wall. I sensed the boys standing behind me at first, but soon boredom must have gotten the best of them, and they wandered off to entertain themselves in the jungle.

"Watch out for mamushi vipers — they're probably all over the place out there!" I called out.

As the mapping progressed my attention began to wander as well. If some problem popped up the system would warn me, so I gradually began to nod off in the humid heat.

I must have fallen totally asleep because all of a sudden, some alarms blared and brought me back to full wakefulness. At first, I was confused — where was I? My eyes darted around, taking in the jungle scene and gaping tunnel until everything came back to me. I quickly looked over the laptop controls for warning lights, until it dawned on me that the alarm sound didn't match anything on the machine — it was my smartphone ringing.

"Hello, this is Tim Hughes," I began as soon as I could fumble the little unit out of my pocket.

The person on the other end was a woman, *"I'm being stalked! They're following me."* she said in a hushed voice.

"Rikochan, is that you?" I addressed the caller.

"Yes, Dad, I think I'm in trouble." She replied in a frantic tone.

Kariko 'Rikochan' was my eldest and happened to be doing a post doc in genetic engineering at Kitakyushu University. The name 'Kariko' was a Japanized version of Calico, a ghost town located in Yermo in the California Mojave Desert. Calico town itself was an open-air museum showcasing the history of silver mining. I had spent my youth in the hills behind the town, exploring miles of tunnels from the old 19th and 20th century silver mines. My whole career in surveying came out of that experience, and later on I had nostalgically made LIDAR maps of the bigger mines like Bismarck, Silver King (the 'mother lode'), and Odessa 'stars & stripes' where the entire top of a mountain had been hollowed out to form a vast cavern. Ironically, Rikochan never showed much interest in exploring the mines or town, unless my college-aged son Masamune brought his friends along who happened to be her age.

"Where are you, sweetheart?" I asked.

Her faint voice came back broken, as if the phone had a bad connection, *'I'm on the Shinkansen Mizuho, heading for Kagoshima. I'll arrive in two hours."*

The Shinkansen was the famous 'bullet train' that wasn't so fast anymore, having been superseded by the superconducting linear motor trains and vacuum tunnels. The first thing that came to my mind was that there was a Shinkansen station in Satsumasendai, within walking distance from the very tunnels we were exploring. Her train would pass through Sendai before going all the way to Kagoshima — maybe we could go get her. But then I remembered that the 'Mizuho' train was an express and wouldn't even stop in Sendai. We'd have to drive to Kagoshima.

"Are you safe? Stay with the crowd honey, we're coming to get you." I consoled, then turned around and called out for the boys to get ready to go.

I had no sooner hung up when the phone rang again — it was my wife Ines Hughes, who was back in Oklahoma.

"How are my men doing? Having fun?" She asked.

I didn't know what to say. We were having fun until just a moment ago. Ines had a knack for getting over-excited about non-issues, so I was hesitant to say anything about Rikochan until I knew more about what was going on.

"We're having lots of fun, honey." I replied.

"Are the boys liking it? Can I talk to them?" She wondered.

We were in the middle of the bushes, scattered everywhere, so I stalled, "Honey, they're climbing all over the mountain."

"Okay, miss my Sweetheart. I'll send you an email." Ines replied and made a kissing noise on the phone.

Thankfully, I kissed her back and we hung up. Luckily, the LIDAR drone emerged from the tunnel just then, having finished the mapping job. I didn't even have a chance to inspect the 3D model before closing the laptop and folding up the little aircraft. With everything buttoned up in the case, I shouldered the equipment and got on the trail leading back to the rental car. A giggling Heebs and Gilly fell into step behind me, having secreted themselves out of the thicket. I explained what was happening as we hopped into the vehicle.

The GPS navigator took us south to the Satsumasendai-Miyako interchange which got us on the Kagoshima-bound expressway. Anger welled up inside me. My first gut reaction was to drive straight for the station, try to find a parking spot nearby, and then confront whoever was threatening my little girl. I was a pretty big guy, and still remembered some moves from back when I was in the US Marine Corps. I imagined myself punching some unwanted suitor and rescuing her out of harm's way. But she had mentioned 'they', meaning more than one stalker. A quick scenario went through my head where I fought off multiple ninjas and left them all passed out on the pavement — even Heebs and Gilly delivering final karate chop blows. A flabby retired marine and a couple of scrawny teenagers, vs the yakuza mafia? No, no we had to get help.

"Heebs, see if you can find a police box at the Kagoshima-chuo station." I peeked back at him through the rear-view mirror.

"Who is following her?" Gilly asked from the passenger seat.

"I'm not sure — she sounded upset though." I replied, "Give her a call and see what she wants us to do."

If Rikochan was in trouble, we had just under two hours to figure out how to get her away from the train station and avoid any followers. Both Heebs and Gilly got on their burner rental smartphones and started doing a little research as I drove us past the Kushikino coastline and through Hioki in the mountains.

Gilly put his device in speakerphone mode. *There might be five or six of them,"* Kariko said, *"they look like hired thugs."*

Alarm bells went off in my head. "What did you get yourself into? We're going to get the police."

"No! Don't get the cops involved!" Kariko's voice came firmly from the speaker, *"I found Professor Hosogawa dead . . ."*

Rikochan's voice broke with emotion. I tried consoling her, but nothing came out for a long while. Finally, she apparently composed herself on the other end and I could tell she was crying.

"I'll fill you in later, Dad. Just get me away from these guys and leave the police out of it — don't know who I can trust." And she hung up.

I was getting angrier by the moment. Who did they think they were, harassing my baby like that? Then I started to think more clearly. Apparently, the stalkers were watching her, and she knew it. She was safe as long as she stayed in the crowd. So how could we lose the tail? Frantically, as I mindlessly drove the expressway, I went over what little I knew about Kagoshima. Suddenly I had an idea.

"Heebs, you remember the game you used to play on the Hong Kong MTR subway?" I gave a snarky grin in the rear-view mirror.

Heebs only thought a few seconds before his reply, "You mean metrospy?"

"Yes, that's it. Now Kagoshima doesn't have a subway system but just a couple of tram lines. Look it up — you only have two lines that run on surface streets with all the other vehicular traffic." I explained, "Between Takamibaba and Kagoshima-ekimae the two lines run together. If you time it right, you can switch directions before anyone can keep up."

"Haha yes!" Heebs smiled.

"You don't have multiple underground exits, so you might have to run out on the surface streets a little and double back. You're going to have to run like you've never run before, with your sister in tow." I said — we were counting on the Kitakyushu thugs being just as unfamiliar with Kagoshima as we were.

Heebs was busy pouring over various maps and satellite views on his smartphone. We were soon approaching Kagoshima interchange, so I quickly laid out a strategy. As soon as we went through the toll booth, I set the GPS navigation to take us by Kagoshima-chuo station, where the Shinkansen train would pull in — we had a little less than an hour to set things up.

Fifty minutes later I was parked illegally with my hazard lights blinking, in front of the Amu Plaza Kagoshima shopping complex which joined onto the Shinkansen station. I had ear buds in as Heebs described everything that was happening over the phone. We had called Rikochan so she knew what the plans were — in fact, she had had to open up her wheeled travel case on the train and swap high-heels for tennis shoes. Heebs had purchased two all-day tram passes and waited at the exit.

"I see her coming." He suddenly said.

I tried to picture my son with his 'tactical' earphones on. They were a full head gear that wrapped over the top of his head, but connected wirelessly to smartphones — he brought them everywhere and didn't have to worry whether they would fall off during rigorous activity. Since I was behind the buildings, I couldn't see the train pull in, so I waited patiently.

"I see some guys following her. Dad, I don't think you want to mess with these guys." Heebs reported "There are only three that I can see — they must have some strategy they're working on."

In my mind I could imagine the gears turning in Heebs' head as he reasoned out metrospy strike and counterstrike.

He had played the game for years with his friends who had all gotten so good I could never keep up. The Kitakyushu ruffians knew Rikochan, but certainly didn't know any of us. Heebs kept his distance and Rikochan knew not to approach him but just follow. In advance we had designated a column just outside a 'konbini' newspaper stand where Rikochan was to park her wheeled travel bag, purse, and whatever other item she didn't carry on her person, then she was to head over to the stand and purchase some small item. Gilly, who was waiting off to the side, would then tow those things away when the thugs were distracted with their attention on Rikochan.

I watched the clock as I sat in the car, occasionally looking around to make sure no one was upset about my parking spot. Unfortunately, at one point I could see a policeman walking in my direction. He came up to the driver's side window and knocked on the glass. I opened the window and heard him say, "Koko wa chūsha kinshi desu yo."

I replied in English, "Oh sorry, I'm just waiting for my son."

With perfect timing, Gilly appeared at the mall entrance and towed his load over to where I waited.

"See look — he's here!" I indicated the boy.

The 'omawari' police officer waited until Gilly and I loaded up Rikochan's belongings and saluted to us as we drove away. Somewhere inside, Rikochan and Heebs were running around trying to ditch pursuers.

Gilly and I immediately set the GPS and drove a few kilometers along crowded city streets to a prearranged parking spot (also illegal) near Sakurajima-sanbashi dori tram station. We rolled the windows down and could smell the scent of yakitori coming from somewhere — my stomach growled since we had not eaten since the inn that morning. If all went according to plan, Rikochan and Heebs would follow a similar route we followed, but with many double-backs, loops, and last second boardings to throw off the pursuers.

Heebs continued to report their progress in real time over the phone. Apparently, the thugs soon tired of the on again off again routine and had two of their men obtain a car from somewhere that would allow them to tail more easily without having to bring all their boys along at every switch, which undoubtedly left stragglers behind. The game of cat and mouse was on, and Heebs took their new approach in stride by running up the wrong way on one-way streets to loop back around as the car tried to head them off.

It almost came as a surprise when I saw the two run into our alley, with no one in pursuit. They hopped into the now-crowded rental car, and I sped away down toward the docks. We had already bought a ticket for the Sakurajima ferry, so I eased the vehicle into the lineup as Rikochan and Heebs exited the vehicle and took the pedestrian route to the boarding area. As far as we could tell we had lost the ruffians, but just in case they wizened up we still didn't want them to figure out how many people were in our party.

Though the adrenaline was still coursing through my veins, we finally had a few minutes to relax. I looked out and could see blue water and blue sky, so peaceful and serene as if all my cares were insignificant. I set my gaze across the bay toward the cone-shaped mountain that had a column of ashes towering up into the sky. At the waterline, it was possible to see a line of structures all along the shore — a cityscape crouching at the feet of a slumbering monster.

"Is that a volcano?" Gilly asked from the passenger seat.

"Yep, that's Sakurajima, an active volcano." I replied.

I started to notice the cars around me all had a thin layer of dust on them. Now that I thought about it, everything — buildings, windows, signs — all seemed a little dusty.

"They say that in Kagoshima, everyone has a garbage day and an ash pickup day. They sweep up the ashes that Sakurajima constantly drops on the whole town." I smiled and looked down at Gilly.

"What about lava day?" Gilly looked at me wide-eyed.

Hmm, never thought of that before. "Sakurajima erupts and spews out ash and rocks. Some ash almost buried a shrine once. I don't recall if anyone has ever seen lava come out."

"That's so cool!" He exclaimed, then changed the subject, "Is that the ferry?"

A huge vessel was approaching, and we could see it maneuvering to line up the ramp.

"Yep, there she is."

A few minutes later we could see cars and trucks driving down the ramp and heading into town. The ferry was large, but I was still amazed at how many vehicles could fit into its belly — they kept coming and coming. Finally, there was a gap, and we could see vehicles driving the other way heading up the ramp. Soon the line of cars we were in started to move.

It was at that point that I saw several men walking up and down the lines of waiting vehicles, peering in the windows. I stared straight ahead and froze as I sensed one man right outside my window, likely giving our vehicle a quick visual search for his quarry. As the man moved on to the car in front of me, I dared to look at his face as he peered in the windows. I'll never forget those cold eyes and beard, rare among the Japanese. He was large, middle-aged and had on a suit, but the necktie was loosened giving him a disheveled look. He was not someone I would have wanted to meet on a dark deserted street. I only hoped that Kariko and Heebs had enough sense to stay low.

It wasn't long before it was our turn to drive up the ramp. The workers directed us in an orderly way, obviously packing in the vehicles by weight, making sure trucks and buses were lined up down the middle and the smaller cars distributed around the outer edges. Our car ended up right against the rail so I could look through gaps in the sidewall down into the water.

We waited in the car until the ferry started moving. Gilly and I got out and felt the swaying motion of waves and vibrations of the engines. The air smelled of diesel exhaust and oil. I followed Gilly over to one of the gaps and looked down at the water, where small bits of trash floated between the hull and the dock. As the vessel moved away, I noticed a group of men on the sea wall gathered around a vehicle with the doors all wide open. They were about 50 meters away. One of the men had his back turned and was shouting at the others. He waved his arms and violently threw something down on the ground. There was an ominous feel about that group. I could almost see them peeling off their jackets and tank top undershirts to reveal tattoos of dragons etched into their backs. As the boat moved away the man throwing the tantrum turned to look our way. Involuntarily I flinched but knew he would have no reason to recognize us. As the distance between us increased, I could barely make out those cold eyes and beard, left behind in Kagoshima.

CHAPTER 2

I stood there with Guilherme 'Gilly' watching the Kagoshima ferry terminal recede in the distance. The whole waterfront came into view, and we could no longer see Rikochan's pursuers. What in the world would they want my daughter for?

"Let's go upstairs, Dad." Gilly implored.

I snapped out of my thoughts and looked over toward Sakurajima — surprisingly we were almost there. "Gilly the ride is only 15 minutes long. I doubt if they even have a snack bar."

We headed for the stairs anyway, with the intent to go fetch the older two. Ferries usually have a vehicle deck topped by a passenger lounge. On longer trips the passenger deck might include concessions or even a small cafeteria. We opened the heavy watertight door at the vehicle level and were about to ascend the steps when we saw Rikochan and Hibiki 'Heebs' coming down to meet us, their footsteps echoing off the metal walls. Something I noticed before seemed a little odd — Rikochan was tightly guarding a large envelope under her arm. Only a half hour earlier I had seen her running with the envelope toward our car in the alleyway. During her escape with Heebs, she was supposed to have shed anything that would hamper a quick dash or slow her down. Of all the items she had with her, why would she have chosen that envelope to hand-carry during a chase? I would have thought, if anything, she might have given priority to her purse or phone. Nevertheless, as we all started walking back to the car, the relief of ditching the stalkers caused me to put it out of mind.

"Did you see them standing on the dock?" Heebs animatedly observed.

Rikochan also seemed happy, "It worked! Thank you so much, guys!"

I wasn't so sure. Once you got mixed up with people like that somehow, they always had ways of finding you.

"Did they see you at all?" I interjected, "Remember these ferries run every 15 minutes — we may only have a 15-minute lead."

"No, I think we're good. Both of us ducked down in the passenger boarding area — thanks to Heebs' quick thinking — when those goons started snooping around. We had a pretty good hiding spot." Rikochan noted.

Heebs added, "After we got on the boat, we found a good spot to spy on them. There's no way they could have seen us."

"Well, let's try to get away from here as fast as we can anyway." I turned to Rikochan just as we started piling into the rental car, "Young lady, why don't you tell us what this is all about?"

As I sat down, I noticed that most of the other drivers had already started up their engines, and probably had not exited their vehicles at all during the short trip. The few passengers who had gotten out were straggling back, and it was apparent that the vessel was already maneuvering to line up with the Sakurajima ramp.

There were a couple of caves I wanted to check out in the Miyazaki area — a good place to hole up for a while. I set the GPS for the small town of Nichinan, which was a little over two hours away. The fastest route went along the south side of Sakurajima, but any pursuers would know the south side is quicker, so it would probably be better to take a bit of a zigzag approach. It was already 1pm and we were getting hungry. Maybe lunch somewhere around the north side? As the vehicles began exiting the boat, I drove past the main highway and did several turns and double-backs to lose anyone we may not have noticed, and set our course onto Highway 26, the 'Sakurajima-minato-kurogami' Route heading north.

As we drove, Rikochan began to fill us in on what she knew. Kariko 'Rikochan' was very intelligent, having recently gotten her doctorate in genetic engineering. She had decided to do a post doc program at Kitakyushu University Graduate School of Environmental Engineering, thinking that a small, well-funded city college might give her some good experience. Wearing glasses, she came across as a smart nerd. She was a little on the plump side but was in fairly good shape, often enjoying her passion of mountain biking. Where Heebs, Gilly, and even my college student son Masamune enjoyed rock music, Rikochan had a wider range of genre tastes that included classic and foreign music. Her favorite were the classical pop tenor artists that could sometimes bring tears to her eyes with their passionate voices.

She looked at me sideways from the passenger seat and tentatively began, "There's a person from another department who was interested in the genetic engineering of microbes to eat up oil spills."

"That's interesting." I replied.

There was a long pause, and I realized she was quietly crying. I looked over and saw her huddled against the door, twitching with occasional shudders as she sobbed.

"It's okay Honey, what happened?" I consoled.

"Professor Hosogawa," in fits and starts between sobs Rikochan continued, "is dead."

"Dead! You poor darling, what you must have been going through," I began, "Was he elderly?"

I imagined an old Japanese man on his death bed, with post docs and graduate students standing around hearing his last words.

Rikochan looked up at me with a brief flash of frustration on her face, "She! It's a 'she', and the professor was only 35. She was killed! And I'm the one who found her body. People around me are dying!"

What the hell! Rikochan turned away and resumed her sobbing. I heard commotion in the back seat — Heebs and Gilly leaned forward as if caught up with some need for gory sensationalism. I didn't know what to say.

A thought came to my mind, "So, you think maybe those thugs might have done it, and they're after you too, for some reason?"

Rikochan went quiet. I had hit upon something and knew she hadn't told us everything yet. I looked around at the neighborhood we were driving through and remembered seeing concrete shelters back in the day, with huge lava rocks piled on top, as if it were a common occurrence for big boulders to fall from the sky around here. We had been driving for about fifteen minutes and I didn't see any of that now. As we passed a little neighborhood called Futamata and rounded a bend, there appeared a cluster of businesses. I thought this area might be a good spot to stop for lunch and pulled into a little bakery-cafe. We parked off on a side street and the four of us went and ordered sandwiches, Japanese style. Rikochan eased out of her dark mood and even began joking with her brothers again as they ate.

We only took a half hour and hit the road again. Rikochan, in a better mood though still somber, began to talk a little more freely.

"I didn't really know her that well. We had met three or four times to look at her ideas for a new research proposal and that was about it. But Hirayuki knew her very well." Her voice caught and she paused, fighting back tears.

"Hirayuki — isn't that your anthropologist neighbor?" I asked.

Heebs piped up from the back seat, "Doei-san, he's your boyfriend, right?"

I glanced over at Rikochan and detected a mix of emotions, almost like she was embarrassed but also grief-stricken.

"They were both transhumanists, and apparently met occasionally with a group." She explained.

Curious, I wondered, "What is a transhumanist? Seems like I've heard the term before."

"I don't understand it very well, but apparently a transhumanist is someone who believes the human individual can be enhanced with greater capabilities. There are various beliefs, such as those benign religious types who think technology and progression into a next life get us closer to God, or there are also the extreme technical folks who are convinced humans can be enhanced using technology and will eventually merge with computers and AI." Rikochan eased out of her grief for an instant, "Dad, have you ever heard of a wormhole? Or 'closed timelike curve'?"

"Isn't a wormhole some tunnel that creates a shortcut through space? I've heard of it in science fiction movies." I replied.

"He tried to explain something to me — it was all so fantastic. He wanted me to give something to Professor Hosogawa. I went to her office in the environmental systems program but couldn't find her. No one knew where she had gone. I was in a hurry, I headed for my own lab to pick up a few things. I sat down and started looking around on my table. I don't know how long I was there — maybe ten minutes, and I felt this strange feeling someone was watching me. The feeling wouldn't go away. Finally, I . . ." Rikochan broke down sobbing again.

Suddenly Rikochan said in a quiet voice, "It was the most horrifying experience. I needed my scissors to open an envelope but couldn't find them anywhere. The feeling of being watched grew stronger."

The entire car got quiet.

Rikochan continued, "As I looked around, I saw her down . . ." she choked up for a moment, "down on the floor through pipes and stools and table legs. She was staring at me with lifeless eyes and there was blood down there. My scissors were stuck in her neck!"

I drove along on autopilot, unable to get that horrible image out of my head.

"I didn't know what to do. I ran away. All I could think of was to jump on the train and find you. I was scared because Hirayuki . . ." she broke down and couldn't continue.

We left her alone for a while and let her cry things out. As I drove, I occasionally reached over to give her a rub on the shoulder. Our route had taken us all around the volcano and south again. At the narrow neck of land where Sakurajima connected to the mainland, we turned northeast along the bay past Tarumizu town. Then we headed inland following the GPS, which directed us onto a narrow two-lane highway with multiple hair-pin turns up a steep mountainside. It wasn't until an hour later as we passed Sueyoshi-cho town that Rikochan settled down again. She looked straight ahead at the scenery in a thousand-yard stare, seeing nothing.

Heebs, Gilly, and I had started doing an alphabet game to pass the time, but using numbers instead since it is hard to find letters on remote Japanese highways. The object was to find numbers on directional signs, mileposts, or wherever and count up in sequence to thirty. It was a lot harder than one would have thought, because once you zip through the single digits you have to find double digits next to each other in order. I think Gilly was leading at sixteen when Rikochan started calling out numbers.

"Look Heebs, there's a fourteen," she said.

"Fourteen on that sign!" Heebs called out.

"Seventeen!" Gilly pointed.

Heebs was doubtful, "Where? I don't see any seventeen. You have to call out where."

"I just saw it on that building back there. We already passed it." Gilly defended himself.

Heebs scowled and looked for a fifteen.

We drove into Nichinan around four in the afternoon, coming in from the historic Obi part of town. I headed straight for Aburatsu-cho neighborhood toward the sea while Heebs looked online for an inn or hotel. First, we stopped briefly in Aburatsu to look at the bridges and houses along the Horikawa Canal. The stone Horikawa Bridge was very picturesque in its surroundings, and the town had done well trying to preserve things. There were several ryokan inns and business hotels nearby to choose from but leave it to Heebs to find another waterfront location. He directed us to a hotel with a view of the coast, right where the Hiroto River flowed into the ocean. This was a perfect location because I had to go do my surveying, and the kids could play on the beach if they wanted to. We checked into the Hotel Seasons Nichinan and they gave us a room on the third floor. The hotel was isolated from the town, with thick, brush-covered green hills surrounding the inland side and riverbanks, leaving the front of the hotel exposed to ocean breezes.

We lugged our bags up the elevator and crowded into the small room which actually only had enough space for two. It was common in our family — check into a cheap room to save money, then have all the boys sleep on the floor with their sleeping bags while women and young children get the beds. Being off the beaten path however, we were surprised at what a nice find the place was. We gazed out the window and could see the waves breaking on a long stretch of sand. Between the beach and the hotel was the coastal road, which crossed a bridge over the river. Heebs wanted to go out and explore the beach, so we put Rikochan to bed and us three boys headed downstairs. I shouldered the LIDAR drone case as we left the room.

Both the caves I wanted to map had historically been made into Shinto shrines, and one of them was literally across the street. It took us only five minutes to walk to Gion Shrine that faced Umegahama Beach. The shrine entrance was a red torii gate facing northeast right on the side of the raised road, which was about three meters above the beach level. Standing under the torii you could look across the street down to the beach, then turn yourself around and look down into the shrine — it was apparent that the shrine and the beach were historically at the same level, possibly predating the road.

We passed under the gate and walked down the steps. A small caretaker's shack and several stone lanterns graced the entrance of the cave, which had a drooping stone ceiling as if a humongous boulder rested on two stone sidewalls. The hill was actually not very big, so it appeared as though the entire mountain had been hollowed out naturally as a sea cave from the constant pounding of ancient surf. Since it was late in the day, I decided to get the LIDAR drone started, and we could follow it in as it mapped the cave. I sat down on one of the benches that lined the path and opened up the laptop. There was snickering behind me.

"What's up boys — anything I should know about?" I asked, intent on reading the screen without looking back at them.

"Hahaha — you'll see." Heebs replied.

That made me nervous. The words 'you will see' never ended up with results I found attractive. I slowly turned and saw both boys grinning widely in mirth. Their eyes focused on me at first, then looked past me at the laptop screen. Both boys burst into a chuckle.

I turned back around and saw that the 3D underground bunker map from earlier was loaded up and displayed on the screen. The millions of laser points in the cloud had been matched with photographic and material spectrography to create a high-resolution virtual environment. One could don a set of virtual reality goggles and take a photographically perfect, leisurely walk through the tunnels. On my screen the viewpoint was from outside the tunnel complex — all I could see was the backside of the negative volume, as if the solid earth were transparent and only the voids could be seen. The multiple parallel tunnels and cross-passages were clearly apparent.

I decided to check the morning data's integrity to make sure it was a good capture. Rotating the entire model, the color mapping appeared continuous with no breaks, in both walls, ceiling, and floors. It was when I turned off the color mapping layers to visualize only the point cloud that something seemed strange. Heebs and Gilly, watching from behind, busted out laughing. Some complicated patterns of point clusters appeared in tight bunches periodically down one of the tunnels. Were there objects inside that got mapped into the model? To be fair, point clouds representing the pile of furniture and scrap wood could clearly be seen in the first tunnel — it was usually not practical to clear out those types of obstacles in order to get clean mappings. But these periodic clusters of points had the eerie shape of humans. I zoomed in on one of them and sure enough, it looked like a person holding arms out in some stance. The next cluster was the same, with the arms posed differently, and so on for a total of six figures. Suddenly I realized the boys had posed for those, making a message out of semaphore alphabet signals!

"You guys!" I cried out and my sons responded in a chorus of laughter.

The boys had taken turns posing in the proper semaphore waiting perfectly still for the drone to pass, then ran outside and around into the next tunnel, looping to the next position to get captured again until all six letters were recorded by the drone. Those genius pranksters! Okay, might as well decode the message: B - O - R - I - N - G.

I looked back at the two with a fake frown and saw smug looks on their faces after having performed a prank well done.

The little shrine dating from 1924 was built by a railroad chief, and apparently contained deities that were believed to protect the locals from ocean storms and floods. The drone passed inside, over a short red wooden bridge, and disappeared in the dark as I held onto Heebs' and Gilly's arms with an iron grip. I didn't want them posing semaphores in the shrine cave. We gave the machine a few minutes to do a good scan then slowly followed it in. The wide passageway was oriented toward the southwest and had several low-hanging rock outcroppings along the way where one had to be careful not to bump their noggin. It penetrated around 20-30 meters into the hill and terminated in a wide room. We washed our hands in a chozubachi water basin before passing into the big volume. Toward the back was a tiny red wooden shrine (this was a small-scaled one, not large enough for visitors to go inside). It was very dark, with just a few dim lights that could be seen in key locations. We stood in the middle and slowly spun around to take it all in — an almost magical place with various religious implements around the walls.

Hidden in the northern wall of the cavern was another crevice that we ducked into, that led to a narrow side tunnel parallel with the main passage. We walked another 20-30 meters, avoiding more low ceilings, and exited the shrine from a tall, narrow, slightly diagonal slot. Immediately to the right was the main entrance — we had walked in one complete loop. The drone had automatically finished its mapping and parked itself on the ground.

"Wow that was really cool!" Gilly exclaimed.

"Yeah! Let's go in again and . . ." Heebs began but stopped as he eyed several teenage Japanese school girls descend the steps and walk into the main passageway.

There it was again — macho awkward Heebs suddenly couldn't keep his eyes off those skirts. I packed away the laptop and drone and shouldered the case, getting ready to walk back to the hotel. It was already 6pm and I needed to get to the second shrine before it got too late.

"Guys, the next place is farther away, only reachable by car. Do you want to come with me?" I asked.

Gilly excitedly volunteered to join me, but we only heard a low mumble come out of Heebs and he waved us away.

"Hibiki Hughes!" I called out and he snapped to attention at the sound of his name. I continued, "You've got the room card key. Go check on your sister and get something to eat downstairs if we're not back in a couple of hours."

Heebs nodded but turned to peer into the cave. It wasn't going to end well for him, and I couldn't bear to see Heebs embarrass himself. Gilly and I walked the short distance back to the hotel and went straight to the car. The trip to Udo Shrine sent us north across the Hiroto River and along the coast for a fifteen-minute drive. We turned off the main highway and drove surface streets through a huge torii gate that marked the entrance to the shrine complex. The sun was starting to set leaving a beautiful pattern of yellow and gold across the sky as we pulled into the shrine parking lot. Storm clouds seemed to be moving in from the west, projecting contrasting bright and dark regions. We parked the car and walked under another torii gate and onto a wide pedestrian walkway. To our left there were a few souvenir shops that appeared to be shutting down for the day, with a wall of vending machines lining the way. As we walked between two large stone lanterns, we could get glimpses of the ocean to our right. The route narrowed down to pass through a red painted gatehouse, constructed using Shinto traditional Japanese carpentry, and immediately opened up to a collection of additional shrine buildings built using the same style. A low, red wooden handrail on the right pointed onward, and framed an unobstructed view of the watery horizon and sunset.

There were still a few people about, so I needed to stop by the main office to get permission to temporarily cordon off the area and run the LIDAR drone. The administrative offices, also built in the Shinto carpentry style, were at the top of some monumental steps on our left. A priest greeted us and thanked us for visiting the shrine. I laid the case on the desk and opened it to expose the LIDAR unit and handed a paper description of my research that had been translated into Japanese.

Having rehearsed in advance, Gilly said, "Kyō wa, Otōsan no tsūyaku yakume no Gīri to mōshimasu, yorishiku onegai itashimasu." Meaning, 'today I am translator for Dad, and my name is Gilly.'

I'm sure the priest, seeing such a young, polite, foreign-looking, half-Japanese boy launch into the formal keigo honorifics must have been impressed.

I explained that I was from Oklahoma State University and described what I wanted to do, waiting for Gilly to translate. I stressed that the cave-mapping task that utilized the flying machine would take no more than ten minutes. The priest asked a few questions and then called a young bozu over (the nickname they use for buzz-cut boys) and assigned him as our guide. The bozu, named Taniyama, could not have been older than eighteen.

We followed Taniyama-san back out to the main path and turned left to pass under a more elaborate Shinto-style tower gate. The path narrowed considerably after that, taking us past other minor shrine structures and giving us a fabulous view of the ocean and craggy rocks down on our right. The troubled sky was impressive and competed with the grandeur of the religious structures.

"Dad, look at those rocks and tide pools! What a great place to go snorkeling." Gilly noted.

Though the complex had several shrine buildings, the main attraction was the famous Udo Shrine built into a cave. Unlike the neighborhood feel of Gion Shrine, the caretakers of Udo were well-off and had plenty of funding for upkeep. The buildings and structures were in top condition. We passed over an arched bridge and began to descend a sloped walkway, passing a small souvenir stand on the right. Stone lanterns lined the way, along with the low, red handrail. After crossing another arched bridge, we descended a long line of steps bordered by the red handrails. The steps seemed to hover in front of a vast cave opening into the side of the cliff on our left side, while exposing us to the rugged coastline down on our right. The stairs ended on a platform that stood right above the pounding waves. A red torii gate to the left of the stairs opened up into the cave.

First, we took a quick walking tour. In spite of its scale, the 38 x 29-meter cavity wasn't as deep as it appeared from first glance. It sheltered a full-on red wooden shrine structure built under the natural rock ceiling. The most striking part was to be inside the dark volume and look back toward the diagonal cave entrance to see the bright red handrails of the staircase contrasted against the sunset and ocean.

Our guide Taniyama-San explained the mapping process to a few straggling tourists who stepped outside the torii and watched as the LIDAR drone entered the cave and did a full round of mapping. After the drone came back out and landed safely, the tourists were ushered back inside. At that point we thanked our host and spent a few minutes gazing out to sea.

"This site is more dramatic than the other one, but what do you think, Gilly?" I asked.

Gilly paused, looked around a bit, and replied, "I like this place too. I would have fun climbing down the rocks to explore those inlets. But I really like that little cave near the hotel."

"Me too. This one is way older and has been around in some form or other since before 782 AD. But I still like the little Gion better." I said as we started climbing the steps. "I'm getting hungry. Maybe we can find some food up there."

Most of the tourists had gone by the time we reached the top, and the cafe was closed. We would have to stop somewhere on the way home or wait till we got back to Nichinan.

Just as we rounded a corner near the parking lot, we noticed some policemen near our rental car. One was looking at the license plate taking notes, and the other one slowly walked around the vehicle peering in the windows. I held out my hand to keep Gilly from walking out into the open. Looking around, I noticed a rock outcropping right next to our car.

I turned to Gilly, "See that boulder? Do you think you could get on top of that and listen to what they're saying?"

Gilly was a small boy, unobtrusive, and spoke Japanese fairly well, so he snuck off through the bushes to get behind the rock. I followed slowly, trying not to make any noise as I lightly stepped over undergrowth and aimed for hard stones or bare earth. We could hear the sound of the surf, but it was not too loud to drown out the radio in the nearby patrol car. The garbled transmissions were intermittent, and occasionally one of the policemen approached the car to engage with the person in dispatch.

"... *(Static static) Hyuzu Kariko (crackle crackle)* ..." came the electronic radio traffic.

I froze. That was us! They were talking about Hughes 'Hyuzu'. I didn't move a muscle as I listened and heard 'Hyuzu' and 'Kariko' mentioned several more times. Gilly came back with concern written all over his face.

"Dad, they're looking for Rikochan. They know you rented that car, and think you know where she is." Gilly whispered.

Not again! First the mob, now the police. Did they suspect her in the professor's murder? I felt an intense urge to get out of there and go get Rikochan to find out what she knew. Should I just walk out right now and give myself up? No, they would probably take her away without giving me a chance to talk with her.

"Okay Gilly, we have to leave the car here." I explained, "let's get back out to the main road and hope we can find a taxi."

We worked our way back to the shrine complex and found a trail between buildings leading through the forest. The path was paved, and I figured any route heading in the northerly direction away from the coast would eventually hit the coastal highway. The sky was dark and heavy with clouds which might help us get away undetected.

Unfortunately, we had only gone a couple hundred yards when my cell phone rang. I pulled it out of my pocket and quickly put it into vibrate mode.

"Hello this is Tim Hughes." I answered, hoping it was not law enforcement calling my private line.

"Dad, they're here!" Heebs' voice whispered.

At first, I was relieved that I didn't have to talk to the cops yet. But that relief soon faded away.

"Dad, it's those yakuza guys. They just pulled up in the parking lot and are coming inside the hotel!" He frantically reported.

I couldn't think straight. Too many things were happening, and I wasn't in control. I had to think of something fast!

"Heebs, wake your sister and get out of there! Just leave everything and run, now!" I harshly whispered into the phone, then quickly added, "follow the riverbank north until you get to a road. There's a little neighborhood called Segai. You'll find a concrete pump house that lets water from the river flow into the canal. Stay there and don't let anyone see you till we get back."

We strained our eyes in the dark, afraid to switch on any lights. Fortunately, the path led down into a gully and up the other side and deposited us into another parking area. I looked around and saw a couple of full-sized buses loading up with tourists. A few taxis waited nearby for potential customers from nearby shops, so we flagged one down. The taxi driver took a different road than the one we had come in on, and it looked like it was the entrance for buses and tour groups. Thankfully this little detour saved us. We passed the drive-through torii gate entrance that we had entered over an hour earlier and saw several patrol cars and policemen starting to set up a roadblock. Had we gone out the same road we had come in on, we would have fallen right into the trap. In our current lane however, the traffic didn't stop, and we came out onto the coastal highway without a hitch.

The taxi drove us south along the winding highway that afforded striking views of the darkening sky and sea. But the colors only became a gloomy backdrop as my mind raced. Large drops of rain started splattering on the windshield.

Gilly looked up at me with a worried look and said, "Dad, I'm scared."

A thousand thoughts went through my head seeing that sweet boy's face. He depended on me. Somehow, we had to get through this together.

"It's going to be okay," was all I could come up with.

The rain soon became a torrent with wiper blades sweeping non-stop. The bad weather complicated things — how would Rikochan and Heebs get out okay? If the two made it out safe, the fastest route would have been for us to cross the bridge at the Hiroto River, drive past the hotel, and enter Aburatsu again before heading north to rendezvous with them. Looking at the map on my smartphone, I found an alternate route leading inland along the north bank of the river. I could see the signal coming up through the pouring rain and told the driver to take a right.

"Koko de migi ni magatte kudasai." Gilly translated.

The new route was a bit roundabout but allowed us to cross the river further north and approach the rendezvous location from the opposite side of town. I needed time to think — I just wanted to go hide somewhere, maybe chill out on the rocky coastline. But we needed someplace dry. The taxi driver turned left and crossed the river at the little cluster of residences in Masuyasu, then turned and followed the river on the south bank.

When we got to Segai I had the driver maneuver the taxicab up onto the levee and proceed with caution. The vehicle clung to the narrow road and slowly pushed through the driving storm. We had not gotten far when we began to approach the rendezvous point. Even in the pouring rain I could see the tall pump house looming off to the side. Two figures huddled under an overhang, cautiously looking our way.

I leaped out and ran over to where Rikochan and Heebs waited, and they jumped up with relief. I gave each of them a hug and we splashed through the puddles back to the taxicab. As the car doors closed, I noticed Rikochan held that envelope close to her. Somehow, I knew even then that whatever was inside that envelope was a key to all of this.

"That was crazy," Heebs began, "we had to climb out a window. It's a good thing we were on the third floor because there was a low roof right there. We ran along the roof, climbed down a downspout to a lower roof, then leapt down to the ground."

Rikochan seemed rested from her earlier breakdown and excitedly added, "It was just as you said, Dad. We could stay hidden in the bushes as we followed the riverbank to the pump house. I don't think anyone could have seen us get away."

I wasn't sure where to go next, but I needed time with Rikochan. If the police were after her as a witness, then we had to turn ourselves in. We should clear her name legally, I thought. She needed to agree that going to the police was the right thing to do. I hoped my worst fears wouldn't materialize — I hoped with all the fiber of my being that she was not criminally involved somehow.

I'm sure I must have cut a stern figure with a scowl on my face. It was getting late, so I directed the driver to take us uptown to a katsu restaurant near the Nichinan Police Station.

"What is going on, Kariko Hughes?" I blurted out as we drove through the rain-soaked town, "Why are the police after you too?"

Whenever I used their formal names, the children knew they were in trouble. Rikochan became sullen and looked straight ahead.

"Dad, it's not just Professor Hosogawa." She slowly began, "Hirayuki had to leave on a trip."

The transhumanist boyfriend again. What involvement did he have in all this?

"Hirayuki gave me this envelope and told me to guard it with my life. He said if he didn't come back in three days, that I was supposed to give this to the professor, and she would know what to do." Rikochan explained, "Three, four days passed, and he didn't come back. But I still waited."

The taxi turned a few corners and made it onto the main street heading through Nichinan city. It was a long straightaway with multiple signals that all seemed to turn red right when we reached them. Just before the train station the driver suddenly turned left on a side street. Immediately in front of us was the Nichinan Police Station — we were heading directly for it! I looked at the driver who focused on the road straight ahead. Rikochan squirmed next to me, my baby girl caught up in something beyond her control. Did the Japanese driver understand what we had been talking about in English? Was he somehow in cahoots with the police to deliver a fugitive? Just as I thought he would drive straight into the parking lot, the driver turned right again, then a quick left — the front reception area of the police station was coming up on our left. I tensed up and was about to tell him not to stop when he kept on past the driveway entrance. Rikochan and I almost gave out audible sighs of relief. Only a few dozen meters further and the taxi pulled up to Katsukaishū Restaurant, which was literally on the same street a block away from the police department.

The driver turned around and smiled, "Okyakusan, tsukimashita yo!"

I was so grateful and thanked the man. We exited the car, paid the fare, and sullenly walked into the restaurant that specialized in pork and chicken cutlets. Our minds were all full of the events that we had gone through the past hour, and on top of that Rikochan's horrific story felt like we were in some thriller movie only it was real. Rikochan asked the waitress if they had a private room, and the woman took us upstairs. There were actually multiple tables up there, but the few customers had all settled into the main dining room downstairs, leaving the upstairs dining room free of guests. A row of windows looked out on the street, and across the road we could see the old brutalist concrete Nichinan City Culture Center building designed by the famous Japanese architect Kenzo Tange.

We were all starving. Everyone ordered various katsu dishes: Heebs and Gilly both ordered tonkatsu, which is a deep-fried pork cutlet cut into strips and served with a pile of thinly sliced crisp cabbage; Rikochan ordered potato koroke, which are mashed potato patties deep fried in a crispy panko batter; and I chose a katsudon, which was a deep-fried pork cutlet served over rice. Everyone scarfed down the food so rabidly that no one could slip in a word edgewise.

I heard the unique up and down wail of multiple sirens first, then I could see the flashing blue and red lights as two police vehicles rushed by down on the street outside our window — they were heading toward the police station with some urgency.

Rikochan's round face had a worried expression as she looked at me through those eyeglasses. She was the most precious child in the world and was utterly incapable of harming anyone. Whoever got her into this was going to deal with my full semper fi wrath.

Without flinching, Rikochan pulled out the envelope and slapped it down in the middle of the table, still looking straight into my eyes, "Somehow everything is connected to this."

We all stared at the envelope as Rikochan continued her story of what had happened only that morning.

"I was getting ready to eat breakfast and then I got a video call from a local police detective in Kitakyushu. He held something up in a plastic bag and asked if I recognized it. My cutting knife — why did he have it? He said he wanted me to come down to the station and answer a few questions and I said 'okay'. I was just about to head out when the news came on. The body of Hirayuki Doei had been found decked out in full scuba gear." She choked and began sobbing again before adding, "Somebody found him floating out in the fog in a small rowboat. He had been cut up . . ."

She grabbed onto me and cried, burying her head on my chest. She forced herself to continue in a broken voice.

"He's dead, Dad. My Hirayuki is dead!"

I didn't know what to think — two horrendous revelations in one day, and our whole world seemed to be crumbling around us. Heebs and Gilly were crying too.

Rikochan composed herself and sat up and said, "I was scared. The first thing I thought of was that envelope — I had to deliver that envelope to Professor Hosogawa before heading to the police station. But I couldn't find her, and then she was dead! I ran away. I needed to talk to you about it, Dad. What should I do?"

CHAPTER 3

Stealthily I crossed the street and inserted myself into the shadows of the shrubbery. The sloped concrete wall of the Nichinan Cultural Center towered above me, but very little light penetrated the alleyways in this part of town. Fortunately, the rain had stopped. I turned around and watched as one by one my children moved from tree to wall to car until they could come join me. There was hardly any traffic at all, and no pedestrians could be seen. First Gilly dramatically tiptoed across the street and ducked in near my feet. Next Heebs purposely came from a different direction and casually slipped into the darkness near us, in case someone was watching.

I saw flashing blue and red lights and tensed up — a patrol car was heading our way. I hoped Rikochan had hidden well. We were still only a block away from the police station, so we all waited until the vehicle passed and watched it pull into the entrance of the station. Rikochan made her move immediately and softly came around the corner.

Gilly was about to say something, and I hushed him up — two men exited a building across the way and stood outside talking. After what seemed like an eternity, the two moved on. The cultural center bordered on a park with high berms around the perimeter. I corralled the boys in that direction with Rikochan in tow, and we were quickly swallowed up in silence as if the city didn't exist beyond the line of trees. We wound our way parallel with the building and found an overhang built into the facade.

"Stay here," I said, "I think the last train is due in a half hour or so. I'll call you, Heebs."

Heebs, Gilly, and I had rental prepaid smartphones we had picked up at the airport. Rikochan's phone was on a regular provider contract, so we had her turn it off in case she was being tracked.

I cut through the park and walked several blocks to the Nichinan train station. There seemed to be cops everywhere, and they were stopping anyone who went inside the station. I put on a surgical mask and pulled my US Marines baseball cap down a little in hopes that from a distance someone wouldn't figure out I was a 'gaijin' foreigner. This would be hard, even in the dark, because I was six foot five and weighed 240 pounds. Fortunately, the Japanese had always been socially sensitive to minor coughs and hay fever, even before the pandemics, so it was not uncommon to see folks walking around in all sorts of fashionable surgical masks.

In front of the train station there was a taxi stand, and a short line of commuters waiting to catch a ride. I started to walk in that direction but saw a policeman standing nearby. I turned and cut through the parking lot where a group of students still in their school uniforms stood around talking.

I made a quick call to Heebs, "Can't ride the train. Call an Uber and tell them to pick me up at the 100 yen per plate sushi restaurant near the station."

I only waited five minutes and a Daihatsu van pulled up. I directed the driver, who didn't speak English, to pass in front of the Tange cultural center where the children were waiting under the overhang. Rikochan, Heebs, and Gilly piled in quickly. Heebs had told the driver we wanted to go to Obi on the north part of town, but on the way, he convinced her to take us all the way to Miyazaki city instead. The 45-minute ride would retrace mine and Gilly's route only a few hours before and take us past Udo Shrine.

I solemnly watched the dark coastline and tensed up a bit as we approached the shrine area, but there was no sign of law-enforcement activity or roadblocks. We passed a local tourist attraction, Sun Messe with its replica Easter Island Moai statues, but the park was closed, and it was too dark to see anything. The Daihatsu van got off the main highway and pulled into the Miyazaki Aoshima neighborhood 20 minutes later without incident. Heebs had the driver drop us off at the little Sosanji train station, where a small convenience store remained open for business.

Against my better judgement, I agreed that it would not have been wise to turn ourselves in to the police until we had more time to figure things out. Somehow both sides of the law had traced us to Nichinan, so we needed an out-of-the-way place to hide for a while. The first thing that came to mind was a 'love hotel'. In Japan, a whole industry of discreet rendezvous locations for lovers had popped up, and no-questions-asked cash hotels could be rented by the hour or overnight. The common understanding was that the hotels were used by those seeking illicit love affairs, but in reality, a lot of Japanese married couples, cursed to live in tiny apartments without privacy, stole away occasionally to get a break from the kids. Some of the love hotels were quite glamorous, and were built to resemble medieval castles, ocean liners, starships, and any number of fantasy themes.

Before exiting the Uber, I did a quick online search and found a love hotel nearby, several blocks away from Sosanji Station so that the driver could not inform anyone of our destination if questioned. The four of us walked out onto Aoshima Kaido Street, then headed inland along the Kaeda River. There were enough streetlights to see where we were walking, but the pools of light left deep darkness in between. The main thoroughfare the Uber had exited earlier was the coastal Highway Route 220, that crossed overhead on an overpass — no traffic could be seen down on the surface street this late at night. We walked under the highway and continued along the side of the river past several residences and came to a walled-off piece of property with a narrow driveway. The entire appearance of the love hotel seemed to be built around privacy, so anyone driving their own car could stay discreet without letting curious neighbors identify them.

Unfortunately, I didn't have any experience in such hotels, having only read about them. This one didn't have the glamour I had seen in other bigger cities, so I was half disappointed that my first, and perhaps only, experience staying in a love hotel would be in a dumpy place half-forgotten up a backwater river.

"Stay here out of sight." I motioned to a niche that was lined with vending machines.

I slipped on my surgical mask and stumbled over to the main kiosk, which again was set up for privacy as a key-dispensing vending machine. I paid cash for two nights and collected the disposable card key. The children followed me to a private bungalow with its own hidden parking spot, and we quickly slipped inside and locked the door.

The inside decor was too gaudy for my taste, with an excessive use of bright red colors. Also, there seemed to be mirrors everywhere, even on the ceiling. Fortunately, there were amenities in the vending machines outside, including toothpaste and shampoo, so in spite of the fact that we had left our luggage in Nichinan we were able to freshen up before bed. As usual, Rikochan and Gilly got the bed, while Heebs and I tried to find pillows, cushions, blankets, and towels that could build some sort of nest on the floor. The remoteness of the location gave me a feeling of relief even if the room left one with a haunting feeling of dirty acts hidden in the very fabric and walls. I worried that Heebs and Gilly might have active imaginations but must have passed into a deep sleep while in the thought.

There was no relaxing. I don't remember what I dreamed about, but we were running from someone, and I must have thrashed about as I tried to escape.

When I awoke again it was still dark and the faint light from a streetlamp outside filtered in through the frosted glass windows. I could smell a faint scent of something, food or snacks that you might find packaged up in a vending machine or newsstand. As I regained consciousness, I could tell there was activity going on. I sat up to see what everyone was up to.

I suddenly felt like I was in the middle of an intelligence gathering operation. The bed was scattered with scribbled notes and wadded-up papers all over it. There in the middle of all that was a single crisp document. A small table off to the side had crumpled wrappers with cookies, juice cans, rice crackers, and dried shrimp in strands — someone must have gone out to raid the vending machines. Rikochan, using a small desk lamp on low power, sat on the end of the bed and bent over to study the document. I looked around and saw that Gilly was researching stuff on one of the rental burner smartphones, while Heebs was talking with someone on another one.

"Funadori — funadori . . . Are you sure it says 'funadori'?" Gilly asked as he scrolled down the page and took another bite out of a cookie.

Sheesh, what time is it? I yawned and glanced down at my watch and saw that it was still only 11pm — I must have been the only one to have fallen asleep.

Rikochan picked up the paper and squinted at Japanese kanji scrawled across the top, "Well, this first character is 'fune' or boat, and the second one is 'tori' or bird. I don't know, maybe try 'funacho'? Or 'shucho'?"

Heebs held up a handwritten note and read the title by the light of the smartphone, "Holographic Schwinger Effect."

I could barely hear the voice on the other end mumble something, to which Heebs corrected, "No, not 'swinger', it's 'Schwinger' S-C-H-W-I-N-G-E-R. Written by Sonner in 2013."

What the heck was Heebs talking about? It sounded like some deep physics, completely out of character for such a rascal. Looking from Rikochan to Gilly and Heebs it seemed like they were all working together on something, then it dawned on me — they had opened up the envelope from Hirayuki Doei, the dead boyfriend.

I rushed over to the bed to see what the papers were about. Strange phrases in Heebs or Rikochan's handwriting adorned each sheet and appeared to be in haphazard piles. Rikochan had organized them into three sloppy stacks that almost spilled over to each other. Heebs had been listening to the voice on the phone and could be seen taking down a few more notes on the page. He set down the paper onto one of the piles, which now read, *Holographic Schwinger Effect and the Geometry of Entanglement.*

"Okay here's the next one," Heebs told the person on the phone as he picked up another memo, "this one is 'EPR Pair Temporal Loops', colon, 'Primordial Closed Timelike Curves' question mark."

The stack appeared to contain a half-dozen or so scrawled titles that might have been physics and scientific topics. I could not make sense of any of them.

"No — nothing. I don't think such a bird or animal exists." Gilly called out to Rikochan.

My daughter was looking at drawings or sketches of various strange-looking objects. The one in her hand had a grid I knew well, with two kanji characters written cursive-style in large script at the top of the page. It was a sudoku puzzle. An irregular amorphous shape or outline wound its way through the puzzle. Below that, what looked like a photo of a ripped piece of manuscript with cursive writing was copied onto the page.

My curiosity caused my eyes to wander over to the third pile. It looked like URL addresses for web pages, with titles like, "*Yata-no-kagami: The Mirror of Yata*, or *Imperial Regalia of Japan*, or *Kusanagi-no-tsurugi*, or *Battle of Dan-no-ura*. It was the strangest set of notes I had ever seen.

"Mas, did you get that last one?" Heebs asked the person on the phone.

Of course — the children had called their college-aged brother to join in their project. 20-year-old Masamune 'Mas' Hughes was studying robotics at Massachusetts Institute of Technology but was currently in Hong Kong for a summer exchange program.

"Hi Mas!" I shouted, causing all three children to glance up at me.

There was a pause, then I indistinctly heard something coming from the phone across the room that sounded like *"Hi, Dad."*

I took advantage of the pause and asked Rikochan, "What are all these things? What do you make of it?"

Rikochan shuffled among the papers to find a small handwritten note and held up both the note and the puzzle. "It says, 'I made a most startling discovery regarding origins of life on Earth — Start with the sudoku'. I think it's a note Hirayuki wrote to Professor Hosogawa."

Surprised, I exclaimed, "Sudoku, entanglement, regalia? What the hell is going on here?"

"Take a look, dad." She handed me the single crisp document she had been studying.

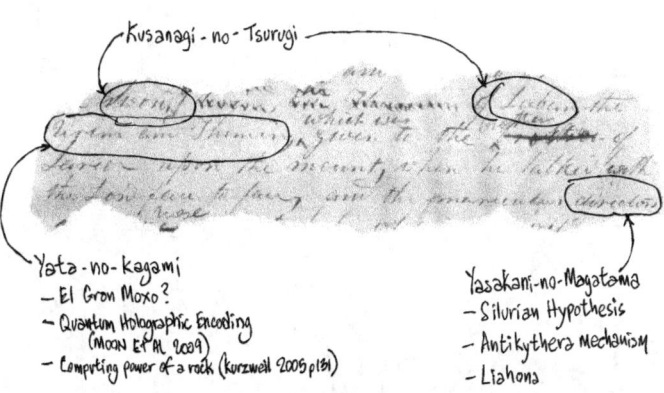

Kanji characters across the top, a sudoku puzzle overdrawn with an amorphous outline, and the black and white photo of the cursive manuscript remnant, all on one page. I looked closer at the cursive writing and could not pick out what was written there except for a few phrases like 'which was given to', or 'upon the mount'. Someone, probably Hiroyuki, had circled a few of the words and written out cryptic Romanized Japanese terms, like 'Kusanagi-no-tsurugi' or 'Yata-no-kagami' — the same as the URLs written on the stack of notes piled on the bed. The children had been taking Hiroyuki's scribbles and looking them up on the Internet.

It was at that point when I noticed something strange about the sudoku puzzle. Instead of numbers, strange symbols could be seen in some of the squares.

"They're Egyptian." Rikochan had been looking over my shoulder, "Look on the back of the page."

I flipped the page over and was shocked to see a round diagram divided into compartments filled with Egyptian hieroglyphics. Again, Hiroyuki had circled some of the symbols and scribbled in notes around the edges. Some of the notes appeared to be English, but Hiroyuki had jotted down other symbols that made even less sense than the hieroglyphs. Glancing down on the bed, I began to be amazed that the children had extracted so many of Hiroyuki's thoughts and had remembered to enlist their brother to help figure out what they meant.

The circular imprint on the document had a row of unintelligible symbols around the perimeter, with a few ideograms recognizable as human or animal stick figures, or resembling parts of the body like an eye or arm. Inside were large rectangular compartments bounded by double straight lines, further divided by single lines. Inside those inner boxes were rows of many of the same symbols that appeared around the perimeter, interspersed with larger figures of animals or humans. The humans all had animal heads such as jackal, falcon, baboon, or crocodile, and were in various stereotypical Egyptian poses. Hirayuki had circled various parts of the drawing and added the cryptic labels.

Of particular interest were two of the inner compartments that had boats with figures riding in them. Hirayuki had labeled one of the boat figures as 'Raukeeyang, 1000-cubit boat of a million year (solar boat) generation ship'. The other boat figure, according to Hirayuki's notes, showed a 'celestial engineer' on the 'throne of the celestial engineer, orbiting Qarob'. A list of technical terms was associated with that one, such as 'self-replication', 'advanced automation', or 'genetic code'. None of it made any sense.

"What the heck are we looking at? Someone was going around killing people for this?" I asked.

Heebs had been watching me from the start as I had studied the page, and shrugged, "Don't know yet. Mas is downloading the papers and will try to read them."

A noise outside caused me to look up. Just at that moment there was the sound of a car motor pulling up outside. These love hotels with their detached bungalows and private parking spaces were meant to provide privacy to the customers, but weren't necessarily sound proof. Had some couple just arrived for a secret rendezvous? Or was it someone else we didn't want to meet? I cautiously moved over to the frosted glass window facing the vehicular approach, carefully parted the curtain, and unlocked the aluminum latch. Without making a noise, I soundlessly slid the pane sideways a crack. Just outside was a wood-slat fence obscuring the driveway. Between each slat was a one-centimeter gap, so I gradually adjusted the window slider so my line-of-sight could afford me a limited view outside.

A couple of streetlamps barely illuminated the area, but hardly penetrated deep shadows. I expected to see a non-descript sedan getting ready to back into one of the private parking spots, but instead something flitted quickly past the vertical slits. I moved my head back and forth to try to use the opening to create a sweeping view outside, when a second figure went by, followed by a third and fourth. Curious — multiple dark silhouettes moving quickly by, silently with purpose. With all the excitement in the past few hours I began to feel nervous — could someone have tracked us here?

"Mas, did you get those titles?" I turned my head, briefly distracted, as Heebs continued the phone conversation with his brother — too loud for comfort.

There was more movement outside. I turned to peer through the slot and saw flickering back and forth. Readjusting my perspective to sweep the yard, I saw that someone was standing across the way, just moving into the cone of light caused by one of the streetlamps. Suddenly I couldn't help but let out a faint gasp — there stood the bearded yakuza-mafioso character waving his arms, signaling to someone out of my view. Involuntarily I ducked down below the windowsill and resisted the urge to slam the window shut, which surely would have attracted attention.

I turned quickly with my index finger held up to my lips urging silence, and whispered, "We've got to go — NOW!"

I turned around once more as Rikochan and the boys gathered the papers together and got their things ready. As I very carefully closed the pane, I could see the man outside sending hand signals to others out of my line of sight, perhaps directing them to do a silent search among the bungalows. I watched as Heebs automatically went toward the rear frosted glass window to see if we could use it as an escape route. Good thinking — the hooligans probably would be watching all the entry doors.

Just as I had done earlier, Heebs soundlessly slid the pane sideways just enough to assess the scene outside. We were in luck! Right outside the window, perhaps only half a meter away was a concrete block wall — it would be possible to stand on the windowsill and climb over that wall. Heebs opened up the window all the way and climbed up to peer over the barrier.

He turned around and whispered, "All clear!" Then he was gone.

Gilly climbed up and leaped over the wall. I stuffed all the cookie wrappers and juice cans into the trash, so they were out of sight and donned my drone case backpack. We had very little possessions on us, having abandoned our luggage at the Nichinan hotel. I followed Rikochan to the window, making sure we left no sign that we had been there. Rikochan stuffed the envelope now full of note papers into her blouse and climbed up on the windowsill. She took a little longer to climb over the block wall, not used to scrambling around like the boys were.

I had one final task. I climbed up, set my feet on the windowsill, and leaned with my back against the block wall. Reaching across without making a noise, I slowly closed the window from the outside. Then I perched upon the wall and looked down where I would land. The entire love hotel complex appeared to have been constructed in the middle of flat farmland. There were no streetlamps back there, only a bit of moonlight that hardly penetrated the darkness below. I could see reflections of stars only a short meter or so away from the wall, meaning that the rice field was flooded. Heebs was already inching along the wall to the right, with Gilly on his tail. Rikochan waited just below, watching me. Without hesitating further, I eased my legs over the edge and hung from the top of the wall. All 240 pounds of me dangled below as my chin and elbows precariously held onto the narrow perch. I could hear someone walking through the parking area, approaching the front door of the bungalow we just vacated.

Rikochan grabbed my legs and whispered, "Okay you're clear."

Without making a sound I let go, but due to the narrow slope, I almost fell away from the wall toward the mud. Fortunately, Rikochan provided just enough support for me to keep my balance.

To the left would have returned us back to the entrance of the hotel, where undoubtedly yakuza men were probably waiting. I silently thanked Heebs for his foresight in heading in the opposite direction. In single file we hugged the wall and headed toward the Kaeda River. I looked ahead and saw Heebs had reached the end of the wall and was about to peek around the corner. From my vantage, there was a dark break in the reflective surface of the flooded field, and it looked like the wall ended at a low levee. With another flooded field beyond, it was apparent that a dirt road on top of the levee came from behind the wall and crossed the rice field we were skirting.

Just then the phone vibrated in my pocket — it was Ines.

"Where are you staying, Honey?" She asked.

What could I say? 'We are staying in a love hotel' — that wouldn't go over very well, especially when I needed to hide in the middle of a muddy rice field.

"Uh, we found a nice little hotel. Listen, I can't talk right now. Love you!" I whispered and hung up.

The rice fields were clear of any shrubs, so we were all exposed — if not for the darkness someone further up the road could have easily been able to see four figures oddly hugging the bare concrete wall. Heebs carefully eased over and peeked around the corner but jumped back in surprise and almost tumbled into the water.

Suddenly a young girl emerged from around the corner running silently along the dirt road. She kept looking over her shoulder as if someone were following her. When she passed our position, we were right out in the open — as she turned briefly to look behind her, she was startled to see us lined up along the wall. Rikochan let out a gasp. Without missing a step, the girl kept running in apparent desperation.

"Sally! What's she doing here?" Rikochan said under her breath.

Heebs peeked around the corner again and took off running after the girl, followed by Gilly. Rikochan launched herself next, and after a quick peek around the corner to make sure all was clear, I ran after them.

Up ahead, Sally threw herself to the ground behind the levee, keeping herself out of sight from anyone on the main road. Heebs and Gilly followed suit in quick dives, while Rikochan and I crouched down a little more gingerly. Sally peeked up over the levee, then began crawling along the ground under the crown of the ridge. One by one the rest of us followed, slowly making our way to a structure up ahead. The levee was shallower than it looked, and I was not up to getting on my knees, so I ended up scooting along on my belly in the moist grass. To the right, the shallow slope eased down into the other flooded rice paddy. Every time a swath of mud broke the grassy slope, I tried to negotiate a crossing by standing up in a low crouch and trudging through, while at the same time maintaining a low profile.

I don't know how we could have succeeded in masking our visibility as we must have looked like dark silhouettes interrupting distant streetlights reflecting off the rice paddies, but somehow, we each made it to the end of the levee. Sally reached the shadows where a building stood between her and the road, and jumped up to continue running, with the rest of us in tow. The dirt road ended abruptly, and we could see a narrow creek or tributary of the Kaeda River blocking the way.

I almost panicked. There was no way out — we could either follow the tributary up to the road, or reverse course and follow the levee back to where we had come. My mind was racing wondering what to do. But the young girl didn't hesitate — she jumped through the dark reeds and headed straight to the water's edge. Heebs, Gilly, and Rikochan followed, and with the adrenaline of the escape, I also leapt onward, my massive 240-pound frame crashing through the brush. My mind was confused — did they intend to swim across? The narrow channel looked to be no more than ten meters across. I steeled myself for an impromptu dunk. The water's edge was littered with junk that my mind had no time to process. It was only when Heebs stopped and called out to me that I realized there was a fourth way out.

"Dad, help us pull!" Heebs shouted.

Sally, Heebs, and Gilly were already tugging at the skiff as Rikochan and I jumped in to help. We were surrounded by small, beached rowboats and other fishing equipment in various stages of disrepair. Some of the boats, including the one we were attempting to launch, were in fairly good condition. With all five of us pulling we got the fiberglass vessel into the river. As I pushed, I felt something fall out of my pocket and splash into the water — my rental burner phone. I frantically searched around in the mud under foot but to no avail. No time! Everyone piled on as Heebs waded in to push us off. Finally, he jumped in and used his momentum to give us one last shove. Sally and I were already on the oars by the time Heebs situated himself.

"Everyone, get down!" I cautioned as I guided the boat along the creek toward the main river.

We still couldn't be sure if the bad guys recognized anyone other than Rikochan and Heebs, and hopefully it was too dark to tell, but I didn't want to take any chances. Who would be operating a rowboat at this hour? Surely, we would attract attention if anyone was looking. The tributary opened up onto the Kaeda River, which fortunately was wide, shallow, and slow-moving. Being fairly large in stature I took over most of the rowing as we turned inland and up-river.

"Sally, what are you doing here?" Rikochan whispered as she hunkered down below the gunwales.

The two girls and two boys were looking cozy among piles of life jackets with their heads near each other. All eyes moved to the mysterious girl who so suddenly had appeared.

Sally hesitated, but stammered, "I . . . I've been on vacation. I'm staying at Aoshima."

Aoshima was a natural peninsula nearby with a narrow causeway connecting it to land. It was almost an island, characterized by washboard rocks, a tropical jungle, and well-known shrine.

"Everyone, this is Sally. She's one of Professor Hosogawa's students at Kitakyushu University." Rikochan introduced.

Everyone mumbled a greeting and I saw that Heebs was already smitten, even if the girl was a couple of years his senior. Everyone but me was laying down on their backs looking up at the sky.

My daughter suddenly remembered and raised up on one elbow to face Sally, "I hate to break it to you but . . ."

Sally turned to face Rikochan and shook her head, curiosity showing in her eyes.

"She's . . . Professor Hosogawa is dead," Rikochan's voice broke as she whispered, "Someone killed her and they're chasing us!"

Sally had a shocked look on her face, and said, "You mean these guys?"

Her thumb pointed back in the direction of the hotel we had just escaped from, referring to the yakuza characters who were probably still poking around the love hotel bungalows.

"Someone has been after me ever since I left Kitakyushu. There are a few sleazy fellows that are stalking me, and I can't seem to get away from them." Sally vented her frustrations, "I've been wandering back streets all night, trying to avoid them."

The experience of the two girls were uncannily similar. I guided the little vessel along the shore where the current was weakest and where we could stay hidden behind the reeds growing along the bank. There were a couple of spots where the river narrowed slightly and seemed to run deep, so Heebs got up and helped row through the faster currents. Only twenty minutes upriver we came to a bridge that passed overhead so I rowed over to the edge and nosed into the growths.

"Well, Heebs, I told you we could ride a boat later," I nervously chuckled.

Heebs glanced up at me and snarled. No one got out of the boat, but we all felt a little safer in the shadowed concealment of the reeds. We needed to consider what to do next.

Heebs brought out his burner smartphone and started looking at local maps. Sally was about to get hers out but we impressed upon her the possibility that account holders could be tracked. She turned the phone off.

My mind began to wander, and I thought about the strange document in the envelope. The only thing that made sense to me were the Japanese Regalia, which were three famous ancient treasures guarded by the imperial family. The treasures were 'Kusanagi-no-tsurugi' sword, 'Yata-no-kagami' mirror, and 'Yasakani-no-magatama' jewel. But what did they have to do with Egypt, and why were folks getting murdered over it? And what did they have to do with quantum entanglement?

"Dad, if we go up just a little further the river passes near the Shio-tsurugisaki Highway. We may be able to catch a taxi there." Heebs pointed out.

"That sounds good, but where do we go from here?" I considered, "Sally are you down here by yourself?"

It was sort of strange to see a white girl all by herself out in the middle of an out-of-the-way spot like Miyazaki.

"I've been with friends this whole time, so it hasn't been so bad. But my friends left early and now I'm alone. I'm really scared!" Sally trembled.

I saw Heebs shift over a bit. It was very subtle, but I could see he was trying to get closer to the new girl, maybe hoping to comfort her.

Gilly suggested, "Maybe we could just go camping for a few days?"

That wasn't such a bad idea — maybe we needed to get away from civilization for a while. How had they been able to track us? If we found a place with no signal, could we rest long enough to figure things out? It was turning into some spy adventure — we probably ought to check our clothes for bugs or something.

"I've got an idea," Rikochan began, "I have a good friend in Nobeoka. Sally, do you know Ichika Ebina?"

For a brief instant Sally had a dreadful expression, as if there might have been some history behind that name. But the expression soon passed.

Sally replied, "We weren't very close, but I know her."

"Her father is an executive of Asahikasei Chemicals — they've got a big house with guest rooms. Ichika's family invited me to come stay with them anytime." Rikochan excitedly advocated.

Nobeoka was pretty far away, too far for a taxi ride. It was unlikely we could find a way to get there so late at night. We needed to find a place to hunker down till morning.

We pulled away from the shore and I continued rowing upriver. Along the way other small boats could be seen beached or tied up in narrow waterways and tributaries. Thirty minutes later we rounded a bend and Heebs pointed over to another dark inlet.

"Head in there, Dad. We can tie up and walk over to the highway." Heebs directed.

"Does someone have any paper?" I asked, "Let's leave a note apologizing to the boat owner."

Safely hidden back in the reeds and tied up with the other boats, we jumped onto the shore and climbed the Bank. Heebs led the way, followed by Gilly and Sally, with Rikochan and I taking up the rear. At the top of the bank was a sluice gate for a small canal. We trudged through brush on the levee and followed a grassy shelf between the canal and a block wall. There were residences and other structures sparsely scattered ahead of us. Heebs stealthily stepped out on a paved road and turned the corner, followed by Gilly and Sally.

As soon as the others were out of sight, suddenly Rikochan turned and held out her arms to stop me from stepping out onto the road.

"Dad, I don't trust myself with this." She reached into her blouse and retrieved the stuffed envelope, handing it to me.

"I don't know Sally very well. I don't want her to know I have anything related to Professor Hosogawa," she whispered.

"Okay I'll hold onto it." I reached out and took the packet, slipping it into a large cargo pocket on my thigh.

I couldn't see her face very well but could tell a big burden had been lifted from her shoulders. She turned around and stepped onto the road to follow the others. The narrow lane came south from the main highway, then stopped short of the levee and turned a corner westward. Looking to the right, I could see dark silhouettes of the children eclipsed by occasional traffic on the main highway. We walked past large, uncovered greenhouse frames on the left, overgrown with tall grass from neglect. On the right, the ground was a meter or so higher, with a rock retaining wall constructed in the 'ishigaki' style. A few residences or industrial buildings were built up on the higher level.

As I turned my head to peer into the dark recesses, I noticed some flashing lights out of the corner of my eye. At the point where we entered the lane, a large convex road mirror had been attached to a pole to give drivers rounding the corner a view of the blind spot. I felt a little panic as I saw red and blue flashing lights reflected in the mirror — a patrol car was making its way east along the other leg of the road.

"Rikochan! Police are coming behind us!" I quietly called out.

All the children heard me and picked up their pace towards the main road. I looked around for a place to hide. On the left, the greenhouse frames opened up to a grassy parking lot scattered with work vehicles. On the right above the rock wall, several large commercial trucks were parked with their engines running. I could see a couple of workers under a streetlamp checking the rigging of the cargo. One of the men looked in our direction and Gilly and I, in unison, both ducked into the shadows of a dark stairway set into the wall.

Suddenly two things happened at once. From the direction of the main highway, several figures with flashlights turned the corner and began methodically sweeping back and forth as if they were searching in the shadows. From the other end of the lane, the patrol car turned the corner at the same time, pointing headlights down the street. From the recessed stairway, I looked across and saw Rikochan, Heebs, and Sally jump behind vehicles and head into the tall grass. There was no way for Gilly and I to follow them without exposing ourselves.

The figures with flashlights got closer, and soon they would be level with the stairway. I motioned for Gilly to crawl up to the top on his belly. The workmen had gone, so we crouched low and made our way to the first truck intending to hide behind it. Fortunately, the sound of the engine drowned out my heavy breathing as I fought to catch my breath. Peeking around the back of the vehicle, I saw a police officer with a flashlight slowly ascending the steps we had just vacated, shining the beam back and forth into the bushes lining the top of the wall.

"We have to keep going, he'll look up here too!" I whispered.

Gilly pointed under the next truck and crouched low to climb under. I followed him and tried to tuck behind one of the massive wheels. The engine noise was very loud, and I could hear the exhaust pipe rattling in its fittings only centimeters from my ear.

Without warning, the truck we were hiding under began to drive away! Gilly and I tucked up tightly, careful to avoid the tires and any low-hanging structure that could drag us underneath. The truck picked up speed and at one point I swear one of the axles seemed to graze my 240-pound belly. Then we were free, looking up at the stars.

I glanced back toward the stairs and saw that the flashlight on the other side of the first truck was still getting closer and we were exposed. Instantly Gilly and I jumped up and ran to the back of the third truck. I don't know if I was thinking straight, but I looked up on the flatbed and saw tarp-covered bumps secured with straps. I lifted Gilly up then put my foot into a stirrup below the taillight, making one final lunge between two covered lumps of cargo just as the truck began to pull away. Gilly and I scrambled further into the midst of the uneven mounds and found a low hiding spot to hunker down in. Behind us the remaining truck also pulled out, its headlights beaming right over the top of my head. I expected our ride to stop any minute and for someone to shout at us to get down, but instead it pulled out onto the main highway and continued to build up speed. We were committed to wait until the truck reached its destination.

CHAPTER 4

In my panic I vaguely recall the truck making various turns as we got farther and farther from the other kids. Nervously Gilly and I kept rock-still for what seemed like hours, until we couldn't stand it anymore. At some point the last truck with its penetrating headlights had fallen far behind and there didn't seem to be much traffic, so the two of us rearranged ourselves to be more comfortable.

My mind turned back to the other three. I had seen them disappear into the grassy field, where it seemed like lots of overgrown greenhouses, trailers, containers, and work vehicles were scattered about. I hoped they had found a good hiding place or evaded the searchers, but I began to worry. I reached for my burner phone but remembered it was not there.

"Gilly, pull out your cell phone and text your brother. See how they are doing," I said.

My son's voice came out of the darkness, "Dad, I already tried but I think the battery is dead. We haven't had a chance to charge it."

"Do we even have a charger? Maybe we left it with the luggage?" I asked.

Gilly held up a cord he had pulled out of his pocket, and briefly a car headlight cast its coiled shadow onto the tarp. Leave it to kids to carry the charge cord around — all we needed was a break to find an outlet.

"Where was it that Rikochan wanted to go?" I asked, hoping she and Heebs had the presence of mind to keep moving, "Maybe we can try to meet them there."

As the truck had made a few turns since we started out, my internal biological compass lost calibration. My mind was already hopelessly confused, and seeing how very few streets in Japan followed a cardinal grid system anyway, who knows where we were headed or how long the trip would be. If we were in luck, we might end up closer to where we wanted to be.

"Nobeoka. I think it's a few hours north of Miyazaki," Gilly replied, "but she didn't say where the address was."

"Let's find some place to charge that phone." I thought out loud.

I must have dozed off after that. The vibration of the truck was soothing, but there was a constant wind tearing at my legs and the lumps of cargo appeared to be hard machinery with the only soft parts being the places where the tarp spanned between hard protuberances. I dreamily recall the truck winding through mountain roads and small villages. I became fully awake as streetlights increased — the truck appeared to be passing through some urban areas. It was still dark, and my watch told me it was in the wee hours of the morning. Beside me, I could finally make out Gilly's slim outline as he snuggled up against my chest. The boy began to stir.

"Where are we?" He asked.

I tried to peek through gaps in the tarp mounds to see if there were any signs, but all I could find were store fronts and commercial signage. Gilly poked his head up as well and we spent a few minutes looking for indications of where we might be. Behind us, the other truck sometimes came right up on our tail when our ride stopped at traffic signals, so we had to keep our heads down at those times.

"I think we're in that city," Gilly pointed at a two-kanji sign, "but I don't know how to read it."

I also remembered seeing those characters repeated in several places. It must have been a good ten minutes later when we saw a Romanized version of the place, which turned out to be a town called Hayato. *Where the heck is that,* I wondered. It could be anywhere — we could have been anywhere in southern Japan!

The buildings started thinning out and the road made several curves through low forested hilly areas. Only another ten minutes later and all three trucks pulled into the wide parking lot of a 24 hour 'konbini' convenience store. It must have been break time — we watched all three drivers hop out and head into the store, with muffled talk and occasional chuckles. Gilly and I quickly took advantage of the stop and piled over the back of the truck bed onto the pavement. It was still dark, around 3am, so there was very little traffic out. We kept the vehicles between us and the store and made our way off to the side to avoid any attention. It was a rural area, with a large industrial building across the street but nothing else other than forests and overgrown fields. Did we get off the truck too early? If we stayed on, would we have been discovered later when the truck arrived at its destination? My mind was desperate to find a way back to Rikochan and Heebs, and I was sick wondering whether they were safe or not.

The konbini was well-lighted with perhaps only one other customer besides the truck drivers. I looked over at Gilly and saw his rumpled shirt had grass stains and dried mud. My own clothes were filthy too — we needed to clean up a bit or we would attract attention. I began thinking about explanations I could tell someone if we happened to be seen, such as we got in an accident, or tripped in a mud puddle, or a half dozen other pathetic excuses.

It was only a few minutes later that we lost our opportunity to get back on the truck, when the three drivers came out and headed for the vehicles. We waited in the shadows for them to vacate the premises, then hesitatingly made our way to the convenience store. Just as we got in front of the doorway another customer came out so I tipped my cap to hide my face and entered before the automated glass door could slide shut. Gilly was right on my tail.

"Irrashaimase!" A store clerk welcomed us from the counter.

I tried to keep my back turned to the young man, hiding the splotches on the front of my shirt and shorts as much as I could. Japanese konbini rarely have restrooms, and this place was no exception. We picked up a few snacks and quickly headed for the register. To my embarrassment, the young man behind the counter looked me up and down. He was too polite to show disgust, but I could see it in his eyes.

"Camping . . ." I explained and gave him a big smile.

Gilly gave a big grin too and posed to match my stance. We grabbed the snacks and headed out into the dark. I had no idea what to do next. For sure there would be no taxis or buses at 3am.

"Dad, look — the Kyushu expressway is that way." Gilly pointed further down the highway in the direction the three trucks had taken.

An illuminated sign could be seen above the road. Knowing Japanese expressways, an entrance/exit ramp could be out in the middle of nowhere. But we had just ridden miles through the forest with very few structures so I figured the expressway direction might have some businesses or perhaps a bus stop at least. We started walking in that direction munching on snacks as we went and tried to duck into the shadows whenever we saw headlights coming our way.

We barely walked a kilometer when Gilly pointed up at another illuminated sign, "Dad, it looks like there's an airport ahead."

We passed the expressway entrance, and sure enough, more and more airport-related structures came into view. There were cargo facilities at first, but we had to go a couple of kilometers further before we reached the terminal building. There in big kanji characters up on the facade read "Kagoshima Airport". I don't really read Japanese, but I recognized the General shape of the characters for

"Kagoshima" at least. This was good news — we hadn't gone so far away after all. Now all we needed to do was find a power outlet for the phone.

Being so early in the morning, very few vehicles were on the road, but I did see a few taxis lining up in front of the terminal. We walked through the front door to face empty check-in counters with one or two attendants getting ready for early-morning flights. Kagoshima was a very small airport, clean and well-kept but probably dating back to the previous century. The check-in counters, gates, arrival, and departure areas all merged together on the same level. Gilly immediately ran over to the seats near the window to see if he could find any electrical outlets. I stood there for a few minutes, pondering whether we ought to catch a flight to Miyazaki. I certainly had enough cash in hand, but unfortunately, we would have to show our ID, and someone might be watching for that. It would still be safer to just stick with taxis, buses, and trains — cash exchanged with no questions asked.

A big information sign caught my eye, so I wandered over in that direction to see what lodging was in the area. The advertisements all showed photos of hot spring inns, mostly using kanji characters. One hotel stood out, mainly because it was one of the few that had Romanized titles, but also because of its name: Kirishima Hotel. Of course! This was the famous Kirishima-Takachiho National Park, with its numerous active volcanoes, cinder cones, and caldera lakes. The hotel wasn't very far away, and a taxi drive was not too unreasonable. It might be a good place to rest, charge the phone, and get cleaned up a bit, especially since we had several hours until public transportation started moving anyway.

I called Gilly over and asked, "Any luck on outlets?"

Gilly replied, "Nothing. I found dead outlets, but no power in them."

"How would you like to go to some hot springs? We could charge up there." I suggested.

"Yes! Let's go, Dad!"

The info board had an old hotline phone still working, that allowed one to dial in a code straight to the hotel of interest. I coached Gilly how to ask for a room even though it was early morning, and the reply came back in the affirmative — they were waiting for us. We rushed outside to the taxi stand and had to pay a late-night premium, but the fellow took us up dark winding roads to the hotel within half an hour. We checked in to a multi-story concrete facility that also appeared to be a relic from the previous century. I managed to pay cash for the room and gave an alias. My excuse for not showing my passport was that it had been lost in an accident — a very muddy accident. Somehow, they still let us in.

When we got to the room, Gilly immediately plugged in the phone, and we stripped off to take showers, donning nice, clean yukata robes. We took turns scrubbing our filthy outer clothes and undies in the sink, hanging dripping articles on a wire over the bath.

Before bed we checked the phone and already a text message had arrived from Heebs — they were safe and holed up for the night. No additional details. I was so distraught that I tried dialing his number but for some reason could not get a dial tone. It dawned on me that his phone might also be dead. We sent a message that we were safe in Kirishima and that we would try to meet them the next day. Gilly also texted his mother and told her dad lost his phone.

Immediately the phone rang — it was Ines calling from America in a different time zone, *"What are you guys doing up so late?"*

"Um, we've been having a little adventure, Honey." I began, "We need to get back to sleep for a full day tomorrow."

I still didn't want to worry my precious wife until things settled down again. Who knows what she might do? Maybe it could get out of proportion, and we'd find she had called in sick at work and hopped on a plane to try to come rescue us or something.

"Okay, can I talk to the boys real quick?" She wondered.

I looked over and saw that Gilly had already dozed off. I apologized that I was the only one awake and we hung up.

It was going to be trouble when she found out the whole story.

Again, I had a fitful night and barely slept a wink. Every few minutes I would hear a sound and jump up to the window to see if any patrol cars or suspicious characters were in the parking lot below. At one point I wandered in the hallways trying to memorize the location of fire stairways or emergency exits. Somehow, we had to get back to Miyazaki where my poor kids were probably huddling in some broken-down shed. These worries merged into restless dreams of constantly being on the run, and only a few hours later it was time to get up already.

Breakfast was included in the cost of the room, and the guests were asked to come down to the restaurant around sunrise. I was still very sleepy but couldn't get any rest. I dragged Gilly out of bed, and we wandered downstairs in the yukata robes. Yukata are lightweight kimonos that have simple cloth belts that tie around the waist, and are so comfortable they are often used as pajamas. It was common to be in yukata while informally walking around or dining inside hotels and inns, and we saw several other guests similarly attired.

The breakfast was a typical Japanese style meal, with rice, raw egg, nori sheets, broiled fish, and local pickled vegetables. As usual, Gilly turned his nose up at some of it. One thing, however, that caught my eye was a small sign wedged vertically in a bamboo stand, serving as a centerpiece at each of the tables. It was a laminated sheet describing a local legend about a mythical god named Ninigi-no-Mikoto typed in Japanese and translated into English on the reverse side. I hadn't studied much ancient Japanese mythology, only being familiar with a few samurai era stories. I probably would have ignored the Ninigi-no-Mikoto story completely, except that as I absent-mindedly read a few lines there was something about the Japanese Imperial Regalia. That caught my attention!

"Wait here, Gilly, I'm going to quickly grab something from the room," I excitedly explained, "put the food you don't like on my dishes."

Gilly had brought the smartphone down and was busy looking at it anyway, so he nodded and went back to what he had been doing. I rushed out, took the elevator up to our room, and grabbed the packet Rikochan had given me. I was back down at our restaurant table within five minutes. Rikochan had gathered all the notepapers up in order by the stacks she had made on the bed of the love hotel. I didn't remove all the material but thumbed through until I picked out one of the papers I had seen. Yes — there was something on the Imperial Regalia! Rikochan had scribbled down the main points of some web page. As I read through the history of the Regalia, the two stories merged together.

"Check this out, Gilly. The Japanese Imperial Regalia came from around here." I showed him the paper.

Gilly gave me a quizzical look, "What is that?"

I explained, "It's one of the clues in Rikochan's envelope. The Regalia are Japanese treasures handed down from the gods to the first emperor. There are three of them — a sword, a mirror, and a jewel. The emperors have been handing them down from father to son for hundreds of years."

"Can we see them?" Gilly wondered.

"No, apparently only the emperor can see them," I began, "they are kept in special shrines. But the origin of the treasures is only 20 minutes away from here. Maybe we can go rescue Rikochan and Heebs and come back here to figure out why they were important to Doei-san."

Suddenly the rental phone Gilly had been looking at chimed — a text message had arrived from Heebs.

Gilly looked at the screen with a puzzled look, "That's strange, all it says is 'wood rose'."

I grabbed the phone and scrolled along the text conversation. Heebs had sent a text the previous night and had been vague, saying they were 'safe and holed-up'. Now an even more cryptic text 'wood rose'. Was he trying to send a code?

"Don't reply yet," I handed the phone back, "maybe it's a clue to where they are."

I tucked the papers away in the envelope, including the laminated page from the restaurant, and slipped it in between the breast layers of the yukata. We gathered up our things and walked out into the lobby.

"Dad, let's go check out the hot springs!" Gilly excitedly pointed to the sign off to one side at lobby level.

The hot springs bath areas didn't start business until 11am but for some reason the doors were open for maintenance or something.

"Maybe we better wait until it opens later on." I replied.

A few photos on the wall revealed that these baths were no traditional Japanese ofuro, but some kind of large hot water theme park or something. We stood there looking through the door trying to get a peek but only the entranceway could be seen.

Just then I glanced over to the front desk and saw three police officers walk up to the host. For a few seconds the world came to a stop. My heart beat rapidly in my chest and I froze — we needed another way out.

"Or maybe now. Let's go!" I pushed Gilly through the door and tried to follow without being conspicuous.

Gilly looked up at me quizzically, but enthusiastically pushed ahead. This time, his eyes were saying, Dad is being naughty with me! Expecting to be stopped any minute, we carefully snuck into the changing rooms and approached the sliding glass doors leading to the bath. The view came upon us unexpectedly, as we realized the scale of the place was astounding. A huge spacious greenhouse several stories high seemed to be filled with clear blue water. A shrine-like structure thrust out of the water and enclosed other pools, with hot waterfalls cascading down various playthings, artificial caves, and plant-filled barriers.

"I saw police in the lobby! How did they find us again?" I wondered, looking at Gilly's fascination with the water wonderland, "we've got to get out of here!"

Without prompting, Gilly pulled out the smartphone and turned it off. Had they figured out how to track rental burner phones? I realized that I had grabbed my wallet before heading downstairs, but I didn't think to bring the LIDAR drone down from the room. We had barely stepped out into the vast bathing area when I stopped in my tracks — should I go back and get it? That laptop had all my research in it! Again, it seemed like time slowed to a standstill as I weighed the options of what we had to do. I can't lose my research, I thought. But Rikochan and Heebs were out there, hiding in some Miyazaki field — I had to go save them!

Gilly tugging on my yukata sleeve pulled me back to my senses. There was some commotion to the side as an older woman with an apron and bandana came out holding a plastic pail. Gilly and I sprinted in the opposite direction and leaped into the vast shallow, warm bath water. I could hear the woman shout "Okyakusan!" but we were already making our way to a pagoda-like structure in the far corner. I thought I could hear other voices, but I didn't bother to look back, and our splashing was drowning out the noise. We reached a bridge-like platform with evenly-spaced pipes flowing hot water into the main pool, and climbed up on top. Artificial rocks with shrubs provided a backdrop cliff of sorts, and the greenhouse wall was on top of that. Was there a door to the outside?

I glanced back and could see several workers making their way across the pool. Gilly followed me as we climbed the cliff to the top. There were no doors nearby, and the glass was frosted with years of calcium build-up. We made our way along the top of the cliff toward the Pagoda and got behind the roof where the cleaning women couldn't see us. On the other side our path came to an end, but down at ground level there was a door to the outside. Quickly we partially climbed and half-leaped down to the floor, and quietly eased open the door to an exterior rock bath area. A sign read, "Kazuko Kuroe Memorial outdoor stone bath".

Gilly found slippers off to the side, and without missing a beat we jumped in them and ran toward the artificial rock wall in the back. I followed Gilly as he climbed over the top, through some shrubbery, and into a back parking lot. We left the cleaning staff far behind.

It was not normal to go outside the hotel in yukata, but it was sometimes done if the customer were just going out to grab a bite at a nearby shop. And gaijin foreigners didn't really know what was proper, so a 240-pound ex-marine and a young boy wearing yukata soaked below the thighs attracted a little bit of attention. Our biggest sin, however, was that we were wearing the wrong kind of slippers. We had the kind that you wear in the bathroom, not the type that could be used on the street. Fortunately, the area we found ourselves in appeared to be a sort of maintenance yard, or work vehicle parking area surrounded by forest. As we stepped out onto the access road, a taxi was just coming down the hill, presumably having dropped off an employee. I stepped out and flagged her down.

I paused for a few minutes, not having thought far enough ahead. I had looked at the maps and there were two train lines nearby, one skirting the north, and the other along the south edge of the Kirishima-Takachiho national park on their way to Miyazaki. But if the cops had been tracking us, wouldn't they expect us to head for the train stations?

A thought suddenly crossed my mind, and I blurted out, "Takachiho-gawara onegai shimasu."

Gilly looked up at me like I was crazy, "Japanese not bad! What is Takachiho-gawara?"

The taxi driver started winding through mountain roads — she must have taken many a tourist there. I put my arm across my chest and clutched the important packet that somehow managed to stay in place through all our gymnastics.

"We're going to find a little more about Ninigi-no-Mikoto," I said.

A half an hour later we found ourselves outside a small, well-designed modern visitor's center built using traditional carpentry methods. On one end was a museum and office, and farther on was a gift shop and shokudo cafe. I steered Gilly into the gift shop first. The majority of products consisted of overpriced, exquisitely packaged Japanese cakes, teas, and crackers, but there were other souvenirs too. Gilly and I luckily each found a pair of cheap flip flops over in the corner, but by way of clothes all they had were flamboyant 'happi' coats or goods one might purchase for a matsuri festival. Happi (pronounced 'hoppy') are short, waist-length kimono-style jackets that use a cloth strip or belt to tie them closed in the front. They often, but not always, have some large graphic on the back, like a kanji character, dragon, or other brightly colored pattern. I looked for the largest, most toned-down happi I could find, thinking that a big dumb gaijin foreigner wearing a happi over a hotel yukata gown might be only slightly less conspicuous than gallivanting around the countryside in just a yukata and toilet slippers. Gilly was too young to have any pride, so we donned our purchases, tossed the toilet slippers into the nearest rubbish bin, and made our way over to the museum.

There were several historical displays about the myth of Ninigi-no-Mikoto, the Japanese Imperial Regalia, and anthropological theories of the origin of the Japanese race. According to one theory mongoloid peoples migrated down from the Korean Peninsula and established mature cultures around Dazaifu and Izumo, where some influence came from the South Pacific islands. It was likely that Kirishima, being on the southern coast of Japan, may have been part of the latter.

Interestingly, there was a history of Ise Shrine in central Japan, thought to be highly influenced by South Pacific grain storehouses. Ise Shrine was where the sacred mirror Yata-no-kagami was kept. I tried to read all the boards to see why the Imperial Regalia would be related to wormholes and quantum entanglement, but there just didn't seem to be any obvious connection. I picked up the pamphlets, tossed them in with the rest of the papers, and thanked the proprietor.

"Dad, let's go," Gilly pulled my arm.

We caught a taxi back into town to the nearest train station, Kirishima-jingu, but we had the driver drop us off a few blocks away. I couldn't think of any other means to get back to Miyazaki, so we decided to take our chances with the public railway. We kept getting strange looks from folks walking down the street but didn't see any police anywhere. I gave some cash to Gilly and had him walk up to the station master and ask for two tickets to Miyazaki station. We only had to wait thirty minutes before a semi-express train stopped at the platform. Looking about we saw no one suspicious so we hopped on board and found a couple of seats. I chose a spot by the window on the boarding side so we could see if any law enforcement would follow us. The door buzzer sounded, and we started moving without incident. We had only a few hours to figure out where to go.

"So somehow the officials can even track rental phones," I began as the train wound through the mountains, whizzing past small unattended stations out in the middle of nowhere, "They must have gotten warrants and were able to track our arrival dates and pinpoint the phone rental service. That means every time the phone is activated, the local cell area gets a blip on their map."

"Is that why Heebs sent such strange texts? Maybe he knows too." Gilly suggested.

"Whatever we do, we can't turn the phone back on unless we can move out of range quickly. But what does 'wood rose' mean?" I considered.

Gilly kept looking out the window, only glancing up at me briefly as he spoke, "It's got to be connected to some place."

The boy pulled out the phone and was about to turn it on out of habit before checking himself.

Seeing his frustration, I sympathized, "I wish we had a paper map."

Suddenly it occurred to me that the train would be passing through the town Miyakonojo, where two lines merged. As a bigger city, the express train would likely stop for a few minutes to allow passengers with first class tickets to find their seats. I pulled out a few thousand-yen notes and gave them to Gilly. When the train rolled into Miyakonojo, Gilly was already waiting by the sliding door, and ran to the nearest kiosk on the platform. It was dangerous to jump out and buy snacks in situations like these, because you never can tell when the doors will suddenly close and leave you there. I waited nervously until I heard the door buzzer, and Gilly had not returned. I immediately stood up trying to peer out the windows at the folks out on the platform, but he was nowhere to be seen. I began to get nervous as the train started moving again and still the boy had not returned — I imagined him running alongside the train calling out 'stop!' Just as I was about to panic, Gilly came walking in from a neighboring car holding a new paper map in his hand — he had quickly boarded a different door just in the nick of time.

Paper maps were pretty much obsolete most everywhere in the world except Japan, so it seemed. For the same reason the Japanese loved their paper books and magazines, maps didn't go entirely digital. We spread the map out between us in the narrow row, using the backs of the seats in front of us as a backdrop. Unfortunately, the map was almost entirely in Japanese. Only major neighborhoods, wards, and train stations had little Romanized characters next to them.

"Do you know the characters for 'wood' and 'rose'?" I asked.

Gilly had been studying the map, but paused to look sideways at me, "I know wood = 'ki' and I know what it looks like, but I don't know the character for 'bara'. It would be 'kibara' I think,"

After showing me the simple four-stroke character, I began to see it all over the map. Apparently 'ki' meant anything from wood to tree to grove to forest, and was commonly found in people's family names too. There was Kiwaki, Kihara, Kibana, Kurogi, and Momiki at first glance, but no Kibara.

"What about this, Dad? This place called 'Kibana' means 'wood flower', and is only about a 20-minute walk from where we got separated last night." Gilly pointed out.

It couldn't be that easy — the cops could figure that one out too. But sweeping the entire map found nothing so close. We finally decided to head that way, but not via train. Instead, we got off at Kiyotake station, a few stops short of Miyazaki, and found a bus cutting across town.

The bus pulled into Kibana Station, a robotic unmanned metro node for the bustling south Miyazaki area. Gilly and I got off the bus in our goofy yukata and happi coats, feeling very out of place. There were shops, restaurants, and 'gaito' malls stretching out in all directions. No one was there to meet us. How would we ever find them! I told Gilly to turn on the phone but leave location services off — we could send a quick message and turn it off again.

Suddenly the phone rang — it was Ines.

Gilly handed the phone to me as we walked along the mall, and I heard my wife ask, *"Hi, Honey, I found that hat you were looking for."*

Just as we rounded a corner, I almost bumped into a group of well-dressed middle-aged men coming toward us. I nearly froze as I realized that I recognized the person in the middle — he was the bearded yakuza fellow that had been tracking us! I steeled myself for a confrontation, getting my flabby 240-pound frame ready to do some serious damage. The bearded man looked straight into my eyes and suddenly stepped to one side.

"Shitsurei shimasu." was all he said and continued past us.

I turned on my heels and stared dumbfounded as the group of men continued onward, eyes sweeping the area as if in search for someone, but apparently not us. As I had thought, the men hadn't seen Gilly and I at all our previous encounters — they didn't recognize us!

"Hello? Are you there?" Ines' voice came out of the phone.

I continued to watch the suits walk down the mall, and said in a panicked voice, "Dear I miss you — hey I can't talk right now. I'll call you later."

I hung up, and the two of us found a sign to hide behind.

"Dad, look!" Gilly pointed in the direction the yakuza characters had gone.

I was still staring as the last man disappeared around a corner, but when I shifted my gaze to follow Gilly's pointing finger, I knew exactly what he was talking about. There, up on a store front was a giant carved flower that was part of the sign saying 'Kibara Internet Cafe'. A giant wood rose.

CHAPTER 5

We found Heebs in the back, hiding in one of the booths. He had his burner phone turned on looking at the photos he took of Hirayuki's document but kept the device offline. He had paid for computer time from the Internet cafe and had been doing generic searches but didn't try to access any of his accounts. There were a few copies of stuff on the desk that he had found online and printed out. As soon as Gilly and I walked up, Rikochan and Sally who had been across the darkened room also crowded into the booth. They couldn't hide the look of amusement on their faces. I suddenly felt very self-conscious of our yukata and happi coat attire.

"You guys look like some gaijin clowns!" Rikochan snickered.

"Way to lay low — did you attract the attention of everyone in Kyushu?" Heebs added.

Heebs stood up and the four of us embraced, with Sally standing off to the side.

Gilly excitedly burst out, "You wouldn't believe what we went through!"

Not to be outdone, Heebs quickly replied, "Us too! We had to stand in the river up to our necks breathing out of reeds."

Rikochan flashed angry eyes at Heebs giving us a hint that he might have been exaggerating a little. She said, "We've got to get you some new clothes. Maybe they tracked you here already! Someone should go out shopping."

Everyone looked at Rikochan and she had to volunteer. I gave her some cash and Sally went along as a lookout. Rikochan put on a big floppy hat and large sunglasses, and the girls inconspicuously exited the cafe. Heebs, Gilly, and I huddled in the booth and compared notes.

"I started looking up some of the things on Hirayuki's document," Heebs began, "I don't know anything about the physics, but the Antikythera mechanism is really cool! Dad, have you ever heard of the 'Silurian Hypothesis'?"

"No, I don't think I have. What is it?" I asked.

"It's like an idea that technologically advanced civilizations may have existed before our history, and somehow, they lost it and turned primitive again. The Silurians came from a science fiction series called Dr. Who — they were advanced lizard people aliens that ruled the earth before humans got out of the Stone Age." Heebs explained.

Gilly perked up, "What? You mean there used to be lizard people?"

"No dummy, that's just science fiction." Heebs crossed his younger brother, "They called it the 'Silurian Hypothesis' as a kind of joke, but they're really bona fide scientists who were thinking about how we could tell from the geological record of a planet whether an ancient technological civilization could have existed there."

"So, what about the Antikythera mechanism? Isn't that some Greek relic?" I probed.

Heebs nodded, "The Antikythera mechanism was supposedly a Greek astronomical calculator, but the precision technology needed to manufacture the brass gears was lost. It's one known example of how technology may sometimes disappear into more primitive dark ages, then get reinvented later. And then there are those examples of diamond drill and saw marks on ancient stone walls."

"So, the lizard people made antikonomical calculators?" Gilly's eyes were wide open with amazement.

Heebs gave his brother a stern look, "Shut up wiener brains! There's no lizard people!"

The boys started getting into an argument that I had to put an end to. I changed the subject and brought up Ninigi-no-Mikoto.

"Apparently this area ties in with the ancient origins of Japanese culture." I mentioned another of Hirayuki's notes, combined with what we had learned, "A Shinto god delivered the Imperial Regalia to the first emperor on the top of Mount Takachiho. Anthropologists believe there were two main origins for the Japanese. The mongoloid race came from the north and includes China and Korea. But ancient Shinto temples like Ise Shrine were patterned after grain storehouses found in the Pacific islands."

Heebs had frozen mid-headlock with Gilly tucked under his arm. He released his brother and asked, "What are the Imperial Regalia?"

Gilly rushed up and faced his big brother, "Gosh turd breath, those are the three Japanese treasures. You didn't know that?"

Heebs reached out to grab Gilly again in a choke hold but the younger boy was too fast and scrawny, so he squirmed out of reach. Heebs waved his hand like he was pushing away and let it go. Instead, he looked to me, waiting for a better explanation.

"If we look at myths back that far, oftentimes the gods were just a highly revered grandfather whose story got bigger each subsequent generation. The three treasures are a sword, a mirror, and a jewel. I wonder why those things ended up being treasures?" I mused.

Heebs remembered something else, "By the way, I looked up Egyptian hieroglyphic numbers to see how they match with the sudoku puzzle —"

"And?" I looked up with great interest.

"There's no match at all! I've pulled out nine hieroglyphs but have no idea which order they are." Heebs shrugged, showing us a sketch he had made of the symbols.

Gilly wandered back and yanked the sketch out of Heebs' hand, "That's easy — all you have to do is make sure one of each is in each line, column, and square! But what do horrorgliffs, swords, mirrors, and jewels have to do with antikathodes and lizard men?"

Just then the girls came back with shopping bags. At some point Rikochan had donned one of those old pandemic face coverings modeled on surgical masks, which she proceeded to take off. The women held up the bags like peace offerings.

"Here you go. Restroom is over there." Rikochan pointed across the dimly lit room to a door faintly visible.

Several minutes later Gilly and I emerged looking a bit more normal. We stuffed the yukatas and happi coats in the trash, which unfortunately would have made good keepsakes if we had been under better circumstances. Rikochan had found a shirt with a big, zippered pocket on the back, large enough to secure the stuffed envelope of papers.

"Nobeoka then?" I asked Rikochan.

My daughter smiled and replied, "Yes! Ebina-san knows we're coming. I used an encrypted messenger app on the cafe computer."

I frowned but didn't say anything as we carefully walked out into the gaito mall. Since the advent of reliable quantum computing, could anything encrypted be trusted anymore? Surely the law enforcement would have those tools available.

There were lots a people about, so we blended into the crowd walking through the shopping mall. Several times we split up, doubled back, lurked behind displays, watched passersby, and determined no shady characters or law enforcement were in the area. Then one by one we entered the train station and scattered ourselves along the platform, waiting for the next train heading north out of town. Once everyone found themselves on the train it was easy to spot followers, should there be any, as we walked down a single aisle with both ends of the train visible at once. I sat down in a private booth and waited as one by one Sally and each of the children joined me.

The train was heading toward Nobeoka and we seemed to be safe for the moment, but something nagged at my mind. I looked out the window and watched the neighborhoods fly by.

"I want to take a slight detour." I proposed.

Everyone looked at me curiously. We were all tired of running and just wanted to find a place to relax out of danger. But we still had a mystery to solve – somehow, we needed to figure out what the next piece of the puzzle might be. I wondered how comfortable Rikochan would be telling Sally what we were up against. Without the ability to consult with her in advance, I decided to take a chance and see what my daughter wanted to do next.

I continued, "I think I know someone who can help us figure out what 'funadori' means."

'Funadori' was written in kanji characters on the page above the sudoku puzzle. Rikochan sat on the far side of the booth, and I kept my eyes on her the whole time. I saw her shake her head almost imperceptibly, as if she wasn't ready to go into detail with the girl. Surprisingly, Sally didn't ask for any explanation, as if finding a 'funadori' bird was completely natural.

If Rikochan wanted to stay mum about the papers, she jumped on board with my proposal, "Agreed — let's do it. The more we get on and off the easier it will be to lose someone if we're being followed. Let's go do some research on birds."

I said, "Okay we'll need to get off soon. I know a former researcher from National University of Singapore in biological sciences. He was a student back then working with Singapore Zoo and Night Safari. We met at a conference because he was interested in LIDAR mapping caves and bat habitats. He ended up right here in Miyazaki!"

We split up into two groups, intent on taking separate taxis to the Miyazaki City Phoenix Zoo. I saw Rikochan, Heebs, and Sally off first at Hasugaike station, then Gilly and I stayed on the train and got off at the following station. The zoo was actually quite small and was combined with amusement park rides, water slides, and a circulating current pool. We found Dr Fumio Okudaira was on-site and he remembered our brief meetings at NUS and the conference.

"Hi Fumio! I guess I should call you Dr Okudaira now?" I greeted him, since he had finally been awarded his PhD, "These are my sons Hibiki and Guilherme, and my daughter Kariko with her friend Sally."

Fumio heartily replied, "Dr Hughes! Please call me Fumio."

"And call me Tim — I don't like being formal at times like these." I returned.

"I remember meeting Hibiki in Singapore. Aren't you the one interested in robotics?" Fumio asked.

I paused for a few seconds, then realized he wasn't talking about Heebs, "Ah Fumio, I think you met my older son Masamune — he's away at college."

Fumio apologized, "Oh sorry, you all grow up so fast! It's great to see you again. Tell me, what brings you to Miyazaki?"

I pointed to Rikochan and said, "Kariko has a question for you."

Fumio motioned for us to join him in his office, where two plush sofas faced each other off to the side of his desk. Each of us took a seat and a young park employee brought in a tray with iced mugicha barley tea.

Rikochan began, "Dr Okudaira, have you ever heard of a 'funadori'? The characters are 'boat bird' but we can't seem to find any such fowl."

Fumio scratched his head and thought for a moment, "No, I don't think I've ever heard of such a bird. Let's see — some species have been named from pre-western eras, meaning that the 'kun-yomi' or 'on-yomi' of the kanji characters reflect exactly how the people of that era called the animal. But sometimes such names are pulled from Latin western names. Let's look this up."

Fumio got on his smartphone and typed in a few characters, "Ah, the Latin term would be 'naviculam avem'. Let's see if such a scientific name exists."

Again, Fumio looked in several sources as he typed away on the smartphone. No luck there.

Kariko revealed the results of Gilly's research the previous morning at the love hotel, "We found a couple of references to minor place names, like Funadori Peninsula, or Funadori Mountain, but those were a little cryptic, in text form but not in any map databases."

Fumio looked thoughtful, then asked, "Where did you hear about this bird? Maybe I can help you there."

Rikochan reached for the smartphone Heebs had used to take photos of Hirayuki Doei's document. From the side I watched as she brought up the image of the sudoku puzzle with the script characters scrawled across the top. She made a copy of the image, then cropped it down so only the two characters remained.

"Here it is — this is where we saw it, in kanji cursive script." Rikochan showed Fumio the cropped image.

The biologist looked at the image and began to laugh, "Hahaha! This is not cursive style, my dear, it's semi-cursive. The formal typeset block script is usually called 'kaisho' with cursive being 'sosho'. In the middle there is 'gyosho' or semi-cursive. Your calligrapher was a little bit sloppy here. This isn't 'funadori', it says 'Funajima'. See how the main radical is identical in both characters but the four dots on 'bird' might start to resemble the little mountain on the character 'island'?"

Fumio paused to laugh again and said, "'Funajima' is an island right here in Kyushu, in the Seto Inland Sea. It's right off the coast of Kitakyushu near Moji, in the Kanmon Straits!"

CHAPTER 6

We took all the usual precautions, splitting up, doubling back, staggering boarding times, but still I couldn't help thinking that the train ride to Nobeoka had unwanted visitors. We sat separately but in the same car. Gilly, Heebs, and I sat in seats that faced each other forward and backward, but Rikochan and Sally sat in the commuter section where the seats had their backs to the windows of the train. I saw no police or yakuza-type characters, but an old man in the commuter section kept watching Rikochan and would turn away every time she looked up. Also, a thirtyish woman walked down the aisle from the neighboring car several times, passing right on through to the next car in both directions. She seemed to slow a bit whenever she passed in front of Rikochan, interested in what my daughter was doing at the time.

As far as I know, there might have been people watching us too, careful to hide their interest. On the other hand, I might have just been a little paranoid. When we got off at Totoro Station in the southern part of Nobeoka none of my suspects seemed to get off with us.

Sally announced that she intended to stay on the train all the way home to Kitakyushu, "I've had enough excitement for the year."

Heebs pointed out, "Someone may still be following you. Is it wise to go home yet?"

"I'll take my chances in familiar territory. Besides, my dad is coming to visit from the United States. I think I'll be safe enough." Sally explained.

We said our goodbyes and left her on the train as we walked down the platform. We saw her waving through the window as the train picked up speed down the track. Little did we know at the time that we would see her again soon, under unfortunate circumstances. But such things were not on our minds as again we slipped into cautionary mode looking out for possible stalkers.

Unfortunately, as on the train, most everyone looked like they could be collaborating with an undercover manhunt. There was the fellow standing near the ticket machines who kept looking in our direction and periodically whispering into his lapel. Or the drunk sitting on the floor with his back to the column.

"Amerikajin!" The drunk man looked up as we passed, "Dis is a pen!"

I smiled uncomfortably as I looked at the poor fellow when we walked past. He didn't have a pen in his hands to show, nor was he even holding anything, but the bottle hidden in a brown paper bag. It looked to me as though he might not even have a clue what the sentence 'this is a pen' meant — the lights were on but nobody's home.

Rikochan leaned over and explained in a whisper, "That's the first English sentence everyone learns in grade school, like 'see Spot run' kind of a thing."

The man was still staring up at me, 'We are all after you' I imagined him saying. He was actually well-dressed in a business suit which was a little crumpled. How could an advanced culture like Japan tolerate something like this right here in public?

Suddenly there was a tug on my arm that made me look up. Two policewomen were heading our way. Rikochan with her floppy hat and sunglasses conspicuously looked away toward a newsstand off to the side. Heebs looked down at his smartphone, which was off, and Gilly put his hands up to his face and peered through his fingers. My heart raced as the women drew closer. There was no place to hide! I couldn't look away — I was so tired of running. I steeled myself for getting caught and closed my eyes, expecting to have my wrists zip-tied any second. Time passed excruciatingly slow.

But nothing happened. I opened my eyes, and the officers were gone. I turned around and saw them leaning over the drunk person.

"Tanaka-san, ikimashō." One of the women said as she reached down to grab the drunkard's arm.

Another tug on my arm and Heebs dragged me out the exit. I was still in panic mode as we ran for the taxi stand where Rikochan was standing near the opened car door beckoning to us. We hopped in the taxi and drove away from the station. I kept turning my head to look back and verify that no police were following us. Ten minutes later I had finally settled down when the vehicle pulled up to the Ebina residence.

"It's okay, Dad, we're safe. Let's go inside." Gilly guided me out of the back seat.

The Ebina residence sat on the end of Totoro Park near Cape Yomo. We couldn't see the ocean due to the trees, but apparently the Ebina back yard actually butted up against the rugged coastal terrain. Across the street from the park there were a few scattered single-family residences and multi-story condominiums.

"The Ebina family owns many of the apartments around here," Rikochan began, "Ichika-san's mother does all the property management, while her father works as an executive for the Asahikasei corporation in downtown Nobeoka."

The neighborhood appeared humble but in good condition. I was thinking that a coastal property like this in the United States would fetch a premium price, but in these remote Japanese villages it was not always the case. Nobeoka in particular had nice long beaches, but just inland between the beach and the residential neighborhoods you would often find wide industrial districts limiting access.

"This is my friend Ichika Ebina, a colleague in genetic engineering." Rikochan introduced her friend.

Ichika-san met us as we approached the front door. She was an attractive young lady, about the same age as Rikochan, but where my daughter was a little rough around the edges, Ichika-san was quite thin, well-poised, and smartly dressed. You could definitely tell she was from a well-to-do family.

Ichika-san bowed and said, "Irrashaimase! Welcome to our home. We have spare bedrooms now that my brothers have moved away."

"Thank you so much. We've had a rough couple of days. You know Kariko. These are two of her brothers Hibiki and Gilherme." I bowed in return.

"Dōzo, please come in." Ichika-san pointed toward the front entry.

Heebs stared at the young woman for a few seconds, admiring her cultured Japanese persona, but avoided any of his usual awkward teenage testosterone-fueled antics. In contrast to down-to-earth Sally, he clearly must have concluded she was out of his league.

She directed us to a small tatami-floored room with a shin-high table. Off to one side was a small ancestral butsudan shrine with rice and mikan offerings in bowls, and faint tendrils of incense wafting toward the ceiling. We could see several kakejiku scrolls hanging on the walls, and a wood calligraphy panel supported at an angle above the shoji room dividers. Of greater interest was the suit of samurai armor protected in a polycarbonate box in a tokonoma niche in the wall. Several samurai swords were on display above the armor.

"Is this real?" Heebs asked as the two of us gravitated toward the armor.

I looked closely at the sword blades and could see the tell-tale layered fold lines that resulted from the forging process — hundreds of cycles of pounding the metal smooth, then folding it over again. The process gave the sword a combined hardness-softness that allowed for razor-sharp edges.

"Yes, my great-great-great grandfather was a retainer for the Shimazu clan." Ichika-san revealed.

We all sat around the table on the floor and Ichika-san brought cold barley mugicha tea and Japanese snacks. The boys scarfed down the snacks and took a few sips of the tea.

"Dad, can Gilly and I go down to the water?" Heebs implored.

I could see they were getting bored, so I waved them on, "Okay, but be very careful! Look out for suspicious strangers. Always keep an escape route."

Gilly looked up with stormy eyes, "Dad, we know!"

"Okay, don't be long." I concluded.

Ichika-san pointed toward a back door and said, "Go out that way and follow the path down. It's a rocky place with tide pools. Good fishing too!"

We watched the boys run out and then Rikochan turned serious. Apparently, Ichika-san had only heard we were going to stay but hadn't heard the details of why.

"We met up with Sally in Miyazaki. She stayed on the train." Rikochan noted.

It was easy to see discomfort on Ichika-san's face at the sound of the name. I recalled the time Sally bristled at hearing the name 'Ichika' too — there must have been some bad blood between the two.

Rikochan looked a little nervous and tried to explain what happened, "There's been a couple of murders in Kitakyushu. The killers are chasing us, and the police think I've done it!"

Interestingly, Ichika-san didn't show any surprise. It was as if the news was completely expected.

"Let me guess." She started, "You've gotten involved with the transhumanists."

Rikochan stared at her incredulously for a good minute or so, then stammered, "I think Doei-san found something scuba diving. I don't know what it was, but they killed him for it."

"Girl, if I were you, I'd stay away. Run away as fast as you can." Ichika-san advised.

"Do you know something? Why would someone want to kill for it?" I asked.

Ichika-san, sitting upright in the seiza style, finally relaxed and crossed her legs. Rikochan and I had long ago stretched our legs out under the table. It looked as if Ichika-san were trying to shoulder a great burden and by just asking, we could share it somehow.

"I don't know any details, but there were rumors that someone had stumbled on something big. I have my suspicions," she said.

I subtly caught Rikochan's eye and gestured toward the stuffed envelope I kept in the back shirt pocket. She nodded and I reached behind to unzip the pocket.

Rikochan spoke up, "Actually, Doei-san gave me some papers. We've been trying to figure out what they mean."

Ichika-san's attention perked up and she sat straight again. Our host eagerly watched as I brought the envelope around and selected Hirayuki's original document out from all the pages of notes the children had produced.

"All these things are related somehow. I think there is a clue as to why Doei-san and Professor Hosogawa were killed, but we just can't figure it out." Rikochan suggested.

Ichika-san began looking at the 'Funajima' characters and sudoku puzzle. I watched as her eyes darted back and forth on the page, observing Hirayuki's Japanese regalia notes and scribbles associated with the scrap of cursive manuscript. Her eyes lit up when she flipped the page over and began reading the hieroglyphics interpretations.

"Egyptian? Strange combination," she noted after turning the page this way and that, "it looks like disconnected topics ranging from biology, physics, anthropology, robotics, and history, all the way to religion. Makes no sense."

Being a genetic engineer, Ichika-san zeroed in on biology-related bullet points. She slapped the paper down on the table and pointed to 'Craig Venter 2010' note.

"I know this one. I'm pretty sure this is Venter's signature work, *Creation of a Bacterial Cell Controlled by a*

Chemically Synthesized Genome." She excitedly remarked, "And *Life at the Speed of Light.*"

Rikochan, also a genetic engineer, excitedly looked on, "Hmm — I thought you'd pick up on those!"

"These are Craig Venter papers." Ichika-san looked up and smiled, "I've followed his work with some interest. This first paper about a chemically synthesized genome is his breakthrough work where his team digitally synthesized the genome of M mycoides and artificially transplanted DNA sequences into the stripped-down M capricolum cell."

"What? What does that mean?" I asked.

Rikochan translated into plain English, "In other words, they artificially created life. A viable self-reproducing cell."

I stared at the girls incredulously, "You've got to be kidding me."

"This is a controversial topic, but because of Venter's work, some of us are starting to look at life from a different perspective. It looks like biological cells are actually programmable molecular machines!" Ichika-san excitedly ventured.

Rikochan jumped in, "Yes! You've got genetic coding that are like strips of DNA commands instructing organisms to grow arms, legs, wings, and whatever."

"The essential parts of a robotic mechanism are all there," Ichika-san continued, "programmable control, sensors, actuators. They're even saying that brain cells in various organisms utilize quantum computing. Did you know that the program required to create a human body is more than ninety percent the same as that of corn? There are alleles out there for vision, touch sensors, spectrometry by way of gustatory senses or taste. You've got genes that control ambulatory mobility, propellers, winged flight, and even jet engines. There are chlorophyll solar panels by far more efficient than photovoltaics, thermal control systems, maintenance systems, transportation systems, wiring networks, molecular assemblers." Ichika-san enumerated.

Rikochan jumped in, "Biological mechanisms can even print 3D metal. Fernando found a plant that can accumulate nickel, Konishi discovered microbes that deposit gold nanoparticles, and there are various creatures that use zinc or manganese to harden body appendages for cutting and drilling."

Suddenly I felt myself stuck in the midst of two specialists going down the rabbit hole. Ichika-san looked at me and pointed at the second publication title, *Life at the speed of light*.

"That's what makes this so exciting!" She said, "Since we can digitally sequence all these genes, and digitally insert them into a cell to program it the way we like, why not send the apparatus out to a desert or underdeveloped country? We could remotely send signals to such a machine and tell it to produce whatever engineered organism we need. That's what Venter was proposing."

"I don't get it. Why would we want to create organisms on demand?" I felt lost.

Ichika-san smiled, "You could send commands to digitally synthesize genes for an organism that eats up an oil spill or breaks apart plastic trash heaps. Could you imagine programming a seed from a pine tree to grow into a house? It would be complete with plumbing, electrical wires, transparent windows, heating, air conditioning, and lockable doors!"

Rikochan added in excitement, "Biology is a most incredible machine. If you stretch out the DNA of a single human cell it is about 3 meters long. Put all the DNA from the cells in one adult human body end to end and it would be 134 astronomical units, or roughly 70 round trips to the sun and back!"

All I could do is stare in amazement. It was still beyond my comprehension, but I could see interesting technologies coming out of it, "Okay, but what does that have to do with wormholes, imperial regalia, or Antikythera mechanisms?"

"Well, that is confusing. But I can at least see a connection with robotics and self-replicating machines." Ichika-san proposed.

I reached over and picked up the document, then carefully inserted it back into the envelope. Ichika-san suddenly had a grave expression on her face and looked at Rikochan.

"That's what concerns me," she said, "someone from the transhumanists must have figured out how it all ties together and is willing to kill for it. Though I can't imagine what the connection might be that would motivate someone so."

Rikochan also got a cloudy expression as the two stared at each other in deep thought.

"Rikochan, I need to discuss something with you in private." Ichika-san seemed desperate.

Both girls turned and looked at me without saying a word. It took a minute for me to get the hint. I returned the envelope to its zippered pocket behind my back.

"Okay, I think I'll go fetch the boys and maybe we'll go out and get a bite to eat or something," I said.

It was late afternoon. I walked out the rear door into a long, narrow backyard. A steep slope on the left was covered with thick brush, offering no way to climb to the top. Trees lined the right side, keeping the yard private but offering views beyond. As I proceeded along the grassy space, I could glimpse the harbor through the gaps in the foliage. The sound of small waves rushing up a beach mixed with a salty, refreshing ocean breeze. I found multiple paths leading down to the beach and chose one to walk out on the sand just enough to see whether my boys were there. On the right the beach ended at a sea wall protecting Totoro Park, sweeping a long arm into the harbor. On the left there was a short jetty made from jumbled concrete tetrapods. Multiple sea birds were roosting out there, hopping across the tops of the tetrapods scavenging for crustaceans. Occasionally one or two of the fowl would take to flight to survey the cracks and gaps along the jetty, then swoop down for a kill. Along this short beach the water was mostly placid, no doubt protected by some unseen wave break beyond the jetty.

Seeing no one, I returned to the long grassy yard and continued following its twisting path past the tetrapod jetty. When I came to the end, another path took me to the rocky coastline of Cape Yomo, where presumably there were tide pools that would attract teenage boys.

I had only gone a few dozen or so yards, skirting crevices and rocky outcroppings, when the hair on the back of my neck stood on end. Something was wrong — my sense of danger was piqued like it hadn't been since I served overseas in the US Marine Corps. Instinctively, I threw myself down behind an outcropping and peered further down the beach. It was as if I had my weapon ready, with all my senses focused on an unseen enemy.

Movement — a head popped up and concealed itself before I could get a good look. I heard the sound of footsteps running erratically towards me, no! Two, three, four sets of footfalls. I looked around for something I could use as a weapon, but could only find odd-shaped, ungainly driftwood pieces or small twigs and branches. The natural igneous rock underfoot seemed to flow in wave-sculpted ridges all cracked and broken, but there weren't even any convenient-sized stones nearby small enough to pick up and throw.

The first set of running feet came closer and a figure stumbled past my hiding spot. It was Gilherme, quickly followed by Heebs, who threw a quick glance in my direction. My presence startled him and he almost tripped.

"Yakuza!" He cried out as he recovered his footing and continued running along the rough surface.

More running footsteps were almost upon me. I had no time to get away, so I tried to squeeze my bulky frame into a crevice and hide as best I could. A middle-aged Japanese man in a dark suit flew around the corner and pounded after Heebs. He was chasing my boy! I was filled with indignant rage.

I leapt up just as I heard another runner approaching. I have no idea how my flabby body responded so well, but the next thing I know I was flying sideways aimed precisely at the middle of another figure rounding the bend. I collided with the person and my momentum caused us both to tumble into a pool of seawater. The other person was well-trained and knew just where to grasp an enemy in hand-to-hand combat. Fortunately, I was also trained, though a little out of shape. I recovered my feet in waist-deep water, and in one fell swoop brought my fist around to squarely connect with her face. A woman! I had just knocked out a woman who fell back against the rocks and lay still.

How could I hit a woman? I had no time for remorse because more runners were coming. I looked back in the direction of Yomo Cape and could see three or four figures in business suits leaping over the rocks toward me. And one of those figures I knew well — the bearded yakuza chief.

I quickly scrambled up the rock and started running back toward the house. I could no longer see Gilly, Heebs, or their pursuer, but I hoped I could catch up to the bastard in time. I ran up the trail to the long grassy yard and could see the Japanese man struggling with Heebs and Gilly near the house. The boys were raging like wildcats, kicking, punching, and screaming, but the man was starting to get the upper hand. I saw Heebs get an elbow in the face, causing him to slink back with his hands covering his mouth. The man was quick, spinning around to restrain Gilly's arms without missing a beat.

"Hands off!" I yelled.

The man didn't even acknowledge my presence but continued to hold an uncooperative Gilly. I caught up to them and packed my incoming momentum into a right hook but missed.

I didn't even see it coming — for a few seconds the lights went out. All went quiet and I didn't know where I was. The fellow must have used some martial arts move with a hand out of nowhere. The world came slowly back, and I lunged toward the tumbling mass of flailing limbs and bodies. I vaguely saw Gilly bite deep into the older man's hand causing him to let go. There was the briefest of pauses as I saw the man's toothy grin smiling down at me. 'You are dead meat,' those sadistic eyes seemed to say. I watched his arm move with astounding speed and there was no chance I could get out of the way. I cringed and braced myself for impact.

Something slammed into my shoulder, but it wasn't what I expected. My groggy mind saw Heebs come into view, wailing on the man with a piece of lumber. I couldn't see Gilly, but objects were flying in, expertly deflected by lightning-quick moves. While he was distracted, I aimed for his legs for a shoestring tackle and caught him off-guard — he went down backwards. Heebs moved in with rage showing on his face, smashing down again and again. The mobster finally lay still in the grass, and I had to insert myself between that motionless figure and the boys.

The three of us stood around panting our lungs out, nursing bruises, sore knuckles, and bloody noses. But the fight was not over — Yakuza beard and his cronies were coming on fast.

"Quick, inside!" I yelled.

We leapt over the unconscious man and closed the distance to the back door in no time. Heebs and Gilly somehow yanked the door ajar and fell through the opening at the same time and I was right on their tail. We slammed the door shut just as the men came into view. I looked down and fumbled with the lock trying to get it to engage. With a final 'click' I pushed the boys further inside with the intent to herd them upstairs and hopefully find a way to barricade ourselves in one of the rooms.

Just then Gilly's phone rang — it was Ines again.

"Can you talk now?" I heard her voice.

Bless her heart, trying to look out for us. Oh, that woman's timing!

"Mom, we can't talk right now." Gilly answered and hung up.

When I took a last glance outside, I could see no one. The unconscious man was still lying there, but 'Beard Yakuza' and the others had disappeared.

It was at that moment we heard a loud crash from the front room. Someone had kicked down the door! The only thing I could think of was Rikochan — I had to go protect her! We rushed around the corner, and it seemed like the whole world came to a standstill. I will never forget the scene that flashed before me. The tatami room we had been in only a half hour earlier was a mess. The suit of armor had toppled, with a cracked polycarbonate case. There were blood stains — dark pools of red liquid seeping into the grass tatami mats. And Ichika-san! The low table had split in half forming a vee shape that cradled Ms. Ebina's body, her eyes staring lifelessly at the ceiling. The short wakizashi samurai sword from the display protruded from her leg with blood all over the handle. And the greatest shock of all! A blood splattered Kariko stood near Ichika-san's head holding the long, bloody katana sword. Multiple stab wounds on the host's torso still spouted blood that dribbled onto the table and floor.

Everything moved in slow motion. The front door had been kicked open. Two helmeted, black-clad Japanese 'Tokushu Kyushu Butai' Special Assault Team (SAT) members rushed in. Each officer held an automatic rifle against the shoulder and peered through optics, fingers hovering over the trigger. Almost simultaneously, the rear door we had just entered crashed open with more SAT team members pouring in. We heard footsteps coming down the stairs. It seemed as though time stopped — we all stood there for endless seconds staring down a dozen rifle barrels.

From somewhere outside an electronically enhanced bullhorn shouted in English, "Te wo agerō! Keep your hands up!"

Each of us slowly raised our hands above our heads. The katana clattered to the table as a blank-faced Kariko released it and raised her hands. The SAT officers continued their ready stance and waited. Soon a 'mawarisan' police officer with a different uniform and no helmet entered and handcuffed Kariko. More officers handcuffed each of us except Gilly.

"I didn't do it!" Kariko pleaded, "I found her like that and tried to save her."

Kariko looked at me with a haggard face. She had blood splattered all over from the chest down. I began thinking maybe she could have done it after all, but quickly quenched the thought. The sweet girl I knew was utterly incapable of such a heinous act. But then again, I had just left those two alone only minutes before — how could Kariko not be involved? But what about the yakuza who were in the area? Yakuza!

I spoke up, "Officer, I'm sure she didn't do it. My boys and I were just now chased by hoodlums. There's an unconscious man outside the back door."

One of the officers led me back there and we looked outside. The body was gone. The officer peered at me skeptically.

"I swear we knocked him out!" I protested.

Both Heebs and Gilly also joined in a chorus of pleading but to no avail. The officers herded the four of us down to the local police station.

CHAPTER 7

Hibiki and Gilherme, being minors, were not implicated in any way. I thought for sure that they would try to pin on me a charge of aiding and abetting, or at least obstruction of justice. But to my surprise they let the three of us free on condition that we surrender our passports and promise to stay nearby in case they needed to question us. I had to explain that we had lost our passports, so we were stuck anyway. Furthermore, I didn't want to get too far away before we figured out how to convince them into releasing Kariko. As for my daughter, no one would tell me anything other than that the investigation was still ongoing.

Fortunately, I still had my wallet, and the police hadn't taken away the envelope of papers. The secret was in there, and we might be able to bargain for Rikochan's freedom if we could just figure out what it all meant. I finally had a chance to talk to Ines in a relaxed atmosphere but didn't have the heart to tell her the real story yet. Heebs and Gilly, also knowing their mother, colluded with me to soften the story until we could find out what was going on.

"We had a great time looking for historical stuff!" I heard Gilly tell her.

Heebs had an even more interesting take, neglecting to mention Kariko, "Mom, it was great! We even got to see the police arrest someone!"

"Okay have fun," she said.

A couple of days later, my boys and I walked out of the Kokuraminami Police Station and trotted over to the Kitakyushu monorail. From there it was a short ride downtown to Kokura station. Part of the deal made with the police included establishing ourselves in a hotel nearby where they could keep an eye on us. The Kokura Station Hotel was a multi-story modern building and was actually quite comfortable even though it was only a two-star rating. We really needed the rest, and besides, I had lots of things to take care of and messes to clean up. We had abandoned a rental car at Udo Shrine, dropped burner phones into the river, left our luggage in the Nichinan hotel, and I lost my LIDAR drone at the Kirishima hotel.

But on this particular morning all those things were working to our advantage. As we stepped inside the hotel and walked up the stairs to the front desk the robotic clerk Joe glided over to a spot directly opposite with its photoreceptors aimed in my direction. The machine was vaguely humanoid, but only in a caricature sort of way. It had a head on a neck that had limited range of rotation, vision sensors where eyes would normally have been, arms with human-like dexterous fingers, and a human-scale torso. Years ago, the life-like receptionists had gotten so realistic that at first glance it was difficult to tell that they were artificial. But some slight nuance always gave them away, and human guests tended to be turned off by the life-like appearance. The backlash resulted in less life-like robotic hosts like Joe, which were not as creepy.

"Dr. Tim Hughes," the robot said in an old-fashioned synthetic voice style, as if he were a genius physicist in a wheelchair, "a package has arrived."

That was quick, I thought. Just then Heebs motioned from the corner of my eye and grabbed my attention, "Dad, I'll be right back. I'm going to print out some articles and make paper copies of the sudoku puzzle."

I turned briefly and watched Gilly follow his brother down the corridor to the business center. Behind the counter Joe shifted over to locate the package. The robot moved back and forth in a miniature autonomous warehouse full of cubicles backloaded by a hidden sorting and supply system. Joe found the package and gently handed it over to me.

"Here you go, Doctor Hughes." the machine said.

Joe could have used any other language had I been a guest from some other country, but English came out in my case. I grabbed the package and turned to follow the boys down the corridor.

Just because the police weren't after us anymore didn't mean that we were clear of danger. The yakuza thugs were still out there, and somehow, they had ways of tracking us. Therefore, it was still unwise to use the rental cell phones. Fortunately, the hotel guaranteed anonymity over their VOIP (Voice over Internet Protocol) system.

I walked into the business center just as Gilly used the VOIP system to call Masamune, my college-aged son. Several desks with computer screens were lined up against a long glass window looking down on the Kokura Station main level. Heebs had printed out a copy of the sudoku puzzle and already started trying to solve it. I had wanted to head up to our room, but since the boys might end up taking a bit of time, I settled down at one of the desks and examined the package Joe had given me. We had only checked into the hotel a few days before, and Gilly had used his Japanese to help me try to track down our abandoned property. Had something been found already? I couldn't read the kanji address, but as soon as I opened the package, I was quite relieved to see freshly laundered, folded clothes and my LIDAR drone case.

"Hey, need some underwear?" I playfully threw an article of Gilly's lost wardrobe onto the keyboard in front of him.

Gilly, deep in remote conversation with his brother, turned to give me a dirty look then brushed the undies aside. I immediately opened the case and found everything in order, including our passports tucked away in the document pocket along with a thick packet of extra 10,000-yen notes.

"Dad, let me see my passport." Heebs called over.

I pulled the three passports out and began checking which one belonged to Heebs. Each of the little booklets was wrapped with a rubber band, and tucked inside was a folded sheet of paper with the flight information for the next leg, since we would all be flying separately. The boys were supposed to fly to meet their brother in a few days, but it wasn't looking good. I picked out Heebs' document and handed it to him.

"Don't lose this. Give it back and I'll hang on to it for safekeeping." I said, returning to the package.

Logging into the laptop, the mapped 3D model of Udo Shrine came up since that was the last survey I had completed. It's hard to put a finger on how attached one can get to their research until you lose your data, thinking you'll never recover it again. I checked the power levels for both the laptop and drone and plugged them in to recharge. I absentmindedly sat back and watched people going about their business on the concourse below.

"What kind of curves? Closed timelike curves?" Gilly with earbuds blurted out, "I don't know what any of that means."

All we could hear was the one-sided response Gilly made in his conversation with Mas. He seemed to be getting more and more agitated.

"What do you mean by science fiction plot?" Gilly asked.

Heebs, being a sci-fi fan briefly looked up from thumbing through the pages of his passport. A still empty sudoku puzzle lay on the desk in front of him. He was running his fingers through his hair, trying to primp his looks — I imagined his teenage vanity must have been triggered by the passport photo. I settled myself in the seat next to Gilly just as the younger boy ripped out the earbuds and put it in speaker mode.

"He wants to talk to you guys." Gilly said and got up to get out of the way.

Heebs put the passport in a button-down shirt pocket and left the puzzle on the desk. He came over and sat next to me.

"Hey Mas, what's up? How was your presentation?" I greeted.

Mas, on summer break from MIT, had been doing an internship at Hong Kong University and had just presented his final research to the faculty.

Heebs gave a "Hey, bro."

Mas' disembodied voice came out of the speaker a little too loud, *"I'm okay, just a little wiped out. I had to stay up three nights in a row to get the programming to work right."*

Heebs quickly reacted by turning down the volume so the discussion wouldn't leave the room. "Did you get packed up yet?" he asked.

"Yes, mostly. I'll be ready to head home to the States with you guys." Mas explained.

"So, what's up with Gilly? How did you get him to run away?" I prodded.

Mas replied, *"I'm trying to figure out some of the physics papers. Check this out — you've heard of wormholes, right? They're tunnels through spacetime that link two distant regions of the universe in a short cut."*

"Like in science fiction?" I confirmed.

Mas affirmed, *"Yes, but it turns out they are real. No one knows if spaceships or people can travel through them or not, but apparently some form of wormholes actually exist, and they may actually be much more common than anyone suspected."*

Heebs looked wide-eyed with excitement — he said, "So there could be some in our solar system?"

"Not only that, but there could be tiny wormholes in every cubic centimeter of space, even inside things." Mas corrected, *"Some percentage of them connect to other parts of the universe, and some tiny wormholes could connect forward or backward in time! In this paper* Construction and Enlargement of Dilatonic Wormholes by Impulsive Radiation *these guys look at how someone could take a tiny wormhole and enlarge the tunnel big enough for people to get through. Or another paper* EPR Pair Temporal Loops: Primordial Closed Timelike Curves? *suggests that some of these*

little wormholes could connect back to immediately following the Big Bang!"

"Come on now! That still sounds like science fiction to me." I scowled.

We couldn't see him, but I imagined Mas shrugging as he backtracked a bit, *"Well, no one has actually done it, but the laws of physics say it's possible."*

"So how can we use that to get your sister out of jail." I brought the discussion back to our problem on hand.

Mas was clearly excited about the wormhole thing. Little did we know how involved he would eventually become with wormholes and supercolliders in the not-too-distant future. Heebs leaned forward a bit as his eyes caught something down on the station floor below us. My gaze followed his and, just as I thought, girls. Three uniformed high school girls were walking past.

"I've got something for you," I began, "You should look up Craig Venter. Rikochan tells us he engineered some designer microorganisms from scratch using synthetic DNA. Apparently, he predicts it could be possible to send a machine to some remote location, and just by faxing commands you could have it cobble together organisms that include anything from wings to legs to biological jet engines."

Heebs leaned forward as the girls headed down the concourse. There was silence at first, then an excited outburst from Mas.

"Wow! That's crazy." Mas exploded, *"Imagine this. Let's say we send one of these machines to the moon. We search through all the alleles of organisms living in harsh environments and find combinations that could survive in vacuum, eat basaltic rock regolith, and poop out oxygen. We could have thriving microbe colonies that gradually produce an atmosphere on the moon! We could have the machine produce more complex organisms that eventually fill out an atmosphere and make it habitable for us."*

Hmm, what an interesting thought. Fax organisms to other planets.

Heebs continued staring unfocused down below — he lost his three loves, but his head was still way out there when he said, "Heck, maybe we could send one of those machines through a wormhole. Maybe there's a tiny wormhole that scientists could fax life far away!"

I stared at Heebs for a while. Sometimes I wondered how genius ideas could come out of such teenage awkwardness. The idea was brilliant, good enough for a science fiction story. But as fantastic as they were, none of these revelations got us closer to something we could use to bargain with the police.

Off to the side Gilly jumped up with glee, yelling, "I solved it! I solved the sudoku puzzle!"

But Heebs and I were barely listening as we considered the possibilities of faxing engineered programmable biological molecular machines through wormholes. How long would it take for us to do that? How many million years would humans have to advance for that to be possible? Just the fact that it was possible almost made it probable. To have such a probability put traditional evolutionary thinking at risk. Maybe life started from chance chemical interactions billions of years ago. But suddenly the idea of chance occurrence seemed less likely than a purposeful capability of advanced civilizations to colonize other worlds. Did Doei-san and the transhumanists stumble upon something?

Mas and I appeared to be on the same page, *"That's interesting Heebs. In another paper* 50-year Window to Establish a Space-faring Civilization *the author suggests NASA could send small packages to distant worlds filled with simple space-hardy organisms. You could pack all the alleles of human DNA in the unused junk DNA of the organisms, program genes to turn on and off as stimulated by environmental cues and use horizontal gene transfer to recombine and populate the germ cell. After millions of years the NASA designer organism package would evolve into humans! Like scattering seeds among the cosmos."*

"And what does all this have to do with Imperial Regalia?" I asked skeptically.

Silence — no one had an answer.

Without warning, Heebs jumped up, pointing beyond the glass, "Who is that, Dad?"

Gilly and I both stood and looked down at the concourse. Three guys in business suits were walking toward the hotel entrance, and one of them was smacking a length of pipe into his palm.

"Over there!" Gilly cried, pointing down the concourse in the other direction.

Two suits, and one of them was clearly Beard Yakuza! Crap, they've got the front door covered.

"We've got to go — now!" I yelled.

Gilly picked up the sudoku puzzle and headed for the door. I grabbed the laptop and drone and stuffed them into the case but didn't wait to put it on my back. I had almost exited the room when I remembered — Gilly had forgotten to pick up his undies. I quickly stuffed them in my pocket and rushed out.

The three of us ran for the rear fire stair at the end of the corridor. Heebs cracked open the emergency exit to peer outside. The stair was not enclosed, but consisted of galvanized steel flights hanging in a cage of sorts. Each flight covered half a story, so above us the stairs zigzagged all the way to the upper floors. Below us three flights landed in a service area.

I gulped — two more guys were loitering down below. If we climbed the stairs our foot-on-steel ascent would surely make a lot of noise.

"Let's take the elevator to the basement. Quick!" I ordered.

The elevator was back down the corridor near Joe. We ran as fast as we dared, then took a more casual pace when we reached the front desk area in order to not draw attention. Gilly, acting like a boy, ran straight to the elevator and slammed the down button before Heebs and I even got past the desk. The door slid open, and we leaped inside. As the panels slid shut, I could see Beard Yakuza climbing the stairs from the entrance — he was looking right at me!

We exited out onto the basement level, which was a flat area located at the bottom of a vehicular ramp that curled down from the street. In the middle of the floor was a large turntable in front of automobile-sized sliding doors. It was one of those robotic parking garages that presumably went deep underground to respect the premium on land area. The driver would descend the ramp, drive over the turntable, and trigger the large doors to slide open. Then carefully the driver would ease inside onto a narrow robotic platform, exit the vehicle, then step back outside where he/she would collect a ticket from the pay station. The large doors would shut again and somewhere below the robotic platform would deposit the vehicle into a numbered cell. Later the driver would retrieve the vehicle by inputting the ticket, paying any remaining balance, and waiting until the robotic platform brought the vehicle back up again. Finally, the driver would back out onto the turntable, which would spin the vehicle so the nose would be aimed outward again.

Without thinking, I hit the override button for the parking garage doors. As soon as the sliding panels opened wide enough, the three of us rushed inside. We found ourselves in a dead-end volume with about the same floor area as a parking stall. A narrow 2 or 3-centimeter gap floated the robotic platform away from the wall. Neither our combined body weight, nor any amount of stomping would trigger the robotic system to move when the controls were outside at the pay station. We were cornered! I stood there in the middle of the platform waiting to be caught by Beard Yakuza or his goons. My mind was filled with the fresh memories of the three of us trying to take that fellow down and getting beaten back again and again. By luck we had finally gotten the best of him. We would have no such advantages this time.

I looked down as Gilly put his arms around my waist and peered up at me with fear in his eyes. Heebs also backed up against me, ready to get into another fight.

Suddenly there was a noise that caused us all to look up in dread. I fully expected to see a group of hoodlums fly out of the elevator or come down the ramp, but it was a false alarm — the large sliding doors had timed out and began closing. Finally, when the doors shut, the lights went out and we found ourselves alone inside the dimly lit machine, safe for the time being.

"Dad, I'm scared," Gilly trembled, "let's get out of here."

I looked at my poor son, barely visible in the greenish glow of a maintenance wall fixture. He was clinging tighter than ever to my waist. Heebs was curiously looking about.

"Hold on, let me think." I soothed.

I knew there was another set of emergency controls by the door. We could simply tap that button and the garage doors would open for a trapped customer. But who knows how long those thugs would be snooping around? Maybe they had already descended to the basement and were ready to capture anyone who stepped outside.

I suggested, "How about we wait just a little longer? Maybe no one will look for us in here."

"I'm good with that, Dad." Heebs said and then sat down right in the middle of the platform.

I took my LIDAR drone case and strapped it on my back, finally finding some spare time to get my hands free. A few minutes later all three of us were sitting on the deck.

Heebs suddenly laughed, "Hey, we forgot to hang up on Mas. No one told him we were done!"

I chuckled and suggested, "He must have been entertained by our quick exit."

There was a distant rumble and vibration that was more felt than heard, coming up through the platform. The three of us briefly glanced at each other and swept our gaze around the room before settling down again — it could only have been a train moving through the station. Since our hotel was built partly over the platforms, hearing an occasional passing train was quite natural even from the hotel rooms. Soon the vibration stopped, only to repeat itself in varying intervals.

Gilly was holding up the sudoku puzzle in the dim light, trying to study it. "Why is there an amoeba shape drawn over the funadori puzzle?" He wondered.

"It's not 'funadori', the zoologist said it was 'Funajima'. I think it's a map." Heebs threw out.

"Don't try to read in the dark, your eyes will go bad," I admonished.

Gilly was about to respond, but we all heard another click and the robotic platform shook. Then the floor seemed to drop out from under us.

"Whoa! Feels like we're going down!" Heebs remarked.

I thought quickly and got to my feet. Heebs and Gilly sensed my urgency and followed.

I said, "I think someone just called for their car. The platform is going down to get it. Anyone have a light? We may have to move quickly if the parking system wants to put a car on top of us."

Heebs switched on the flashlight on his rental phone and shone it about. We waited only seconds before the platform came to a stop. In front of us a vehicle sat spanning between load points. A set of moving beams started extending from the platform under us and proceeded to reach under the parked car. My mind was racing, and I looked around — there was another vehicle parked opposite.

"Jump up onto that hood!" I yelled.

Heebs and I made the leap onto our bellies, spread-eagled on the parked vehicle, and I turned around to help Gilly scramble up. In the dim light I could see the first car already moving onto the platform — we would have been squeezed off with no place to stand. Heebs must have harbored the same thoughts because he briefly flashed the light downward through a tangle of beams and girders into a bottomless pit. The three of us scrambled up onto the roof of the car and turned around to watch the robotic platform carry the other vehicle up the shaft to be reunited with its owner. This time we were stranded deep in the bowels of the machine, with no apparent way to get back out again.

I turned and continued to climb across the roof of the vehicle feeling the thin sheet metal buckle as I put my weight on it. The two boys followed, careful not to slip off the side into the dark hole. Fortunately, against the far wall Heebs' light illuminated a narrow maintenance catwalk that we eagerly lowered ourselves onto. The catwalk circled the entire vertical parking structure, just outside the radial fan of vehicle parking stalls.

And we were in luck — as we walked around the catwalk, we discovered a niche in one wall with a series of steep ship ladders going up and down. I paused for a moment with my hand on a ladder rung, looking down into the abyss. Nothing for us down there, I thought. The upward direction didn't seem as dark, and I could see another dim light up there somewhere, as if to beckon us on. I hefted myself up and began to climb and could hear several footfalls below marking the progress of the boys following after me. At each level I stepped out onto a landing, spun around behind, and started up the next ladder.

The reverberation of the robotic mechanisms soon ceased, leaving our stomping feet hitting steel rungs as the only thing that could be heard. But that didn't last long — the machine came to life again as another vehicle was inserted into the system. We listened as the platform came down from above, passed our level, and continued on below carrying its dark cargo. Several mechanical noises echoed up and suddenly the sound of spraying water. A whole new set of swishes and clinks and clanks made us all pause.

"Dad, I think there's a car wash down there! Customers get their cars washed as part of the parking experience." Heebs observed.

I smiled wryly, though no one could see me, "Indeed you're right. Good thing we didn't ride it all the way down."

I finally started climbing a ship ladder that was different from the rest. Instead of landings made of expanded metal decking, this one passed through a rectangular opening in a thick concrete ceiling. As I passed through the hatchway, I found myself in a narrow, dimly lit maintenance room. There was a metal trap door that could have sealed the hole but was now hinged open to lean against the wall. The room had shelves of spare parts and the floor was scattered with boxes and larger assemblies, all in various stages of retrofit or repair. In the far wall was a door leading to the outside, because I could see a brilliant light leaking in under the threshold.

"This is it, boys, our way out. Let's be careful in case someone is watching." I cautioned.

We tiptoed through the debris, then Heebs slowly opened the door to take a peek outside. To our surprise, a train passed by just outside with all the racket and close-up detail. Passengers' faces looking through windows whizzed by in a blur that increased as the train built up speed. We were at track level near the boarding platforms. I squeezed past Heebs and looked both ways down the track for something to hide behind and saw a large galvanized electrical transformer cabinet to our right about thirty meters away.

Just then I saw the end of the train coming and ducked back inside, leaving only a narrow, inconspicuous slit to look through. When the train had gone, I could clearly see the faces of passengers up on the meter-high platform lining up to catch the next train.

Below me Heebs had the same pose as I, peeking out the door crack, and Gilly was below him. We were like three stooges in trouble again, but I wouldn't want to be anywhere else than with my boys. Another train came and stopped right in front of us, blocking our view of the platform.

"Okay now! Keep low and hide behind the silver cabinet!" I pushed them through the door and shut it behind me.

Down at this level, crouching low, it was hard to be seen by any passengers looking out, but no doubt someone could have spotted us. As soon as we piled behind the electrical cabinet the whistle blew and the train doors shut, signaling that it would be on the move again. We squeezed against the metal wall to keep a narrow profile as the train passed by.

Suddenly Heebs' phone rang — it was his mother.

"Heebs, you know you left your stuffed cat at home. Are you brushing your teeth every day?" Her voice sounded from the phone.

Embarassed, Heebs replied, "Yes, Mom. We're having a great time, don't need that cat. I've got to go now!"

Heebs hung up and fumbled with the phone until it was safely back in his pocket.

Gilly was the first to peek around the corner, "Dad, there's a stairway on the end of the boarding platform."

Sure enough, the electrical cabinet was situated just past the end of four or five platforms each lined up with small maintenance staircases descending to track level. This time no passengers had lined up, meaning there was no train scheduled to stop there. We should be free to cross the track.

"Okay go! Wait at the bottom." I directed.

I watched as Heebs and Gilly stealthily leaped over the steel rails and tucked themselves below the end of the platform. Gilly was running around with that paper in his hand, not about to let go of it. I heard a train coming, but with five parallel tracks I figured something was passing further down the line. I quickly jumped out to leap over the track and almost made a deadly mistake. I had forgotten that some express trains barrel on through, scheduled to only stop at the bigger stations. I was already in motion as the front of the train drew ever closer. I cleared the first rail and almost tripped on the second before skidding down next to the boys. I could feel a draft of air as the train rushed by. Fortunately, the trains were all automated, so no one would alert my presence to the station master. The three of us quickly scrambled up the steps and put on an air of passengers innocently walking along the platform.

Heebs asked, "Where do we go next?"

The hotel was out of the question. We needed to find a rail map and figure out what to do next. The answer came as we walked up the stairs to the main station level. Gilly suddenly stopped in front of a travel poster touting some interesting local spots of interest.

He clutched the paper tightly in his hand and said, "Dan-no-ura. The battle of Dan-no-ura!"

On the poster a samurai arrayed in armor held up a bow about to let go an arrow with an odd tip. A short description in Japanese was accompanied by an English translation.

"The battle of Dan-no-ura was a sea battle fought in 1185 in the Kanmon Straits. Come see the place where Yoshitsune routed the Taira clan, and the Kusanagi-no-tsurugi (Imperial Sword) was lost at sea when the young child emperor Antoku jumped to his death." Heebs read.

The Imperial Regalia! Down at the bottom of the poster was a rail map and directions. The destination was only a few stations away.

****

Only an hour later we stepped out onto a narrow coastline park. On the left, the waterway opened up to the Seto Inland Sea. To our right was the massive connecting bridge of the Kyushu Expressway that arched overhead and dwarfed a steady parade of ships and boats moving back and forth through the Kanmon Straits. The long strip of landscaped park hosted a series of monuments, statues, historical cannons, and seating areas that framed views of the island of Kyushu across the water. Looking under the long span of the bridge, it was possible to see the Kokura skyline where I hoped we had left the yakuza fellows behind.

Heebs and Gilly, seeing a row of cannons, immediately sprinted over to inspect the old weapons. Apparently, this location was famous for more than one battle in its history.

I strode over to where two statues were frozen in dynamic battle pose. One statue was of a famous samurai, Minamoto-no-Yoshitsune, who was the Genji general that destroyed the Heike forces. The next statue was the enemy general Taira-no-Tomomori standing on the prow of a ship with a massive anchor. The famous battle was fought right out there in the narrow part of the straits. When Yoshitsune overwhelmed the Heike, many of them chose to jump overboard rather than die at the hands of the Genji.

I walked over to the low fence at the sea wall and looked down into the murky waters. Trying to maintain their legitimacy, the Heike had taken with them the child emperor Antoku and the Imperial Regalia. In a last-ditch effort to keep the symbols of sovereignty out of Genji hands they were tossed into the sea, and Antoku's grandmother leaped overboard holding the child.

Apparently the Yasakani-no-magatama jewel and Yata-no-kagami mirror were immediately recovered by divers, but it is unclear whether the Kusanagi-no-tsurugi sword was recovered, or whether the current item in possession by the Japanese government was a replica forged later.

I looked around at the other historical items on display. Heebs was posing behind one of the cannons while Gilly had climbed up on the barrel. Apparently, those were replicas of weapons used in a later Bakan War skirmish between the Chōshū clan and foreign fleets in the 1800's. Okay, we're here where the Dan-no-ura battle was fought — what now? My mind was reeling with wormholes, designer organisms, Antikythera mechanisms, and Imperial Regalia — nothing made sense!

"Heebs, Gilly, let's go for a ride!" I called out.

At the end of the park was a ropeway gondola that carried visitors to the top of a mountain called 'Hinoyama'. It was just the sort of fun that could take our minds off the dilemma at hand. Heebs and Gilly excitedly strutted ahead as we boarded the glass-walled ropeway car. The view was quite spectacular with the gondola climbing the steep mountainside. We alighted at the upper station which was an elevated platform with steps leading to the viewing deck on top.

The vista of the Kanmon Straits was magnificent framing a bird's eye view down to the park and bridge. We could see all the way back to Kokura and Shimonoseki, and I thought I could even see light reflecting off the distant East China Sea.

The viewing deck was a circular glass-enclosed balcony perched on the ridge. We took our time walking along the glass, taking in the sights from all directions. At intervals a photo of the view from that point had been made into a guide panel, with labels pointing to mountain peaks, bays, islands, piers, buildings, and other points of interest. While I carefully picked over the guide panels, the boys soon got bored and ran on ahead to find other entertainment. I had only gotten past the second panel when I heard the boys arguing.

"I told you, it's 'Funajima', not 'funadori'!" Heebs scolded.

Gilly still had that paper clutched in his hand, rolled up into a tube. He would point it at Heebs whenever he wanted to emphasize something.

He said, "Rikochan had me look up 'tori', boogerface!"

"That's before we talked to the zoologist, tori-brain!" Heebs countered.

There were other guests admiring the view and my boys were about to make a scene. I hurried over to where they stood in front of a third guide panel.

"Quiet down, guys," I said, "what's up?"

Heebs stepped over to the guide panel, pointed to something annotated in the photo, and chided, "This does NOT say 'funadori'. It's 'Funajima'!"

Astounded, I looked at the spot Heebs was pointing, "What did you say?"

"Buzzard-brain, here, is wrong!" Heebs returned.

I stepped closer to the panel and brushed Heebs' hand away. Many of the major annotations were translated into English, but this one was in raw Japanese kanji. I reached down and snatched the rolled-up paper from Gilly and spread it flat on the guide panel next to the tiny feature. Yes, the characters matched! The guide panel had an insignificant amorphous-shaped island labeled 'Funajima'! Just a short taxi ride away.

"Boys, I think we know where to go next," I said.

CHAPTER 8

Getting to Funajima turned out to be a little more complex than we thought. Catching a taxi to the shoreline nearest the island was difficult, because industrial shipping and cargo facilities lined the waterfront. A second issue was how to get over to the island. As it turned out, we found a public pier that formerly hosted an old water taxi to Funajima but had since gone out of business. I spot-checked a few fishermen along the seawall, but no one wanted to take me up on my offer, even for a little cash.

We finally settled on purchasing a vinyl inflatable raft at a fish & tackle store. And just in case we had to get into the water, we picked up a couple of mask & snorkel sets. I was at the counter with a big box under my arm and a cheerful cashier in her forties told me the amount. Heebs was quietly waiting near my side, but Gilly kept picking things up nearby and trying to convince me to buy them.

"Dad, I think we might need this." Gilly held up a compact, folding shovel based on the old type soldiers used to carry.

"No, why would we need that?" I asked.

Instead of answering, Gilly went over and picked up a survival knife, explaining, "We can use this to cut things."

I frowned, "Don't get that thing anywhere near a rubber raft!"

Time after time Gilly snatched up compasses, flashlights, lighters, and a myriad of other small items.

"It's a bright, sunny day outside." I countered for the umpteenth time as he picked up a mini lantern.

In retrospect many of his choices turned out to be prophetic, but we didn't know it at the time. My attention went back to the purchase. It was necessary to look at the value on the cash register since my Japanese was virtually non-existent. I had already freed up a few ten-thousand-yen notes from the LIDAR case and began fishing for them in my pocket when I felt some wad of fabric. I pulled the thing out to free up my pocket and set it on the counter. My probing finally located the folded bundle of notes and brought them out.

The cashier, who had been very sweet only moments before had a scowl on her face and was staring down at the counter. I looked down and to my utter horror saw a pair of little boy's undies laid out wide open. I quickly looked up and met her gaze.

"No, it's not what you think!" I slapped my palm down on the offensive article of clothing.

The woman had no idea what I was saying but just looked at me like I was some kind of pervert or something.

Just then Gilly came up and cried, "Otōsan hazukashii! Katazukeru no wo wasureta. Those are mine!" and whisked them away.

I motioned with various hand gestures trying to convince the woman it was an embarrassing mistake, and she finally let out a healthy laugh and took my cash.

"Maidō arigatō gozaimasu! Itte irrashaimase!" She smiled and waved as the three of us took our purchases out the door.

With all the back-and-forth travel via taxis and buses, at last we found ourselves standing on a sea wall on Hikoshima island, directly across from Funajima at its closest point. It was already late afternoon and the sun hung low over the hills and jagged silhouette of residences behind us.

Funajima, also known as 'Ganryū-to', was a low, uninhabited island with very few structures that could be seen. To us it appeared to be a flat, sandy beach with a bit of foliage, and the distant Moji highlands peeking up over the top.

We set up shop on the sea wall and I got Heebs employed on the foot pump to inflate the raft. Gilly sat down nearby and pulled out the sudoku puzzle to study. I let my eyes wander to find a suitable place to launch. The concrete apron we stood upon was fairly high above the water, high enough to allow deep-sea fishing vessels to tie up. Off to our right a couple of hobby fishermen could be seen on a small pier that jutted out some fifty feet or so. One of the figures sat in a folding chair and the other one stood nearby and repeatedly cast his line into the choppy water. Behind the fishermen were rows of solar panels configured in a sawtooth pattern that gave way to industrial warehouse structures.

To our left, tall gantries peeked over the top of dock buildings, leaving a narrow strip of thick trees right at the water's edge. My eyes focused on a concrete ruin, which might have been a short, collapsed pier, that eased into the water — an easy place to launch an inflatable raft.

Heebs was taking his time with the boat. I was about to kneel down to lend a hand when I noticed one of the fishermen walking toward us. I stood up straight with my hands on my hips and a smile on my face and waited for him to approach. As he got closer, I suddenly did a double-take — the fellow was also a foreigner.

Relieved, I waved and called out a quick, "Hello!"

The fellow looked up at me as if seeing me for the first time, "Oh hi there," he said.

The man looked Caucasian but was a good ten inches shorter than I. As he got closer his hand went up as if he wanted to point something out, and he had a peculiar nervous batting of the eyes — they blinked rapidly each time he wanted to say something. He looked off to the side and started speaking.

"Sorry to bother you," he began, eyes blinking wildly, "but do you happen to have a knife?"

When the words came out, the fisherman's eyes came up to meet mine briefly, then nervously shifted to the side as he waited for a reply. If only we had bought that knife Gilly asked for!

"No, I'm sorry. Don't have one this time." I apologized.

The fisherman's shy demeanor caused him to look past me, then briefly connect with my eyes. The rapid blinking began again.

"We saw you arrive and thought you were coming to fish," the man tentatively theorized.

I replied in the negative, "We just want to explore that island over there."

The fisherman continued to look past me either to one side or downward, not daring to face me straight on.

He said, "Oh, are you interested in the great duel between Musashi and Kōjirō?"

I had never heard those names before but decided to agree — we had forgotten to do any research about the island, and now I was a little embarrassed.

"Do you know anything about the lore of this place?" I queried.

Apparently, the man was a fan of history, because his usual shy approach gave way to a short streak of confidence, "It was in the early 1600's. Must have been a spectacular fight out on that flat stage."

The fisherman looked out across the water toward the island, with no sign of nervous blinking.

"Nobody knows for sure, but it is thought that the Hosokawa's and other spectators may have either set up a viewing area out there on the island or maybe up on this hill," the man pointed up the slope that stood above our sea wall.

"That's very cool. We'll go check it out," I politely returned, "How is the fishing going?"

His rapid blinking returned, and his old pattern of looking to the side until the sentence ended repeated itself.

"We're waiting to do some night fishing," he said, "Maybe stay a few days then move on."

I was feeling a little bit uncomfortable, and hoped the man would get back to his business, "Okay good luck with your catch."

There was a long awkward pause before he turned and started heading back. I thought to myself, who won the duel? I didn't even know which samurai had won the fight. I watched him walk along the sea wall briefly before turning my attention back to my boys.

Just then Gilly, who had been studying the sudoku puzzle suddenly piped up, "Look! There's a pattern here with all these 'sword'-looking symbols."

The fisherman, who had only gotten a few dozen feet away, turned around and stared at Gilly. I waved again and after another awkward pause he resumed his walk back to where his companion waited. Strange man, I thought.

I crouched down to look at the amoeba shaped drawing overlaid on the puzzle. Gilly had expertly recreated all the hieroglyphic symbols so that the entire sudoku puzzle was filled out.

"Take a look at all the symbols," Gilly explained, "See how the drawn outline never intersects with the 'swords'?"

Once he pointed it out it was quite obvious. The amoeba outline roughly coincided with the shape of Funajima, with a few glaring exceptions. Whenever the outline got to a square with a 'sword' symbol, it subtly jogged out of the way a little, but plowed right through all the others. Surprisingly, seven of the 'swords' lay on the outline.

"You've missed these two 'swords' that are floating off the map outline. Maybe it is a coincidence." I noted.

But the obvious intersection of the 'swords' and avoidance of all the other hieroglyphs still seemed to pop out.

"Don't you see? 'Sword' marks the spot!" Gilly looked at me and smiled.

Of all the genius — !

"Instead of using an 'x' Doei-san used a 'sword' symbol to mark something. Maybe there is treasure buried there!" Gilly excitedly contemplated.

It made so much sense! But still there was a problem.

I pointed and said, "You mean 'swords' mark two spots."

Gilly studied the map a bit and suggested, "Well, one of the 'swords' is over water so that one doesn't count."

Sure enough, one 'sword' marked a spot in the middle of the island where the other non-engaged 'sword' was out in the water.

"Good work Gilly! Hirayuki Doei must have buried something there," I began, "give me that map. I think we have a helper tool for this."

I took the LIDAR case off my back and opened it up. Setting the map on the ground with rocks on two corners to keep it from blowing away, I removed the drone from the case and used its camera to take a still photo. Then I got on the laptop and tweaked a few settings.

"Check this out." I called to the boys.

Heebs was just finishing the inflation of the raft, so he disconnected the pump and came over to watch the laptop screen with Gilly and I. As I moved the drone around, the camera returned a live feed of the video back to laptop, with one minor difference. The lines and symbols of the sudoku map were now superimposed on the live video feed — all white areas from the paper were now transparent.

Heebs caught on immediately, "Ah, you can use that to fly above the island and we won't have to pace out a real grid!"

"Exactly!" I smiled.

We took all our stuff out to my proposed launch site and put the boat in the water. I had the LIDAR case on my back again, and we threw all our things into the boat except the pump, which we intended to pick up later on our way back.

It took us only a half hour for Heebs and I to row across, but twice we were almost run over by passing fishing vessels. As I worked the oar, I noticed a line of small military destroyers, or patrol boats or something, lined up on a distant dock. Occasionally we got glimpses of the coast guard patrol zigzagging its way between vessels out on the open channel — likely checking papers and shipments. Once or twice our boat spun around and I could see our launch point, with the two fishermen watching our progress. I waved at them.

As we got closer to the island, the foliage began to appear a lot thicker than it had seemed from a distance. There was a thin beach that got wider at the southernmost point, which appeared to be a suitable landing location. The approach was shallow, and we could see scattered rocks protruding from the surface. The further south we paddled, the more the beach turned into an artificial wave break made out of jumbled stones. Just as we made our final approach, we passed by an automated light beacon cemented onto a jumble of small boulders.

By the time we reached the shore the sun was just about to set behind the hill. The boys quickly hopped up on the rocks and I had Heebs carry the raft up to the high point where a concrete path ran parallel to the waterline. The smooth route made for easier walking, so Heebs and Gilly each grabbed the handles at both ends and began a slow jog along the path. On our left the foliage started to thin out and soon opened up to a wide field. Offshore to the right a couple hundred yards was an old rusty freighter at anchor.

The last beams of direct sunlight disappeared so we were about to run out of daylight. I let the boys go on ahead and sat down on the cement in order to initialize the drone. When I switched on the camera, the sudoku puzzle and map merged with the video stream and the drone took off straight up into the sky. I set the camera view downward in the nadir direction and watched the island zoom out. Soon the entire island was in view, and I slowed the ascent. Using fine yaw control to slowly spin the drone, I adjusted altitude until the map lined up exactly with the actual island coastline. There it was, just as Gilly said — seven of the 'swords' traced out the shore, with one detached 'sword' in the island interior. The last 'sword' was off-shore a short distance.

The sky was still a brilliant blue and I looked back toward where the sun had gone down. To my surprise the two fishermen had gotten themselves into a small motorboat and were not too far from the island. I could not guess where the boat had come from, but the two were busy casting lines and setting multiple poles off the side. If I knew they had had a boat, we could have gotten a ride, I thought.

Leaving the drone in station-keeping mode, I got up and hoofed after the boys who had found a small beach to play on.

"Okay guys! Let's find some treasure!" I called.

Heebs and Gilly left the raft on the beach and excitedly came up to look at the laptop screen. We could see ourselves as little specks on the video feed and began using the video to orient ourselves toward the detached 'sword' symbol in the puzzle. When we got to the spot there was still a large square to search. We took four stones and used the video feed to locate them at the corners of the square. The sandy area had no special markings, nor was there evidence of recent disturbance. My second regret for the day — we should have purchased the shovel.

Using our bare feet, we dragged along the square in tight rows, scraping a few inches off the top. To our delight, right smack in the middle of the square Heebs uncovered the top of a small cylinder. We all three dove down and used our hands to dig it free. Heebs enthusiastically unscrewed the cap and pulled out a note from inside.

'Betsu no katana (the other sword)' was all that was written on the paper.

The three of us looked up at each other in excitement. The note proved Gilly's theory was correct. It also meant that whatever Doei-san had been hiding was underwater! I snatched up the laptop and case and the three of us ran toward the eastern shore which was closest to the last isolated 'sword' symbol.

"Didn't Rikochan say Doei-san's body was found in scuba gear?" I panted as we ran.

Heebs concurred, "I hope it isn't that deep!"

Our route took us right between the statues of two dueling samurai. These guys must be Musashi and Kōjirō, I thought. Back when the water taxi visited the island regularly, tourists must have come here to see the statues and get a feel of the location where the duel took place. Again, we found ourselves on a narrow cement path at the top of sloped jumbled stones on the water's edge. It was getting dark, and I remembered my third regret — Gilly suggested buying a flashlight or lantern.

Quickly I sat on the edge of the apron and pulled out the laptop. The drone, still hovering in station-keeping mode faithfully showed the video feed and sudoku map in perfect alignment. I selected the final 'sword' square and changed the mode to tracking. The square glowed with a red outline. Then I turned off the map overlay and let the drone spiral down in autopilot, which kept the square of water centered on the screen. The glowing red border grew in size. When the drone had gotten low enough to fill the screen with the square patch, it ceased maneuvering and slipped back into station-keeping again.

"Boys, get the boat!" I directed, "Row out to where the drone is hovering. Hurry!"

Heebs and Gilly were gone in a flash. We had to move fast because the little flying machine was low on power, and the sky was getting dark. Fortunately, the square was only about fifteen or twenty meters offshore, near the beach where Heebs had dropped the raft. I looked out and saw the boys frantically paddling out. Heebs had stripped off his shirt and already donned the mask, ready to go for a swim.

I had never used the spectral radiation function over water before but thought that maybe some wavelength might penetrate deep enough to see something. I sent down a burst of infrared, but the cold watery surface blocked everything. Ultraviolet also didn't seem to penetrate very far. Then I remembered those underwater lasers we used to use on our scuba dives to point out various critters to each other. Which color laser was it? Green! I turned on the lower LIDAR units and had them do a green sweep. Bingo! Only 20 feet down, right in the middle of the square was a long, rectangular object.

The boys maneuvered to a spot, looked up at the drone, then readjusted their position. It was quite dark already and hard for them to see the little thing up in the sky. I half looked at the screen and half watched the boys.

"This way a little!" I yelled.

On the screen the raft clipped the glowing red border of the square. I frantically waved my arms this way and that until the boys, following my directions, ended up right in the middle of the square. Heebs immediately dove in while Gilly tried to keep the inflatable from drifting away. Using the drone to watch the action was like having a front row seat. Twice Heebs came up for breath then dove under again. Those times he had played 'fetch the golf ball' with his friends in lakes and pools was paying off.

Without warning Heebs' head broke the surface but he was struggling with something. Gilly paddled closer and reached over to give him a hand. Together they pulled a rectangular object out of the water and onto the raft. Heebs was too tired to climb in, so he swam while pushing the boat toward shore as Gilly paddled with the oar.

The drone had done its job, so I shut down all the instruments. Feeling elated, I decided to take her up one last time to get a night view of the city that glowed on the distant shore. On the screen, my boys could be seen making their way to shore. The camera was using low-light mode, and as it rose to a higher altitude, I could see the two fishermen off the southwest tip of Funajima, still checking lines and recasting. I pointed the camera northward toward Shimonoseki town and admired the birds-eye view. Dozens of boats could be seen, with lights blazing, moving back and forth in the channel. One particular boat broke away and started heading in our direction. I dropped altitude and zoomed in to follow out of curiosity. Something was nagging at my mind — the vessel was speeding way too fast for the typical cargo traffic. Then all at once the boat did a slight turn toward the pier on the north end of Funajima. Whoever it was, they were heading our way!

I did one more maneuver to get close enough to see what was going on. It was then that my heart dropped. Those persistent bastards! I could swear I glimpsed Beard Yakuza with several other suits standing on the deck.

In record speed I shut down the camera and recalled the drone. Because of the distance it would take a while to get back to home. The boys had almost reached the shore, so I put the laptop away in the case and stood up to warn them.

"Stay there! I'm coming!" I yelled.

The buzz of the drone got closer. I peeked over toward the north and saw all the boat traffic from ground level. One set of lights was closing in. The drone finally landed, and I quickly folded it up and returned it to the case. I could see the lights from the speedboat slow up against the dock, and several dark figures jumped out.

I rushed down to the water and waded out to the boat. Heebs had already gotten in and put on his shirt, so I fell in backwards and pulled my legs out of the water as the boys frantically paddled away. My head hit something hard, and I realized it was the long object they had recovered. Careful not to capsize the raft, I sat myself up and took over Gilly's oar.

The rusted old freighter was right in front of us. We could reach the stern in only a few more minutes of hard rowing. Back on the island, I could see dark silhouettes of running figures eclipsing the lights coming from the town and boat traffic. Just a few more yards . . .

A huge shape loomed out of the darkness. Our little boat got close and almost scraped the rusty hull. The dim light from the town illuminated the red antifouling paint line high above the water level. We worked our oars silently and slipped around the stern. I looked back on shore and watched as three sets of powerful flashlights sent beams out over the water. Occasionally one of the beams flashed brightly when it pointed directly at us, but passed by and continued its sweep.

Without warning our little craft ran into something in the dark, separated a few meters from the hull. Alarmed, I used my oar to touch the object and traced out a curved metal panel protruding from the water. We worked our way around the thing trying to get behind the freighter. As we rounded the side of the hull, I turned back to see what the obstacle could have been, and my heart almost leapt to my throat. I could see the silhouettes of huge marine screw propellers sticking partway out of the water! Just the thought of those things mere inches from us put me into a panic — what if the ship had started its engines just then?

At that moment Gilly's phone rang, and Ines was on the line. Gilly handed it to me.

"Hi, Honey, it must be evening there. Have you all eaten yet?" She asked.

The thought of food briefly got my stomach growling, but I was still in panic mode.

"Hi love, we're on a boat right now, just about ready to get off. I'll talk to you later. Love you!" I schooled my voice to try to maintain a steady, happy demeanor.

It was very dark, but I could tell Heebs and Gilly were looking at me shaking their heads. We floated near the rusty hull out of reach of the hoodlums' lights. It was a safe location for the moment, but my mind kept thinking, those goons had a motorboat and could come looking.

"We've got to find a way aboard this ship." I whispered.

"Are they coming after us?" Gilly sounded scared.

Heebs said in a low voice, "They'll come eat our brains!"

It wasn't total darkness. There were lights on the Kitakyushu side of the Kanmon Straits that illuminated the wall of metal. I could see a sort of break in the rusty expanse and told Heebs to head toward it. When we got near, we could see a rope ladder hanging off the side.

"Okay son, do you think you can climb to the top?" I asked Gilly.

The small dark figure nodded and began climbing. The long object Heebs had pulled out of the ocean appeared to be a plastic case with several handles on it. I pulled one end and balanced it on my shoulder, using a one-armed marine weapon carry technique to inch up the ladder. Heebs followed, hanging the rubber boat precariously on his head as he used his hands on the rungs. At the top, Gilly helped me muscle the case over the gunwale and soon all three of us were laying on the deck panting our lungs out. We did one last task before we could rest — pull up the rope ladder.

CHAPTER 9

Heebs, Gilly, and I lay still below the gunwale as sounds of other vessels could be heard nearby. Motorboats would speed past, go out a short distance, then double back. To me it sounded like several engine types and hull sizes slapping the choppy surface. My mind's eye imagined spotlights sweeping back and forth unable to illuminate their quarry. This went on for a couple of hours then gradually decreased in frequency. Finally, all we could hear were the distant sounds of a busy city.

I sat up and looked around. The deck around us was dimly lit by the light of the half moon, which placidly hung in the starless sky. I could barely make out ambiguous frames and structures that might have been lifeboat or cargo davits. The main crew cabins and operational superstructure towered above us. Coils of cables, barrels, and small containers were neatly lined up or strapped against the metal wall. The scene was sobering — the light salty breeze blowing through the spooky tangle of metal structures smelled of diesel and engine oil.

I was reminded of the ghost ships from Japan that had been found drifting off the Pacific coast of Washington and Oregon. They were in perfect working order, but no one was on board. All sorts of theories were brought forward, such as the crews abandoned ship during a storm, or the ship had been torn from its moorings during a tsunami. But no one came forth to lay claim on the salvage — it was rumored that the crews continued to sail on toward hell.

I saw Gilly began to stir, but Heebs appeared to have fallen asleep atop the rubber raft.

"Dad, what are we going to do now?" Gilly worriedly asked.

My eyes went to the plastic case Heebs pulled out of the water. There was no telling how long it had been submerged. Though it was dark, my handling of it didn't reveal any growths or barnacles.

"Let's see what we've got!" I said, "Gilly, do you have a phone light?"

Gilly pulled out his rental phone and turned on the flashlight. I pulled the case over to a clear area on the deck. It was heavy, and a quick mental calculation from a rule of thumb learned in the marines told me that a case that large would have to be heavier than its equivalent volume of water or else it would float. The case wasn't locked but had six heavy-duty latches that I opened one at a time with a loud 'clunk' noise.

Before I had the last one open, I sensed a presence over my shoulder. Startled, I turned around and saw a dark figure there. It was just Heebs, who had been awakened by our commotion and had silently come to watch.

"Sheesh! You scared me boy!" I choked.

Heebs came close and leaned over the case, "Open it, Dad," he said.

The rectangular shape was hinged on its long side, like a rifle case. I flipped open the final latch and opened the lid to reveal some long item wrapped in cloth protected by foam padding. At both ends of the case most of the foam had been hastily cut out and the holes filled with lead diving weights, the older kind with belt slots molded into them. My eyes returned to the protected item, and I carefully unwrapped the cloth to reveal a dark, discolored metallic object partially covered with layers of hardened coral, barnacles, and growths. The protruding parts revealed an exquisite alloy that must have resisted oxidation. Was that gold underneath?

"Dad, this is really old!" Heebs observed.

Yes, it reminded me of some artifact freshly pulled by divers from an old galleon wreck, that might be cleaned up and restored to its golden luster. It was like those first photos of the Antikythera mechanism! Was this another connection between Hirayuki's notes on the document? Could this artifact be the remains of an ancient device?

Gilly pointed at the exposed end, which might have been buried to escape attached barnacles.

"It's a sword, I think." Gilly suggested.

I looked again at the patinated surface and tried to imagine the overall shape. Yes, there wasn't really a tang, but the entire hilt was forged in metal also, integral with the blade.

"I think you're right!" Heebs agreed.

Gilly wondered, "Doesn't this seem like the sword from the Imperial Regalia? It's one of the three Japanese imperial treasures!"

Gilly's observations hit me like a ton of diver weights. We had been thinking about the Dan-no-ura story all day. Of course, this was it! Doei-san must have been searching for this during his scuba-diving trips. The crusted artifact did not have the characteristic curve of the typical samurai sword, but was straight, almost like something you would find in Viking history.

"If this is the real Kusanagi whatchamacallit, we're in big trouble!" I lamented.

Gilly looked up at me with a worried look and said, "Doei-san was killed for it."

"Those yakuza guys! They must be combing the town for us along the coast." Heebs considered.

A million things were going through my head. It wasn't as though finding the sword solved the mystery of the torn manuscript remnant or the round hieroglyphic imprint. But I didn't really care about those anyway — what I wanted was a way to clear Rikochan's name and get her home safe.

Suddenly the great interest in the information we possessed made sense. Any single piece of genuine imperial treasure would be worth a fortune! Some may even be willing to kill for it. If this was the actual sword that sunk with Emperor Antoku, we could make the deal of the century!

"Give me that camera, Gil." I barked as I snatched the smartphone away, "Heebs, I need your light too."

While Heebs shined his light on the sword, I used the flash to take several snapshots of the artifact. What we needed was a safe place to hide it while we used photos to negotiate with law enforcement. Apparently, the local organized crime knew about the sword, and would do anything to get their hands on it. Was there any place that would be safe? The men in suits were searching everywhere. When would they think of climbing on board a rusty freighter?

I stood up and looked down the length of the ship toward the bow. It was a small freighter, and thinking back on my training with the marines I would guess it to be about 4,000-ton capacity, much smaller than the giant 30,000-ton modern behemoths. There would be all sorts of places one could hide a plastic case.

I kneeled back down and began pulling out all the heavy diving weights and passed them to the boys, "Toss these overboard," I said.

When the weights were gone and Heebs clunked shut the latches, the case had become much lighter.

"We've got to find a place to hide this, in case the yakuza come back." I explained.

Heebs and Gilly hurried down the length of the ship while I snatched up the case. We all began poking into crevices and stacks of old containers looking for a good place to hide the artifact.

Suddenly I heard the sound of a boat motor. Gilly came running back, feet pounding on the painted metal decking.

"It's coming this way, Dad! A boat is coming!" He yelled.

Next to us was an empty pair of lifeboat davits with the curled-up rope ladder, but beyond there were several more davits with dark shapes hanging from them. I ran to the nearest and discovered a small rowboat with an outboard motor, covered with canvas. The edges of the canvas were tightly cinched down — I would never be able to get it loose in time. However, at the rear of the small craft the outboard motor only had a few simple straps holding down the cover that I quickly unfastened. I took the case and slid it under, letting it drop to the floor of the little boat, then retightened the straps.

"How did they know we were here?" I wondered.

Gilly, always the smart one, nailed it, "Dad, every time you took a picture of that sword it lit up the side of the ship!"

Heebs walked up and the three of us crouched behind the gunwale. My mind was frantically trying to figure out what to do when the hoodlums began boarding. I imagined kicking them off into the water or playing hide and seek in the engine room. Would we eventually have to swim for it?

The motorboat got close and cut its engine. We dared not peek over the gunwale just in case the others were casting about by chance — maybe they hadn't actually seen flashes of light from our camera.

"Hey up there!" A perfectly accented English voice yelled up.

We waited, holding our breath.

"Hey, Musashi, it's me — Kōjirō!" The voice said.

The fishermen? The familiar-sounding voice used the two samurai names from the famous duel on Funajima. Suddenly I thought there might be another way out of this. I stood up and looked over the side.

"Did you catch anything?" I asked, not knowing what to say.

I could see the dark shape of the little motorboat bobbing in the rough chop but could not see our friend.

"Yes, we did! What are you doing up there?" the disembodied voice said.

"We're trying to avoid some bad guys on motorboats!" I called out, "Can you give us a ride to shore?"

"Yes, we can!" The man answered, "How will you get down?"

I looked over and saw Heebs was already throwing down the rope ladder. He immediately began climbing down to the little vessel, which was maneuvering to the base of the ladder. In the dim light I could finally see the man we had met on the shore at the wheel, while his partner huddled slumped over with the hoodie covering his head.

Gilly paused at the top, waiting for the ladder to stop swinging. I rushed over to the rowboat hanging from the davit and began to undo the straps again. Crap! I was just thinking about how I would have to crawl under the tarp and retrieve the sword, when suddenly there was the sound of another motorboat. This was no little fishing vessel, but the thrum of a powerful speedboat engine. The sound got louder, then without warning I could see lights on the vessel coming around the side of the freighter.

I yelled, "Come back for us!" and ducked back down again behind the gunwale.

"We'll be back my friend!" The voice came from below — the little fishing vessel started its engine and took off at full speed with Heebs safely aboard.

Gilly and I waited as the new vessel approached and were startled as a spotlight lit up the side of the freighter's superstructure. Behind the gunwale we were still bathed in a deep shadow.

A blast of cursing in some foreign language cut through the night. I could hear the grumble of several men who seemed to have a similar frame of mind as the first person.

"Who's up there on my ship!" A heavily accented voice yelled out.

Gilly pulled at my sleeve and said, "I think the crew came back."

In my head I sighed in relief. It wasn't the yakuza after all. We were still in trouble, but maybe we could talk our way out of it. Frantically, I tried to come up with a plan as I once again stood up to show myself.

"I'm sorry, sir!" I called out, "my boy and I are trying to get away from someone, so we hid on board."

Gilly stood up to join me. I continued to hear cursing in some language and saw the vessel maneuver up to the ladder. A man jumped over and clung to the rungs, then started climbing up.

"Stay where you are, #*@$ Leo pirate!" Another man still standing in the motorboat called out.

I was afraid these ruffians might decide to throw us overboard. My mind was reeling as I watched the first man reach the top and climb over the gunwale. Rather than confront me, he pulled out a flashlight and went straight for the empty davit controls. An electric winch noise marked the lowering of cables that would bring the speedboat back up onto the deck of the freighter.

What the heck were we doing out here, I thought. We should have been over there across the water, safe in that Kokura hotel, like we told the police. Who would have thought we could get into such a mess? The sword was unreachable under the small skiff canvas cover, Gilly and I were standing there vulnerable, about to get into deep trouble. And somewhere out there, Beard Yakuza and his men were intent on skewering us like they did to Doei-san and poor Miss Ebina, and maybe even Professor Hosogawa. At least Heebs had gotten away.

Below, the men attached cables to the speedboat. The davit windlasses started up and pulled the powerful vessel out of the water. I watched as the operator used skill to balance the speed of the two electric motors and keep the boat level all the way up — it looked like an old system, probably custom designed and maintained. I didn't realize it at the time, but my attention to the davit operation would prove helpful later. A line of fierce-looking faces rose above the gunwale.

The cusser from before, apparently the captain, called out, "Leo, you *#$@& come to visit us!"

I studied the man's face in the dim light, but there didn't appear to be any anger. In fact, the fellow had an ear-to-ear grin. He jumped down on the deck and rushed over to give me a big hug. The greeting was so unexpected all I could do was just stand there.

The other men had all jumped out and headed toward their various work tasks. Someone must have flipped a breaker because the superstructure lights suddenly switched on and the deck blazed brightly. The captain backed off and did a double-take.

"You're not Leo! By gosh, it's Tim Hughes!" The captain incredulously blurted out, "What a surprise to find you on my ship!"

I was dumbfounded — expecting to be thrown overboard by a bunch of ruffians, the captain knew me by name. I studied his face but could not recognize him.

"You have the advantage of me." I said in complete shock, "Do I know you?"

The captain stuck out his hand and replied with a grin, "Captain Alyosha Nephus at your service! You don't know me, but I have followed your research."

I didn't know what to say. The past few days we had been beset with so much misfortune that it was hard to believe we may have found a friend in the middle of the Kanmon Straits. I smiled and enthusiastically grabbed his hand for a good shake.

Alyosha looked at Gilly, who stood near me with a dazed look on his face and asked, "Is this your boy? How are you doing, kid?"

"This is Gilherme my fourth child." I proudly introduced.

"Well come on, let's visit for a bit in my cabin." The captain showed us toward the nearest door leading into the superstructure.

"By the way, who is Leo?" I asked curiously.

The captain let out a hearty laugh, "That ol' pirate is my cousin. Sometimes he follows us around, arriving by plane to meet us in some distant port."

Gilly and I followed along, still a little dazed. The door into the superstructure was a water-tight hatch with rounded corners and a threshold one had to step over. When we got inside, a long corridor had mostly blank walls on the right, and a line of doors evenly spaced on the left. We stopped in front of a door with a sign saying 'Captain Nephus' and he opened it for us to enter. The room we found ourselves in was small, but the first thing I noticed was that the walls were covered with computer graphic printouts. Captain Nephus had printed out dozens of partially transparent 3D LIDAR scans of caves. This man was an armchair surveyor!

I stopped in front of one printout in amazement. Stone columns formed a colonnade carved wholly out of solid rock, with multiple chambers penetrating the mountain.

"You've got the Mumbai Elephanta Caves!" I remarked as I studied the detail.

Captain Nephus smiled, "I thought you would appreciate my collection, my friend."

There were other rarities: the Treasury in Petra, an ancient Roman brick sewer, Basilica Sistern in Istanbul, and even Zedekiah's Cave and the Siloam Tunnel from Gihon Spring in Jerusalem. I stopped at another tunnel mapping I didn't recognize.

"That one is an underground passage in Kaymakli town in Cappadocia." The captain explained in an authoritative tone, "It's eight kilometers long and connects the neighboring town of Derinkuyu."

"Cappadocia!" I couldn't contain my excitement, "How did you get in there? I thought that whole area was closed to outsiders?"

Captain Nephus spread his arms and replied, "It's another shipping port for me. I can't keep up with the big boys, so I try to pick up specialty loads that the big boys won't take. Delivering a Mercedes to a regional governor opens many doors!"

I stared at the captain incredulously. This man had access to locations that had long fallen behind red curtains and under dictator thumbs, and exotic seaports. What an adventurous life he must lead. Behind the man my gaze settled on several drone cases secured with straps in a side cabinet. One could have been a twin to the one I carried on my back.

"Have you ever published?" I asked curiously.

Captain Nephus frowned, "I've attended a few conferences, where I heard you speak, Dr. Hughes. But never had time or training to write a paper."

I was thinking starry-eyed about a potential rich partnership where we could co-author papers on caves, ruins, and excavations never before seen by the surveyor community, when Gilly began tugging at my sleeve. I was being dragged back to reality again.

"Dad, I got a text from Heebs. He says he's safe on land." Gilly reported, "The text looks like it came from another number though."

Alarmed, my full attention went back to our current predicament, and I looked squarely at my young son. I resisted the urge to grab the phone away from Gilly and text back a few questions. Whose phone did he use? Was he really okay? How could a sixteen-year-old boy make his way around Japan with Yakuza on his tail? My hand went out toward the phone but stopped in mid-air. What if we were tracked? Our phone numbers were known.

Gilly noticed the confusion on my face and observed, "Dad, he probably used the fisherman's phone so he wouldn't get tracked."

Of course! I was instantly relieved that Heebs would be taking such a precaution. He'll be okay, I thought. An incoming text would not be traceable on the receiving end, so our anonymity would be preserved.

At that moment another text came in. It said, *'The fishermen are asking if it is safe to come get you.'*

The fishermen had sped away, assuming the incoming motorboat carried the folks who had been chasing us. But now that we had met Captain Nephus, we were no longer in danger. It would be to our advantage to stick around a little longer, at least overnight until the search died down.

"Could they find us if we borrowed Captain Nephus' phone?" Gilly came up with an obvious solution.

I turned to the man and began, "Captain Nephus," but was cut off.

"Call me Alyosha, my friend." The captain corrected and graciously handed me the phone.

Gilly read off the number from the rental phone and I typed it in. I sent the message directly to Heebs' handset, since incoming texts couldn't be traced. I told Heebs to immediately get back to the Kokuraminami Police Station and ask for protection. We would follow in the next day or so. Only seconds later an answer came back from the fisherman's phone. *Will do, I'm leaving now'* it said.

Gilly and I arranged to stay on board for the night, and Captain Nephus invited us to join him for dinner after a short tour of the ship. The name of the vessel was 'Cave Diver', very appropriate knowing the exotic hobby of the captain. It was very old, constructed way back in 1958 as a United States naval vessel with an original designation being the 'USS Comet' sold for scrap. The superstructure was located right in the middle of its 150-meter length and spanned the entire 24-meter beam. The engine room was below that, with propeller shafts running aft under the cargo areas. The cargo capacity of 5,000 tons included a bow hold and stern hold with permanent towering gantries. The unique feature of the 'Cave Diver' was that it was originally a ro-ro type cargo vessel, with a hatch that allowed vehicles to roll on and off. The system of vehicular ramps was impressive, but unfortunately the loading hatch had long ago been welded shut. Captain Nephus often carried high-end vehicles as cargo but had to use cranes and gantries for loading and unloading the old-fashioned way.

The life of an independent free trader was tough, apparently. The 'Cave Diver' had delivered an exclusive collection of original mobile homes to a client in Shimonoseki (mobile homes had become outlawed in the States and were now collectors' items), but floated idle for three weeks as they tried to secure another shipment. It was tough competing with Maersk, Uber, and the other giants that had regular customers. Even tougher was the requirement to get enough tonnage for a safe trip, to make sure the screws were deep enough to stay on course in rough seas.

"I've had collections of rare snakes pay for the entire voyage, but still had to find enough bulk to give us a healthy draft and decent trim." The captain mused over dinner.

"You carry animals too?" asked a wide-eyed Gilly, who had been full of questions the entire tour.

"Yes, my boy, I've had some very interesting passengers, including a whole family of monkeys who escaped their cages. One smart one figured out how to open the lock, then went on to free all the others. They stole things, messed with equipment, and took days to recapture." Captain Nephus laughed.

We both laughed with him, trying to imagine such a scene. Gilly loved everything about the ship and couldn't get enough of the captain's never-ending stories. The evening wore on and we were able to forget the traumatic experiences of the past few days.

"Tonight, we finally secured a shipment to Singapore. Tomorrow we're going to pick up containers of faulty titanium parts that will be scrapped and reprocessed. Very valuable!" Captain Nephus concluded toward the end of the evening as Gilly began to nod off with all the excitement.

Tomorrow — back to reality. We'd have to figure out how to get the sword out of the rowboat without the crew noticing. We'd have to think of a way to trade the sword for Rikochan. We still had to avoid the underworld characters running around all over the place. This left us with a dilemma: how to hide the sword or carry it back to the police station without anyone noticing. If only we could take it out of the country! If I could keep the sword in a safe place away from Japan it would be a much stronger bargaining chip. Tomorrow . . .

With sleepy eyes Gilly looked up and asked, "Dad, can we stay with Captain Nephus?"

The solution hit me like a ton of cargo. I'm so slow at figuring out things like this — as usual it took a genius little boy to get me thinking out of the box.

I turned to the captain and asked, "If you take animals on board, what about passengers?"

Captain Nephus smiled a big grin, "Of course! We often take passengers, for a fee of course."

"How long would the voyage take to get to Singapore?" I pressed further.

After that, things got a little fuzzy, but the next day we were still on the ship as the 'Cave Diver' made its way down the east coast of Kyushu Island. We had purchased passage to Singapore for the two of us, and a few hours later the tugs helped 'Cave Diver' maneuver into the Oita dockside.

I arranged a hotel room near the airport for Heebs to stay in, since he was supposed to fly out in a couple of days anyway. I borrowed the captain's phone once more to send a message to Heebs, gave him the hotel and flight info, and told him we would be heading to Singapore. He still had his passport and could travel on his own. A text came back acknowledging the info. As long as Heebs could avoid bumping into the yakuza folks we would be home free.

I called my lovely wife Ines and warned her we would be out of signal range for a week or so, "We're taking a boat out to some islands."

"Oh, that sounds fun. I'm going to miss you," she replied.

I knew that she was just making small talk. She was the last person on Earth who would want to go off on a boat without a phone signal or Internet. During that week, she probably would go spend a few nights with her sister in a five-star hotel.

"I'll call you when we get in range again." I consoled.

Gilly and I watched the container loading process with fascination. We had a birds-eye view of the bow hold from the wheelhouse. It took a little over two hours to get the job done, and Gilly religiously counted every one of the containers.

"I counted 46. So, if they all weigh the same, there must also be 46 in the stern hold too, making 92 containers total." Gilly noted with a big grin on his face.

"It's probably a lot more complex than that." I pointed out, "I'll bet they've bundled all the titanium parts onto pallets, then loaded those inside the containers. They probably don't all weigh the same."

Gilly was determined to ask the captain later. We were boarded by Japan immigration officials at one point, and the captain introduced us as passengers. Our papers were in order, but the officers asked to do a more thorough inspection of our cabin beyond the cursory questioning of the other ship crew members. I was relieved when no one made an attempt to peek inside the rowboat hanging from the davit cranes — the sword was still safe under the tarp.

We watched the final buttoning up of the holds, and the excitement of moving away from the dock. The 'Cave Diver' apparently had enough fuel for the voyage, and Captain Nephus appeared satisfied he could get a good price for full tanks in Singapore. It was later in the afternoon when we found ourselves leaving the relative calm of the Seto Inland Sea for open Pacific waters. I could feel a noticeable deeper sway of the decks than before.

The next day the 'Cave Diver' had made good time and came within view of Tanegashima Island. Tanegashima is the next island below Kyushu, and Captain Nephus had secured another cargo destined for Singapore. Tanegashima was where Japan's main space launch complex was located. A Japanese agent had sought a small freighter that could carry a second stage rocket to Singapore space port, and the 'Cave Diver' was uniquely configured to carry specialty cargo. The ship would need to bypass the normal deep harbor at Nishinoomote and go straight to the loading facility at Takesaki.

Gilly and I stood on deck as the vessel cruised southward along the eastern coast of the island. Nephus had loaned us a pair of binoculars to spot things on land. More and more signs of Japan's space infrastructure became evident the further south we sailed. We were in good spirits as we saw rocket launch gantry towers in various stages of use, including one being prepped for launch with a fully stacked rocket.

A small tugboat helped the 'Cave Diver' ease up to a recently completed deep harbor dock protected by Kojima Island and artificial breakwaters. On the concrete apron we could see the cylindrical second stage rocket on its side, wrapped in tarps and enclosed in a steel handling frame ready to be loaded.

"Dad, isn't there something about space in Doei-san's notes? I wonder if we could find out some clues?" Gilly looked up at me in curiosity.

Not a bad idea, I thought. As if in perfect timing with fate, Captain Nephus serendipitously appeared from the wheelhouse and stopped in front of us.

"We'll be here a few hours. If you like, see that cluster of buildings across the sand? That's the Tanegashima space museum. You could take a couple of bicycles over in a few minutes." The captain pointed.

Excitedly, Gilly led the way and watched as one of the crew members used a davit to lower two bicycles over the gunwale. Gilly and I went below decks and disembarked via a ramp that had been attached to a lower hatch near dock level. We rode the bikes past the wrapped-up rocket stage being rolled over to the 'Cave Diver's' loading gantries, passed between some buildings, and found ourselves on a long, paved concourse traversing a very wide sandy beach. The whole place was like a tropical paradise, and I wish I could have just laid out in the sand for a few hours. Ahead, a full-sized launch vehicle rocket laying on its side, mounted on pylons could be seen in a park, where visitors could leisurely walk around looking up at monstrous engines and fuel tanks. The concourse intersected a highway just short of the rocket display, and we turned left toward the museum. Another rocket was on display, this one fully erect, with guy wires keeping it from falling over.

We pulled up to a large building on the left and parked the bicycles before going through the front entrance. The space museum was fascinating, with lots of prototype hardware and recovered spacecraft on display. But there was one exhibit that caught my attention. It was a historical look at rocketry, which included the 13th century gunpowder rockets invented in China. The old Chinese characters on display got me thinking about how kanji characters were similar to hieroglyphics in many ways — symbols that told a story rather than specified how to pronounce the word. In

Japanese, the borrowed Chinese characters became the root word, and were conjugated using the phonetic hiragana alphabet. I wondered whether hieroglyphics were the same. More importantly, if the Chinese were able to invent rockets hundreds of years ago, was there also a precedent in other ancient civilizations? I seem to recall the idea of spaceships imagined up in ancient tales from India. Mythical flying palaces were described in 4,000 BC Sanskrit texts. Were such stories also found in Mesopotamia or ancient Egypt? Hirayuki Doei's notes referred to space-faring colonizers and generation ships. It must have been a sophisticated civilization to dream up such concepts.

Just at that moment a docent walked by and greeted, "Irrashaimase."

"Excuse me," I quickly called out as she was about to turn a corner, "do you know any more about ancient spaceflight?"

I meant to say 'rocketry' but my mouth betrayed my thoughts. The woman's eyes lit up and she did a double-take.

"Did you say 'spaceflight'?" She confirmed in perfect English.

I stammered, "Well, I . . ."

"Have you heard of 'vimana' from India? Or the 'boat of Sokar' described in the 'Sarcophagus of Princess Anchenneferibre', which was symbolic of the orbit of the sun?" She returned as she came walking back to where we stood.

Something told me this person was obsessed with spaceflight history, and we had just turned on the spigot. We could be trapped here for hours, I thought. However, the docent, Reiko Imamura, turned out to be an extremely interesting host and gave us a deeper tour of the historical display than we could have gotten on our own. We ended up sitting at a nearby table as Gilly pumped her with questions.

"Speaking of sarcophagi, I've got an interesting document you might want to take a look at." I ventured.

I reached behind and unzipped the pocket on the back of my shirt and pulled out the envelope. I carefully retrieved a copy of Doei's document we had made at the hotel and set it in front of her. Immediately her eyes got big, and she read aloud the notes describing the '1000-cubit boat of a million years' and 'solar boat generation ship'. But when she got to the bottom of the page her brows furrowed and she looked up at me suspiciously.

"Where did you get this?" Imamura-san asked.

I broke down and told her about the transhumanists, careful to keep anything about the Japanese regalia out of the conversation.

"We need to find out about what these things mean, because my sister is in trouble." Gilly jumped in with innocent desperation.

Imamura-san's face softened, "No one could know about 'stellar white holes', and I'm sure the binary Sagittarius A* is unknown — Dr Murakami hasn't even published yet!"

"What does it mean?" I asked.

Reiko Imamura stared at me for a long while, then swore us to secrecy.

"Can I keep this? I've seen something like this before. I think it's called a 'hypocephalus', and was part of the *Book of the Dead*," she pointed to the round, hieroglyphic-filled circle, "they used to customize them and place them under the head of deceased persons, as a set of instructions for eternal progression. But what's more, I think it may be an ancient star map. See, look — your transhumanist friend has already labeled the names of some of the stars. Our sun, 'Enish-go-on-dosh' (that's what these phonetic symbols are referring to), is represented by this figure. And this figure in the middle is called 'Qarob', with a stellar white hole 'Oliblish' nearby. And he somehow assumed these two stars on either side are 'Hakkokabim' black holes."

Imamura-san excitedly pointed to a boat symbol in the upper-left and exclaimed, "And look at this! I've seen this before! 'Raukeeyang' is the 1000-cubit boat of a million years that Osiris legend says circles the sun. And over here," again Imamura-san pointed to another boat symbol on the right, "this figure apparently represents some 'celestial engineer'. The ship is the throne of the celestial engineer, and it orbits Qarob! I find it fascinating that the Egyptians used 'ships' to show this. Maybe the Raukeeyang solar boat was indeed a mythical generation ship!"

"What's a generation ship?" I asked.

"It's a theorized way of transporting colonists across the vast distances of interstellar space, where generations would live and die before their posterity eventually reaches another world to settle." She paused for a moment, looking at me with excitement in her eyes before continuing, "Those Egyptian astronomers were well beyond what we thought they knew. I guess it won't hurt to explain since the paper should be published next month. Dr Murakami is a JAXA (Japan Space Agency) astronomer who occasionally uses the Miyanoura Observatory on Yakushima. There's a large array telescope that has installations spread out on all these islands down here. Recently, observations of the Milky Way Galaxy core revealed that the supermassive black hole Sagittarius A* is actually a binary black hole, or in other words, two black holes orbiting each other. Interestingly, the binary Sagittarius A* seems to fit well with the Hakkokabim double orbs in the hypocephalus!" Imamura-san revealed.

"So, no one should have known about two of them?" I wondered — Hirayuki's notes had described 'Sagittarius A*' major and minor.

"No!" She began, "And what's more, his theory of stellar white holes is something only a few of us know about!"

Gilly jumped in first, "What's a white hole?"

"Well, Einstein's general relativity predicts black holes," Imamura-san paused.

Gilly was just at that age when black holes were a thing of endless fascination. He would read all about them and tell us that a black hole the size of a grain of sand could suck up our whole house. The boy stared wide-eyed and absorbed everything the docent said.

"But," she continued, "they also predict white holes. Light cannot escape black holes, but light cannot enter white holes. Cosmologists suspect the two are connected. Light and matter getting sucked into a black hole emerges from a white hole, whether in our universe or somewhere else. It's an Einstein-Rosen Bridge."

"Cool!" Gilly spurted out.

If all of this was new cosmology, did Hirayuki somehow figure it out from the hieroglyphics?

Imamura-san continued, "It was conventionally assumed that white holes occur all at once, like a Big Bang. But lately there have been doubts about the hydrogen atomic fusion model of stellar energy. There doesn't seem to be a match on energy output. So, what Dr Murakami has theorized, is that most stars may also be connected to a black hole, or conversely, black holes may be feeding energy through to stars as stellar white holes. Rather than self-generated fusion furnaces, stars get their light through some other medium."

Like a wormhole, I thought. Gilly and I rode the bicycles back to the 'Cave Diver' deep in thought. I was beginning to understand the meaning behind Hirayuki's notes, but just couldn't figure out how everything could be related. In fact, I was getting frustrated with the whole thing. In a few hours we were at sea again, with two new JAXA passengers who were accompanying the rocket stage.

In the next few days, typical of a 13-year-old, Gilly explored everything about the cargo on and off-loading, and absorbed as much as he could about the ship generally. Though my mind was blown by what I had learned, I was feeling happy and carefree. With all our problems almost solved, I had a moment of impulsive abandon and threw Rikochan's stuffed envelope in the trash can — no need for all that nonsense anymore! We had our bargaining chip, and surely the Kitakyushu police would agree to a trade.

The two of us were put to work in the galley helping the cook prepare meals from stores that had been separately loaded in Oita Port. The slow roll of the decks began to work on me and I couldn't shake a persistent headache. At first, I was able to bear it, performing the galley tasks and even finding quality time to talk surveying with Captain Nephus. But it was on the third day out from Tanegashima that we saw really rough water and I lost it. I got so sick and felt like the world had ended for me. I confined myself to the cabin and every clap of thunder or flash of lightning kept me awake, and every wave splashing up on the porthole enhanced the queasiness. I lost track of the days.

One day during this time Gilly, who seemed to be wholly unaffected by the motion popped in and reported, "Dad, Mas sent an email and said Heebs never arrived!"

"Heebs? Heebs. Who is that?" I vaguely recall myself saying.

"Dad, Heebs is lost! No one can find him!" Gilly persisted.

Deep inside I had a flash of panic but there was nothing I could do about it. The delirium caused me to overlay the plight of Rikochan and Heebs, and I alternated between thinking Heebs was being cared for by the police and being chased by yakuza thugs.

Sometime later our worst fears were realized. In my delirium I recall Gilly rushing in all flustered in alarm. He must have run the entire length of the ship and was out of breath.

"Dad, Heebs has been kidnapped!" Gilly said between gasps, "A text message came in from his phone number."

Weakly I tried to get my wits together and croaked, "What did it say?"

Gilly just handed me the phone. I have no idea how the unit could have picked up a signal way out there — maybe from Okinawa or Ishigaki island? The message read, *'Hibiki die if not give us three treasures. Give us sword, Urim & Thummim, and Directors when you arrive in Singapore.'*

CHAPTER 10

The seas finally calmed down a bit and I began to pull out of my delirium. The last cryptic message from Heebs' captors likely helped sober me up a bit. 'Urim & Thummim'? What the heck was that? Why hadn't I heard of it before?

The mystery was getting deeper and deeper, and even though the Kusanagi-no-tsurugi Japanese imperial sword ought to have been the greatest archeological find of the century, something was still missing. I got up, stumbled over to the corner, and rummaged through the trash can to find Rikochan's envelope. I laid out the various piles as we had organized them and began looking for anything about the Japanese Imperial Regalia. I pulled out a description of each of the three treasures that I knew I had seen before. I took each note and taped it to the cabin wall, trying to keep things in some related order. Something was very odd — the three treasures were supposedly the sword, a mirror, and a jewel. There was nothing about 'Urim & Thummim'. My mind was confused, and my stomach hurt more from worry than the rough seas. Nothing made sense. I desperately needed to get back to Japan and find my boy!

In retrospect I should have looked through the papers again, but I was still feeling sick and was still on the verge of tossing the whole lot. It was at that point I saw a pamphlet I had picked up a couple of days previously with Gilly when we had looked through that Kirishima-gawara Museum. I began reading absent-mindedly about Ise Shrine, where the sacred imperial mirror Yata-no-kagami was supposedly kept. The pamphlet mentioned several sister shrines, including Moto-Ise Shrine on the Japan Sea. I recognized that name! A Japanese colleague of mine lived there — he was a former architect and produced many scholarly articles on LIDAR-scanned temples and historical structures. Ryuichi — that was his name. I needed to talk to Ryuichi. I determined to look him up later, as he would probably know more about the Imperial Regalia.

Just then Gilly bounded in again and sympathetically patted me on the back, "Are you feeling better, Dad? Captain Nephus says we have several days of smooth sailing ahead."

"Thank goodness! I felt like I was going to die." I replied.

"Come with me up on deck. You'll feel much better." Gilly said as he grabbed my hand to lead me outside.

My son was right. The cool salty breeze felt refreshing, and the steadiness of the horizon somehow relieved the motion sickness. To my astonishment, I saw a stretch of land starboard, or off in the distance to the right.

"Captain says that's Ishigaki Island, last of the Japanese Archipelago. We might go past the southern tip of Taiwan. Then the next land we'll have a chance to see will be the Vietnam peninsula in a couple of days." Gilly explained.

That was a bit disheartening. The entire trip was supposed to take ten days, and I was thinking it would be like a cruise. If we hadn't even passed Taiwan then we weren't even halfway, and I was already needing to get off on dry land. Now our troubles had multiplied. Rikochan was in jail suspected of homicide, Heebs had been kidnapped and somehow the crooks thought I could deliver some impossible artifacts. I needed to come up with a plan before the 'Cave Diver' arrived in Singapore.

Again, I debated whether it was wise to contact the police or not. The kidnappers were willing to kill to get the artifacts they sought. On the one hand, I figured that as long as I had control of the sword, I had leverage. On the other hand, how could I be sure they hadn't already harmed my son? Somehow, I needed to contact the perpetrators and get them to put Heebs on the phone.

My eyes wandered from the horizon onto the gently pitching deck and I began to pace along its length with Gilly in tow. When the nausea returned, I took a deep breath and looked out to the horizon until the feeling passed. I felt so helpless — why did I let him go?

Though the ship was old and in need of repairs, Captain Nephus kept everything quite neat. Gilly and I walked along between organized piles of materials as I pondered the situation. My gaze settled on some rolls of metal bands used for strapping crates together and I suddenly got an idea. I felt strongly that I needed to hang onto the sword as long as I possibly could.

Gilly sensed a change in my demeanor and looked up at me with hope, "You've got a plan, Dad?"

"Yep, let's get to work." I enthusiastically responded.

The next few days I kept busy in the machine shop trying to shape a piece of scrap metal into a decoy sword. The ruse didn't have to fool anyone who performed a close inspection but needed to pass as genuine if viewed through an x-ray machine. I sent Gilly off to explore the ship stores and rummage through closets to find another box or padded case long enough to hold the piece. We had to aim for around 80 centimeters, which was the published length of the sword. Several times Gilly came back with excellent containers that must have held sensitive electronics or engine parts, but they were either too long or too short.

I got Captain Nephus in on our plan, without giving him any critical details. I let him know that the same unpleasant fellows who forced us to hide on the 'Cave Diver' were convinced we knew the location of a valuable collector's item.

"I suspect someone might be waiting for us in Singapore, and they will want to steal the original if they can. If we go empty-handed, they might try to rough us up a bit.

But if we had a decoy that we could toss at them when cornered, it will give us a chance to get away." I explained.

"I'll help you any way I can, my friend." Alyosha offered.

Captain Nephus helped Gilly find a suitable container, and even emptied it of its previous contents. Gilly and I discussed details over and over again. By the time the 'Cave Diver' made its approach to Singapore we were ready.

There was a noticeable change in the sky on the last evening. Captain Nephus had the cook set up a table on deck and invited us to join him for dinner. A brilliant sunset revealed a painted sky with breathtaking colors, but it was not against a smooth horizon. Rough bumps and dips traced a line of dark mountains hugging the distant skyline.

"That's Malaysia. There are some fairly high mountains on the peninsula. The highlands to the right are probably Mount Tahan over 2,000 meters in elevation." The captain pointed out.

I did some quick calculations and came up with 7,000 feet and said, "Not too bad. Not comparable to the Rockies or Sierra Nevada however."

"No, you're right. But the tallest peaks in Malaysia are on the island past Sarawak over that direction." Nephus pointed off the port side toward a smooth horizon, "Kinabalu is over 4,000 meters but we can't see it from here."

Gilly craned his neck and moved his head side to side as if trying to see Kinabalu past the huge deck gantries.

"13,000 feet — now you're talking!" I replied.

The captain turned back toward the distant chain of mountains and continued, "We'll sail on past those, then cut in just before Bintan Island in about an hour."

We ate slowly, watching the coastline get closer and closer. A few scattered lights could be seen on the shore, which must have been towns or urban areas.

"Any idea where you'll head next?" I asked.

"I'll go wherever they pay me to go, but if I could choose, my shortlist would include Egypt or back home to Greece — seems like I always miss those." Nephus lamented, "I've always wanted to scan the temple of Luxor. I also don't have the Parthenon even though I grew up in Glyfada. And El Gran Moxo — that would be interesting!"

'El Gran Moxo' — wasn't that one of Hirayuki's notes? It was written as a footnote for Yata-no-kagami the mirror in the Japanese Regalia.

I ventured to ask, "I've never heard of El Gran Moxo. Where is it?"

Nephus turned and jokingly replied, "That's what the Conquistadors were after — the hidden city of gold. No seriously, it is a supposed Inca or Mayan ruin somewhere on the plateau Matto Grasso in Brazil. There are eternal lamps constantly lit by some ancient power source no one has been able to figure out."

It could have been a small hint referring to the Japanese treasure item — did the Yata-no-kagami mirror have some connection to eternal lamps? As interesting as the conversation was, I couldn't think of a way to follow up on the idea.

"Let's keep in touch. Your work should be published! I can help you with that." I noted.

Captain Nephus had to get back to the wheelhouse, so he stood, shook our hands, and left. Gilly and I relaxed on deck and watched the dark coastline pass by. Suddenly, a bright fiery light rose up from the south end of the landmass. Like a burning flare, there was a flickering of sorts, and a glowing tail contrasted with the darkening sunset. Momentarily a faint roar could be heard coming from that direction.

"What is that, Dad?" Gilly asked.

"Wow, that's great, eh? I think it's a chemical rocket launch from Tekong spaceport." I presumed, "I'll bet that rocket stage we're carrying is going to end up there."

Tekong Island was part of Singapore and launch facilities had been established on the east side out of Changi Airport flight paths. The bright rocket flare continued to rise and curved over to the side, as if it would arch back down to the ground.

"It's heading for orbit now. Keep watching and you'll see the boosters come back down for a landing." I noted.

Gilly was the first to see the points of light that marked the retrofiring of the boosters. We followed the points back down until they slowed and winked out at ground level. As if that was a cue, a steady line of well-spaced lights soared overhead, marking the resumption of aircraft on the runway approach to Changi. The action wasn't confined to the sky. We began to pass all sorts of marine traffic, including massive tankers and freighters. Soon the 'Cave Diver' entered the Singapore straits and we saw well-lighted cities on both sides. Amazing silhouettes of towering structures with bridges and spires were clearly illuminated against the dark sky.

As we approached Singapore proper, we passed literally dozens of ships at anchor, brightly lit and floating serenely like clusters of jewels. Soon we felt the 'Cave Diver's engines reduce and observed activity as the crew went through the sequence of tying off to one of the massive permanent parking buoys. The 'Cave Diver' would now be in queue for unloading, which might be several days hence.

Singapore immigration officials wasted no time boarding the 'Cave Diver' and checked our papers. Since Gilly and I were passengers, we got our passports stamped for entry.

Captain Nephus came back again and informed us that he needed to go ashore to take care of some business. He would probably be back in the middle of the night, so Gilly and I should just relax for the evening, and he'd see us in the morning. The two JAXA engineers went as well, and the crew of the 'Cave Diver' must have been bucking to go ashore, because every one of them lined up to board the jetboat with the captain. We had learned that the original crew complement was almost 300 back in the day, but since the ship had been refitted with autonomous equipment there was only need for 15 under Captain Nephus. Gilly and I watched the men jump onto the craft leaving one man behind to lower the vessel using the davit winches. When the speedboat hit the surface, the crewman operating the winches threw the rope ladder over the gunwale and climbed down to meet the others. We watched the boat speed off to the west. Gilly and I were alone on the rusty freighter once again.

Several smaller ships and passenger vessels passed back and forth between us and the shore — I could see countless vessels moving in all directions around us. Gilly and I stared off in the starboard direction at fantastic high-rises and other structures that were less than a kilometer away. Somehow as luck would have it our berth was right off the west end of Sentosa Island, which was a resort of sorts, full of hotels, casinos, beaches, gondola skyways, and even a Ferris wheel (one of several in Singapore).

The bright nightlife ended abruptly at the west end of the island, which was mostly still a dark silhouette of its natural terrain. If my memory served correctly, the western tip of Sentosa was preserved as a museum of Fort Siloso, which had been used as late as World War II.

Suddenly a thought occurred to me. I looked across the way and could barely see the old Fort Siloso concrete observation towers standing lonely on the dark beach. I decided to change my plans. I left Gilly at the gunwale and went to our cabin, returning with the long container carrying the dummy sword. How many eyes were out there watching us already? Could I pull this off in darkness?

"Gilly, follow me. I need to run an errand," I said.

The two of us passed the empty slot where the pair of davits now hung over the gunwales waiting for the return of the speedboat. I stopped at the rowboat with its tarp hiding our prize underneath.

"Did you watch the crewman as he worked the windlass?" I turned to Gilly and asked.

"Not really. Well, maybe sort of." Was his reply.

I quickly unstrapped the canvas in the back and folded it over just enough for one person to sit. I peeked down on the floor and saw that the long case had not been disturbed, though it might have slid a little bit during the heavy weather. I put the false sword case in beside the real one. I showed

Gilly how to operate the winch, in the same way the motorboat operation had been carried out.

"Stay here and watch me. I'm heading over to those concrete towers," I began, "when I get back, you'll need to lift the winch like this."

The little outboard motor was electric, and its batteries were hooked up to a charger with alligator clips that I disconnected. After confirming that Gilly knew what to do, I climbed aboard and sat down next to the two long cases. I had to make a decision on what would be the best way to protect the sword. On the one hand, if we were to make a wild dash for the airport in the morning carrying the sword, there would likely be too many chances to get intercepted. On the other hand, hiding the sword somewhere also had its risks.

The two cases were not identical. It would be safer if Captain Nephus saw us with the case he had given us. That meant Doei's original case needed to be hidden. Depending on which choice I made, I might have needed to switch contents. Fortunately, both the original sword and the decoy, if found accidentally by an ordinary person, may likely have been considered useless junk. I thought long and hard about which route to follow. Finally, I made up my mind and chose which one to hide and got both cases ready. I pulled a paper out of my pocket that I had written in advance and slipped it inside — 'if found, please contact Tim Hughes' and I listed my State-side address and contact information. If the hidden case were found by someone, I had no doubt it would find its way back to me. I re-closed the fasteners on both cases, and prepared Nephus' contribution to be the one we would hand-carry to the airport.

I waited as Gilly expertly lowered both winches evenly until I was riding on the choppy surface. I unlatched the cables and started the motor. Silently I began to cross the kilometer distance over to Sentosa in the darkness. Three times I had to avoid large vessels passing perpendicular to my path, but it only took about twenty minutes to get across. I identified a smooth area to approach and shut off the motor, lifting the outboard until the propeller was out of the water.

The waves were quite calm, so the landing was very gentle. With case in hand, I leapt into the surf and pulled the boat onto the sand a bit — no need to tie it off. I strode the short distance over to the base of the right-hand observation tower. In the dim light I could see rectangular concrete pillars and diagonal cross-bracing anchored to the rock. I shouldered the case and climbed one of the diagonals as best I could until it intersected another vertical column. Somehow, I made it to the base of the observation structure and found a crevice under the floor large enough to stow the case where it would not easily be seen or knocked loose by storms. Task accomplished.

Twenty minutes later Gilly once again expertly operated the davit windlasses. I got back aboard the 'Cave Diver' and replaced everything as I had found it. I picked up the remaining case and smiled at my young son.

"Time for bed, Gilly." I said and tousled his hair.

We returned to our cabin for much-needed rest. A tremendous load had been lifted from my shoulders and I could barely keep my eyes open.

****

The next morning Gilly and I had a quick breakfast with the captain and began to get our things ready. I took down all the notes from the wall and re-stuffed the envelope, returning it to the zippered pocket on my back. We emptied out our cabin and put the long box and a few other items in a pile on the deck. The jetboat was still tied up at the base of the rope ladder where it had returned the previous night and was ready to take us ashore. I placed the LIDAR drone case on my back and paused at the starboard gunwale to look out across the water. The daytime view of the city was quite a bit different from the illuminated nighttime. Instead of brightly lit pinpricks set in dark frames, walls of mirrored glass and steel broken by abundant roof gardens met the eye. The marine traffic had been incessant the entire night, and hundreds of boats of all sizes still crisscrossed the waterways. The morning brought small fishing boats as well. One small fishing boat drifting nearby had multiple fishing rods mounted along both sides with their lines out.

On the port side a small tanker had moored across a span of open water from the 'Cave Diver', with dozens more visible in the distance. Each of the ships was tied to a buoy at the bow and were allowed to pivot around that mooring as the wind came in from the northwest orienting all the vessels parallel to each other. Gilly watched a drone flying around the tanker and the steady buzz of the propellers reached our ears. The little craft flew over to a second boat toward our stern and began circling the other vessel as if doing some sort of inspection. Port authority making the rounds, I assumed. The buzz sound of the propellers got louder as the drone came our way across the water and began circling the 'Cave Diver'. I knew a little bit about various drone models, having used them often in my profession. This one was not a typical consumer model but looked like a commercial grade delivery drone, complete with dangling manipulators. The drone made two rounds of the main deck, then hovered for a while near where I was standing.

Suddenly without warning, the drone swooped down and landed on top of the sword case. Before I realized what was happening, the manipulators tightened themselves around the case and began to slowly lift. I ran toward the small aircraft and attempted to grab onto the case, but the remote operator easily sidestepped and avoided my lunge. The payload must have weighed in at the maximum capacity of the drone's lifting ability because it sluggishly crossed the deck as it tried to gain altitude. I chased the thing and again tried several times to reach for it but missed as it dodged about. The drone successfully flew past the gunwale over open water.

Shocked, I stared after the little craft as it struggled to gain lift. Apparently, someone thought the case contained the actual Kusanagi-no-tsurugi sword and didn't want to wait until I exchanged it for Heebs' freedom.

"No!" I yelled.

In a moment of desperation, I took my own drone off by back and quickly set it up for flight. The laptop took painfully long to boot up, but finally I was able to send the little aircraft speedily on to intercept. Using first-person dead reckoning I was able to overtake the struggling craft and come in overhead from behind. Following the same flight path, I could see through the camera one of the fishing boats straight ahead must have been its destination. I swooped down in front to head it off, but the aircraft avoided my maneuver. Twice more I tried to get the craft to move aside but it corrected course right away.

I had one more tool up my sleeve. Flying backwards, I locked onto the intruder's flight path and set my drone into formation right in front of its cameras. The two aircraft were staring at each other as they sped across the water. Then, with the flick of a switch, I sent a concentrated burst of laser pulse right into the other's lens and burned out all its CCD imaging circuits. The intruder was now flying blind and began to wander off the straight path it had been on. Unfortunately, I was still losing ground. A good pilot would be able to see his distant remotely operated aircraft and compensate with line-of-sight visuals.

I continued to try to disable the other drone, using my landing gear to perhaps clip one of the propellers. The maneuvering was very difficult, and the other pilot skillfully avoided most of my attempts. When I finally did connect, the commercial drone's propeller was so powerful that it knocked my aircraft into a free fall. I recovered at the last minute and swept my cameras up from below as I tried to play catch-up. It was then that I noticed a third drone swoop in. The newcomer had something hanging from its underside, and when I finally got full control of my aircraft back, I could see that it was a makeshift net.

"Dr. Hughes, come on!" Captain Nephus' voice called out behind me.

I briefly turned around and saw him about to descend the rope ladder, but his eyes were covered with a VR headset. The captain snatched the headset away for a second and looked in my direction.

"Let's go get it!" He said and disappeared below the gunwale.

I ran over to the ladder and practically slid down the ropes while trying to cradle the laptop. I saw that Gilly was already onboard, and one of the 'Cave Diver' crewmen had started the jetboat engines. Captain Nephus and I settled down to continue the battle.

The jetboat accelerated at a surprising rate but I didn't have a chance to look up and enjoy the ride. I could see through my cameras that the intruder drone was getting close to its destination fishing boat. The other small vessel was also speeding toward the aircraft to try and shorten the distance it would have to fly. Suddenly Nephus' drone dove and expertly released the net into the intruder's propellers causing it to go down. I saw the case hit the water with a splash.

The captain yelled over the sound of the boat motor, "Get ready to snatch up the case!"

I set my drone to home in on our location and finally had a chance to look up and get my bearings. The wind hit me full in the face, as the jetboat sped directly to where the case bobbed in the choppy waves. From the west the fishing boat was also making a beeline toward the floating object. At first it wasn't clear who would arrive first, but our expert driver stepped things up a notch.

"Wrap this around your waist a few times!" Captain Nephus yelled and handed me a rope.

I obediently coiled the rope around my waist, tied it in a knot, and handed both ends back to him. The captain braced himself between the seats and used his eyes to point down over the right side. Gilly also braced himself down on the deck. This was going to be exciting, I thought. I leaned over the side and lined up my arm to the fast-approaching floating rectangle. The other boat was close too, and it was apparent that they would try to ram us if they didn't get what they wanted.

At the speed we were going, I would probably have broken my wrist trying to snatch the case out of the water. But our driver did a sudden turn on a dime, and the case was right there in front of me for a few agonizing seconds. I reached down, plucked it out of the water, and embraced it for dear life as the jetboat came out of the turn. This is where the ropes around the waist came in handy, as I was almost ejected out into space. The captain held on, I embraced the case, and by the time we had all lost our flying momentum the jetboat was speeding off in a new direction leaving the other fishing vessel in our wake.

The other boat kept coming. At first, we sped out to sea, winding our way around huge tankers and freighters waiting their turn to either drop off or pick up cargo. In the distance we could see islands with what looked like hundreds of petroleum tanks lined up along the shore, giant maritime refueling stations like Sebarok and Bukom Islands. The drones caught up with us and did carrier landings right onto our moving craft. I buttoned up my aircraft and laptop and put everything away, getting ready for our dash to the airport. Our jetboat made a wide arc and headed for St John Island. When we thought we had lost them, the pursuers would somehow reappear, having guessed our trajectory.

"We'll drop you off at Raffle's Place. You can catch the MRT rail system to the airport from there." The captain yelled, "I'll miss you, my friend!"

"Thank you so much! Let's get together soon." I returned.

The boat driver took us east along the coastline to Marina Bay. The narrow bay entrance had at one time been dammed up to create a fresh-water reservoir but had since been restored as a salt-water estuary when high-proficiency nuclear desalination plants had come online. The boat zoomed past the remains of the dam and entered the narrow waterway. We had gained quite a lead, but those others were always visible behind us. Gilly and I stared in wonder as we passed the two domes of 'Gardens by the Bay' or the bridging structure atop the Sands hotel. Unfortunately, we had to slow down as we passed under the helix bridge and crossed the bay. Our pursuers had to slow down as well, but it seemed as though they had made up lost ground. The jetboat pulled up to a dock called Clifford Pier Jetty next to a round restaurant built over the water.

"You can see the entrance to the subway station across there." The captain said.

There it was — a sleek glass structure across the plaza. I snatched up the sword case and we sprinted for the Raffles Place station. We bought tickets and got down onto the platform, only taking a brief few minutes to figure out that a straight shot on the green line would get us to Changi Airport. Crowds of people were waiting for a green line train to arrive, which was apparently a few more minutes away. On the other side of the platform a red train had just pulled up.

My heart skipped a beat as a group of men in business suits appeared at the top of the escalators — Beard Yakuza and his henchmen. Gilly saw them too and without a word, we crossed over to the red train and hopped on board. The red line wouldn't be as direct as the green line, but the hoodlums wouldn't be able to reach us before the doors closed. Gilly still had the Japanese rental phone, which was worthless in Singapore, but the camera still functioned. We watched as the suited men rudely pushed their way down the escalator through the crowd, ever keeping us in their sights. Gilly held up the camera just as the doors shut and Beard Yakuza's face was perfectly framed outside the window — click.

CHAPTER 11

My mind was swirling with thoughts as I tried to unravel what I assumed were the three treasures, namely sword, mirror, and jewel. We had achieved our primary objective, which was to get the Kusanagi-no-tsurugi sword out of Japan, hopefully to use as bargaining leverage to free Rikochan. But now someone had kidnapped Heebs and thought we also knew how to find the mysterious Urim & Thummim, and something called the 'Directors'. Did the mirror and jewel have alternate names I didn't know about? Somehow, I had to talk to my friend Ryuichi and see if he could help me figure things out.

In the meantime, Rikochan was in jail, and I had to somehow string Heebs' captors along and keep them thinking I had what they sought. The thing that worried me the most was the fact that folks who knew about Rikochan's envelope somehow ended up dead. I didn't deceive myself into thinking that if I gave away the sword and other information that we could possibly be safe — we knew too much. The only thing we could do now was to see this thing through to the end, and somehow reveal the culprits.

For the time being, we were at a disadvantage. The thugs knew we were in Singapore and saw us jump on the train with a long case. And they probably guessed we would eventually be heading for Changi Airport. As Gilly and I stood on that train passing through darkened tunnels my mind went through alternative scenarios.

"Remember metrospy?" Gilly asked.

I smiled as I looked at the Mass Rapid Transit (MRT) subway line map on the wall of the train car. The two of us stood near the door holding on to stainless steel grab bars. The car was not so crowded, but every seat lining the windows was taken. Even though we had hopped on the red line, we may have given ourselves away — the yakuza men had seen us waiting for the green airport-bound train across the way. I had never seen someone so determined as Beard Yakuza to get that sword. It was likely they would send some of their guys straight to the airport to look out for us.

"Shouldn't we try to take the fastest route to the airport? Maybe we can beat them to it. We can play games some other time." I reasoned.

"Not if we do the City Air Terminal." Gilly pointed at a poster.

The poster advertised a new service where airport passengers could go to the City Air Terminal downtown, check in their bags, and take their time getting to the airport luggage-free. The trains serving Changi Airport practically ran right up to the check-in counters, but having a pre-checkin downtown would allow passengers to relax unburdened with business colleagues or loved ones sending them off.

According to metrospy unofficial rules of engagement, as Gilly explained, one needed to do things the pursuers did not expect. Certainly, the yakuza would intend to forcefully take the case away if they could. If we showed up at the airport without the container it would be unexpected, and the crooks would wonder where we had hidden it.

Gilly added, "Look Dad, the terminal is at Dhoby Ghaut, only two stops away!"

I was sold. We got off the train and followed the signs toward the terminal. The smell of food wafted through the air and we passed all sorts of ethnic restaurants that beckoned us to enter. There were Malay satay, Indian prata, Chinese bao, Japanese ramen, Korean chicken, Philippine adobo, Mexican tacos, halal Muslim and non-halal Chinese pork dishes. There were even ethnic variations of each other such as Japanese Mos Burger with their version of the popular American fast food. It didn't take much to go for a small detour to fill our bellies.

The terminal was located in the same underground complex as the Dhoby Ghaut station, which was a confluence of the red, purple, and gold lines. We had had no means of making reservations in advance, since the 'Cave Diver' internet system had been unreliable. However, there was a flight to Hong Kong that afternoon upon which I booked Gilly and checked in the sword case in his name. The mobsters saw us enter the train station with the long package, so checking the case in would extend my bargaining leverage even if we got caught. I found a flight the next day destined for Kansai in Japan which I nabbed. We emerged happily without anything to carry, ready to make a run for it if needed.

Our next task was to get clothes. We had found ourselves on the 'Cave Diver' with only one set of clothes each, but fortunately Captain Nephus had a lost-and-found box full of items he had collected from forgetful passengers and crew. We were able to cobble together a couple of outfits that covered us when we did our laundry. I don't think Gilly realized at first, he had picked out women's clothing for a smaller person but was beginning to feel self-conscious about it. Entering a nearby clothing store, we purchased sweat shorts, sandals, sunglasses, surgical masks, hats, and thin hoodies that could cover our heads in a pinch.

Singapore was a shopping Mecca. The store appeared to be a fashionable place for all ages, even the elderly, with one section displaying hip canes and character walkers for the mature generation that grew up loving the various cinematic franchises. We slowly walked down the aisle in amazement, looking at the various flamboyant products. The cane collection included several versions with cartoonish mouse ears, superhero logos, magic wands, and a few popular sports teams.

We decided to change into our new clothes immediately and walk out of the store in disguise. Heading for the checkout counter the thought hit me — I couldn't get my mind off the light-up laser saber or light-sword walking cane (or whatever you call it) from the famous Star Battle sci-fi movie series that was still popular. I had never gotten into any of the franchises, so maybe I got the name wrong. On impulse I turned around.

"Gilly, go grab one of those space sword walking sticks!" I asked.

Gilly might have been into the franchise but wasn't enthusiastic about buying a cane. It was a gimmick that old sci fi geezers could carry around and do mock saber fights with their elderly buddies. Gilly rushed off with a scowl on his face, probably thinking I was some kind of nutcase dad. I walked up to the register holding the price tags of our new items.

"Excuse me," I asked the salesclerk, "do you have gift boxes for all the products in the store?"

"Certainly." The young man returned.

Just then Gilly walked up with the cane and handed it to me.

Placing the cane on the counter, I asked, "Can you put this in a gift box? Thanks."

The salesclerk rang up our purchases, packed the cane in a long box, and gave me a few hundred Sing dollars cash back.

Gilly had finally figured out what I intended to do and smiled, "Dad, you have a really sick sense of humor!"

I couldn't help it. We left the store and found an out-of-the-way corner with a bench. If the yakuza didn't see us carrying the case we walked in with, at least we had something else to distract them. I scribbled an address on the box which, if they tracked it down, would turn out to be the Kokuraminami Police Station back in Japan.

We reboarded the red line train, intending to take a wide roundabout route to the airport, but Gilly insisted that we change trains and even backtrack a few times. We finally ended up taking the blue line to Expo, then riding the final leg of the green train into Changi Airport like we had intended to do from the beginning.

At this point the metrospy game turned serious. With every other person wearing a business suit, we couldn't be sure who, if any, our pursuers might be. Both of us had hoodies up, with hats, masks, and sunglasses in place so we looked normal in the tropical environment. Being a tall foreigner was no problem because there were a lot of other big white guys walking around to blend in with. At first no one gave us a second glance, but as we approached the check-in counters, I saw two suits that I had definitely seen before. We walked right by them without being recognized. Since we had already checked in via the City Air Terminal, we already had Gilly's seat assignment and we didn't have to line up at the counters. I walked Gilly straight for the gate.

I pulled him aside and said, "Gilly let me have the Japanese rental phone. Mas will be waiting for you when you get to Chep Lap Kok Airport in Hong Kong. I'll see you in a few days."

Gilly pulled out the phone and charger from his pocket and handed them to me. I took out his passport and boarding pass and handed them to him, along with some Sing dollars for a little snack.

"Whatever you do, don't lose this. And don't stop playing metrospy until you are with Mas. Tell him to bury the case at Piccadilly and Haymarket." I added.

"What do you mean?" Gilly began, "Isn't that a place in England?"

"Mas will know what it means." I replied.

Gilly nodded and walked through the gate, showing his documents to the immigration officials. I stood there waiting until I could no longer see him as he walked toward the gate.

Since my flight was early the next morning, I set out with the long box under my arm to find a place to stay for the night. It was then that I noticed a couple of suits following me from a distance. At first, I thought it was a coincidence, but soon I realized they were the same two fellows we had passed earlier, and they seemed to always be somewhere in the vicinity. It was time for me to try my own game of metrospy.

I walked into a crowded gift shop full of passengers seeking souvenirs. Keeping my head low, I removed the mask and sunglasses and went out another exit. I immediately ducked behind a display and watched the men exit the same way, frantically trying to find out where I had gone. This time I tracked them for a while, until I was sure they had not seen me. I doubled back and tried to put as much distance between us as I could. Unfortunately, fifteen minutes later they were back on my tail. Once again, I used a crowd to lose them again, then ducked into a restroom toilet stall. I pulled my old, crumpled shirt out of my LIDAR backpack and slipped that on over the hoodie, then ditched the hat. Seeing no one outside, I made my way over and caught a ride on the monorail-like airport train that ferries passengers between terminals.

The next terminal over was a huge dome with an amazing garden inside. A waterfall poured through a funnel in the roof. After wandering about I found myself walking on a vast rope net suspended just below the glass ceiling. Again, I thought I had lost the two fellows but there they were again, with one more colleague. Down in the garden I tried to duck into a full-sized maze made of immaculately trimmed shrubs, but most of the narrow passageways ended up being dead ends or were blocked by the yakuza fellows coming the other way.

The party of suits grew, and I recognized that bearded fellow among them. Then things got interesting — they no longer tried to hide the fact they were following me but engaged in active pursuit. I glanced back once and saw Beard Yakuza send a couple of guys in another direction to head me off, but I succeeded in slipping out a side passageway. Again, I managed to use a crowd to lose the bunch.

Just then something completely unexpected happened. I tried to inconspicuously lurk behind some displays when I heard a familiar voice.

"Hey, Musashi," I heard coming from behind, "It's Kōjirō!"

I turned around and there was the fisherman from Funajima. The man walked up to me in his shy manner, batting his eyes until the last word came out, whereupon he would look me in the eye for only a brief moment.

"Fancy meeting you here," he said.

I looked incredulously at the man, who appeared to be alone this time. He had a box of fishing gear that he appeared to treasure, with a long plastic tube, presumably containing a fishing rod or two.

"I didn't expect to see you in Singapore," I replied.

The man batted his eyes and shyly looked this way and that without focusing directly on my face, "We've been making the rounds in several Asian countries. What a coincidence!"

"Where's your friend?" I asked.

The fisherman seemed to fix his gaze on the long box and pointed off to our right, "Getting something to eat."

I looked in that direction but didn't see the other man. Instead, Beard Yakuza and several others were coming our way fast.

The fisherman saw my reaction and turned around, "Not these guys again!" He mumbled.

We both started running at the same time, and I accidentally plowed through a group of teenage girls. The fisherman shot out ahead.

I held tight to the box and yelled, "Sorry!"

Glancing backwards, I saw guys in suits zigzagging and leaping all over the place. I caught up to the fisherman and his eyes went to the box again.

"You know those fellows?" I asked between breaths, pounding pavement as fast as my legs could carry me.

"It's a long story." The fisherman kept glancing at the package, "That's going to slow you down, must be important."

The fisherman had abandoned his gear back where I had first seen him. He kept looking from side to side for a place to hide. I should have told him that hanging on to the package was just part of a ruse, but somehow the words didn't come out.

"I've got to hide it somewhere. I can't allow them to get it." I said instead as I tried to match his stride.

The man pulled out ahead and pointed to a recessed corridor, "There!"

I saw him disappear around the corner and followed, but suddenly everything went dark. I found myself on the floor with vague impressions of two figures struggling nearby. Somehow, I managed to crawl behind a column away from the commotion and had just enough energy left to roll under a line of seats. A man with a dark suit, one sleeve partially ripped at the shoulder, embraced the long box and sent blows in the direction of the sprawled fisherman. In a surprising turn of acrobatics, the fisherman flipped over on top of the thug and yanked the box clear. In one smooth motion he regained his feet and started to run off. However, the thug expertly kicked out his leg and caused the other to trip. The package changed hands again and I watched as the two sparred as they made their way down the corridor. I wanted to shout that the box was not important, but they had already gone.

Looking from under the row of chairs, I could see pairs of running legs shoot past, following the two fighting over the box. By the time I recovered enough energy to stand again, I had counted six pairs of legs, including the last who leisurely followed along behind the others.

I got up and followed behind a bit until the narrow concourse opened up into a wide area lined with shops. A brawl had broken out and the fisherman looked surrounded. One of the men managed to get the box away from him but the fisherman pounced. With one powerful blow he lashed out and floored the yakuza fellow, then leapt over a handrail with the box under his arm. If it had been me, I would have given up by that time and handed over the package, but to my surprise the fisherman fought back with a fierceness I wouldn't have suspected. It was almost as if both parties were desperate to obtain that box no matter what. I was touched by his defense of my property, but there would be a very embarrassing apology to that fisherman someday I thought. I lost sight of the group after that, and all was quiet.

I wandered about for more than an hour but didn't see anyone again. Surely if one of those thugs obtained the box and opened it, they wouldn't be amused. It was sure they would come looking for me.

I checked into a capsule hotel for the night and went inside to stay low for the evening. I was still playing metrospy early the next morning as I headed to the gate to catch my flight back to Kansai Airport in Japan. There was no sign of the men in suits or my fisherman friend.

Suddenly I had a sick feeling the fisherman would not make it out alive.

CHAPTER 12

The clickety-clack, clickety-clack repetitive sound of steel wheels on rails coincided with power poles whizzing by. Nine hours later I was on a train in Japan heading out of Kyoto Station. I had the fully charged rental phone in my hand and could not resist looking at the screen every few minutes. The phone was my only link with whoever had kidnapped my son Hibiki, and I had already sent out a text upon my arrival. I had the sword in a safe place but had no idea how to approach the Urim & Thummim or Directors without bluffing. I had attached a photo of the sword we had taken that night on board the 'Cave Diver', then asked for a phone call to speak with my son to make sure he was alive and well.

But there was still no reply from Heebs' captors. Could it be that Heebs' phone was at that very moment tucked in the pocket of one of those mobsters running around Singapore? If so, where were they keeping Heebs, and who was going to give him meals? My mind would not dare go to the place that seemed horrible and inevitable. I was worried sick that some harm might have fallen on him, and I was irritated because my first attempt at negotiation returned dead silence.

My thoughts plagued me, and between worrying and nodding off the train made its way into the mountains. It was already late afternoon when the train pulled into Miyazu for a brief stop, then reversed direction onto another track. I could see the beautiful coastline finally, and for about ten minutes the train hugged the shore before pulling into Amanohashidate Station.

Exiting the train, I marveled at the slick, hi-tech construction that had completely replaced the remote backcountry station I had visited decades earlier. The building had an attractive mix of contemporary materials and heavy timber construction that reflected some of the unique indigenous architecture in the area. I crossed the street and saw an entire neighborhood revitalized, with waterfront buildings taking on the imagery of the 'funaya' or boat house from nearby Ine-cho town. In Ine-cho the fishing boats were traditionally housed in the funaya boat garages built over the water, tightly lining the shoreline of the entire bay of Ine. Since becoming a World Heritage site, the funaya had been restored, rebuilt, beautified, and the entire area was popular with tourists and vacationers. Unfortunately, on this trip, as much as I loved staying in rooms overlooking the water, I did not have time to visit Ine-cho.

I found a small upper floor funaya style restaurant overlooking the Amanohashidate sands, which would be the closest I would be to an actual funaya. I sat by the window and ordered an udon noodle and quickly ate as I watched fishermen and jet boats full of tourist zip by in the waterway below.

Again, I could not stop myself from glancing at the screen of the rental phone, hoping to get some reply from the kidnappers. I finished my meal and there was still no answer. I descended back down to water level and decided to walk the length of the Amanohashidate sand spit rather than take a bus or taxi. My destination was the Moto-Ise Kono Shrine where my friend and colleague Ryuichi Hebiwara had retired as a Shinto priest. Since the hike was only forty minutes, a taxi would hardly get there much faster.

Amanohashidate is a natural narrow forested sand spit that crosses the Asoumi Sea like a bridge. The scenery was beautiful, and I walked on the well-beaten path only part of the way before kicking my shoes off and passing through the trees and grassy meadows to the beach. The soft sand and cool water increased the length of the walk but provided an escape from the stress. Soft rushing sounds of small waves breaking on the beach though relaxing, did not stop me from taking a peek at the phone now and then. But no answer came.

The Moto-Ise Kono Shrine lay at the northern end of the Amanohashidate strand in a small neighborhood of residences and shops. Ryuichi Hebiwara welcomed me warmly in front of Mikado gate and led me to the Haiden ancient wooden temple structure, where we could peer through heavy columns at the Honden main shrine. The priest was wearing a men's kimono, made from what looked like rough, subdued materials. His bald head was new to me, but I could see the dark, several days' growth framing a face and eyes I knew well.

"It's good to see you again, my friend." I greeted.

Hebiwara-san reached out and we shook hands, "The pleasure is mine." He said, in immaculate English pronunciation.

We stood side by side admiring the simple lines of the carved timbers. "It's magnificent." I observed.

"I never get tired of its beauty," the priest began, "Legends say that this was the original shrine to the sun goddess Amaterasu, before Ise Shrine was built."

I recalled reading about Moto-Ise being the 'original' Ise, and therefore the two shrines had a special association. I asked, "How much of this structure is original?"

Hebiwara-san smiled and noted, "That is the most asked question. Actually, only a few pieces of sacred wood are original, and are protected. Everything else has been rebuilt in the original style and craft."

"Do you rebuild it every twenty years?" I wondered.

"No, my friend," the priest chuckled, "It's not as rigorous as Ise Shrine, which has national funding. We just have repairs done as needed, but still make use of the traditional craftsmen."

The most significant reason for me to visit the shrine was because of the Yata-no-kagami mirror connection from the Imperial Regalia. "You served many years at Ise Shrine, right? I have a few questions about the sacred mirror," I said.

Hebiwara-san looked at me and put a hand on my shoulder, "Come, let's get comfortable. I've got a very Spartan room for you that I hope will help you relax."

We took a walk over toward the shrine offices. "Most of our priests live nearby in regular houses with their families, but we do have a few special rooms. A dorm perhaps." He explained.

We entered the building which was also constructed in a less ornamental style of the Shinto tradition, and walked past the offices which were closed for the day. Hebiwara-san indicated an open door, and I peeked in. I felt an acute sense of Deja vu as I observed walls covered with LIDAR plots of Shinto temples, intermixed with exquisite floor plan and sectional drawings produced by hand. The room very much resembled Captain Nephus' cabin on the 'Cave Diver'. Instinctively I entered the room, which appeared to be Hebiwara-san's office. Ironically, the priest had spent his life as a high-tech architect, artistically expressing steel columns, ducts, and exposed plumbing using very simple, cleverly designed joints and connections before retiring. He soon took up LIDAR scanning as a hobby and began attending surveying conferences where I met him.

"Your work is astounding — always well- done without any unnecessary artifacts!" I praised.

Where most surveyors, such as myself, only removed unsightly obstacles before the scan if it was convenient, Hebiwara-san must have painstakingly removed every single foreign object, such as shoes at the entry, waste cans, umbrella stands, desks, furniture, and even exposed power conduits to make sure only the pure, original Shinto architectural surfaces remained in the scan.

"Thank you, you're always very kind." He said as we moved further into the building.

A narrow corridor smelled of Hinoki Japanese Cypress and a strong hint of incense. Hebiwara-san led us past several sliding wood fusuma doors and stopped in front of the last one. Inside was a small 6-mat tatami room looking out onto a Japanese garden. In the middle of the room an electric pot and small tray of porcelain cups sat on a low table.

"Take a seat, Dr. Hughes," Ryuichi motioned to the floor beside the table where several zabuton cushions were stacked up.

I took one of the cushions to sit on the floor, and pulled my LIDAR drone case off my back as I settled in. Hebiwara-san took two cups and poured some hot tea as he sat down across from me.

"Sorry our accommodations are not very elaborate." He apologized.

I looked around the room. It was definitely not five-star luxury, but in my mind the simplicity made it much more comfortable and homier. The deep Hinoki cypress wood smell was intoxicating. And of course, nothing could compare with the beautiful view of the garden.

"This is very nice, thank you so much!" I countered as I reached into my backpack for Rikochan's papers, "I'd like to ask some questions about the Imperial Regalia."

Hebiwara-san watched as I separated the papers into the topical stacks the kids and I had organized. Most of those were handwritten notes the children had put together, but we did manage to print out a few articles at the hotel. I watched the reaction on the priest's face as he ignored most of the piles of papers, such as wormhole physics, remote editing of DNA, and self-replicating machines which were apparently of no interest to him and went straight for the historical information. The priest picked up the papers and began to look through them.

"I know a little about the Japanese treasures, especially the mirror," he said as he looked over the top paper which was a simple printout from the Internet describing the Yasakani-no-magatama jewel, Kusanagi-no-tsurugi sword, and Yata-no-kagami mirror.

"Is the mirror kept at Ise Shrine?" I asked.

Hebiwara-san nodded his head, "I started my Shinto career at Ise, soon after retiring from my architecture practice. I never saw the mirror personally but have heard some interesting things from the older obosan priests."

Hebiwara-san turned the page and seemed to be taken aback. I peered over at the page and saw the title *The Jews and the Japanese: The Successful Outsiders* which I had glossed over before as seeming out of place. It appeared to be a scan of a book cover with several pages stapled onto it. Heebs had found it online and thought it worth keeping after hearing about various origin theories for the Japanese race.

"Now this is interesting," the priest whispered, "it reminds me of something I've been studying. Hold on a second."

Hebiwara-san stood up and walked across the tatami floor in his sock feet, stepping into the slippers on the wooden floor out in the corridor. For a few seconds he disappeared, presumably to fetch something from his office. When he returned, he had another thick set of papers stapled together. As he sat back down, he handed the document to me. It was a scholarly paper by Alice Elsa Smith from 1949.

"*Comparative Study of Judaism and Shinto* — what's going on here?" I asked.

Hebiwara-san was silent for a while as he picked up Heebs' printout of the book excerpt and poured through some of the pages.

"In Nagano Prefecture there is a mountain called Moriya, where a Shinto ritual is performed called 'Mi-Isaku-Chi'. They tie up a boy to a wooden pillar and a Shinto priest acts as though he is going to sacrifice the boy. But the boy is released, and an animal is sacrificed instead. It's like the Jewish story of Abraham sacrificing Isaac on Mt Moriah. Or there is the tradition of carrying the portable omikoshi shrine on poles, like the Ark of the Covenant. The Ise Shrine supposedly could be a wooden version of the ancient tabernacle of Israel. Or how about the torii gates painted red like blood on the door from during Passover?" Hebiwara-san excitedly described parallels between the two religions.

I looked incredulously at the older man and wondered, "Are you saying there is some non-coincidental link between the two?"

The priest momentarily set the papers back down and explained, "There is a theory that one of the lost tribes of Israel may have traveled along the Silk Road and settled in Japan as the Hata and Inbe clans. Another researcher thinks that the Japanese emperor might have descended from the tribe of Gad — 'mikado' signifying the empirical family supposedly is an honorific 'mi' prefix to 'kado' or Gad. There are many connections like this."

I continued to eye my friend skeptically. Was this something that was well-known? Why hadn't I heard of this before?

As if to answer my unspoken question, he added, "I haven't seen this published in English. But if you look through Japanese publications, you would see dozens of titles from various authors."

"Does this have anything to do with the Imperial Regalia?" I asked.

"Yes, it does. Among the priests in Ise and Moto-Ise Shrines, everyone knows about the Hebrew written on the back of Yata-no-kagami." Ryuichi smiled with great pleasure.

I almost fainted — Hebrew on the back of a Japanese imperial artifact?

Hebiwara-san saw the disbelief on my face and said, "After World War II one of our early Ise priests worked with a scribe named Yutaro to copy off the characters written on the back of the mirror. The symbols spell out the name of God in Hebrew, specifically 'eheyeh asher eheyeh' found in Exodus 3:14, which translates to 'I AM THAT I AM'. You can find this easily with an Internet search."

"But how can this be? Did the early Gadites bring the mirror? Was Ninigi-no-Mikoto from Gad?" I pressed, referring to the story Gilly and I had found in the Kirishima hot springs hotel.

The priest responded, "That's only one theory. There's also the idea that Jewish exiles in the 9th Century made their way to Japan and mingled with the Shinto priests. But that doesn't support the fact that the Yata-no-kagami is a 3rd or 4th Century artifact. So, there are those who say Katakana and Hiragana scripts may have somehow been influenced by the Hebrew characters written on the mirror."

My eyes glanced at the smartphone to see if some message had come from Heebs' captors — nothing. Something still didn't seem to fit. I remembered reading about how the Ise Shrine architectural style probably came from the Pacific Islands modeled after the raised grain storehouses. It seemed more likely that there must be some influence from the Pacific cultures. And how in the world could Judaism and Shintoism be connected? Hebiwara-san took Heebs' Judaism-Shinto connection article and slipped it under the pile.

"Is there any connection between the Jews and the other artifacts?" I inquired, "I mean besides the mirror?"

Hebiwara-san nodded, "Hebrew Regalia supposedly consisted of three articles — a staff, a jar, and the Ten Commandments. The treasures had always been wrapped up in cloth, with the common priest not allowed to open them up. The priests still handled them, nonetheless. A wrapped metal staff would ring when struck or knocked about. After generations, who knows what went through their minds about the contents of the wrapped items. Maybe there could be some connection between a long metal rod and the sword from the Japanese treasures? I'm just stabbing in the dark here, but if Hebrew exiles found themselves far away from home, and needed to recreate important religious artifacts, the memory of those wrapped articles might have resulted in a sword instead of a staff."

It sounded like a long shot, but Ryuichi's reasoning made some sense.

Hebiwara-san stared down at Doei-san's original document with the sudoku puzzle and scrap of ancient manuscript. The torn remnant floated at the bottom of the page with handwritten notes pointing to some of the cursive words. The three Japanese Regalia were jotted down. Under Yata-no-kagami were three sub-bullets: 'El Gran Moxo', 'quantum holographic encoding', and 'computing power of a rock'; and under Yasakani-no-magatama were three more sub-bullets: Silurian hypothesis, Antikythera mechanism, and 'Liahona'. Hebiwara-san moved his finger from Hirayuki's scribbled notes up to one of the original cursive words written on the torn remnant. His eyes lit up with excitement.

"Hmm, maybe we need to add one more item to the ancient Hebrew regalia: the 'Urim & Thummim'!" He enthusiastically proposed.

There it was again! Shocked, I looked at the cursive word Hebiwara-san pointed to and could see it plain as day: 'Urim and Thummim'. Why I had not seen the words before I could not tell, only that cursive script had so many bumps that ran together that my mind must have shut them out.

I quickly snatched up the paper and looked closer at the cursive words. Yata-no-kagami was pointing at 'Urim and Thummim', and my mind was already telling me what I would find under Yasakani-no-magatama — yes! It was 'Directors'! Two of the three Japanese Regalia could apparently be matched up with 'Urim & Thummim', and 'Directors'. The third regalia item was not so clear, but was probably also a sword, just as Heebs' kidnapper had demanded.

"I think I have something on this." Hebiwara-san said as he again stood up.

He made another trip to his office and came back with a second article that he laid on the table. I leaned over and read the title, *The Urim and Thummim: A Means of Revelation in Ancient Israel* by Cornelius Van Dam. Hebiwara-san thumbed through the pages.

My friend briefly put me in a tailspin, "What is a Urim & Thummim — is it some kind of mirror?"

Hebiwara-san seemed deep in thought, as if I had brought some clue to a secret he had been searching for, "It was an instrument supposedly made by God, that appeared to be in the form of a pair of goggles or glasses, connected to a breastplate. The priest could look into the glasses and have all sorts of information revealed to him. If the Japanese Imperial Regalia was inspired by the Hebrews, maybe Yata-no-kagami was some representation of Urim & Thummim!"

Hebiwara-san shuffled across the tatami with his mind already gone on to wherever the new revelations would lead him. I watched the older man disappear into the corridor and slide the fusuma door shut.

My eyes dropped back down to the table where the phone and papers still lay in neat piles. No message from Heebs' kidnappers. Finally, I had the time and privacy to take stock of what was in the envelope. Somehow, I had to figure out how they all linked together in order to negotiate for Rikochan and Heebs' freedom. I reached out and picked up the first stack, which happened to be notes on physics papers:

- *Holographic Schwinger Effect and the Geometry of Entanglement*
- *Construction and Enlargement of Dilatonic Wormholes by Impulsive Radiation*
- *EPR Pair Temporal Loops: Primordial Closed Timelike Curves?*
- Gilbert Fulmer 1983 (not looked up yet)

Just a quick glance through them all left me completely drained — who would understand what they were talking about?

The next pile, which had historical discussions, was quite a bit easier to understand. I think I got a little more insight into their significance after my discussion with Hebiwara-san:

- sudoku puzzle overlaid on Funajima map
- *The Jews and the Japanese: The Successful Outsiders*
- *Comparative Study of Judaism and Shinto* (just obtained from Hebiwara)
- *Imperial Regalia: three Japanese treasures*
- article on the Antikythera mechanism
- pamphlet on Japanese origins
- pamphlet on Ise Shrine

The last two Gilly and I had picked up at the museum in Takachiho. The priest had taken the other paper, *The Urim and Thummim: A Means of Revelation in Ancient Israel* so I would have to look that one up later.

Finally, there was the group of engineering manuscripts that had kicked off the creepy genetic manipulation discussion between Rikochan and the late Ichika Ebina:

- *The Silurian Hypothesis: Would it be possible to detect an industrial civilization in the geological record?*
- *Quantum Holographic Encoding in a Two-dimensional Electron Gas*
- *50-year Window to Establish a Space Faring Civilization*
- *Code of the lifemaker*
- *Advanced automation for space missions*
- *Creation of a Bacterial Cell Controlled by a Chemically Synthesized Genome*
- *Life at the speed of light*
- *The Wow signal of the terrestrial genetic code*

Again, I recalled the mind-bending discussion between Ebina-san and my daughter about faxing DNA code sequences to remote locations. The *Advanced automation* document looked like a NASA report of some kind, and *Code of the lifemaker* appeared to be part of a science fiction story. Unfortunately, though I had made some progress, none of the paper topics seemed related to each other — I was still at a dead end.

Another thing nagged at me — were all of Hirayuki's notes translations from the ancient hieroglyphs? This seemed unlikely because they referred to modern works. Rather, it seemed more probable that the hieroglyphics might have been an ancient discussion from perhaps an advanced civilization long dead, a Silurian civilization if you will, that may have been rediscovered in the modern papers.

I put the papers away and got ready for bed, making a quick trip to the ofuro bath. I washed myself thoroughly, seemingly for the first time in a long time. I lifted several planks covering the raised wooden tub and stacked them off to the side. The water was hot, almost too hot to stand, but slowly I eased myself inside one foot at a time until the liquid went up to my neck. The aroma of Hinoki cypress seemed to be enhanced by the steam coming from the bath and had a hypnotic effect. My frenzied mind was calmed and for several blissful minutes I forgot all about swords, regalia, genetic engineering, or entanglement physics.

About a half hour later I found my way back to my room, dressed in a yukata robe. Someone had pulled out a futon, which was a thin mattress and duvet covered with crisp white sheets. I turned on an oscillating electric fan and collapsed onto the futon spread-eagle fashioned as I basked in the peace of the moment.

But the peaceful feeling was not to last. I reached over to the nearby table where the phone sat plugged into its charging cable. A message had arrived from Heebs' number!

"Too late. Your son die!" The message said.

CHAPTER 13

I had a fitful night with very little sleep. I started off begging them to protect my son. I sent messages saying I knew where the sword was hidden, if only they brought him back unharmed. I would nod off waiting for a reply that never came, then find some other way to beg for his safety. By morning I was a nervous wreck and had sent over a dozen texts without hearing any response.

I briefly saw Hebiwara-san as I rushed out. He had just gotten into his office and looked deep in thought as he studied images and text related to the Urim & Thummim.

"My son is in trouble; I've got to go." I said in passing.

Ryuichi barely looked up and said, "Hope it isn't serious. See you soon, my friend."

I had no time to explain exactly how serious it was as I ran out to the parking lot and grabbed a taxi that had just been vacated by one of the priests arriving for work. I had no clue where to go, but somehow, I had made up my mind to return to Shimonoseki, and perhaps Funajima which was the last place I had seen Heebs. The taxi drove the long way around Asoumi inland sea, but still took less time to arrive at Amanohashidate Station than I had taken to walk the sand spit the previous day. I caught a train to Kyoto and again waited impatiently as the clackety-clack sound of the mountain railway weaved through valleys and sleepy farm towns.

I felt relieved when I finally took my seat on the bullet train out of Kyoto, which was only a two-hour trip to my destination. But my mind was still in a panic as my imagination kept conjuring up ways yakuza hoodlums could torture people. All those classic Japanese flicks where fingers got cut off, or worse, continued coming to mind. I braced myself for bad news and kept glancing at the smartphone screen.

The Japanese Shinkansen, or bullet train was supposedly one of the fastest of its kind in the world. They had upgraded the main lines with linear motors, and the train didn't even make contact with the rails but levitated several centimeters above the surface. Even at those speeds the time passed agonizingly slow. No further text messages came in answer to the dozens of pleading texts I had sent over the previous twenty-four hours.

Imagine my surprise when, instead of a text message, the smartphone began to ring with an incoming call. I fumbled with the device and almost dropped it on the floor. The call was from an unknown number.

"Hello?" I answered, my hands trembled as I feared the worst.

"Dr. Hughes?" Came a middle-aged Japanese male.

The person seemed familiar, but I couldn't quite place where I had heard the man before.

"Yes, I am he." I replied in a hoarse voice.

It seemed like there was a long pause that was probably only a second or two, *"This is detective Fujii."*

My heart dropped. I remembered that awful scene at Ebina-san's home with blood everywhere and imagined law enforcement crawling all over the place taking photos of a murdered young boy. So close! I was almost there!

Suddenly I remembered the voice. Detective Yui Fujii was the person from Kokuraminami Police Station that had arrested Rikochan. Would he also investigate homicides in the neighboring prefecture across the channel? I felt sick to my stomach and it felt hard to breathe. My head was feeling dizzy. I'm sure that if I had been standing, I likely would have passed out. I leaned back in the train seat, closed my eyes, and took a deep breath.

"There's someone here who would like to talk to you." Detective Fujii's voice came through the little phone's speaker.

My mind was already resigned that I would hear a terrible announcement regarding my precious son Hibiki. But the detective didn't seem consoling. I waited for what seemed like an eternity as the phone on the other end was passed on to some other person.

"Dad?" Came a weak voice.

It was Heebs! I choked up and couldn't say a thing. My eyes teared up and I began heaving in great sobs. I can't explain it, but suddenly I felt the most happiness I had ever felt in my life. My boy was safe!

It took me a while to realize that Heebs was talking to me, *"Dad, are you there?"*

I must have been whimpering because Heebs started to console me over the phone.

"Are you alright? Dad, are you okay?" The voice said.

Finally, I calmed down enough to speak. I wiped my tears and took another deep breath.

"I'm here, son. I'm okay. I'm so glad you're safe!" I managed.

The bullet train was only ten minutes from the station. Sometimes with these high-speed mass transit systems you have to overshoot your destination or get off early and take a local train to the smaller stations. My plans changed. Heebs was right there near the Kokura station, and I wouldn't have to hop on the local line to backtrack across the Kanmon Straits. Twenty minutes later I walked into Kokuraminami Police Station and gave Heebs a giant hug.

We sat at a conference table with Detective Fujii and took our time drinking cold mugicha barley tea.

"I don't know what happened," Heebs began, "I had only gotten off the fisherman's motorboat and walked about a block when, out of nowhere, somebody sucker-punched me from behind. It was dark and they threw a black bag over my head. I tried to fight back but the dude was strong! No, I think there were two or three of them. They zip-tied my wrists and ankles."

"What happened then?" I asked.

Heebs continued, "I must have blacked out. The next thing I knew I was in some room by myself. I could feel the tatami floor under me, but it was dark. I tried calling out, but no one would answer."

I looked down at his wrists and saw deep grooves where the zip-ties had cut into his flesh. He had a black eye and a few cuts on his face that were already scabbed over.

"I finally ripped the bag off my head and could see a little bit of the room. But my hands were still zip-tied behind me. I think I must have been out for days, because I was so hungry." He explained.

Heebs described a small traditional Japanese room with a kitchenette at one end. A window above the sink was boarded up but let in cracks of light during the day. Someone had left packaged snacks and water bottles that he had trouble opening.

"It was miserable. I couldn't get out of the zip-ties no matter what I tried. At night I would fall asleep and dream I was being smothered, only to wake up all tied up. Then I remembered how flimsy the old Japanese homes used to be, so I got on my back and used my feet to pound the door." Heebs animatedly demonstrated.

I looked at my beautiful son and was amazed at how cool he was taking it. The wolf was there with determination in his eyes. His foot battering ram knocked a hole in the door, but it was still too small to get through. The next room was dark, with old musty construction materials and debris on the floor. The building had apparently been abandoned a long time ago. Heebs used the same technique on the walls, which were mostly solid. But one section collapsed, allowing sunlight to stream inside. The gap opened onto a narrow alley two stories above street level. He yelled through the hole and almost went hoarse, but finally an 'obāsan' old woman stood on the street below staring up at him. Shortly thereafter police officers arrived to get him out.

"Where is Gilly?" he finally asked.

"He's safe." I assured.

Detective Yui Fujii, who had dispassionately watched us during the exchange, finally spoke up, "The old building was to be demolished to make way for a factory building. The owners thought it was locked and secure, but apparently the kidnappers broke in."

I tiredly watched the middle-aged detective and remembered back on the events of the past weeks. We had been running, hiding, avoiding thugs, ditching 'omawari' police. I just wanted this thing to be over.

"You have my daughter in jail. Can't you see what this is doing to my family?" I said with a hint of exhaustion.

Detective Fujii frowned, "Your daughter was involved in a heinous killing. She's our only lead to several homicides. I'm sorry, Dr. Hughes, you and your son are not suspects, but you must understand our perspective. We just don't have any contrary proof."

Heebs leaned up against me and wrapped his arms around my shoulders. I almost felt like sagging in the chair and yielding to my exhaustion. They had plenty of proof! We had described the yakuza fellows, but no one believed us. If only —

Suddenly I remembered the smartphone photo Gilly had taken as we had boarded the Singapore MRT subway train.

"I've got some proof!" I exclaimed as I pulled out the phone.

I quickly parsed through the photos until I got to the one where Beard Yakuza was staring at us through the glass train car door. I held the phone up so Detective Fujii could see the photo.

"Here he is. This guy is the ringleader. They've been chasing us and harassing us these two weeks. Here's your murderer!" I blurted out.

Detective Fujii dispassionately looked at the photo while Heebs vigorously nodded his head in agreement. The detective slowly got up from his chair. The conference room we were sitting in was adjacent to a larger room with rows of desks and cubicles, and various police personnel going about their business. Plain-clothed detectives sat at desks writing reports, as uniformed officers brought in suspects and other persons of interest.

"Mariko, Nakaya no — hora," Fujii-san called out to a smartly uniformed lady standing a few cubicles away, "desuku no shashin motte oide."

Officer Mariko looked up in momentary confusion and asked, "Shashin? Ano higegao shashin?"

The woman must have been in an accident recently, because her left eye appeared bruised and there were partially healed cuts and abrasions on her face. Something seemed familiar — had I seen her before?

"Mnn." Fujii returned with a single syllable meaning 'yes'.

The woman turned and headed toward a row of doors on the far side of the room — high-ranking officer territory. She opened one office and went inside, returning holding a small, framed photo stand displaying a bust image. Detective Fujii took the photo and stood it on the desk for us to see. It was Beard Yakuza all decked out in a crisp police dress uniform. A label on the bottom had both Japanese and English: 'Chief Detective Kusato Nakaya'.

Involuntarily I gasped, echoed by Heebs. The photo had been taken recently, with full beard and those cold, calculating eyes. A myriad of thoughts passed through my mind. We had been avoiding two distinct parties: some underworld murderous characters and law enforcement. If Nakaya and his gang had also been on the side of the police, who were the real bad guys? Also, I recalled the skirmish we had had on that rocky Yomo coast outside the Ebina home. My boys and I had taken one of them down, and I had clearly knocked out a woman by mistake. I suddenly looked up through the glass windows into the room of cubicles and saw Officer Mariko looking back at me with her bruised face. Next to her a second man stared back at me with a mostly healed beat-up face. I knew those eyes —

"Detective Nakaya has been on this case from the start. I believe he and a few others are in Singapore following up some leads right now." Fujii explained, "Does this look familiar?"

The detective held up a photo of the plastic waterproof case Doei-san had submerged at Funajima, and I had rowed across and hidden in the concrete foundations of the Singapore Fort Siloso spotlight tower. In the photo the case was open, and a phony, crudely fashioned metal sword-like object lay across the top. My mind flashed back to the hours I had spent in the 'Cave Diver' machine shop playing with metal scraps. I also recalled switching out the real Kusanagi-no-tsurugi sword with the fake one before hiding the case under the tower.

Suddenly it dawned on me. Detective Nakaya, aka Beard Yakuza, never was looking for murderers. A high-ranking detective in Kitakyushu had a much more important mission for his country all along — to find the genuine Imperial Regalia artifact that had been lost since the 1300's. We had been avoiding two groups of Japanese law enforcement because the regular police were searching for killers, and Nakaya's special detective force was hunting down the sword. Fortunately, we had checked the real sword in at the Singapore City Air Terminal, and my son Masamune had received it when Gilly arrived in Hong Kong.

"You still seem to be hiding something, Dr. Hughes." The detective wryly sneered.

I looked up at the detective and asked, "Have we broken any laws, officer?"

Fujii turned dark. We had brawled with his personnel — could they get us for that? No, apparently such mishaps were part of the job. We were free to go but would probably continue to be stalked by the Japanese detectives. It was clear that Rikochan's freedom was not merely a matter of clearing her from the homicide charges. There was some other deeper motivation that probably went over the heads of Fujii and Nakaya, possibly all the way to the top of the Japanese government. After all, the actual Kusanagi-no-tsurugi sword was at stake. What could be of more worth than that?

Regardless, it was time to end all this. I had to get the sword and make a deal with the police before the real bad guys could do any more harm.

Four hours later two dog-tired beat-up guys hobbled down the Fukuoka departure gate and boarded a flight to Chek Lap Kok Airport in Hong Kong. We had used all our skills playing metrospy to avoid any followers and had even ducked into a store to pick up new clothes. I gave Heebs the window seat and settled myself in for a three-and-a-half-hour flight. I didn't see any detectives following us, but that didn't mean the law enforcement folks, or criminals for that matter, weren't tracking us somehow. Even with a change of clothes and diligent backtracking, it would be hard to miss a large American on Japanese streets. We had finally surrendered the rental phone at the booth in the airport terminal but had to relinquish our deposit on the other two smartphones that had fallen in the Kaeda River and had been taken from Heebs by the kidnappers.

I immediately fell asleep and the next thing I was conscious of was the shock as the plane's landing gear hit the Chek Lap Kok tarmac. We exited the plane and went through immigration to the train station. I recalled years before when the communists had shown a larger presence and guards walked around the terminal building with submachine guns. Thankfully, Hong Kong's indomitable spirit had gotten them through the unrest, and they had returned to the wild free markets from yesteryear. We took a train into Central, then switched trains and got off three stops later at Hong Kong University Station in Pokfulam.

"They're here!" I could hear Gilly's voice excitedly call out.

I looked toward the voice and saw my oldest son Masamune walking through the crowd, with the younger Gilly hopping up and down. Heebs and I gratefully headed in their direction, and we all hugged each other in a big group hug.

Mas led the way up to street level, which was just below the HKU Haking Wong building where his lab was located. We took an elevator up several levels and walked across a pedestrian bridge. Mas led us through a series of buildings and humid gardens across the HKU campus. I recalled that life on Hong Kong Island could be confusing, and it was difficult to know where the real ground level was. In some cases, a pedestrian bridge connected the tenth floor of one building straight across to the ground floor of the next. In between the two buildings was a fantastically steep slope. Looking out over the city, one could see pencil-thin towers 40 stories high poking up through forested hills. The city planning laws of Hong Kong created hard boundaries where extremely dense high-rises pushed up against, and pristine forests were preserved on the other side. It was interesting that, including the New Territories, Hong Kong was ninety-one percent uninhabited natural areas with an extremely dense city on the remaining nine percent. I recalled in my younger days leaving my rental flat in Kennedy Town with a small backpack and drinking from pristine streams only twenty minutes later. Those streams sounded very nice as sweat poured down our faces.

Our trek across campus brought us to Robert Black College. This was not a school or place of higher learning as the name 'college' suggested, but a residential building for visiting professors and grad students. Mas opened his apartment door and we gratefully flopped about his living room enjoying the air conditioning.

I took the relaxed occasion to ask, "Is everything set up for tomorrow?"

Mas looked at me and smiled, "Yep, I've already arranged a local fisherman to meet us on Tung Wan beach."

The next day we were going to do a little island hopping, and Mas had set up a complicated tour route that would help us avoid any followers. We were going to get the sword.

"Everyone, take a short break. I've got lots of cool stuff to show you." Mas excitedly called from the kitchen as he prepared four glasses of ice water for all the collapsed deadbeats.

I was still lacking in sleep and was not enthusiastic to go out again in the Hong Kong humidity, but my boys were all safe here with me and I was getting hungry. I called Ines and told her we were all safe in Hong Kong, helping Masamune get ready to return home to the States. An hour later the sun had already gone down and the sky was a deep blue. HKU was up on a hill, and we could get glimpses of the town between towers. The million lights of the city lit up like jewels. Mas led us back to the Haking Wong Building and took us through a series of open cubicle labs, where researchers and students had set up their various projects. Even though it was getting to be evening, the whole space was active with students working on machinery or sitting around talking with snacks and drinks.

"This is mechanical engineering. Everyone is doing some kind of mechatronic project." Mas explained.

"Is that a transformer robot?" Gilly asked as he looked around in amazement.

Mas laughed out loud, "Haha no, 'mechatronic' means some mechanical aspect integrated with electronics. It's highly compact devices that could be robotic, or a 3D printer, or an automated steering system. Lots of things are possible."

Heebs looked over at several Hong Kong girls poking at some gadget with two spheres inside a rat's nest of tubes, pipes, and wires. I could see him morph into the macho man. Careful, I thought — you always embarrass yourself when the testosterone takes over.

"Gosh, even the nerds are cute here." Heebs remarked.

We arrived at Mas' workstation, and he proceeded to open up a locked cabinet. He pulled out a large contraption that had a directional Yagi antenna and microwave beamer mounted to a two-axis gimbal, all wired up to a twelve-volt car battery. Yagi antennas are long aluminum tubes with multiple shorter aluminum cross pieces mounted perpendicular to the main tube along its length — they are usually used to beam a radio signal. He hefted the unit and set it on the floor in the middle of the walkway. Next, he reached into the cabinet and pulled out a tiny device that looked like a grooved sphere, which he set on the ground. Heebs and Gilly were enthralled and couldn't take their eyes off the little ball. Mas pulled out his smartphone and opened an app. The little grooved sphere jumped, and some of the ridges expanded outward to become tiny legs. The sphere had transformed into a spider robot.

Suddenly the spider moved. It ran across the floor and startled Gilly into crying out. Heebs also moved quickly away. I was, well, very calm. Not! I could have leapt up on the table except that my gaze went toward Mas' smartphone screen, and I realized that he was controlling it with a tiny stereo camera. Mas expertly caused the spider to shift directions and run in a circle around Heebs. Then it sped off down the aisle avoiding strangers along the way. Occasionally a girl would let out a yelp, but mostly the passing folks seemed to be used to strange little machines running all over the place.

I noticed that the Yagi and microwave beamer constantly pointed at the little spider, with the little gimbals allowing it to precisely track the device. The Yagi's long aluminum main-member tube and multiple cross-elements maintained aim directly at the spider.

Mas saw my interest in the Yagi and explained, "My control signal goes through the Yagi, and the spider is getting power beamed through the microwave. Now watch this!"

The little spider was now about ten meters away, and suddenly dropped a little spiky jack-looking thing. The spider then turned out of the aisle, but the Yagi kept pointing at the spiky jack.

"That's a repeater. Now the spider can go anywhere line-of-sight with the repeater." Mas explained.

With the spider out of sight, the three of us crowded around Mas trying to see what the little thing was transmitting back via its cameras. We watched as the little machine dropped a second spiky jack micro repeater and went out into the main corridor. The Yagi and microwave beam were still focused on the first repeater.

"Now watch this!" Mas smiled and turned the little robot straight toward the wall.

Instead of stopping short of the vertical surface, we watched the little screen as the multi-legged device scampered up it without missing a beat. It kept climbing until it reached the ceiling, then to our surprise the robot transitioned over to that upside-down surface without slowing down. Mas directed the little thing to walk upside-down along the corridor ceiling as students walked unknowingly beneath it.

Mas came to the elevator hall and paused, "Now check this out," he said.

We watched as the robot dropped another repeater, but this time the spiky jack clung to the ceiling.

"It can go miles away and still maintain its power link and signal through multiple repeaters," he said.

The robot turned the corner and came to a stop. Mas controlled the cameras to make a sweeping view, including down where the people were. Several university personnel and students were waiting for elevators below.

Mas grinned and said, "Okay let's say the little guy gets discovered."

He fiddled with the controls, and we heard a loud electronic cat call come from down the corridor where the robot had disappeared. In unison, all the folks down below waiting for the elevator looked up at the little machine. Mas executed the return command and in very fast motion the spider retraced its steps. When it got to the third spiky jack clinging upside-down, the robot quickly collided with the repeater and absorbed it. We could see a few curious onlookers try to follow it as it scampered across the ceiling at lightning speed. In general, it followed the same path backward, but seemed to make new avoidance decisions on its own at times. The robot descended the wall and returned to floor level, absorbing the second spiky jack. As the original repeater filled its camera sights, we looked over and watched the machine race around the corner, latch onto the spiky jack, and make a beeline toward our feet. We heard the little gimbal motors whirring in protest as the Yagi antenna swept around and stayed perfectly aimed straight at the robot.

The three of us broke out into applause. At the time, I had no idea how significant a role that little spider would play in our efforts to free Rikochan.

After Mas finished putting the equipment away, we began walking down to street level. We found ourselves in a canyon of high-rise apartments, with a variety of buses, taxis, delivery trucks, motorcycles, and private vehicles whizzing by in both directions.

"You know, Dad, I've had some thoughts on those papers Hirayuki-san referred to." Mas said as we crossed Pokfulam Road.

The bus stop was right ahead of us, and a rapid succession of hyper-modernized two-story London buses pulled in to pick up passengers, then quickly continued on their way.

Mas continued, "Think about the *Silurian Hypothesis* — Doei-san must have suspected that some advanced culture lived on Earth before us. Perhaps there were multiple times when civilization rose and fell, reverting back to hunters & gatherers. The Antikythera mechanism must be some historic proof of it, or so he thought."

We arrived at the bus stop and waited with a large group of HKU students. I looked back westward and saw another bus coming our way.

"That's not a bad theory," I began, "I've heard of similar things in regards to ancient stone structures and such — no way primitive peoples could have built those things."

"Here's where I think a couple of papers fit together on the engineering side. Everyone thinks life began on Earth as simple RNA molecules that somehow began to self-replicate." Mas suggested before stepping onto the bus.

We followed him and held our 'octopus' transportation cards up to the fare reader. Mas led us upstairs and we took a seat near the front with its wide panorama window.

"Everyone knows the Wells Paradox that suggests the Earth can't be old enough for pure chance to have allowed complex humans to have evolved, right?" Mas looked at me.

"I've heard that, but isn't it controversial?" I returned.

Heebs and Gilly had taken the very front seat and were watching passengers board whenever the bus stopped. Probably looking at pretty girls, I thought.

Mas continued, "Well, one of the books on the list, *Code of the Lifemaker* is a science fiction book, but actually seems to be a parody of evolution."

"A parody?" I took my eyes off the scenery and looked directly at my son.

Mas chuckled and said, "Yes, just before the book was written, the NASA workshop on space automation was held. The workshop proposed building a self-replicating factory on the moon, using only raw materials found in Lunar regolith. A self-replicating factory was too much of a temptation to pass up for author James Hogan, who liked to buck the orthodox. *Code of the Lifemaker* begins with the premise that some advanced alien race sends out self-replicating probes, such as those proposed by von Neumann, out into the galaxy. The probes land on planets, establish factories, like the one NASA proposed, then make copies of themselves. The copies go on seeding the universe, and manufacture goods that are sent back to the home world."

I knew Mas was enjoying himself. Mas had always been interested in space exploration, and his favorite planet was Mars. There was a space boom of sorts going on, and various outposts and small pressurized towns had grown up tucked in craters and lava caves. It was Mas' ambition to get a job at one of the research centers on Mars, like Grindavik or Novissima or such. He devoured science fiction stories like this, especially when there was a mechanical theme.

"Okay, very interesting. So why is it a parody of evolution?" I wondered.

Mas looked about him outside the bus, and instead of answering me, called out, "Mid-levels. Okay guys, this is our stop!"

Heebs and Gilly held onto the grab bars and started to walk back toward us, swaying with every acceleration of the still-moving bus. Mas and I joined them and waited at the top of the narrow spiral stairway. The bus came to a stop and we all got off with half of the other passengers — Mid-levels must have been the main destination for the nightlife.

I looked around and there was a gap in the buildings on the downhill side, affording a view of the brightly lit downtown area. Several spotlights swept the sky from somewhere, and hundreds of electric passenger drones crisscrossed and avoided each other on their various flight paths. Similarly, we could see glimpses of Hong Kong Bay where hundreds of vessels going back and forth mirrored the busy skies.

Right in front of us was a set of outdoor escalators that went down the hill all the way to Central. We followed Mas as he stepped onto the crowded way. Off to the left and right, passengers got on and off the escalators to explore side streets where restaurants and bars proliferated.

Mas turned to me and continued, "So *Code of the Lifemaker* is about one probe that loses its navigation instruments and gets lost, and its original purpose to send products back to the home world is forgotten. It crashes on Saturn's moon Titan and tries to set up a self-replicating factory, except that the machinery is damaged, and the proper machine coding is not available. Instead, the main artificial intelligence running everything locates a full set of coding spread out in pieces among multiple machines and sets up a workaround that is similar to male and female roles in biology. For each copy of self-replicating machinery, one of each type of machine must contribute a copy of its coding in order to have a complete set."

We continued to descend the escalators which sometimes were stairs, but mostly consisted of sloped travelators or moving walks.

"So, I see a parallel in biology. How does it become a parody?" I asked again.

"So far, I have only described the prologue. The actual story starts here: subsequent generations of products and self-replicating factory copies continue to have defects and are self-aware robots. They build entire communities and economies, mirroring human cities. The protagonists from Earth discover these robot communities but find out the machines have no clue that they are actually robots." Mas reported.

I stared at Mas for a minute or so — fascinating concept! So, the implication was that self-replicating biological molecular machines in the form of cells proliferate Earth's biosphere and don't even realize they are machines! *I definitely have to go read that book*, I thought.

We finally reached the bottom of the escalators and walked toward Central. Mas led us to the Hong Kong International Finance Center (IFC) and we found a nice restaurant overlooking the harbor. It took a full twenty minutes to overcome the distraction of so much boat traffic out on the bay, so we could finally order our food.

Mas opined, "So here's where I think the engineering papers fit together. Remember when we talked about faxing life to colonize worlds? The *50-year Window* paper was written in 2015 and thank goodness humankind didn't fall into any of the traps it warned about. It described lean ways to colonize other worlds, particularly Mars. It mentioned that the most efficient way to colonize a faraway world would, instead of sending people who need huge habitats and power and propulsion, we could just program junk DNA into biological cells to turn on and off in response to environmental cues, and plant them on bare rock worlds. The DNA programming could be set up so that at the end of the evolutionary process humans are guaranteed to emerge."

"I remember our discussion about faxing life to remote locations. What do you think?" I asked.

Mas gave his conclusions, "Remember the *Silurian Hypothesis*. I think Doei-san and the Transhumanists think that some advanced race out there, maybe our ancestors, faxed us here to Earth."

It wasn't all that surprising, I thought as I looked out at the passenger ferries moving between the islands. Our discussions kind of concluded this might be so. But now it was down to the line. Someone had some wacky imagination and found some papers to back up the crazy ideas.

"Okay, I'm inclined to trust each of these papers individually, but why should we conclude that our biosphere was engineered rather than evolved by chance?" I asked.

Mas sighed, apparently already convinced the theory might be correct, "Well, there's one more paper. The *Wow Signal* paper. The Search for Extraterrestrial Intelligence (SETI) folks have long established a set of characteristics to judge a signal coming from outer space, that would tell us without question whether it came from intelligent beings. The *Wow Signal* paper takes each of those characteristics and shows that they could be used to describe the genomes of Earth biological life. Every single one of SETI's requirements are met. Life itself is apparently a signal that may contain unambiguous signatures of the advanced engineers that faxed us here."

I didn't press him on the thought that we've never found a prehistoric 'fax machine' for transmitting genome data. If the *Silurian Hypothesis* were true, any such technology would have rusted away eons ago. We continued to eat our meals, but the topic of conversation went in other directions.

The first indication that our problems were still not over came later that night as we dragged ourselves up through the HKU campus and returned to Mas' Robert Black College apartment. The door was slightly ajar, and the whole place had been ransacked. The four of us surveyed the scene with dismay. This was not a police sort of operation — the underworld had traced us there. Fortunately, with the experiences we'd had the past few weeks, I learned to never let my LIDAR drone and laptop out of my sight. His luggage had been rifled through, but anything of importance that Mas might have owned was shut up in the locker down in the lab. One last item needed accounting for —

"Mas, is everything safe at Piccadilly and Haymarket?" I asked.

Mas was dumbstruck as he looked at the room in shambles, but coolly replied, "Wow, these guys play dirty pool! Yes, everything is safe."

I figured things might come to this and had a backup plan to protect the sword. I knew a place in Kwai Chung right next to the container port that would ship anything, no questions asked. It was the last leg of getting the artifact safely back to the States until this whole mess could be unraveled. All we needed to do was to deliver the sword to Kwai Chung without anyone knowing . . .

CHAPTER 14

The next morning the four of us set out for the HKU Mass Transit Railway (MTR) station. Besides my LIDAR backpack, we carried nothing but water bottles, with flashlights hidden in our pockets. This time we bypassed the double-decker buses and Mid-levels escalators and rode the train to Central. On the harbor side of the IFC complex there were a half dozen or so ferry piers, including the historical Star Ferry. Mas had done his homework and led us straight to Pier 6. We had timed it fairly precisely to arrive right on schedule to catch the ferry to Peng Chau Island.

We walked down the ramp and crossed the gangway into the air-conditioned interior. Heebs and Gilly headed straight for the stairs and climbed to the upper deck, with Mas and I in tow. We settled into cushioned seats and looked out the window at all the shipping traffic in the harbor.

"Dad, what is that old boat coming in next to us?" Gilly pointed.

The vessel he indicated was painted dark green and was symmetrically oval shaped both front and back. The decks were open to the sea breeze and filled with tourists. The ferry was well-cared for but looked like something from previous centuries.

"That's the historical Star Ferry. Might be fun to ride on it someday if we get the chance," I said.

Our ferry departed next, and we watched as the piers fell away. On the other side of Pier 7, a second Star Ferry was pulling out as well, matching our speed. Our two vessels soon lost formation as we vectored toward separate destinations, but the harbor opened up and we watched other shipping activity instead. One common type of boat that we hadn't seen in either Japan or Singapore was the small freighter that would go out to meet the big super freighters and help them unload their container cargo. They could only carry a few containers at a time, so dozens of them crisscrossed the shipping lanes, gradually helping the big ships unload. Many other small craft crossed our wake as well, such as fishing boats and patrol vessels.

Our destination was Peng Chau Island, one of a dozen or so islands with small fishing communities that had gradually catered to tourists and vacationers. The trip took a little less than an hour, and the ferry pulled up to a dock almost identical to the one in Central.

"Okay guys, we've got to run quickly," Mas suggested, "someone will be waiting for us on the beach side. Follow me and don't get lost!"

Hong Kong had a few popular islands that were roughly hourglass shaped like Peng Chau, with ferry terminals on one side of the pinched, narrow neck and beaches on the other. We disembarked from the ferry and jogged through a crowded small town that had tourist shops and seafood restaurants. As we got closer to the beach side, there were a smattering of private homes and places to stay overnight.

Running through one final alleyway the beach suddenly came into view, with families, groups of young people, and tourists playing or walking along the sand. Our trip to Peng Chau was just a ruse to throw off anyone who happened to be following us. The boys were having fun riding the various means of transportation, even if we didn't have time to play on the beach.

There was a small fishing boat pulled up to the sand with a middle-aged Chinese woman waving at us. We rushed over to the boat, splashed in the shallow surf, and climbed aboard. I glanced around to see if someone had been following us but no one stood out. The woman had kept the diesel engine idling and immediately backed out into deeper water. Turning the boat around, she opened up the throttle and headed out of Tung Wan Bay.

"Boys, stay low. We don't want anyone to recognize us." I warned.

I was a little bit disappointed at the slow speed, even though the woman swore she was going as fast as the craft was capable. As we exited Tung Wan Bay, we could see the main Hong Kong harbor off in the distance again. Our pilot turned northward to follow the coastline of nearby Lantau Island.

Heebs got excited and pointed straight ahead, "What's that over there?"

I looked over on Lantau and saw an eclectic assortment of historical rooftops mixed with futuristic buildings and immediately recognized what it was.

"That's Hong Kong Disneyland, or what used to be. I think Disney mothballed the place a few decades ago." I explained.

The loud diesel engine took us past the old Disney site and headed toward the gap between Ma Wan and Tsing Yi islands, which were connected by the Tsing Ma bridge soaring high overhead. As we approached the bridge and passed under it, our little boat paled in comparison scale-wise, and the massive structure almost seemed intimidating.

"Dad, check out seven o'clock. What do you make of it?" Mas warned.

It took me a few seconds to calibrate myself, imposing an invisible clock face onto the little craft, and swinging my head around. A small motorboat was keeping pace with us about half a kilometer away.

Without turning my head, I asked Mas, "How long has it been out there?"

"I think it came from Discovery Bay direction, but I'm not sure." Mas replied.

Our diesel boat changed course and started to follow the Tsing Yi Island coastline in a clockwise direction. The distant motorboat followed us for a while but seemed to turn away at some point. I couldn't be sure if the other boat was one of our pursuers or just an innocent coincidence.

About twenty minutes later the Chinese woman steered our diesel fishing boat up to a dock on the coast of Tsuen Wan town. We had picked that location because only about 50 meters away was the entrance to Tsuen Wan West MTR subway station. Again, we clambered off the boat waving to our pilot in thanks and ran to the station entrance.

Heebs smiled as all four of us got ourselves into metrospy mode. In order to throw off anyone who might have been following us, we first headed toward Mei Foo station, then transferred trains back to Tsuen Wan on a branch line. Exiting the train, we used evasive strategies in the maze-like underground to shake off any potential followers, then climbed back up to the surface again. Our chosen exit got us to the terminal where we found a bus heading for Shing Mun Reservoir up in the mountains. There were already a large number of passengers lining up to catch the next one.

"Boys line up here; we're going to ride this one. I'll be right back. I've got one more errand to run," I said.

Mas, Heebs, and Gilly saved spots in line while I quickly ducked into a nearby grocery store. I purchased a couple of bags of potato chips, garlicky bread, and a few other highly scented foods and filled up some plastic shopping bags.

The bus left soon after I had returned. There were lots of riders this time with no more seats, so we had to stand and hold onto the loops. Due to the press of riders, I was almost hanging over a couple of seated young women conversing in Cantonese. Both of them were well-dressed in mid-calf skirts and had small stacks of books or magazines in their laps. I suppose if I had been Heebs' age I might have seen the magazine sooner. Or maybe I would have been distracted by the skirts. But as it was my mind was rehearsing over and over in my head what we needed to do to get the sword to safety, so it took a while for me to focus on the title of the publication in her lap.

Liahona was what it said on the cover. I did a double-take. It definitely said 'Liahona'. It was the same name as the one I had seen scribbled in Hirayuki's handwriting on the remnant manuscript and sudoku puzzle. My mind backed up a bit and my focus went to the young women. Surprisingly, one of the girls appeared to be Caucasian. I wanted to ask about the magazine, so I started with an unrelated comment.

"Your Cantonese is pretty good!" I complimented.

Both girls looked up at me at the same time. One was Asian, and the other was definitively a foreigner. For the first time, I noticed both the girls were wearing black name tags that were mostly in Chinese characters. But 'Sister Jones' was written in English on the foreign girl. 'Sister ___' something was on the other tag, but I couldn't quite make it out.

"Thank you." The foreigner replied in American English.

That was enough to break the ice for me, so I ventured, "Excuse me but I noticed the magazine in your lap. *Liahona* — is that the name of an artist?"

Sister Jones looked down at her lap and smiled. She pulled the publication out from under some books so I could see the entire cover. Surprisingly, there was a picture of an Urim & Thummim sitting on pieces of parchment that had what looked like Egyptian characters scrawled on them.

"L-ee-a-hona," the girl corrected my pronunciation with a long 'e' sound on the 'i'. Sister Jones looked up at me again and said, "No, it's not an artist. This is our church magazine."

Puzzled, I probed a little deeper, using the correct pronunciation, "But what does 'Liahona' mean?"

The two women looked at each other briefly, then Sister Jones turned to me and said, "Oh the name is an ancient ball-like Directors, or a compass."

Just then a buzzer sounded, and Mas indicated it was our stop. The bus slowed and several people started pushing from behind.

"Listen I have to get off here. Did I hear you correctly? Did you say 'Liahona' was a 'Directors' thing?" I asked.

Sister Jones briefly looked at the magazine then thrust it into my hands, "Yes! Here take this, I can get more," she said.

By that time the bus had stopped, and the press of riders became too great. I wanted to get some contact information from her, but it was too late. I was whisked out of the bus with the crowd. The doors closed and the bus began to move. I could see Sister Jones and her friend inside waving at me enthusiastically.

I looked down at the magazine in my hands. Not only was the Urim & Thummim depicted there on the cover, but the word 'Liahona' was the same as the mysterious Directors that had been mentioned by Heebs' kidnappers. This magazine somehow held a clue to the connection with the Japanese Imperial Regalia! Sister Jones had mentioned it was her church magazine. Was she Jewish? Were we getting to the core of the real Hebrew ancient regalia that Hebiwara-san had suspected, that included the Urim & Thummim? Something was wildly crazy about all this, and my mind was going numb just trying to process it all. I didn't have time to look at the magazine then — all I could do was to pull my backpack down and stuff it in for later reading.

"Which way, Dad?" Gilly came over and tugged on my arm.

We were in sight of the lake, and the route followed the water's edge for a short distance. We walked along, observing the telltale muddy slope that was evidence of low water levels. As soon as we passed a public barbecue area, the route split off into the mountains. The famous Maclehose Trail passed by the reservoir at that point, so we started to climb up the trail towards Smuggler's Ridge.

Immediately I had the impression that we were being watched. I got a glimpse of a head peeking at us from a location off the trail, but when I turned to get a better look, it disappeared.

"Careful guys, we may have company." I whispered.

The interesting thing about Hong Kong hiking trails is the absence of switchbacks. Though the overall elevation wasn't too high, the hills are extremely steep and sometimes there will be hundreds of steps going straight up a mountain without any landings. I was definitely out of shape from my Marine days, and huffed and puffed as I dragged my 240-pound frame up every rise.

On both sides of the trail there were disturbances in the bushes, as if someone had just been there and ducked down. Mas, Heebs, and Gilly walked along with heightened awareness, turning their necks this way and that as sudden noises spooked their senses.

We went around a bend and right in the middle of the trail a female monkey hugged her newborn infant and faced us defiantly. It became apparent that she wanted something from us. She used her baby to elicit a compassionate response from us and began begging for food. Mas smiled knowingly, but Heebs and Gilly had to do everything in their power to refrain from feeding the wild animals. A scurrying in the bushes on both sides caught the boys by surprise, and we saw several male monkeys peering at us through the foliage. The males were using the mother and baby to get food, which they would undoubtedly rush out and take away from her if given the chance.

I recalled that further down the Maclehose Trail the Kam Shan country park was famous for having several monkey bands living in the forest and near the lakes. The monkey population must have exploded, pushing some tribes into the Shing Mun area.

"You'll be okay if you don't feed them. But some of the males further up the pecking order chain could get aggressive." I warned, "Better get some good sticks in case we need to shoo them away."

We eased past the female with the cute little one and continued on the trail, keeping an eye on the males hiding on either side. Soon we reached our destination. Heebs, who had been walking ahead, started whooping and hollering in excitement. The rest of us caught up and saw what he had found. Off to the left side, there were two concrete tunnel entrances. Both were dark and deep.

"This is it," I said, "Right down one of those tunnels."

Full of curiosity, Heebs peered into one of the tunnels and asked, "What is this place? How far do they go?"

I walked up behind him and peered over his shoulder, "During World War II, the British had set up a series of forts, tunnels, and bunkers that cut across the entire Hong Kong peninsula called the 'Gin Drinker's Line'. This tunnel complex is called 'Shing Mun Redoubt'. It's where the Japanese first penetrated Hong Kong."

"Can we explore them?" Heebs wondered.

"Yes, but let's take a look around and make sure we are alone." I suggested.

Heebs hesitantly backed away from the tunnels and grabbed Gilly's arm, "Let's go up the path a little bit," he said.

Mas and I found a path that led to the top of the hill and climbed up to where a galvanized power transmission tower had been constructed much later. A stretch of old concrete slab nearby had a broken hole that gaped into darkness below. I walked up to it and peered inside. It was the roof of a tunnel, probably blown open during that invasion over a hundred years earlier. If all went well, we would be exploring that tunnel later.

"So, this is where the battle happened?" Mas asked.

I looked around and said, "Part of it. The Japanese came up the hill over here, from the Shing Mun River," we walked through the brush over to a precipice where we could look down the hill, "they took the under-sized British units completely by surprise."

Mas and I surveyed down the hill and saw the Shing Mun dam. There were people down there, including local Hong Kong young people taking photos down the gorge.

"Looks like the invasion is on again!" Mas pointed down the hill.

I followed his arm and through the trees there were several Asian men in dark suits climbing the Wilson hiking trail. They were too far away to make out individual faces, but one of them stood out with a beard — it could only have been Detective Nakaya, aka Beard Yakuza! The Japanese were climbing the same route that Colonel Doi, Major Nishiyama, Lieutenant Kasugai, and especially Lieutenant Wakabayashi took leading the Japanese 228 Infantry Regiment on 9 December 1941.

"Damn, that Nakaya!" I mumbled under my breath.

I wasn't ready to hand over the sword until I had gathered all the evidence. However, at least we could feel assured that we were not in any bodily danger. Nakaya was not the killer we had suspected him to be.

I turned to Mas and said, "Okay let's get moving. It will get interesting here soon enough and we want to be out of here."

Mas and I walked back toward the Maclehose Trail to meet up with the boys. I had plastic shopping bags full of surprises that I could use if the Japanese tried to move in.

Just as we descended down to the main trail, Heebs and Gilly came running down the hill, "Dad, there are more tunnels up there. Looks like the route crossed the trail!"

"Yes, I know. I think we only have about a half hour before our Japanese detective friends arrive. You two can go explore but meet back here in twenty minutes." I implored.

The tunnels were all named from famous places around London. Heebs and Gilly immediately took out their flashlights and entered the left tunnel Heebs had first discovered. Into the concrete above the tunnel was cast the letters 'Regent Street'.

Mas had been to Shing Mun Redoubt only a few days earlier, when he climbed up in the late hours of the evening to hide the sword. He walked over to a bush off the side of the path and retrieved a small folding shovel that he had hidden.

"Let's go," he said.

We turned our backs on the two side-by-side tunnels the boys had entered and walked in the opposite direction. Only a few meters away, hidden by overgrowth, was another tunnel labeled 'Piccadilly'. With our flashlights on, we ducked low due to the build-up of sand on the tunnel floor. The sand cleared out quickly and we could stand up tall. Soon the tunnel sloped and turned into a set of stairs. Beyond the stairs sand filled the tunnel again and we had to walk bent over.

From the left a new passage came to a tee intersection. Tunnel names and directional arrows were cast into the concrete walls. The side passage was named 'Haymarket'.

"Right here, this is where I buried it." Mas pointed.

The sand was deep, and he had done a good job hiding the evidence of his digging. Mas immediately got to work again and began to dig up the case. I got down on my knees and used my hands to scoop loose sand out of the way.

It wasn't long before Heebs came running down the tunnel. He was breathing hard and mostly out of breath.

"Dad, the yakuza are here in the tunnels!" He exclaimed.

"Okay, go get Gilly and come back here. On the double!" I yelled.

Damn, those Japanese were here earlier than I had anticipated. Heebs ran off again while Mas and I dug faster. We uncovered the case and removed sand from its entire length. Mas reached down and pulled out the case, giving it a shake to remove any residual sand.

"Open it up. I've got a decoy measure we can take," I said.

Mas unfastened the case — it was the decoy case Captain Nephus had found for us on board the 'Cave Diver'. Inside was a long cloth-wrapped object cushioned with foam that I had swapped out. I reached in and unwrapped the cloth a little bit to expose the ancient barnacle-encrusted sword, then lifted it out altogether. It was the genuine article.

I handed the plastic shopping bags to Mas and said, "Remove the foam, and open up all these bags of chips and snacks."

While Mas was doing that, I used some string to tie a sling onto the cloth bundle. We emptied the snacks into the case, closed the lid, then poured sweet-smelling soda all over the outside. We kept one bag of candies separate.

Just then Heebs came running back yelling, "They're here! They're here!"

I slung the sword under my shirt to keep it from being obvious. Mas picked up the case, without closing the fasteners, and tucked it under his arm. I grabbed the extra bag of candies, and we began running down the Haymarket tunnel.

"Hughes! Dr. Hughes! Come back here with the Kusanagi-no-tsurugi!" Someone yelled from behind with a deep Japanese accent.

I could hear their footsteps right behind us. The tunnel wound around with sloped floors here and there, but mostly seemed to be following the contour of the hill. Suddenly we came to an open gap, which I was expecting.

"Climb up, left-hand side!" I yelled.

Mas scrambled up with the case under his arm and I saw Heebs near me as we climbed together. But there was no Gilly!

"Where's Gilly!" I frantically grilled Heebs.

"I couldn't find him. The yakuza were in between us!" Heebs exclaimed.

Footsteps pounded toward us as we worked our way up the hill. Out of the candies bag I pulled handfuls of pieces and tossed them into the bushes and trees. Monkeys were watching us, and a few of them followed their curiosity to see what I had thrown at them. If my mental map was correct, we could continue to scramble up the shallow gully until we reached the 'Strand Palace Hotel', which was an underground complex consisting of a galley and other facilities the British had used.

I turned back and saw Detective Nakaya pop out of the tunnel, followed by three others, "Hughes!" He yelled.

Mas had gotten to a small clearing and waited for us to meet up with him. We all turned our gaze downhill, and Mas carefully set the case on the ground, still unclasped, making sure the Japanese could see it. I then emptied out the candy bag around the case and the three of us continued to scramble up the hill.

Behind us the trees came alive as hundreds of monkeys swooped down to eat the candies. I have no idea how the word spread so fast, but the entire monkey troop must have showed up! Those British hired the wrong guys, all they needed was a pack of rogue rhesus simians! I couldn't help but continue to glance down the hill to watch the action. Nakaya and his buddies almost got level with the case, when one of the larger creatures figured out how to pull the handle. The case flew open and spilled all the chips and snacks onto the ground. An army of monkeys descended, rushing past the poor Japanese contingent.

We finally located the 'Strand Palace Hotel' but there was no way to get into the tunnel system. All we could see were two grilles in the ceiling.

Without warning, Mas' phone rang, and Ines was on the other line.

"Mom!" Mas cried out before tossing the phone to me.

I looked down the hill and saw monkeys jumping all over the place. One of the creatures decided to use Beard Yakuza's head as a springboard and the detective let out a yowl before glaring up at me in anger.

"Honey, I . . ." I began.

"Oh, Timothy, I'm glad it's you. Did you know Joyce's niece had her baby? It's such an adorable thing." Ines jumped right in.

"Sweetheart, there's a little bit going on right now. Let me call you later." I said and hung up, passing the phone back to Mas.

The concrete slab making up the roof of the subterranean tunnel of the 'Strand Palace Hotel' was exposed a bit, so we continued to follow it up the hill until we found a square chimney-like structure — an air shaft.

"Mas, see if you can shimmy down there." I suggested.

Shining the flashlight down, it was apparent that the sloped passage was a staircase. Mas quickly climbed up on top and let his legs dangle inside. Slowly he lowered himself down and used the walls of the shaft to brace against.

"Hold my arms." Mas reached both arms upward for us to grab.

Heebs and I both took his hands and he gradually scooted down the shaft until he was ready to drop his legs out the square ceiling hole — there was no more shaft to push against. At that point Mas let go and hung freely from our outstretched arms.

"Okay I'm going to drop." He said and let go of our hands.

He hit the bottom square on, keeping himself braced for the differences in step heights.

"Okay I'm good." He called up.

Heebs went down next, taking advantage of Mas' steady hands. I lowered the cloth-wrapped sword, but realized I was too fat to fit in the hole.

I called down, "You guys go ahead. I'll meet you where 'Charing Cross' meets the Maclehose Trail."

I could hear Mas and Heebs stomp up the steps down below. I looked up-slope and knew that it was a straight shot if I could just get through the overgrown, thick jungle. Down-slope, Nakaya and his men were still having trouble fighting off the monkeys. One by one they got free, and I could see their heads bobbing up and down through the thick foliage.

I moved forward as best as I could, where the thicker parts made it so that I had to take a zigzag course through the undergrowth. As I fought my way through, I became aware of a buzzing sound, like the hum of multiple electric motors. It was a drone. Somewhere up ahead, an electric passenger drone was trying to maneuver.

I popped out onto the Maclehose Trail near where the 'Charing Cross' tunnel entrance was supposed to be, but I couldn't see Mas or Heebs. Directly across the trail was the entrance to another tunnel, 'Shaftsbury Avenue' — which way did they go?

Faintly, I heard Mas' voice calling out from the 'Shaftsbury Avenue' tunnel, "Gilly!"

Detective Nakaya and one other fellow jumped down onto the trail at the same place I had made my entrance and began running toward me. Without hesitation I leapt for

'Shaftsbury Avenue' and ran along the narrow confines, calling out for my boys.

"Mas! Heebs!" I managed.

Nakaya was right behind me. I lost all recollection of whether I went up or down stairs, or whether I turned into side tunnels or not. I followed the ruckus in front of me, and the sound of occasional scuffles. Nakaya and his man never missed a beat and stayed hot on my trail. Finally, I caught up to everyone at the bottom of a stairway. In retrospect it might have been 'Regent Street' but I cannot be sure. Mas was standing there, with Heebs right behind him. They were looking up the dank, dark stairway toward a circle of light, which was one of those rough, blown open holes in the roof of the tunnel. I could hear the scream of electric motors outside, as if the flying craft were hovering above the hole.

A dark figure stood there, completely dressed in black, including a black balaclava with barely a narrow slit to see through. The ninja-looking fellow had his arm around Gilly, and a gleaming knife at the boy's throat. Whenever Mas tried to move forward, the black-clad figure viciously made a shallow cut in Gilly's skin, and the boy cried out in fear and pain. Detective Nakaya slammed into my back, and I could feel the eyes of the two Japanese men staring past me at the ninja fellow.

Suddenly I became aware of a second figure, slowly easing his way from behind the ninja. The second person was also dressed in black, but his head was uncovered.

"So, Musashi, we meet again." Came the words from the new person.

"Kōjirō!" I blurted out as I recognized the fisherman.

"Hand me the sword or the boy dies!" The fisherman ordered.

Just to show that they meant business, the ninja figure again made a shallow cut on Gilly's face, resulting in the boy screaming in fear. 'Kōjirō' the fisherman pulled out a walking cane that had been made into a lightsaber. He switched on the glowing simulated light blade and threw it at me, which I had to duck to avoid.

"Quite amusing, Musashi. Looks like I win the duel," he said.

The sunlight beamed down on the fisherman like a spotlight in a stage play. There he was, characteristically looking down at our feet until the last syllable, then glancing up at us in what now seemed like a shifty gesture. Mas looked back at me and what could I do? I nodded in return and watched as he handed the bundle to the man with outstretched arms. 'Kōjirō' graciously took the bundle as if he were receiving a gift, then backed up behind the ninja who hadn't budged.

I don't know how he did it, but somehow, he quickly scrambled up the walls and disappeared through the hole. The electric passenger drone motors picked up a pitch. Without warning the black clad figure gave Gilly a shove that blocked any possibility of our moving forward, and grabbed onto a line which pulled him out of the hole. By the time we rushed forward to look up, all I could see was glimpses of the flying craft rising high in the sky.

CHAPTER 15

On the one hand, I felt that a great load had been lifted off my back. The sword was no longer in my hands, and both the Japanese detectives and criminals knew it. None of my children were in bodily danger, and most of us were free to move about without fearing for our lives.

On the other hand, unfortunately, Rikochan was still being held in custody, and was the only presumed link with the fisherman 'Kōjirō' and his ninja buddy. I still felt like I couldn't let go — somehow, we needed to figure out how all the pieces fit together and discover how to track down the fisherman before Rikochan could be released. Since 'Kōjirō' was in possession of Heebs' burner phone, he would have had access to Hirayuki Doei's documents that Heebs had photographed. My mind was swirling with all kinds of loose ends. Would the fisherman stop now that he had obtained his valuable prize? Or did he also recognize Hirayuki's deeper clues, that something else was going on?

A few days later I sat back and relaxed in my Cathay economy class seat, on a long flight to Los Angeles LAX. Heebs sat by the window and Gilly was between us. Mas was in the same row but across the aisle from me.

"Dad, if they ask us about meals, I don't want any fish." Gilly said as he peered up at me.

I looked at my poor boy's face, with that bandaged neck so recently scarred by evil intent. It was another reason I couldn't let it go yet — these killers had left a trail of murder and destruction and would not hesitate to do so again.

"No worries, I asked for a kid's meal for you." I responded.

Gilly looked indignant, but it was clear that he was calculating the odds of how edible a kid's meal might be as opposed to the default adult version. He turned his attention back to the screen in front of him, following Heebs' lead on getting a head start with the best movies. Mas had leaned back to get some much-needed sleep, so now it was my time finally.

I pulled out the magazine Sister Jones had given me and looked at the cover. The magazine title said *Liahona*, which the sister had said meant 'Directors' or a compass. Her church wanted the magazine to function as a compass for their readers, much like other faiths had done with 'Guideposts' and the like. But what was so special about a compass? And why would 'Liahona' be listed as a bullet point under Yasakani-no-magatama jewel?

The more I thought about it, the more convinced I was about Hebiwara-san's theory regarding a Hebrew regalia that must include the Urim & Thummim. Perhaps these theories really did have substance, that Judaism somehow anciently influenced the Japanese, or surprisingly, could have been handed down by ancestors that were Jewish. If that were the case, mightn't the Hebrew regalia also have included a sword rather than a staff? And the fisherman, as Heebs' kidnapper, had sought three articles: the sword, Urim & Thummim, and Directors. If such a set of treasures actually existed, then finding just the Japanese Imperial Regalia, though significant, might pale by comparison to finding actual Hebrew regalia.

Opening the magazine to the publisher's info page, my hopes were dashed a bit as I discovered the 'church' Sister Jones had referred to was not Jewish but was some long-titled organization that could have been a tongue-twister:

'The Church of Jesus Christ of Latter-day Saints'. Still, in all our searches about Imperial Regalia, Japanese origins, and Jewish connections this magazine somehow promised to tie together a great many loose ends.

I sat back to read the article featuring the Urim & Thummim. Right from the beginning the historical background of the Urim & Thummim piqued my interest. I glanced across the aisle at Mas and noticed that he had woken up, so I decided to fill him in on new insights.

"Check this out. The Urim & Thummim was used by the Levite priests. This was along with the Ark of the Covenant!" I highlighted some of the text.

Mas was curious, "What was it for?"

I scanned the paragraphs and found some description, "The Urim & Thummim was like a pair of spectacles that the priest could attach to a breastplate. When he looked into the lenses, supposedly he could see visions or information that could help Israel. It was an instrument for receiving divine revelation."

"That's kind of silly, did they believe it?" Mas shrugged.

"I don't think anyone, but the priest was allowed to look into them. He could have made up anything. But the point is that it was a historical artifact revered by Israel for centuries." I replied.

Mas nodded and looked over at the artist's representations on the page of the magazine. I continued to scan the article. Hebiwara-san had not given me his paper on the Urim & Thummim, but to my delight, I soon began to wonder if the *Liahona* article might have been even more complete regarding descriptions of the ancient item.

"It says here that there could have been multiple versions of the Urim & Thummim. Populations of Jews living apart or remote from each other might have each had their own. These people called the 'Jaredites' seemed to have one set, and they were apparently living on the American continent!" I summarized, "A person called the 'Brother of Jared' took 16 small stones to the Lord (if you believe in that sort of thing), who touched them and caused them to continually glow. The Brother of Jared used the stones to light up the interior of their boat-submarines as they crossed the great ocean. Apparently, two of those stones were set into a frame to create the Urim & Thummim. Maybe the Japanese trying to recreate an Urim & Thummim from cultural memory resulted in the Yata-no-kagami mirror."

I glanced over and Mas appeared intrigued by the idea. I thought back on the story of El Gran Moxo that Captain Nephus had related and wondered — if two of the 16 stones were used to make the Urim & Thummim, then 14 more stones should be out there in the world somewhere. Was the perpetually lit lamp at El Gran Moxo one of those stones?

"Hmm — another group left Jerusalem around 600BC and eventually made it to America as well. They ended up in possession of the Jaredite Urim & Thummim." I noted, "It became one of the prized artifacts of the newcomers, who were called the 'Nephites'."

Suddenly a paragraph jumped up at me. I looked over at Mas in astonishment.

"What? Did you find something relevant?" Mas asked.

"Look here!" I pointed to the page, "The Nephites had three sacred treasures — the Urim & Thummim, a sword, and the Liahona! This is it! The Yasakani-no-magatama jewel must have come from the cultural memory of the Liahona!"

The ancient Hebrew regalia, in the remote Nephite culture, seemed to fit with Hebiwara-san's theory. More pieces seemed to be falling into place. But the more I thought about it, ancient regalia, quantum entanglement, and faxing genomes to other worlds just didn't seem to mix.

Mas was nodding off, so I turned the page and began reading another article. The church with the long, tongue-twister name was apparently based in Utah, and had many years ago constructed nuclear bomb-proof granite vaults in the mountains outside of Salt Lake City. Hmm, a Utah church, maybe like the Mormons?

"Mas, this looks interesting. These folks have constructed huge granite vaults to house genealogical records. It sounds like they also store historical books and other things too, from the 1800's." I looked over at Mas, but he had already fallen asleep again.

I turned back to the magazine to continue reading but my eyelids were heavy too. I wondered if the church had ever hired someone to survey the vaults with LIDAR? I started to slip into slumber but suddenly jerked awake. The magazine was gone from my lap, probably had fallen to the floor. My slumber had been rudely interrupted by a female voice in the row behind us.

"Excuse me sir, I need to get out." A young woman said.

The voice sounded familiar. I turned to see who it was and saw a face I knew.

"Sally! What are you doing here?" I asked.

Startled, the girl looked back at me like she didn't know what to say. She was standing there, waiting for an elderly male passenger sitting in an aisle seat to move and let her out.

"Mr. Hughes! You're on this flight too?" She asked.

The elderly man slowly got up and Sally moved over to the aisle, letting the passenger sit back down in his seat. Heebs and Gilly caught wind of the interaction and looked up at the girl.

"Yes, we're heading home back to the States." I replied.

Heebs, seeing the cute girl who had spent so much time with us a few weeks earlier perked up and gave her his full attention.

"Hey, Sally, you're here!" Heebs said coolly after that macho mood tried to take over.

Don't overdo it Heebs, I thought, *you know what happens when testosterone ties your brain in knots*. Sally looked a little panicky but smiled.

"I heard what happened to Rikochan." Sally began, "Those goons were questioning everyone at Kitakyu-U."

"Yes, well, we hope to get her released soon. It was all such a big tragedy." I frowned.

Sally looked quite nervous, as if her mind were on other things. She had her purse hanging from her shoulder, perhaps needing to visit the girl's room. But she didn't move.

"My father has had some weird things happen lately, like being anonymously threatened. I decided to take a quick trip home and see if everyone is alright," she said.

Heebs jumped in and asked, "Do you guys live in a rough neighborhood? Give me your address, we can beat them up!"

I rolled my eyes and saw Sally's expression that she was trying to be polite but would have rolled her eyes too. Then I just realized — we were on a flight out of Hong Kong.

"Usually, Japan is the stopover between the United States and Hong Kong. I thought you were in Japan. How did you get way out here?" I wondered.

A flash of panic again crossed her face, but she quickly said, "Oh that's the weird timing of the airlines. I could only afford Cathay and everything routes through Hong Kong."

"Well, I hope everything is well with your father." I waved, not wanting to keep her any longer.

"Yes, see you soon I hope." Sally returned the wave and started backing down the aisle.

Heebs also raised his arm and called out, "Let's get together soon!"

Sally did a quick turn and continued walking down the aisle. We watched her disappear into the next passenger section and then returned to facing forward. I remembered the *Liahona* magazine and started to look under the seat, but it wasn't there.

"Did you see that magazine I was reading?" I asked Gilly.

My youngest son looked at me and shook his head, then returned his attention to the movie. A hippopotamus could have run down the aisle, and he wouldn't have noticed. I looked down, checked between the seats, the floor of the aisle, and even over under Mas' feet but to no avail. Perhaps a flight attendant or someone had picked it up as we were conversing with Sally. I would have to keep my eyes out for it, in case one of the nearby passengers had seen it.

I stopped a flight attendant as he walked by and asked whether he had seen anything. The well-dressed Asian man said he had picked up a few lost items on the floor and put them back in the galley. However, the pile of items was open for anyone interested to rummage through, so it was not guaranteed that the items were still there. I was getting a little exasperated thinking that it could not be good practice for flight crew to carelessly pick up items without asking nearby persons, but I realized that something falling into the aisle could have been unconsciously kicked down the row. I did make one attempt to visit the galley, but none of the lost items were familiar. At length I gave up on getting the *Liahona* magazine back and hoped that there would be some opportunity later to pick another copy up once we landed.

The rest of the flight proved boring, so between meals I ended up sleeping or buried in some movie right alongside my sons.

The Cathay flight landed around 6pm at Los Angeles LAX airport. We were all jet lagged, so the time waiting for the plane to taxi in, pull up to a gate, and prepare to deplane was miserable. Fortunately, it was evening so once we got to our hotel, we would be able to sleep it off. We stood up in our seats and got our hand luggage ready — I lifted my LIDAR drone backpack and put it on my back so I wouldn't have to carry it.

Heebs looked up at me and pointed to the empty seat behind us, "I wonder where Sally went. I didn't see her return to her seat."

I had almost forgotten about the girl, but Heebs was correct. She had mentioned her father getting threats, and I suddenly had an unpleasant thought. Could the fisherman and his gang be harassing Kitakyushu University students and their families? We still didn't understand how all the pieces fit together. Were there others at the university who had been having unpleasant experiences like us? If Sally hadn't returned to her seat, could someone from that gang have kidnapped her during flight? Where would one hide a person in a commercial airline cabin? As the plane emptied out, I had my boys stay back until we could more leisurely exit without the press of the crowd. I went all the way to the back of the aircraft and checked every restroom, hoping my worst imagination of a poor girl duct-taped to a toilet seat would not come true. All the restrooms were clear, but we never did see Sally anywhere on the plane or thereafter in the terminal.

LAX had finally moved from a third-world airport to become the pride of the West Coast. Where it used to be a horrible mess of buses, taxis, Uber, and private cars that took almost an hour to get around the loop of terminals, an efficient rail system had finally been constructed that linked everything to the green and blue lines. As tired as we were, we still had a couple-hour drive out to Riverside, and the ease of the rail system and car rental pick-up got us on the road quicker. We rented a four-wheel drive vehicle with plenty of ground clearance, because we intended to go camping on our multi-day road trip back to our home in Stillwater, Oklahoma. We finally reached the Mission Inn Hotel in Riverside around 9pm and headed straight for our room to crash.

None of the boys paid much attention to the interesting design and castle-like features until the next morning when we had all rested up. It was hard to keep Heebs and Gilly corralled as they ran all over peeking in corners and over balconies. We avoided wedding parties near the chapel and found ourselves at the top of a circular stairway that spiraled around the multi-story colonnaded courtyard called the Rotunda. Excitedly, Heebs and Gilly couldn't refrain from noisily descending the steps in what felt like an echo chamber. We made our way behind retail shops, past the pool, and into the main lobby where we were directed to the Spanish Patio for breakfast.

Mas, who had found an old-fashioned paper printed newspaper kicked back and read the headlines with the whole thing held up in the air like in the old movies. The rest of us found comics and other secondary stories printed on the back, and never got through any particular story before Mas turned the page.

Without warning, Mas folded the paper and set it down on the table so that one particular story popped up.

"Look at this, Dad, someone stole a portable fission unit early this morning. I wonder how much power those things put out." He pointed.

I reached over and pulled the paper closer. The fission unit was military grade, stolen from the Marine Corps Logistics Base out past Barstow. Along with the unit a heavy plasma cutter was also missing.

"I guess there would be enough power to run a heavy plasma cutter." I suggested.

Mas looked dreamy-eyed, "Can you imagine how cool it would be to have one of those nuclear units? I could set one up to beam power to my spider and wouldn't have to recharge the battery for decades!"

"Are they available for civilian use yet?" I asked.

Mas was designing all sorts of gadgets in his head that could use such long-term storable energy, "I don't think so. Imagine installing one in a car — it wouldn't ever need fuel. That's why all the tanks and military vehicles are fly-by-wire electrical nowadays. The electric motors on tanks are massive!"

"Talk about Barstow, boys I'm thinking we ought to head out to Yermo tonight and camp near the Calico silver mines. What do you think?" I suggested.

Heebs and Gilly were ecstatic, and even Mas looked excited. Calico was a ghost town open-air museum partially restored back to its old western days but had modern restaurants. Because of my boyhood love of the place, I had named my daughter after it — Calico became Kariko when fitted to Japanese alphabet characters. Our destination would not be the ghost town, but the abandoned mine tunnels behind the town, where generations of Boy Scouts had gone out to do countless adventures.

First, I had a job to do. The owners of the Mission Inn had recently joined with other businesses in the area to unearth and restore the old Prohibition-era tunnel system that ran from Mount Rubidoux through many of the basements of the old buildings. I had recently obtained funding to use my LIDAR drone to map the underground passages in sections as they were restored.

I left Heebs and Gilly with Mas, and the three of them headed for the swimming pool. Anita Cartwell, the Mission Inn general manager, led me from the Lobby down into the Music Room, and took me down a narrow stairway on the north end.

"This is the old Refectory where the original owner Frank Miller had parties and private guests were served meals. Your scan should include this area." Cartwell explained.

She led me toward the East wall and down a long dark corridor with periodic nooks and small stained-glass windows overhead. The corridor opened up to the 'Catacombs' where Frank Miller used to keep his art collection, then wound around the inn's footprint ending up in the Catacombs again. Parts of the corridor had vaulted brick overhead, and arched doorways everywhere.

"Some of these passages are actually outside the floor plan of the building, running under the sidewalks instead." Cartwell noted as she led me to what looked like a narrow passage with pipes on racks along one wall, "And this is one of the tunnels."

After Cartwell left, I set up shop in the Refectory and started up the drone. The entire sub-basement had been barricaded off until I finished the scan. I hung back as the drone autonomously worked its way down the tunnels, pausing to fully map nooks and side passages. There were a couple of hidden stairways that would have been interesting to explore but were blocked off. I suspected they led into secret panels in apartments or other rooms.

As the scan progressed, my mind kept going back to those granite nuclear bomb-proof vaults in Little Cottonwood Canyon that Sister Jones' church had constructed. One interesting point in the Urim & Thummim article impressed upon me that this was no ordinary church. Apparently, unless I read it wrongly, early members of the church at one time had possession of an Urim & Thummim, and regularly used it to do translations. I was skeptical that such an ancient thing, should it have been genuine, actually had the ability to assist with translation, but just the fact that this church had somehow gotten possession of the artifact wouldn't leave my thoughts. Besides my academic interest in LIDAR mapping underground vaults, I began imagining that any such ancient Hebrew regalia still in existence could be stored down there.

The Mission Inn Catacomb scan finished, and I reported back to Anita Cartwell. I herded the children and checked out of the hotel. We stopped at an outdoor store where we picked up a few camping supplies, then headed north on Interstate 15. Driving up through Cajon Pass the tops of the Victorville high-rise financial district came into view, which had become a bustling city center after the nuclear terrorist attacks had decimated the Los Angeles Bunker Hill area back in the late 2020's. The long haul across the Mojave Desert to Barstow was just as barren as ever, but the additional overhead air traffic flooded the sky with passenger drones going to and from Las Vegas. Just beyond Barstow we began to see military vehicles lined up out in the desert, with heavy armored tanks sitting on railway flat cars about to be shipped to who knows where. It was the Barstow Marine logistics base.

"Check those out!" Mas excitedly pointed, "Each one of those tanks has enough fission power to stay in a remote desert for years without refueling."

Heebs and Gilly tried to identify some of the vehicles, but they were only visible for a few minutes before we had to turn off the freeway.

The majority of tourists got off at Ghost Town Road to visit the historical Calico Ghost Town, but we continued on one exit further to Yermo. Some of the biggest historical silver mines were right behind the town inside the Calico Mountain such as Silver King and Maggie Mine. I recall sneaking up there as a kid, climbing down a shaft near one of the giant 'C' letters, and going down level by level exploring miles of tunnels. Some levels were only accessible by shimmying down vertical shafts that we had no idea whether we would be able to crawl back out of. At the end of the day, all covered with dust, we had emerged from a horizontal, half-buried tunnel in Wall Street Canyon.

But the ghost town folks were getting stricter with patrol drones and they had buried many tunnel openings, so it was almost impossible to climb up on the mountain without getting caught. Instead, I drove the boys up Odessa Canyon back behind the Calico Mountain where the other big operations like the Bismarck, Silver Bow, and St Luis mines were open for exploration. Doran Scenic Drive and Mule Canyon Road provided rough four-wheel drive access to countless dirt tracks and trails.

At a couple of points in Odessa Canyon, huge boulders choked the way and I had to switch into limbed articulation mode in order to crawl over the obstacles. Heavy treaded tires attached to four folded mechanical appendages stretched out from our rental vehicle and literally climbed and tiptoed over and around the boulders, getting us safely across.

High up on a canyon wall a special set of mine tunnels, likely part of the Bismarck operation back in the early 1900's, had been nicknamed 'Stars & Stripes' by countless adventurer Boy Scouts due to some graffiti that looked like parts of an American flag. Once entering the horizontal tunnel, the entire interior of the mountaintop opened up in a sequence of huge, excavated volumes. In places small openings penetrated the ceiling, so one didn't even need a torch, flashlight, or lantern in the main spaces. One of my brothers in his romantic younger years had once brought in a folding table and all the fixings for a candlelight dinner for some special girl — they dined as beams of sunlight slowly raked across the rock outcroppings.

One short side tunnel opened up onto a sort of rocky balcony overlooking Odessa Canyon below, that had enough flat area to lay out a few sleeping bags. After we had gotten all set up, Mas and I found a big sitting rock inside the hollow mountain and relaxed as Heebs and Gilly climbed up dusty chutes and ladders exploring the branching tunnels.

"All this rock," Mas noted as he swept his gaze around the rough-hewn walls of the mine shaft, "I wonder how much computing power is around us?"

"What do you mean?" I asked.

Mas explained, "Under the Yata-no-Kagami mirror note, Hirayuki referenced Kurzweil's 'Singularity' book about the computing power of a common one-kilogram rock. He said that the 10^{25} atoms in just that small sample share electrons with each other, change particle spins, and generate rapidly moving electromagnetic fields, exactly like a computer."

"Huh? You mean this lump of stone is electronic?" I said as I picked up a nearby chunk.

Mas continued, "It's not meaningfully organized as computations in a computer, unless you think of each rock computing the truth about itself for us to observe by way of the light reflecting off of it. But apparently a one-kilogram rock at any one moment has at least 10^{27} bits of memory. He argued that all that computing power in the rock equals about 10^{45} calculations per second. If you only look at the neurons in a human brain, the calculations going on in a one-kilogram rock is about ten-trillion times more powerful that all the human brains on Earth!"

I did a double-take with my mouth open in surprise, "What!? That's kind of hard to believe!"

"That's what he came up with. People just don't look deep enough at common things around us." Mas said.

Microscopic biological molecular machines, self-replicating programmable cell factories, and now this — super computing rocks! I looked at the hard surfaces near me, trying to imagine computing going on. Little did I know how that fact would be relevant later, in ways I couldn't have imagined.

"You know I've been thinking," Mas began as we watched flashlight beams from the boys sweep across distant stone surfaces eclipsed by rock outcroppings, "suppose a galactic civilization out there is faxing life to other worlds. They have some means, which we haven't figured out how, of remotely turning genes on and off. What's the purpose?"

I sat back and considered for a moment before countering, "It sounds like Venter and those folks actually have machinery that they can use to remotely send coding representing sequences of amino acids. The coding is sent, and the machinery outputs strips of DNA or RNA. Don't you think it's ridiculous to think some machine was out there sitting near the primordial soup?"

"Well, as long as life can be planted, maybe the 'faxing' function actually consists of molecular machines already in the cell." Mas pointed out.

"How do you mean?" I wondered.

Mas looked at me and said, "We sort of know a little bit about the engineering side, but we've been neglecting the physics papers. You've heard that quantum effects seem to have no distance limits. There are papers on entanglement in there, and I found a few more."

It was not obvious what Mas was getting at. Everyone has heard of quantum entanglement, but very few people understood what it meant, including me. The confusion must have shown on my face.

Mas continued, "Entanglement is the way particles in the universe communicate and bond with each other. Most of us imagine particles existing in a big volume that we call space, but it turns out such a volume does not exist. The paper *Building up spacetime with quantum entanglement* goes a step further and says that space emerges from the connections between particles. In other words, entanglement is the fabric of space woven together by the many threads of particle-particle connection."

"What did you just say? Explain it simpler." I asked, confused.

Mas sighed in exasperation, "Okay, let's say there are only two particles in the universe. A communication wire stretching between them is entanglement. What do you think would happen if you tried to send a signal in the opposite direction from that wire, away from the other particle?"

"I don't know, maybe go out into space?" I guessed.

"Wrong!" Mas seemed to enjoy my misunderstanding, "That single wire is all there would be of space and time. A signal could go to the other particle and another signal can follow the wire coming back, but all you would have would be a single wire one-dimensional universe where absolutely nothing exists outside that wire."

"Okay," I started to see, "How far apart are they?"

Mas came back quickly, "Zero. Entanglements are zero distance. And zero time. You would have to get thousands and billions of particles all connected via a tapestry of entanglement threads before 'distance' or 'time' starts to emerge and become understandable."

Mas' description started to make sense. Somehow the very fabric of both space and time emerged from billions of back-and-forth signals passing along these entanglement threads.

"So, what does that have to do with faxing life to another world?" I asked.

Mas wiped his forehead and proceeded to explain, "The quantum entanglement paper suggests that each particle is its own universe. Each thread of entanglement is actually a quantum-sized wormhole connecting those two universes. So, our macro-sized universe consists of a tapestry of untold gazillion networked wormholes."

The conversation paused when one of the younger boys could be heard calling out, "Hey over here — we didn't explore this one yet!"

Mas continued, "Think of an advanced race millions of years ahead of us. I can't imagine such a race not having figured out how to tap into such a powerful network. Those advanced engineers could likely plug into, intercept, or edit any signal they want. In fact, another paper on the list, *Construction and Enlargement of Dilatonic Wormholes by Impulsive Radiation* talks about how these quantum entanglement wormholes that have existed since right after the Big Bang might be hijacked using radiation. The third physics paper too, *EPR Pair Temporal Loops: Primordial Closed Timelike Curves?* talks about the same thing. This means that such an advanced technology would allow access to any point in space, or even any point in time!"

Mas just blew my mind as I began to grasp the enormity of the concept, "So this is real? It could really happen?"

"There was a physicist several decades ago who used to explain deep physics concepts to everyday people. Michio Kaku even wrote a book about how advanced a civilization needed to be in order to conquer warp engines or traversable wormholes. He projected that some of the most exotic ideas might be within our reach if we continued to progress millions of years." Mas laughed, "What I find funny is that once an advanced civilization figured out a way to hijack wormholes back in time, say from right after the Big Bang, then nothing is out of their reach."

I mused, "So if an advanced civilization could reach back in time and manipulate any part of the universe, wouldn't we have seen them? Someone could have taught people technology back in historical times."

Mas shook his head, "No, there's a problem with paradoxes. A physicist named Aharonov showed that not only is there forward causation of events creating effects, but a future state might also reverberate backwards as a kind of inverse causation to ensure its own origin is preserved. In other words, somewhere in the linear timeline, each technology must have a set of causal events that bring it about."

Mas cleared his throat and took a swig from his water bottle. We could still hear occasional sounds from the boys. The 'stars & stripes' mine didn't have miles of tunnels, nor were there any overtly dangerous spots, such as bottomless shafts. There was just the right amount of danger to make it fun.

"There's another thing to note," Mas began again, "I think it would be hard for a civilization with such advanced technology to keep from destroying itself unless every individual were completely benevolent to each other. Even the slightest malice toward others could not be tolerated. Otherwise, it would be easy to go back and do tweaks that reverberate forward and backward until nothing is left. Your entire civilization could be edited out of existence."

I looked at Mas wide-eyed. There was something about time that I had heard, and the movie industry was finally starting to avoid stupid time travel illogical mistakes about 'changing the past'. Logically speaking, time could not be 'changed' by going back a second time around. If you were able to visit an era twice, it meant that you witness the same exact events twice. If you were able to change something, then the only logical explanation is that the changed events would result in a parallel universe rather than change the 'original'. I could see that an advanced civilization able to edit the past might end up with an unmanageable number of parallel timelines without solving the problem.

"That's a scary thought." I mused, "I suppose that editing oneself out of existence links back to the discussion about the Drake Equation and Fermi Paradox. We don't see any evidence of aliens because they have wiped themselves out somehow?"

"Yes, that could be true. But there's likely another possibility too. I read a book by Jared Diamond titled *Guns, Germs, and Steel* that had some interesting thoughts about this. Some of the discussion centers around what might happen when an advanced civilization met up with a less advanced culture." Mas explained, "Either the advanced culture would destroy the lagging folks, or the latter would get technology too fast to understand the ethics of its use and would become a menace to themselves and to everyone else."

It made sense, I reasoned, "So smart aliens can't just come down and teach us how to solve our problems, eh? We have to learn everything ourselves along the way, making incremental mistakes so we understand the consequences of misuse."

"Exactly," Mas confirmed, "any sufficiently advanced race would have to keep themselves hidden. They can't be involved with the causal development of child race technology but would have to allow them to make their own mistakes."

It felt as though more pieces were coming together. At least the engineering papers and physics manuscripts felt like they were working together.

"So back to the beginning," Mas concluded, "Let's say our million-year-old civilization figured out how to hijack entanglement wormholes. Maybe out of all the millions of entanglements within the germ cell, only a few would be needed. All you would need to do would be to instruct the gene editing machinery of the cell to change a few sequences of amino acids and viola — new genes faxed into the organism."

Mas and I both sunk into deep thought. We had started out our conversation wondering what the purpose would be for faxing life to other worlds, and now the purpose seemed a little bit clearer. The motivation must have been colonization, to propagate the species in as wide a way as possible, like planting seeds. Hopefully some of the seeds would land in fertile ground and continue to grow and develop. But that thought opened up another big question: did the life-faxing advanced engineers intend on their biological molecular machinery to self-replicate at the cell level, but allow any kind of organism to emerge? Or did those engineers maintain tight control over the development to steer life to resemble them? Was the purpose to plant biospheres on as many worlds as possible and let them customize themselves befitting the new environment? Or was it an actual conscious goal that made sure thinking, reasoning beings came out of the other end of the process?

Mas seemed to be thinking along similar directions and said, "Would it make any sense to grow up on one world, design a super-advanced self-replicating, programmable molecular-scale factory, then send it out to other worlds on a slight chance that a biosphere might take hold?"

I agreed, "It would make more sense if they either made the system smart enough from the start or continued to fax instructions for guided development. The emergence of intelligent life must not be left to chance. The colonies need to grow the capability of seeding other worlds, generation after generation."

Mas smiled and looked at me out of the corner of his eye, "Self-replicating biosphere, eh? Mature worlds giving birth to baby worlds."

We heard some ruckus and knew that Heebs and Gilly were on their way back. We moved out of the tunnel and set up shop on the flat camping ledge overlooking Odessa Canyon. I continued to think about our conversation as I pulled out the camp stove and freeze-dried meals.

"Heebs, get some water boiling for us." I said as the boys arrived in camp, "Gilly grab your eating utensils."

Mas perched on a nearby rock and continued our conversation, "Okay, so they've got the biological cells which are molecular factories. They've also got the means to send fax instructions to the cells. How did they deliver the cell colonies to the planet surface?"

Heebs, who had just filled a big pot with water, answered as though he had been listening from the start, "There's already a proven, demonstrated mechanism for that. Just use space capsules."

We all laughed at the obvious answer.

"Okay Heebs that will work. But what's a good way to send cell colonies if you can't be there to take care of them when they arrive on the surface?" Mas prodded.

I had heard of these 'panspermia' theories before, so I contributed, "Bury them deep in water ice comets and send them out in all directions."

Mas brought up one more big problem, "There's still too much chance involved. If the goal were to build a successful colony that could eventually become a parent as well, then there would be too many pitfalls ahead of the emerging colony. The chances of that child civilization getting through without destroying itself would be pretty slim. How could the advanced parent race coddle the child race when they have to stay hidden?"

"Yes indeed — how would that work?" I agreed.

The four of us had an enjoyable evening sitting around camp, talking about the old mining days. I had explored all the Calico mines since I was a kid, and of course I had already used the LIDAR drone to map the more prominent ones. We decided to take a 'selfie' of the four of us sitting on the ledge at the mouth of the tunnel. I set up the laptop and got the drone airborne ready to take the shot.

"Okay everyone be perfectly still." I cautioned.

The drone swept the cliff face around us, capturing the upper walls of Odessa canyon. I also programmed the flying vehicle to go inside all the nearby caves about 3 meters deep.

When the drone landed, I brought up our 'selfie' scan and spun the 3D image around for us to see. Mas and Gilly were perfectly captured, and the scan showed me off to the side watching the laptop screen. But Heebs — such a prankster! He had been around the LIDAR scans so often that he knew he had to freeze when the first scan came, then quickly change position before it came back around again. He had kept his body and head perfectly still but ended up with four arms doing menacing superhero poses.

The next morning, we got up early to try to beat the heat. Our cliff-side balcony faced east and would get the brunt of the morning sun. As we were rolling up sleeping bags and putting things away, we heard the electronic sound of an incoming text. It was from Mas' smartphone. Mas pulled out the device and looked at the message. A deep frown came over his face.

"Dad, I think you had better see this." Mas looked up at me.

I stopped what I was doing and took the phone from him. There was no message, but just a single photo. To my surprise the *Liahona* magazine that I had lost on the plane, or one just like it, had its cover torn off. The bold 'Liahona' title and image of the Urim & Thummim were clearly visible. That single cover page was haphazardly laying across the rest of the magazine which was opened up to the article describing the granite vaults. But the thing that was most shocking was the object laid on top of everything: the barnacle-encrusted blade of the Kusanagi-no-tsurugi sword was clearly visible.

CHAPTER 16

Mas and I walked out of the Salt Lake City Police Department feeling frustrated. We had told them about the discovery of the Kusanagi-no-tsurugi sword, the series of murders, and the recent photograph showing the sword and *Liahona* magazine, but no one believed any historical artifacts were in danger.

"For one thing, those granite vaults are impenetrable. We work with those guys and their security is top notch." Explained Officer Sutherland, "Second, it's not likely that those artifacts are even in the vaults — all they would find would be old microfilms, some old leather-bound books, computer servers, and endless shelves of backup drives."

A woman, Officer Harriman, stood off to the side and said, "Some of us doubt they even exist."

Sutherland looked up at Harriman and countered, "Oh they exist alright. Just probably not there."

The two officers eyed each other as if they had had this argument before and hadn't resolved their differences yet.

"Do you know who this fisherman guy is?" Sutherland turned back to us.

"No, I never got his name." I regretfully admitted, not even able to give a good description of the fellow.

"You wouldn't believe the stories we hear coming out of that place. Every world-class criminal seems to find their way up to the vaults. We've had some famous names in our jail." Harriman rolled her eyes.

Officer Sutherland mentioned that all they could do was to give the vault security folks a heads-up and sent us away.

"They have no idea who they are dealing with." I grumbled as we got to our rental vehicle.

Mas had a confused look on his face and said, "One thing still bothers me. How did they get the *Liahona* magazine?"

I shrugged and made a guess, "I suppose those are available anywhere. You might be able to just do an Internet search for 'sword, Urim & Thummim, Directors' and find it."

"But don't you think it's strange that just as you fall asleep, this Sally person leaves the seat behind you never to be seen again?" Mas suggested.

I hadn't thought of that. But how could Sally be involved? She was such a sweet girl. Still, I had always thought it rather odd that she happened to show up behind that Miyazaki love hotel just as we jumped over the wall. Her story made sense, but Rikochan didn't really trust her. Was it possible someone had been pressuring Sally's family, forcing her into collaborating?

The fisherman had sent us a message — why? Surely sending such a provocative photo would pique the curiosity of any poor soul and send them running to the law. Or was it just me? I had no skin in the game, especially since the sword was out of my hands, and Detective Nakaya had witnessed it forcefully removed from my possession. Could it be possible that Rikochan might be released soon? Every logic cell in my brain was screaming to stay away. And yet there we were, way off course from our intended Interstate 40 straight shot home to Oklahoma. Insurance — we needed to get that sword back as insurance for Rikochan's release. Fortunately, Ines was understanding when I told her I had to take a small detour before going home.

"Maybe Sally sent the picture and wants to be rescued." Mas proposed.

When we got in the car and closed the doors, Heebs was just then helping Gilly try on a climber's harness. We had rented some climbing equipment to use on the Alpenbock Trail Network in Little Cottonwood Canyon near Salt Lake City. The Alpenbock trails were rock climbing routes suitable for a variety of skill levels. And even better yet, many of the routes were in walking distance of the Granite Mountain Records Facility parking lot. We would be able to look at those atomic bomb-proof vaults from a closer perspective.

"You got it figured out, Gilly?" I asked.

Gilly gave me a flash of exasperation, "Dad, it's not like I haven't done it before!"

"It's just like our climbing wall trips, right?" Heebs nodded toward his little brother.

I started up the car and we made our way through town to get on Interstate 15 south. The view was magnificent, with the majestic Wasatch Mountains towering like a wall along the east side, and the smaller Oquirrh range clear across the valley to the west. The two ranges created a wide populated corridor running north and south. We continued until we got to the 215 Beltway, then headed for the canyons. As the Beltway turned north at the foot of the mountains, we exited the freeway and followed Wasatch Boulevard south past the mouth of Big Cottonwood Canyon. Our destination was the gap in the massive granite wall, Little Cottonwood Canyon.

"I can't believe how high that is!" Mas looked up at the line of tall granite cliffs.

Heebs and Gilly were also peering out at the sight, seeming a little intimidated. It was looking as though the climbing wall might have been outclassed by a long shot.

"What's up, boys? Got butterflies in your stomach?" I chided.

Mas had been splitting his attention between the outrageously scaled granite outside, and his smartphone.

He said, "Dad, it looks like there are two vault facilities up there. The 'Perpetual Storage' vault, a little farther up, is like a bank deposit box on steroids."

"Okay, let's drive up and check out the canyon." I acknowledged.

Mas couldn't stop admiring the massive stone mountains, and let out a low whistle, "Think of all the computing power from Kurzweil's calculations."

"Ah, the one-kilogram rock," I recalled.

"You know, there was another, um, Hirayuki reference for the Sacred Mirror treasure," Mas remembered, "Some guys achieved a data storage density of three exabytes per square inch using 'electronic quantum holography'. They say such a density could store all the world's data on only a seven square-foot surface. If we can get that sort of density with our current-day technology, imagine what a Silurian civilization millions of years old could accomplish."

Gilly's eyes went wide again, "Is that the lizard people?"

Heebs rolled his eyes and shook his head.

"So, you're thinking all that granite out there could be calculating unimaginable amounts of brain power, and the data is stored right on the face of the cliff?" I snickered.

But in all seriousness, the thought was mind-boggling. It was always there but none of us made the connection. I for one would never look at common stone again without imagining sophisticated microelectronics. It was one of those things that made one wonder if we were all living in a matrix simulation after all.

Right away, as soon as the residential neighborhoods ended, a parking area spread out on the left. We could see folks with trunks and rear hatches open gathering their climbing equipment, pads, coolers, and backpacks.

"I see some guys up there on that face!" Gilly pointed up at the massive granite wall.

Heebs joined in, "Yeah, and over there! And there!"

Some of the deciduous trees were gradually changing color, a little ahead of the main fall colors. Hikers were going back and forth, heading toward loop trails that accessed dozens of well-established climbing routes. A few stragglers seemed to just be strolling along without any interest in climbing. The whole scene was beautiful and could have attracted all sorts of folks interested in being outdoors.

We continued past the parking lot and after only a couple of gradual curves we could see the Granite Mountain Records Facility perched up on a ledge. All that could be seen were out-buildings, and a road cut into the side of the cliff. No bomb-proof tunnel entrances were visible from our perspective. If you didn't know what you were looking for you would miss it.

I kept my eyes glued on that road cut, and tried to follow it down the side of the mountain until it became hidden behind a copse of trees. On our left there was another parking lot below a steep bank of rock tailings that might have been the remains of granite that had been blasted out from the construction of the vault decades earlier. 'Grit Mill Trailhead' read a sign at the parking lot entry. There were several vehicles parked in the lot, perhaps belonging to climbers or hikers. But the thing that caught my eye was the presence of law enforcement vehicles stopped next to each other, ostensibly chatting at each other through open windows.

"Maybe they did listen to us." Mas commented.

A little further up we passed the point where the vault entry road cut met the main highway. There was a gate a short distance up, complete with guard booth and a pole bristling with security cameras. We passed another law enforcement vehicle coming down from further up, and a few uniformed officers walking down the side of the road placing tickets on a few straggling parked cars. Security was indeed very tight.

We passed another turn-off packed with cars and saw more climbers on the granite face above.

"Perpetual Storage coming up on the left." Mas pointed.

The next vault facility was harder to spot, hidden behind a rocky slope choked with deciduous trees. Again, a gate blocked the access road. We continued up the canyon on the winding road, past trailheads and campgrounds. The deciduous trees gradually faded into evergreens, and we found ourselves in a real forest.

Heebs, peering out the side window, suddenly spoke up, "Dad, I just saw something that looked like a cannon. What the heck was that?"

"They use those in the wintertime. They get very deep snow drifts up here. Apparently, these slopes are so steep that they have to use cannons to preemptively trigger avalanches before they become dangerous to highway traffic." I explained.

"But why would they keep these roads open in such weather?" Heebs asked.

The answer became apparent as we rounded another bend and saw the extensive Snowbird ski resort facilities. Mid-rise hotel buildings clustered around sports shops, restaurants, and private condominiums. Dozens of chairlifts could be seen shooting up slopes and side canyons. A large enclosed aerial tramway went straight up a mountain face, then disappeared over the ridge.

"They rebuilt that tramway a while back — it links four resorts together for skiers who purchase a super ticket. I think it's Snowbird, Alta, Solitude, and Brighton." I explained what I had read recently.

We got as far as the Alta ski resort, but the road ended there so we turned around. The boys started to get excited about climbing, but I could tell there was an underlying nervousness that punctuated their conversation. We continued back down the canyon headed for the parking lot that would give us access to the Alpenbock climbing routes. Mas and I peeled our eyes as we passed the nondescript driveway entrance for Perpetual Storage, where no sign marked the location for curious onlookers.

As we began to approach the entrance to the church-owned vaults, I slowed down and craned my neck trying to look up the hill through gaps in the trees. It was here where I made a critical mistake. As often happens on mountain roads, between the time we had gone up the canyon and returned back down, one of the banks on the uphill side had crumbled a bit and spilled small rocks all over our lane. The car in front of me deftly swerved over into the opposing lane when there was a gap in oncoming traffic and avoided the pile. But I was distracted right then and in spite of having rented the special off-road articulated suspension system with heavy mud tires, one particular sharp piece of stone pierced a sidewall. The vehicle was out of control at first, but I was able to slow down and gain control of the steering. There was no place to immediately pull over, so we rode the flat a short distance until we got to the church-vault driveway which was wide enough to pull over. The vehicle ground to a halt and we all sat there looking at each other.

"What do we do now?" Heebs asked.

I thought for a moment then looked back toward where the massive spare was hanging off the rear of the vehicle, "How hard could it be? You've helped me change tires before."

Mas spoke up, "I'll call the car rental folks — maybe they would rather we use their road-side assistance."

There were a couple of parked vehicles nearby with paper traffic tickets flapping on their windshields, but across the street a single car sat with its motor idling, occupied by a girl with the windows down. All of us got out and I started looking for the lug wrench and tire jack. I remembered back in the day we used to need some sort of heavy-duty hi-lift for these raised vehicles, but there was nothing to be found. By the time I made one round of the car, Heebs had already found the lug wrench.

"I've got this!" He confidently exclaimed, eyeing the girl in the parked car across the highway.

The rental company informed Mas that a person could meet us in four hours, which would eat up half the day.

"Tell them to forget it." I threw my hand toward Mas as if to waive them away.

Gilly wandered over near the gate blocking the entrance to the vaults and longingly eyed the granite wall farther up, and Mas kept looking up the road where the granite vault out-buildings must have been right around the bend. He walked around the back, swung open the spare tire tailgate, and began rummaging through his things in the rear luggage compartment.

"Hey, Gilly, let's go check out those rocks." Mas pointed up the slope.

Eagerly the two started climbing the bank at the side of the road, ostensibly aiming for the base of smooth rock not too far up the slope.

"Dad, I don't think we need a jack." Heebs observed.

My attention was brought back to the issue of how to change the tire. I was about to be entertained again by the chemistry between Heebs and the young woman staring at us curiously. Heebs was looking at a small diagram pasted on the back of the tire carrier, which showed the vehicle in limbed articulation mode. On this vehicle, the four heavy tires were actually mounted on fold-out mechanical arms tucked against the chassis until they are needed for traversing rough terrain. The way to change a tire, the diagram illustrated, was to put the vehicle into limbed articulation mode where the three good tires readjusted their stance into a tripod, leaving the flat tire off the ground ready for removal.

I got into the driver's seat, and it only took a few minutes to figure out how to specify which tire, and get the vehicle to stand up on its haunches, as it were. The distance down to the ground had changed so I had to use built-in stirrups to climb down. I backed away from the vehicle to see what sort of pose it had gotten itself into. Three articulated arms reached out in various directions like some wild animal about to pounce on its prey. The headlights looked like eyes staring down its next meal, with front limbs aggressively reaching outward. I heard the clink of metal on metal and realized that Heebs had already started to remove the flat tire from the tucked-up fourth limb.

I walked around and stood behind my son as he expertly got the lugs loose. Slowly, the limb lowered itself so that the heavy tire was almost touching the ground, and a sixteen-year-old boy could just pull it off and roll it to the side out of the way. In his mind I'm sure he thought the girl across the street was impressed. The tailgate also had an easy lift mechanism, so it was not difficult to switch the good and bad tires.

I was just thinking that maybe the testosterone macho man might get away with the task without tripping over his oversized feet, when an alarm sounded up the hill. Heebs had finished mounting the spare, but still hadn't lifted the punctured tire up onto the tailgate. We both turned around to find out where the sound was coming from and realized there was activity up at the Granite Mountain Records Facility. I scanned the slope to see if I could discover where Mas and Gilly had run off to and saw them rock-hopping from boulder to boulder off to the side — they were coming down the mountain in a hurry.

Across the street the girl had gotten out of the car to get a better view of the action. Heebs appeared deflated — not only had the alarm hijacked his performance, but it was obvious that the female leaning back against the parked van was probably in her thirties — way out of his league.

The granite vault facility alarm continued to sound as Mas and Gilly reached the base of the bank. Several additional sirens started blaring from up and down the highway, and suddenly two security vehicles came into view rushing from the direction of the ski resorts. Mas and Gilly bounded over just as the two cruisers menacingly pulled up to frame in our rental car. A third vehicle, a patrol car, abruptly appeared from around a curve in the road below us, sirens blaring.

Two uniformed security officers, one male and one female, leapt out of the cruisers just as the patrol car arrived and shut off the siren. Bright red and blue lights flashed from all the vehicles, giving eerie colored reflections off exposed surfaces.

"What is your purpose here?" The woman demanded.

My mind went back to that time in Nobeoka when Japanese law enforcement surrounded us with their guns drawn. These officers were well-armed but hadn't pulled out their service weapons. The patrolman in the other car stayed put in his vehicle but appeared to be reporting to someone over the radio.

"Sorry, officer, we got a flat tire." I explained.

The woman saw the punctured tire, still sitting on the ground, and looked at each of us in a sweeping glance. Her gaze centered on Mas.

"This area is closed to rock climbing. There's a turn-off just up the hill, or you can go back down to the Grit Mill Trailhead or Alpenbock parking area." She warned.

I apologetically motioned to Heebs and the unmounted punctured tire and pleaded, "Okay we'll be on our way as soon as we finish this."

The woman looked up at the larger male who had emerged from the other security vehicle and nodded, "Officer Beck will give you a hand. Please clear the area as soon as you can."

The woman turned and hopped into her own car, shutting off the emergency lights and pulling out onto the highway. She could be seen with a radio mic held to her mouth as she sped up the hill. The patrol officer continued to sit in his car a short distance away, but with the female officer gone we had a clear passage onto the pavement.

The big fellow, Officer Beck, quickly lifted up the punctured tire without using the tailgate lift mechanism and placed it squarely on the lugs. Heebs placed the lug nuts and tightened them one by one. Officer Beck stood there waiting with his hands on his hips — they were not messing around when they meant for us to leave right away. I looked over and saw the patrolman still in his squad car, watching us while talking on the radio. We quickly piled in and got back on the road. I noticed that the girl across the street had already gone, probably not wanting to get caught up in the excitement. As we headed toward the mouth of the canyon, I looked in the rear-view mirror and saw the big security man still standing there watching as we slid out of view around a bend.

"Dad, let's skip Alpenbock and just climb at the Grit Mill area." Mas implored.

It only took me a second to agree. At that point I had no idea what we would do next, other than climb up the rock face and get a good look at the outer doors of the vaults.

Mas directed us into a good parking spot where we could see both the climbing cliffs and vault out-buildings. We laid out a tarp and began to organize our harnesses, kernmantle ropes, carabiners, nuts, hexes, and cams. We divided them up according to experience, where Mas and Heebs were better at placing cams and hexes in rock cracks so they would lead. Gilly and I were good followers and would have the role of gathering up the devices as we trailed along.

I thought we were ready to go and were about to head up the trail when Mas stopped me.

"I need to do one more thing," he said.

I watched him unpack the unit he had showed us in Hong Kong, that had the gimbal Yagi antenna and microwave beamer.

"What are you going to do with that?" Heebs asked the question on all of our minds.

Mas didn't say a word as he set the unit on the roof of the car on a tripod and began securely fastening the tripod legs to the roof rack. We all watched in curiosity. Was he going to send the little spider robot up the granite rock face after us so we could take selfies?

The last time he demonstrated the unit it was attached to a heavy 12-volt car battery, which he couldn't carry home on the plane with us. So instead, he pulled out some jumper cables, opened up the hood of the rental car, and connected them to one of the car batteries. Finally, he shut the hood, making sure the cables weren't pinched anywhere.

"Almost ready." Mas said as he pulled out a set of virtual reality goggles.

So far, I hadn't seen him take out the little spherical package that was the spider robot in its stowed configuration. Mas pulled out a game controller and with the goggles on, began fiddling with the controls. Suddenly the Yagi antenna came to life and began to rotate on the gimbal. It seemed to sweep back and forth, up and down as if it were searching for something.

It only took a few minutes for the antenna to find its target. The Yagi consisted of a single aluminum pole with multiple cross elements pointed up the hill — straight toward the vault out-buildings!

"What!?" I blurted out.

Mas removed the goggles and looked up at us in a cool manner.

"While you were changing the tire, I planted the robot spider right on the edge of the road up there," he said.

CHAPTER 17

We set ourselves up at the base of the cliff, right where the jumble of granite scree began to slope down to the parking lot. Mas teamed up with Gilly and laid out a mat at the starting point as they got ready to climb. Heebs and I set up our stuff right next to them. The area we chose had been flattened out and cleared of debris, and there was evidence that many climbers had used this area before. Looking up the rock face, we could see anchor bolts set into the granite, meaning we would not have to use many nuts or cams but just needed to attach carabiners to the bolts. Since we didn't have a guidebook for this location, we had no idea how difficult the routes were. I made the boys promise to take it slowly, and only proceed if it was safe and appeared right for their skill level.

All that raw stone, I thought, *the ultimate weather-proof microelectronics*. Heebs and I hung back as Mas started up the face. Gilly had found a good spot to anchor himself in and knew how to belay someone twice his weight. Seeing that the climb was going smoothly, Heebs started up a parallel route with me on belay.

Rock climbing always scared the hell out of me. As soon as I got going, the sheer fright of being up so high blocked out the entire world, so all that was left was my climbing partner, the little outcropping of granite I happened to be clinging to, and my sweaty palms. I frequently reached into the chalk bag meant to make the hands less slippery and gradually went from protrusion to protrusion, hanging on for dear life. Only when it was my turn to belay, and I was firmly anchored in could I relax a little. I made sure Heebs found a good deep niche for that.

On one such occasion I looked over and saw Gilly and Mas both anchored in on a ledge. Gilly was sitting around, peeking over the edge while Mas had donned his virtual reality goggles and was manipulating the game controller. I turned my head and looked toward the church-owned vaults and realized that we had gotten to a point high above the parking lot. I could see multiple truck-sized door openings along the flat granite surface with one large out-building on the end.

I turned back to Mas and called out, "Mas! Don't do anything illegal! You're not supposed to be in that area."

"Don't worry, I'm just checking things out around the parking lot." He replied.

I imagined the little spider scuttling around from hiding place to hiding place, going completely unnoticed by anyone working at the facility. The little thing was probably too small to set off motion sensors, and even if the security folks zoomed in on CCTV camera recordings later, it would just seem like some little animal. When Mas first planted the thing, he probably set it right on the edge of the driveway where it had a full view from the parking lot. I imagined the first thing he did when he slipped on the goggles was to drop one of those little spiky jack micro repeater repeaters so he could go around corners.

"Okay but be careful. The security folks already know something is up. We don't want them coming after us." I returned.

Each team got to a point where it looked like there might be overhangs or tricky lateral traverses, so everyone rappelled back down. We did multiple routes with a few pitches each and traded partners a few times.

On the last climb, I decided to lead with Gilly on a simple route. Mas and Heebs finished early and headed to the car. Gilly and I were still on the mountain as the sun threatened to dip below the peaks at the mouth of the canyon. We quickly rappelled down and gathered all our equipment just as the sun set, but the sky was still bright enough to pick our way to the parking lot. However, when we reached the car no one was there. The older boys' equipment was safe inside, but the two were nowhere to be found.

A thought had been nagging me and briefly put me into panic mode. We couldn't figure out why the fisherman 'Kōjirō' would send us that photo of the sword and *Liahona* magazine. What if he were trying to lure us here to kill us? So far, all the witnesses had been eliminated — it seemed to be his style. Were my boys in danger? Were he and his cohorts watching us from nearby in the twilight?

I quickly reached inside and pulled out a large flashlight, switching it on as I swept its beam toward the far corners of the parking lot. Gilly caught my nervousness and squeezed up against me, staring into the gathering darkness with fright in his eyes. The flashlight lit up the taillight reflectors of a few remaining cars, but I couldn't see anything suspicious.

Up the hill, electric streetlamps blazed away in the church vault parking lot. Hmm, I wonder . . .

The flashlight beam made its way over to a pile of scree, where two figures sat on top of granite boulders. At first, I was taken aback, and Gilly jumped a little too. But then I noticed both of them had virtual reality goggles over their eyes and they appeared to be staring out into space. Gilly and I walked over in that direction.

"Mas, aren't you done looking around?" I called out to one of the figures.

Mas was frantically fiddling with the buttons and levers on the game console.

Heebs, who apparently was watching the same scene as Mas, held up his hand and let out a loud "Shhh! He's at a tricky part right now!"

I climbed up the pile of scree with Gilly in tow and snatched the goggles off of Heebs' face. The boy looked up in frustration as he was denied watching the action.

"Hey!" He called out.

I slipped the goggles on and was immediately immersed into a stereo scene where tiny scales appeared enormous. Right in front of me there was a huge castor wheel, similar to what one might see attached to the corners of a movable cabinet, except that it appeared to be four or five feet in diameter. Above, the castor wheel appeared to be supporting a smooth ceiling soffit that opened up into a massive volume overhead. About twenty meters further on, or so it appeared, was an identical huge castor wheel holding up another low ceiling, only the castor was aimed in a slightly different direction. Beyond that I could see a long line of massive castor wheels holding up low ceilings in what looked like infinite regression. Shocked, I took the goggles off and found myself standing on top the scree pile again surrounded by nighttime darkness.

"Dad, you better take a seat," Heebs helped me sit down on the boulder, "you're lucky he wasn't running."

I settled myself in and replaced the goggles. Instantly I was there next to the giant castor wheel. As I began to analyze the scene, it seemed like I was looking down a row of wheeled cabinets that were monster sized, so large that it appeared as though I could stand up under the gap between the cabinet bottom and floor without bumping my head. The cabinets were in rows in an immense volume, and I could barely glimpse a ceiling up there, perhaps what seemed a quarter mile up in the sky. Around on the floor, especially under the humongous cabinets, were large pebbles, foot-tall tufts of cottony substance, and occasional piles of unrecognizable debris — giant-sized dust bunnies.

Suddenly, a couple rows over, a massive pair of shoes came walking in from the side. The footsteps paused, then a giant knee came down and palms of a huge hand pressed against the floor. What came next gave me a shock — a humongous face of a person appeared almost touching the floor, and a giant eye looked under the cabinet. The security guard looked this way and that, finally spotting us and focusing in our direction. In an alarmingly swift move for something of that scale, a gigantic cylindrical object was suddenly thrust underneath and made a sweeping motion that slammed into the castor wheel. It was a broom handle of unimaginable size and didn't seem to behave according to intuitive laws of momentum that I knew in my human-scaled world. The security guard was trying to flush us out!

The scene quickly spun around 180 degrees and I could see spider legs on both sides move at fantastic speeds to carry us in the opposite direction from the guard and his broom handle. The stereo vision was not smooth at all, and I started to get motion sickness. Up ahead, the receding row of giant castors came to an end at what might have been a wall. The forward action of the spider headed toward that barrier so fast I thought there was going to be a collision and I involuntarily brought my arms up to shield my face. When no arm appeared in the scene I had another shock and had to remind myself I wasn't really there.

The spider came to a quick stop just short of the barrier and made a sharp right behind the last castor. At that point it secreted another spiky jack repeater behind the wheel and changed directions. I'd had enough and removed the goggles again to find myself in the darkness feeling as though I was about to spin off the boulder I had been sitting on.

"I told you guys not to do anything illegal!" I reprimanded, "The spider robot is inside the facility!"

Calmly, without removing his headset or taking his mind off that other world, Mas replied, "I let Heebs drive the spider for a while, and he made it run right in the door!"

"Yeah, the guards thought we were a fast rodent or something. There are several of them chasing after us. Once I ran right between a guy's legs!" Heebs bragged.

I gave Heebs a stern look and his bravado moved down a few notches.

Mas joined in as he swiftly worked the buttons and levers on the console, "Now I'm just trying to get out of there."

"Did you see the Urim & Thummim?" I excitedly asked.

Mas briefly paused and peeked at me from under the goggles. Heebs and Gilly looked up at me as if to say, you're just as naughty as the rest of us!

"Nothing but shelves and cabinets." Mas replied as he slipped the headset back into place, "Heebs drew a map."

Heebs showed a sketch pad that he had been doodling on as he watched the spider's progress. Parallel lines penetrated the cliff face showing several truck-sized entrance tunnels, each of which intersected a large cross vault. From there, three narrower tunnels staggered from the entrances continued deeper into the mountain. According to the *Liahona* magazine, these narrower tunnels connected to six main vaults under 700ft of granite, each 190ft long x 25ft wide x 25ft high. Heebs' map had only just begun to sketch these out.

It was a typical bomb shelter design only much larger than anything I had visited. I had used my LIDAR system to map hundreds of similar smaller scale tunnel shelters in Japan — an entrance that heads straight in, intersecting a cross tunnel, with sheltered volume staggered from the entrance penetrating further in. In case a bomb went off at the entrance tunnel, the staggered design would prevent any explosion from penetrating past the cross tunnel.

Briefly deprived of the goggles, Heebs had figured out how to watch the action on his smart phone, and Gilly was looking over his shoulder.

"Give me that!" I made a swipe for the phone and watched the spider from a new angle, probably clinging to a wall.

Heebs, temporarily empty-handed, reached over and picked up the spare goggles again. Gilly shifted over to my side and continued watching the chase on the phone. Soon all four of us were watching, shouting out instructions, or cursing at the guards. The spider would run along the floor, climb walls, ceilings, and scamper along shelves. A semi-transparent graphic occasionally appeared overlaid on the spider's camera view showing coverage from various repeaters. It was apparent that Mas used the graphic to tell him when to deposit another spiky jack.

The cat and mouse game continued, with at least two guards trying to corner the little robot. It wasn't clear whether the men thought they were chasing an animal, or whether they had gotten a clear view of its mechanical nature, but whatever they thought of the nature of the spider, it definitely did not belong down there.

Several times during the chase Mas had been able to double back and pick up previously placed spiky jacks, only to redeploy them elsewhere as they continued deeper into the mountain. Rounding one bend, there appeared to be water pooling on the floor in places. The original engineers had dug the vaults at a very shallow angle for this very purpose, knowing that a certain amount of groundwater seepage might occur. Several times we had watched the spider stumble on a system of drainage ditches built into the floor to take care of the seepage. But this particular spot must have been a source of continual problems because cones and mop buckets surrounded the area, and typical cabinetry and furniture had been cleared away. The spider ran right out into the open.

Suddenly from both sides security personnel pounced and Mas frantically drove the little machine this way and that to avoid capture. I looked away from the little smartphone screen to keep from getting motion sickness. Even Heebs had to momentarily take his goggles off for a breather.

The next time I looked at the screen the spider had scampered up a wall above the men's heads and they were throwing things at it. There was a stain on the wall in that area, as if decades of seepage had mis-colored it. Mas continued zigzagging back and forth as he climbed the stained surface. Up ahead, there appeared to be a round opening in the wall through which water must have flowed in the past. Mas did one final leap and climbed into the hole just as a mighty shoe slammed against the little robot.

Suddenly the screen went blank. I looked up and Mas was trying to do some kind of recovery procedure in vain. He finally gave up and took off the headset.

"The power was getting low, and there wasn't a repeater that could beam down the hole." Mas explained, "We might still have a chance, but the car battery needs to be recharged."

The four of us climbed down off the pile of scree, hopping from boulder to boulder. Leaping into the vehicle, I tried to get it to start, but there was just a slow turnover that immediately ceased as the engine could not be moved by the starter. The next time I tried the starter button, the only response was a faint 'click'.

The articulated limb rental car did not have direct mechanical drive from the engine to the wheels, but each wheel had an electric motor in the hub. The engine was just a generator that recharged a main battery. Fortunately for us, Mas had wired up his Yagi antenna tracker to the system battery which was not the main power source. In other words, the vehicle had back-up power. Soon I had the engine revved up and the system battery began to recharge.

Mas donned his headset again and retried the recovery procedure. We all looked on with bated breath. I tried to imagine what might have been happening inside the vault. Undoubtedly, the security folks would try to go find a ladder so that they could look into the drainpipe the spider had entered, and perhaps poke some long object like a broom handle down the hole. There was no time to waste if we wanted to get that robot out in one piece.

Without warning, an image appeared on the screen. The little spider robot was just inside the hole looking out at the vault volume. It had, on its own autonomous response, dropped a spiky jack micro repeater right inside the opening. We all cheered and clapped at the recovery.

But there was still no time to waste. We could see a guard far down the aisle lugging a ladder along. Was there another outlet to the drainage system that the spider could use to escape? Mas quickly turned the thing around and headed deeper inside, switching on tiny headlights to illuminate the path. Only a couple feet further on and the pipe ended, with the spider crouching on the edge of a dark abyss. The tiny headlights swept back and forth to reveal a drainage cistern of sorts. It was a nexus of drainage pipes all emptying into the same place.

Mas dropped another spiky jack and scampered over to a neighboring circular opening. It was one of many alternative routes that hopefully could take the little machine out of there. Mas paused at the entrance and aimed the cameras down the pipe but all we could see was blackness. He moved over to the next opening and looked inside — nothing. At the third pipe there was a flicker of light. Up ahead there was some source of illumination. Mas ducked inside and scurried toward the source. A dimly lit circle of light got larger and larger until the little spider once again crouched on the precipice of a vertical shaft.

At first it was hard to understand what we were looking at. From the perspective of the tiny cameras, the shaft appeared quite wide, but considering the scale difference, it was probably only a couple feet square. Cables hung from above, and a very powerful beam of light shown down the hole. The cables were lifting something up the shaft. A dumbwaiter? Why would an underground records vault have a dumbwaiter? And why would a drainage pipe flow into a dumbwaiter shaft?

The answer came slowly, as I saw the crude markings on the bare granite wall of the shaft — it had been roughly hewn by some kind of high-energy mining system, probably a plasma excavator. From our vantage on the lip of the round opening, I could see an identical pipe opening across the way. It became obvious that this shaft had been dug recently and interrupted the drainpipe which led to who-knows-where. This was a heist operation — someone topside was trying to steal things from out of the hole!

CHAPTER 18

Mas dropped a spiky jack micro repeater. Cables were slowly raising a load of goods up the shaft that the spider's tiny cameras could not quite make out.

"Jump on top when it gets to our level!" I suggested.

Masamune nodded and set his fingers on the set of controls that would pull it off. Hibiki followed along through the second headset, and Gilherme and I watched on the small smartphone screen. As the load got closer, it appeared as though multiple bundles of white fabric were taped shut with what might have been duct tape. Just as the bundle got to be level with the pipe opening, we watched as Mas caused the little robot to leap onto one of the bundles. The spider burrowed between the layers of fabric and turned itself around so that it could point the tiny cameras out the crack.

We watched the pockmarked and scored walls move downward as our ride winched its way toward the top of the shaft. Without warning, partly transparent digital instrument displays overlaid onto the video feed. I could see compass (yaw) markings, along with roll and pitch indicators flash on the screen.

"Something is odd," Mas noted as he thumbed through the displays, "I don't think the shaft is vertical. It's dug at a steep angle."

We watched the spider ease out of the hiding place and point the cameras down in between the load of bundles and the shaft wall. The whole thing was a cart with wheels, rolling up a steep slope. Turning around to look upward, we could see the spotlight beam getting closer as we neared the top of the hole. Mas returned the little machine back into its hiding place.

As the cart cleared the top of the hole, we got glimpses of the operation. The scene swept past piles of newly excavated rock, a plasma excavator, portable fission power unit, and off in the distance an electric passenger drone. The whole world outside shook as someone manhandled the wrapped items, getting them ready to load into the drone. Then, for a brief moment the tiny cameras swept past the perpetrator and captured an expression I knew well.

It was the fisherman.

Then everything went blank. All the feeds stopped transmitting and signals bounced back unanswered.

Mas tore off the goggles and yelled out, "Crap! The security guards must have found the repeater!"

Heebs also took his headset off and opened the car door. We all followed suit and exited the vehicle to stand around staring up at the massive granite wall.

"Up there somewhere — they drilled down from the back of that mountain!" Heebs pointed.

Suddenly there was a buzzing sound of propellers echoing off the cliffs. A passenger drone rose above the peak and set off toward the mouth of Little Cottonwood Canyon.

"Damn, we'll never catch them!" I said as I moved to jump back into the driver's seat.

But Mas held back my arm with a calm demeanor and pointed toward my LIDAR drone — of course! Maybe there was a way after all. I quickly pulled out the drone and booted up the laptop.

"I've got something that you might need, Dad." Mas said as he rummaged in his bag.

He pulled out a spiky jack micro repeater with power leads and alligator clips.

Mas advised, "Pull out your battery and clip these leads on instead."

I fastened the alligator clips onto the power leads of my drone but let the spiky jack hang underneath the little aircraft.

"Now hold up the drone so you're in range of the Yagi." Mas directed.

I held the drone over my head and watched the Yagi begin to seek back and forth until it zeroed in on the hanging spiky jack. The drone motors roared to life, and I let it zoom into the sky. The long aluminum antenna pole and cross pieces aimed straight at the repeater and tracked the little aircraft. We now had unlimited beamed power.

Tending the LIDAR drone and driving the rental car at the same time was quite challenging. Mas had slipped his goggles back on, trying to see if he could pick up the little spider again. I finally left the drone piloting up to Heebs who had taken the passenger seat anyway, and we sped down the mountain.

"Dad, I can barely see them. I think they are faster than our drone." Heebs complained.

"Stay with them, Heebs!" I shouted.

I peeked over at the laptop screen and saw the tiny dot go down and land on a large parking structure. They must be transferring the goods over to another vehicle!

By the time the LIDAR aircraft got close enough to pick out the passenger drone in its landing spot, it was apparent that its doors had been left wide open, the cargo hatch gaping, and no one was around. They had gotten away!

Heebs had the drone circle around the parking structure to see if any cars exited. Unfortunately, the place was busy and there was a constant stream of vehicles going in and out. I could hear the gimballed Yagi antenna motor whirring on the roof of our rental car as it continued to track the LIDAR unit.

We were still on the ground a few kilometers away from the parking structure and closing in as fast as I could drive, but Heebs had no luck figuring out which vehicle might be carrying the thieves. As we got closer, the circling drone continued to go on and on without needing to swap batteries.

Suddenly Mas let out a whoop and holler, "I've got the signal! The spider is still hiding where we left it."

Mas directed the little machine to sneak out of its crevice and look outside. Peering out the front of the thieves' vehicle, he began to call out landmarks as they passed.

"Their vehicle is a hatchback, and the color might be white or cream-colored. They just passed a family restaurant, then a donut shop." Mas rattled off.

Heebs did wider and wider loops, and Gilly kept a lookout for the landmarks. Soon our team was able to zero in on the right vehicle, and Heebs kept the drone high on their tail. I still needed to close it up a bit, as we were over a block behind them. Whenever the fisherman's vehicle took a turn, both Mas and Heebs called out the change, and I would enter the exact street. We finally got close enough so that I could see the hatchback up in front. Heebs had both vehicles on the laptop screen from above, and Mas turned the spider around so we could get a selfie of ourselves out the rear window of the crook's getaway car.

Unfortunately, our luck didn't last. The bad guys drove near to the TRAX rail line and crossed the tracks just before a signal turned red. We were stuck in traffic as their vehicle put distance between us. Additionally, something malfunctioned with the Yagi tracking. Both the LIDAR drone and spider feeds ceased, and we were completely blind. We lost them.

"Crap!" Mas exclaimed.

Without the power beam, the drone couldn't fly anymore. As the traffic started moving again, we came to a place where something had shattered on the street. I looked out the window and recognized pieces of propeller, broken body parts, and a smashed spiky jack micro repeater scattered across the roadway.

Frantically, I tried to guess where the other vehicle might have been heading. We drove around in circles with no luck. They seemed to have disappeared into thin air!

We were just about to give up when we heard the Yagi motors start to gimbal around. Mas quickly pulled on the goggles and shouted a victory cry as the Yagi had once again acquired a signal. With the spiky jack smashed back there on the street, it could only mean one thing — the Yagi had found a line-of-sight connection with the spider itself. We were very close!

"Gas station! They're stopped at the pumps!" Mas called out.

Gilly found them first and pointed, "Over there!"

I started to head for the gasoline station and suddenly got an idea. The thieves' car appeared to be unoccupied, meaning they had all gone inside the store.

"Mas, give Heebs your headset. I need you to drive. Hurry!" I shouted.

It happened in a matter of seconds. I pulled up to the neighboring pump as if we were going to refuel, then quickly leaped out of the rental car and rushed over to the thieves' vehicle. I hopped into the driver seat, assuming that Mas would take care of things. The fisherman ran out of the store and came pounding in my direction. I quickly locked the doors. The hatchback did not have a key but must have needed a fob. There was no fob anywhere! 'Kōjirō' caught up to me and tried to open the door but it held. I had my finger on the lock button just in case. When the fisherman pushed the unlock button on his key fob there was a 'click' but I immediately locked it again.

From the corner of my eye, I sensed a second person approaching the passenger side, who began to beat on the window. I watched 'Kōjirō' pull out a big knife and aim for my window. In desperation I pushed the start button and the engine responded! The second passenger must have left their fob inside the car somewhere. The wheels peeled out as I put it in gear and stepped on the accelerator all at the same time. The big knife came against my window and shattered little cubes of safety glass all over my chest and thighs, but I was already gone. I pulled out onto the street and didn't look back.

Once I had put some distance between us, I realized that I hadn't given the plan much thought. I wasn't sure what to do next. I would have to call Mas and rendezvous with them somewhere, then drive the thieves' getaway vehicle back to the church vault and return the items. Or should I go straight to the police? Somehow, we had to stop 'Kōjirō' once and for all.

It was at that point that I realized I had made a deadly mistake. The phone rang and it was Mas.

"Dad," he said.

I started thinking about where we could meet, when all of a sudden, another voice came on.

"Bring me the Urim & Thummim, Directors, and plates, or I'll kill everyone!" The fisherman threatened.

A text message appeared on my phone, with some Salt Lake City address. I could hear Gilly crying in the background. Somehow the thieves had coerced my boys into becoming hostages.

CHAPTER 19

Don't panic! As long as I had their treasures, I had leverage. I made a couple of turns and parked on a dark street. The actual Hebrew regalia were apparently right in the back of the car!

Turning around, I saw bundled up shapes and, poking out from the fabric, the little spider legs. I had to get rid of the spider or 'Kōjirō' would be able to commandeer Masamune's controller and track me. Quickly, I walked back to the rear and opened the hatch. I reached over and pulled out the lifeless spider and dropped it into a drainage culvert on the street. If we got out alive, we could always come back here and tell it to climb out of the hole.

My attention went back to those bundled pieces. I knew I didn't have much time, but I was dying to take a look. There were three cloth-wrapped items and a long case. It occurred to me that the long case probably held the Kusanagi-no-tsurugi sword. Or maybe, could it have been the other sword? The original Hebrew regalia sword kept by the Nephites? I tried to pick up the largest of the three fabric-wrapped items but could barely get it off the floor, like it was made of lead. I didn't know where that fit into things, but the other two smaller shapes probably were the ones I wanted so desperately to see. One was a ball-shaped package, so I opened that first.

In the dim illumination of the dome light, I pulled out a very strange object. Instantly I knew the thing was the mysterious Directors, or Liahona. It was round in shape and was fashioned with exquisite detail. As I touched the ball and turned it around, there were two things that came to my mind. First, I knew it was an ancient artifact — there was no mistaking the tremendous age that seemed to permeate its very existence. I had felt the same way with the Kusanagi-no-tsurugi, but this was even older. Second, the detail carved into the skin of the ball was not the work of a primitive culture. There was no decorative vines, flutes, or gaudy rococo art carvings. Instead, the impression I got was that it must have been highly machined, perhaps using methods of precision lost before the prehistory of our modern culture. It looked like every indentation was there for some utilitarian purpose. The ball felt like an Antikythera mechanism, only far more advanced.

As I held the Liahona and turned it around to view the various details and surface features, a surprising thing happened that almost made me drop the thing. Suddenly on a smooth metallic surface that had been blank only moments before, a sentence had appeared. The words were in plain English and looked somewhat like a liquid crystal display contrasting on a silvery background but much more subtle. It was almost as if the metal itself shifted some molecular-scale polarity only where the letters were. The sentence read, *"Look in the Urim & Thummim."*

The sentence began to fade and soon was not visible at all. Whatever molecular polarity had created the contrast on the polished metal surface returned to its original value.

The Directors told me to look in the Urim & Thummim. I carefully wrapped up the Liahona, reapplied the strips of duct tape, and respectfully set it down next to the large heavy object. Next, I picked up the other small package and unwrapped the fabric. Before I could get the cloth undone, a small brownish-gray stone fell out. To my surprise the surface of the stone had a faint glowing letter radiating seemingly from the very center of it. It was an *'L'*. When I picked up the stone, three more letters became visible and formed the word *'Look'*. That faded away and another word took its place: *'in'*. One by one in sequence the words came and went reading the same sentence, *"Look in the Urim & Thummim."*

It hit me that the rock was an even more astounding Antikythera mechanism than the 'Liahona directors' — an advance Silurian civilization must have taken advantage of the computing power of the stone, or super-dense data storage, and hijacked the entanglements between particles for the ultimate LED display technology.

By this time my curiosity was burning so badly I could not stand it. But as I finished unwrapping the two clear lenses held together by a crude metal bow, I wondered if, for some reason, I was not allowed to look. Weren't there stories about how only the head priest was permitted to look in them? Didn't legend say that if someone were to look for the wrong, selfish purpose they might be destroyed?

Whether I would die right there on the spot or live to see another day, I had to look into those lenses. In the dim light I lifted them up and examined the various parts making up the Urim & Thummim. The bow was very crude, almost as if some primitive metalworking wrought and formed the way it clasped the edges of the crystals. But the lenses were very surprising in their detail. As I turned the object around, I could just glimpse deep patterns manufactured into the material, but the patterns disappeared when the angle shifted slightly.

I can't say when I noticed it, but each of the lenses had a glow of their own. The illumination seemed brighter every time I looked at it. It was like the El Gran Moxo lamp, or the sixteen stones molten out of the mountain by the Brother of Jared. Without further hesitation, I held the Urim & Thummim up to my face and looked into the lenses. The first thing I noticed was the impression of untold knowledge just waiting to be released with the right word. It was just beyond my grasp, but part of me felt like it was MY knowledge, that I had forgotten something, and it wanted to come back to me. Another part of me sensed knowledge that far exceeded the imagination and should not be sought after because we are not ready.

But somehow all that blurry intellectual feast ended up being a bush in the desert. I couldn't explain it, but I could see several healthy growths rooted in a sandy soil. In the lens the scene moved closer, and I saw the Kusanagi-no-tsurugi in its long box, the heavy fabric-wrapped package, and both the Liahona and Urim & Thummim, also wrapped, sitting in the sand. The bushes created a nest of sorts so that the artifacts could not be seen. I had the impression that if I put all the artifacts thusly, they would be safe.

The image suddenly faded and all I could see was the rear cargo area of the car. I felt an urgency to find those bushes and that sandy stretch of desert floor, wherever they might be in the world. I arranged all the packages in a neat and orderly manner and jumped back in the driver's seat.

I started driving again, but my mind was distracted. I had no idea where I was going. How could such a scene have presented itself? Was it a recording? The Urim & Thummim and Directors were no ordinary ancient artifacts — they certainly should not fall into the wrong hands. Over and over again the vision of the bushes and sandy ground impressed itself in my thoughts.

I faced a dilemma and needed time to think. Somehow, I had to negotiate for my kids' freedom, and the artifacts must be hidden in a safe location. The fisherman would not just let the children go if I told him the hiding place — he would demand for some guarantee. How could the trade happen? On the other hand, knowing what 'Kōjirō' did to witnesses, it's likely that he had some machinations to kill us all. It seemed like he had all the cards. He would use my children to get me close, then brutally get rid of all of us and take the treasures. I could not see a scenario where we all got free and were able to return the items to their rightful owners. Somehow, I knew that the bush in the sand, wherever that was, had to be the right place and all would be well.

As I peered up at the starry sky, I imagined some ancient race in a Silurian scenario, faxing life to colonize worlds, and thought they must have manufactured the Liahona and Urim & Thummim. I felt like a medieval peasant trying to make sense of a contemporary smartphone. Suddenly a feeling of indescribable joy filled my whole being. I looked out and saw the stars, all in order, with endless entanglement connections weaving the fabric of reality. My mind wandered and thought upon the trees, plants, and people around me actuated by billions of self-replicating factory cells. Even the crude houses and vehicles around be felt to be in harmony with — something. Just the thought of some distant civilization of engineers out there among the stars who had figured things out pounded me with wave upon wave of burning hope, and tears came to my eyes. I don't know how long it lasted, but somehow, I knew I would never be the same again.

Suddenly I had an astounding realization. If our human race continued to grow for millions of years in knowledge until we learned all the laws of the universe, and had the wisdom to use that knowledge ethically, wouldn't we be like gods? And if our advanced posterity eons from now could hijack entanglements or create traversable wormholes forward and backwards in time, wouldn't it be tempting to go back to the beginning, shepherd their ancestors past the Fermi Paradox great filters, to ensure all the historical causal paths turned out right so that their own existence was assured? Maybe I wasn't understanding the nature of time correctly, but could it be that God came from the future?

I must have wandered around all night — driving down various unknown streets, mindlessly waiting at traffic lights, or slowly creeping along in the slow lane as everyone honked at me. When I came to my senses, I found myself west of Salt Lake City airport driving along wide avenues between warehouses and logistics buildings. The eastern sky was a bright blue, and the sun was about to peek over the Wasatch mountains. I passed huge parking lots full of cars and saw dozens of automated freight haulers pulling in and out of loading docks. I passed a large warehouse and spontaneously turned north on 6550 West. Only a few hundred feet and a well-travelled dirt road appeared on the left. The shores of the Great Salt Lake were in that direction.

The impression of that sandy stretch of ground was clear in my head, and somehow, I knew I needed to get off road. As I left the pavement the bumpy un-maintained surface kicked up dust but the street suspension system on the hatchback seemed to take it rather well. The dirt track continued north and crossed over a couple of canals before looping around on a winding course through ponds and wetland areas. The road branched off and merged with others, followed water-filled ditches and skirted mud holes.

Then I was there. Ahead of me salty flats stretched away on both sides of an unkempt causeway, whose traces led all the way to Antelope Island. On both sides of me sandy soil sported desert shrubbery intermixed with sparse patches of brown grassy tufts. I stopped the car and got out and walked a few paces away from the road. The bushes all looked similar to what I had seen in the Urim & Thummim — would it be alright to just pick a spot? Somehow, I knew the location had to be exact.

As I turned to look back toward the car, immediately I saw the precise arrangement of bushes that had appeared in the lenses. I opened the back hatch of the car and first pulled out the sword case, setting it on the sand exactly the way I had seen it in the — what was it — Video? I snapped open the fasteners and checked that the Japanese Kusanagi-no-tsurugi was as I had seen it last.

Next, I went to get the heavy wrapped artifact, but as I tried to pick it up, part of the fabric covering fell away. I was shocked to see a glimpse of engraved gold, with hieroglyphic characters that were obviously of ancient date. I felt the surface and ran my hands along the side to discover that the entire artifact consisted of thin gold pages like a thick book, bound along one edge with rings. Looking closely, it was fascinating to see small scratches and imperfections around each character that must have resulted from the engraving process employed by an ancient artisan. I quickly rewrapped the plates and hefted them over next to the sword case.

Finally, I carefully added the Urim & Thummim with the Liahona to the collection.

Just as I returned to the car, my cell phone rang. As expected, someone was still calling from Mas' device.

"Musashi, I see you have led me right to my prize." The fisherman's voice came through the little speaker.

"Kōjirō!" I exclaimed and began to look around to see if anyone was nearby.

Over on a small rise, our rental car was sitting in off-road articulation mode, with all four folding limbs stretched out in a predatory stance. Large knobby aggressive tires were ready to tear up the ground. Mas' Yagi antenna tracker was still sitting on a tripod, lashed to the roof rack. 'Kōjirō' leaned back against the vehicle with phone in hand as he watched me sweating in the morning sun. When our eyes met, he took the phone away from his ear and used it to wave at me.

"Damn!" I exclaimed.

To the rear of the vehicle, I could see the little black-clad ninja-looking character holding Mas in a choke hold. A big ugly knife was held to his neck. I could not see the other boys anywhere.

Briefly I had a panic attack — could they be dead? Had the fisherman and his pal already done away with them? My fear suddenly turned to anger.

In one swift motion I jumped into the hatchback and squealed the tires in the loose dirt. The vehicle was not made for real off-road punishment, but I didn't care. I drove over bushes and rocks in a beeline toward 'Kōjirō'.

The folks surrounding the rental car reacted too slowly, thinking it was a bluff. I saw Mas take advantage of the situation and twist out of the ninja's grip. He dove off to the side and stumbled but quickly recovered and gained speed. The fisherman and his buddy stepped back from the car at the last second. I steered the hatchback straight into the other vehicle's right headlight and crunched both front quarter panels. It was demolition derby time.

As I backed up to make another run for it, 'Kōjirō' moved with astounding speed and hopped into the driver's seat of the rental car. By the time I moved in to ram him again he was ready. The nearest articulated limb lifted up and slammed down on my hood, allowing the other vehicle to roll up the windshield and along the roof of my car. Safety glass partially gave way without shattering and put a big dent in the windshield.

The rental car jumped off the rear of the hatchback and aimed for the cache of artifacts. Out of nowhere the ninja came and hopped into the passenger seat as articulated limbs took on the uneven ground. I did a tight turn and followed right on their tail. The Fisherman did a sort of breaking turn maneuver, where the electric motors in the wheel hubs caused him to turn on a dime. I crashed into his side, causing my forward momentum to aim in the wrong direction. I drove back up onto the dirt road heading back toward Salt Lake City, and 'Kōjirō' stayed with me trying to run me off the side.

The dirt track was only one lane wide, so at any one point either I was on the road, or his vehicle stayed centered on it. We continued bashing each other back and forth, fighting to stay on top. Up ahead, I could see green algae-filled ponds on either side, and I determined to try to get him off the road. As we were almost even with the water it looked like I was getting the better of him as he veered away from the road. But I was mistaken. The fisherman swung wildly back toward me and used his momentum to knock me right into the muddy water. I was permanently stuck.

I watched helplessly as the fisherman slowed down, turned the beat-up rental car around, and leisurely drove back to the spot where I had stashed the artifacts.

I climbed out on the hood, walked on the car roof and jumped off the back onto dry land. *How did this happen*, I thought. Wasn't the hiding place supposed to keep the cache safe? I jogged down the road and watched the two load up the car in the distance.

"Dad!" Mas called out and joined me in the run.

But by the time we reached the hiding spot, we could see the rental car speeding across the salt flat toward

Antelope Island. Both of us just stood there trying to catch our breath.

Finally, I turned my gaze away from the speeding vehicle and asked Mas, "Where are your brothers?"

Mas leaned over and propped himself up with his hands on his knees, getting out between breaths, "Heebs escaped at the gas station last night. Then early this morning I helped Gilly escape. I have no idea where they are."

The answer came with the sound of choppers. Three military helicopters flew overhead from the direction of SLC airport with deep aggressive blades tearing up the sky. Something told me someone was about to get their ass kicked. A fourth law enforcement helicopter followed but broke off and headed toward us. I could see dozens of emergency vehicles with red and blue lights blazing up the road, and the sounds of sirens reached our ears.

The police helicopter landed a few dozen feet away and Heebs and Gilly hopped out and ran in our direction. I could also see Officer Sutherland from the Salt Lake Police Department climb down and walk our way. Mas, Heebs, Gilly, and I did a big group hug.

"That's quite a fine bunch of boys you have, Dr. Hughes." Sutherland remarked, "Hibiki aimed us in the right direction without losing any time. We were able to pinpoint the area using Masamune's cell tower data."

"Thank you." Was all I could muster.

We watched the Utah National Guard choppers drop off a few dozen soldiers who set up a perimeter around the distant rental car. Several swat team vehicles drove past our position and soon caught up with the guard.

"Shall we?" Sutherland asked and motioned to the police helicopter.

We all climbed aboard and made the short hop over to where we got a bird's eye view of the two crooks finally getting captured. We saw swat officers forcefully extract two persons from the vehicle. The police helicopter took us down and landed, and Sutherland escorted us to where officers had set up a quick field office. There were two civilians standing nearby who didn't have uniforms on.

A. SCOTT HOWE

"Dr. Hughes, this is Elder E. James Martin of the Quorum of the Twelve Apostles from the Church of Jesus Christ of Latter-day Saints." Sutherland introduced a grinning elderly man in an immaculate suit.

Elder James reached out his hand and warmly greeted me, "Thank you for your help."

I shook his hand and said, "Nice to meet you."

Sutherland also introduced Dr Patricia Hernandez, who specialized in ancient scripture at Brigham Young University.

Police officers walked the two suspects toward a waiting van. The fisherman scowled at me, but the other person just hung her head. Her? I did a double-take — it was indeed Sally, dressed in black garb. We watched them, handcuffed, get into the back of the van which drove off.

Dr Hernandez was called over to the rental car where she oversaw the handling of the artifacts.

"You know, no one alive has ever seen these before," Elder James said as he watched the artifacts being packed in special crates, "It looks like our predecessors sealed the artifacts in a special anteroom back in the sixties when the granite vaults were constructed. They didn't want it known."

I got the hint, "Your secret is safe with me, Elder James. But I have so many questions!"

Elder James put his hand on my shoulder and reassured, "That's understandable. We've arranged for all of you to have lunch with Dr. Hernandez. She'll be able to give you quite an interesting explanation."

We watched the crew carefully pick up the Kusanagi-no-tsurugi and opened the case in front of Dr. Hernandez. The professor had a confused look on her face. Just then another law enforcement vehicle pulled up, with a different color scheme painted on its side from the rest. A man climbed out of the back seat and walked over to Dr. Hernandez. We knew that face well — Detective Kusato Nakaya from the Kitakyushu Police Department — 'Beard Yakuza'!

But there was no time to ponder the coincidence, because two others emerged from the back seat of the car. We looked on dumbstruck. It only took a moment for Mas,

Heebs, Gilly, and I to rush over and give Kariko and Ines a big hug.

"All that playing around!" Ines scolded me, "Didn't you have any clue that Kariko was in danger? That nice Japanese man brought her home."

CHAPTER 20

Our lunch with Brigham Young University ancient scripture Professor Patricia Hernandez had been scheduled for the afternoon of the following day, after which we would finally be on our way home to Oklahoma.

"Dad, check this out. I've been looking at the hieroglyphic symbols used in the sudoku puzzle." Hibiki announced as we packed our things in the hotel room.

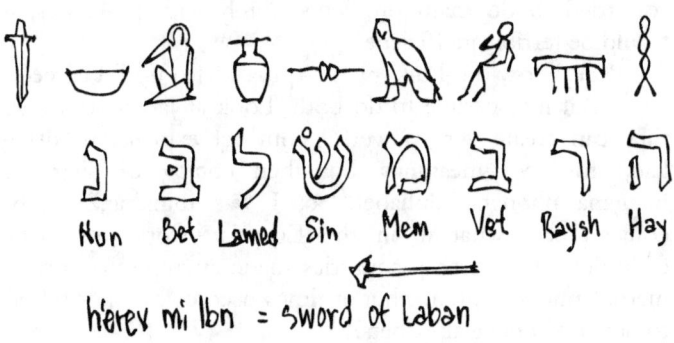

I looked at the sketch Heebs had drawn and was surprised to see Hebrew symbols in the mix.

Heebs continued, "The thing you told us about the Hebrew on the back of the Japanese mirror gave me a hint. They weren't numbers, so I suspected perhaps they were from some hieroglyphic alphabet."

"I thought Egyptian hieroglyphics were ideograms. Don't they have meanings attached without phonetics?" I wondered.

"Yes," Heebs agreed, "They're like Chinese characters. There are so many countries around China who borrowed the kanji characters and kept similar meanings but pronounced them differently."

I carefully put my laptop in the LIDAR backpack, but the little aircraft was gone. I was proud of Heebs, because he had grown so much over the summer. It was good to see him passionate about something other than girls.

I paused and turned to face him, "It seems as though most cultures grow into phonetic systems."

"I think there are pros and cons to each." He said, "Ideogram languages can be extremely powerful. Take mathematics for example. The symbol '2' has no indication on how to pronounce it, but just retains the meaning. Therefore, as an ideogram it becomes universal, and each language or culture can pronounce it any way they want. If you tried to do math problems purely with phonetics, it would be terribly inefficient."

"Yeah, t-w-o p-l-u-s t-w-o e-q-u-a-l-s f-o-u-r!" I agreed.

"But it's possible to do both. Look at Japanese, where they can create very powerful compact expressions using kanji for root meanings, but then conjugate using the hiragana phonetic alphabet. So, I was thinking," Heebs conjectured, "what if in the Egyptian world, over the centuries, other nearby countries made attempts to borrow hieroglyphic ideograms, but at times used common symbols to derive phonetic alphabets?"

His line of thinking seemed reasonable so I followed up, "So you think the sudoku puzzle characters might have been phonetic?"

"Yes!" He excitedly agreed, "And they weren't chosen randomly. Apparently early attempts at fitting phonetics to ideograms were done by the Coptic Christians. They tried to fit Greek characters to starting sounds in the Egyptian. I think there might have been earlier attempts to borrow hieroglyphic radicals for phonetics too."

Gilly, who was nearby listening, didn't quite understand what 'ideogram' meant, but seemed to have an intuitive grasp.

"Like the little sword in the puzzle?" My youngest son suggested.

Heebs reverted back to a teenager and protested, "No, dummy! The sword was actually a made-up symbol, not real hieroglyphics!"

"So, what did you find out?" I asked.

Heebs got serious again, "I found equivalent sounds for all the sudoku symbols except for the sword symbol. But the most interesting hint I found was inspired by that remnant of manuscript with the cursive English words."

Curious, I pulled out Hirayuki Doei's sudoku page and looked closely at the remnant. We had figured out the cursive words 'Urim & Thummim' and 'Directors', but there were other words that were hard to figure out.

Heebs pointed to one of the cursive words that Hirayuki had circled, with a hand-drawn arrow from the Kusanagi-no-tsurugi sword, and asked, "What do you think this cursive word says?"

I looked closely but could hardly make it out, "Does it say 'Laban'?"

"Yes," Heebs agreed, "Now watch when we unscramble these sudoku hieroglyphs, and match them with Hebrew, who didn't traditionally use vowels."

Heebs wrote the Hebrew character names under the symbols in order: hey-raysh-vet-mem-sin-lamed-bet-nun. Next, he wrote an arrow indicating the direction right to left.

"The sudoku puzzle needed nine unique characters. I looked these up in Hebrew, and 'mem' means 'of', as does 'sin'. The sword symbol gave me another hint. Altogether the sudoku symbols say h'erev mi lbn, which translates into the manuscript remnant cursive English phrase as being 'Sword of Laban'." Heebs smiled at having solved the deeper puzzle.

It was a brilliant effort on Heebs' part.

"So, if the Japanese Regalia were recreated from the memory of much older artifacts, you're saying that the original Hebrew regalia that inspired the Kusanagi-no-tsurugi was something called the Sword of Laban?" I deduced.

Heebs nodded and said, "Maybe."

"But why would the sudoku puzzle say Sword of Laban if the Japanese sword was just a recreation of its memory?" I wondered.

"I think Hirayuki Doei thought that the artifact was actually the genuine Sword of Laban. Like the original Hebrew artifacts were scattered and the sword ended up in Japan." Heebs conjectured.

"Could it be? Maybe he was right!" I returned.

It was another question for Dr. Patricia Hernandez. After checking out of the hotel, Ines, Rikochan, Mas, Heebs, Gilly, and I drove south out of Salt Lake City to a college town called Provo. We had gotten a new rental vehicle, after having a difficult time explaining what had happened. No one would believe me when I attempted to tell the company I was trying to prevent someone from stealing gold plates. I didn't quite understand it, but the topic of 'gold plates' must have hit a sore spot for many people in Utah. Either they glowed when the plates were mentioned, or scowled and rolled their eyes. Regardless, neither party took me seriously when I explained the part about driving around with them out near the Great Salt Lake.

We drove up in front of the Joseph Smith Building on the BYU campus and met Dr. Hernandez. From there we took two cars and drove along Campus Drive, then went on 820 East all the way to the foothills. There was a parking lot there, and a short gondola ride up the mountain to a small cluster of buildings in the shape of a gigantic 'Y'. Professor Hernandez had booked a table at a restaurant with a fabulous view of Utah Valley.

"First of all, thank you so much for protecting the artifacts." Dr. Hernandez shook both of my hands at once, "I'm amazed at the adventure you've had the past few weeks!"

"It was a bit crazy, I admit." I noted.

Gilly was already getting bored with the pleasantries, so he blurted out, "What happened to the bad guys?"

The Professor smiled at Gilly and began, "Eric Spaulding and his daughter Sally will be tried and convicted here, then probably extradited back to Japan and tried for multiple homicides."

Heebs wondered, "How did they get involved in the first place?"

"That's a good question. I think he was just a hardened thief who heard about an opportunity from his daughter." She said, "Sally had gotten involved with the transhumanists and told her father about it. They intended to silence anyone who knew about the Japanese sword because it was a high-priced item."

Rikochan jumped in, "The transhumanists aren't all like that — Doei-san was pretty mellow. Ebina-san told me about the sword after Dad went outside to the Nobeoka beach to find the boys. I didn't have time to tell anyone before the police raided the house."

"There's also something else. As soon as Mr. Spaulding heard about the connection with the Church, he apparently cooked up a plan to get some revenge for his great-great-something grandfather, who had an unpleasant run-in with Joseph Smith and other early church members back in the 1800's." Hernandez explained, "Some of those old anti-Mormons ended up joining us, but others held grudges for generations."

"Something still bothers me," I began, "how did Spaulding drill down from the back of the mountain and find the precise location of the artifacts, when church leaders like Elder James didn't even know about it?"

"That's a good question. Spaulding was a very smart man, an evil genius. He's not very cooperative I'm afraid. But apparently, he found original construction drawings of the excavations, and compared them with later published documents. The earlier drawings had all sorts of details like culverts, cisterns, air vents, and as-built excavations. The published drawings reflected finish walls and surfaces which were smooth compared to the rough blasted rock face behind them. Spaulding noticed a slightly wider dug-out portion in the drawings, that had smoothed-over walls later. Serendipitously, the wider volume had an air vent. He climbed up on top of the mountain and located all the old air vents, which had mostly been buried or sealed, and made approximate estimations as to where that particular vent might have been. I suppose he must have used some kind of endoscope inserted down the vent to make sure (but I've never heard of a 700-foot endoscope before). He might have had access to a ground penetrating radar unit that hung on a cable down the hole. Remember, he knew about the gold plates, so all he needed to do was find some reading showing an object of the appropriate density and he knew he would be close. After that the plasma excavator made short work of the granite, as he widened the vent all the way down." Hernandez speculated.

"But the *Liahona* magazine was only stolen from me a few days ago on the plane. How did he find time to do all that work?" I protested.

Professor Hernandez furrowed her brow and thought for a minute, "I don't know for sure, but I suspect he realized the connection with the Church earlier, when he first saw 'Liahona' in the documents. He had a head start on you and might have had other willing collaborators doing the hard excavation work. Sally probably didn't know what her father had been doing and took the opportunity to steal the magazine in case it would be of use to him."

The explanation made sense. I imagined Spaulding being a double-crosser. They would probably find the bodies of a couple of laborers and wouldn't have any evidence of how they had met their demise. I looked up and saw Ines scowling at me. My stormy wife was Brazilian Japanese but had enough Latino fire in her that I thought I might have to give her a less watered-down version later. I tried to smile back and diffuse things as much as I could.

Next it was Mas who had a question, "Okay I assume you are familiar with ancient languages. What do the Egyptian hieroglyphics mean that we've been trying to figure out — Dad, show her the paper."

I reached behind my back and unzipped the secret pocket, pulling out the stuffed envelope. First, I removed Hirayuki Doei's original sudoku/hieroglyph sheet with notes and handed it to the Professor. Then I began to lay out our scribbled papers with Heebs' help.

"Yes, I know this very well." Dr. Hernandez pointed to the round diagram full of hieroglyphic symbols, "This is 'Facsimile 2' from the Book of Abraham in the *Pearl of Great Price* volume. It's what we call a 'hypocephalus'. It's a discussion about astronomy and progression into the next life. It turns out hypocephali were commonly used in funerary text, passed down and modified since ancient times. We believe it was originally authored by Abraham or some of his associates. You can find lots of them if you do an Internet search, always unique in their own right, but including the same elements each time."

My eyes widened and I couldn't hold out any longer, "This is really a star map?"

Dr. Hernandez got distracted by Hirayuki's notes and didn't answer for a while. She pointed at each note and either nodded or showed a perplexed expression.

Finally, she looked up and said, "These are very interesting notes. It looks like you have found most of them."

Hernandez looked at the arrangement of papers on the table.

"I'll be happy to hear what you have discovered. This is the first time I've seen Kli-flos-is-es and Hah-ko-kau-beam described as black holes." She continued.

Mas nodded his head and jumped in again, "There are two ships in the hypocephalus diagram. Could these really be talking about space-faring people?"

"Well, we don't usually explain it that way — maybe that was Hirayuki's speculation. We have a different belief about God — we believe the mantra 'As man now is, God once was; as God now is, man may be'. We believe He is a physical being, an advanced human who has progressed and reached a perfected state. But you could just as well say that we believe there is a community of extremely advanced celestial engineers out there whose purpose is to terraform planets and colonize worlds, including this Earth."

Hernandez added, "But what Egyptologists do know is that Raukeeyang is said to be a 1,000-cubit boat of a million years, or 'solar boat' that orbits — something. I've never heard this particular perspective, but yes, maybe it is talking about a colony ship, or some means of establishing people on various worlds."

"If that's the case," I began, "wouldn't there be some evidence of it? There must be some artifacts, or even stories or myths that have survived."

But as soon as I said it, I knew that I had seen the evidence — the Urim & Thummim and Liahona, real live 'Antikythera mechanisms' from some ancient Silurian techno-civilization.

Dr. Hernandez reminded me, "I think you of all people have seen the evidence, Dr. Hughes. Consider this. If you had an advanced programmable system of molecular machines and self-replicating factories that could be sent out as a means of terraforming and colonizing dead rocks in space, would you just leave it alone and hope it takes root? You don't just build an advanced AI fighter jet, or autonomous electric vehicle, or space planetary rover and send them out without any contact. You'd keep some kind of watch over them, perhaps using remote wireless communication. And yes, there are multiple stories from various cultures that we still have. The Creation Story describes a planetary terraforming process that most people are familiar with."

"I've never heard of that before." I objected.

Hernandez held up her hand and explained, "Most people know the Adam & Eve creation story from the book of Genesis in the Bible. There are two more accounts in the Book of Abraham and Book of Moses. And a fourth version is in our temple ceremony. The book of Moses hints that the terraforming process was first planned in advance. Abraham says that it was accomplished by 'celestial engineers' if you will. The story talks about gradually getting the planet ready, first using plants, then lower forms of life, then humans. Adam and Eve first found themselves on a world that was a harsh wasteland, and only in the Garden of Eden was it possible to survive. There are accounts of automated sprinkling systems that watered the plants. Who knows, but perhaps they first lived in a controlled environment or habitat until the technology started to break down and they had to figure out how to live outside using local resources and their own sweat and tears. The Genesis creation story figuratively talks about seven days, but the other accounts hint that it might have taken eons to terraform Earth."

The food started to arrive, so I carefully picked up Doei's paper and all the scribbled notes and returned them to the envelope.

"Okay," I said as I slipped the fat envelope into the pouch behind my back, "That kind of brings us back to the Hebrew regalia. What was the gold-paged book with hieroglyphic characters?"

Dr. Hernandez explained, "That is the original ancient record that Joseph Smith translated into the *Book of Mormon* using the Urim & Thummim and small seer stone. The *Book of Mormon* is a history of a branch of Hebrew people called the Nephites who broke off and came to the Americas, and it can be found online. 'Mormon' was the name of one of the authors of that volume of history. In that ancient record, there's an account of a ship builder named Hagoth, who built many ships that launched into the Pacific Ocean. There's a theory that the South Pacific and Polynesian peoples originally came from Hagoth, and that one of several Japanese origin theories include these Pacific cultures. All along these migrating groups may have remembered the Urim & Thummim, Liahona, and Sword of Laban that the Nephites treasured in America. This could be the deep cultural memory that produced the Japanese Imperial Regalia. The interesting thing about the gold plates was that they were written in Hebrew, borrowing the Egyptian hieroglyphics as the written medium."

I looked over at Heebs and he smiled back at me with a wink.

"You mentioned the seer stone. I think I saw that — it spelled out instructions for me. I got the impression that hiding the artifacts in that exact spot would protect them, but Spaulding got them anyway." I noted.

"Were they not protected? If Spaulding hadn't actually taken them, he wouldn't have gotten what he deserves. Maybe you were instructed to put the artifacts in that location so Spaulding could easily find them and thus incriminate himself. You can't outguess how things will turn out, especially when people's free agency is involved." Hernandez pointed out.

Finally, after a long break where everyone enjoyed their food, Heebs had the last question, "We saved all the other Hebrew regalia, but where was the Sword of Laban? Is it true that the Japanese Kusanagi-no-tsurugi was actually the real Sword of Laban?"

Dr. Hernandez smiled and leaned back in her chair after taking a bite from her hamburger, "Funny you should ask. But first one correction — these are only 'Hebrew regalia' of one branch of the House of Israel. We think there are more Urim & Thummim out there. And remember, no one has found the Ark of the Covenant yet. Has anyone met the real Indiana Jones?"

Everyone let out a chuckle. The Professor took a few more bites of her burger. We were all fully engaged in our meals by that time.

Hernandez finally looked up again and said, "Hmm — the Sword of Laban. There are other older stories about treasured swords in Israel lore. For example, the sword of

Goliath, that David took after slaying the giant, was one of David's prized possessions, and became an article of kingship of sorts for subsequent kings. We don't know what happened to that sword of Goliath. But seeing how Laban ended up with many cultural treasures of the Jews, some speculate that the Sword of Laban was actually that same sword from Goliath. According to Church lore, the golden plates, Urim & Thummim, Liahona, and Sword of Laban were all given back to a heavenly being after the translation was finished. But there are many of us who have believed that anything that was made here on Earth would have stayed here, kept in a safe place. The general public think they are out of our hands, to keep curious folks from prying too deeply. But with your help, and no thanks to Spaulding, we now know the safe place was here all along. As for the sword, we have a team of archaeologists at BYU that work on stuff like this. I got a call from one of my colleagues just the other day. They had been using ground-penetrating radar on old mounds and hills around the upstate New York area and found an underground volume that was a little too squared off and regular to be natural."

The Professor paused and reached down for her purse which was hanging off the back of her chair. She pulled out a photograph and slid it over in my direction. It wasn't very clear, but it looked like a long object mostly wrapped in some leather protective covering. It was like having a Deja vu moment — what looked like a sword hilt was partly visible. The wrapped artifact was sitting on a table, with stacks of rectangular objects scattered about.

Hernandez continued, "The team drilled a core down and used a pressurized tent to fill the volume with inert gas to preserve the contents from decay. This photo was taken by an endoscope immediately afterwards. The team plans on widening the access shaft, and they want to first do a noninvasive LIDAR mapping of the chamber."

That got my attention. All sorts of things went through my head regarding what sorts of scanning instruments would need to ride on such a LIDAR mapper drone. Then I got to thinking about who in the surveying / mapper world would be capable of doing the task correctly.

"Do you want the job?" Dr. Patricia Hernandez asked.

My mind began reeling — it sounded like a fantastic opportunity, branching off in a direction I hadn't tried before. I had lost my own drone, but I was ready for an upgrade anyway. Maybe I could team up with Captain Alyosha Nephus at some point.

But the thing that I couldn't get over was the idea that these ancient artifacts existed in the first place. Whether the Urim & Thummim or Liahona were really Silurian civilization technology, or the seer stone actually functioned as an entangled information-dense pipeline from an advanced race of celestial engineers could still be a matter of speculation. It was a strange mix of science and religion that I had never heard before. But the very existence of programmable biological machinery that we all witness everyday was the most astounding 'Antikythera mechanism' of all! How could we have all been so blind? Space colonization and planetary terraforming using modular, programmable self-replicating factory blocks to fill out a biosphere, and all the celestial engineers had to do was to fax instructions to the molecular assembly lines using hijacked paths of entanglement. Mind blown!

Should I take the job, or run away from this madness? I looked over at Ines who was nodding her head with a smile.

"Yes — count me in!" I replied eagerly.

EPILOGUE

Around midnight, a maintenance robot in the Kokura Station Hotel in Kitakyushu Japan finished cleaning the floor of the business center and began wiping the tabletops. Near one of the computer workstations overlooking the concourse below, the robot found a stack of papers neatly stapled on the upper left-hand corner. It was an article written by Gilbert Fulmer from 1983 titled, *Cosmological Implications of Time Travel.* The maintenance robot had no capacity to understand that the Fulmer treatise was an argument about how any sufficiently advanced race who had mastered time travel, would likely not resist the temptation to travel back in time to guarantee the causal roots of their existence. The robot was programmed to pick up wadded papers, scraps, and refuse and put them in the incinerator chute. But books, writing instruments, electronics, and other items would need to be turned in to the front desk in case a customer came looking for a lost possession.

The maintenance robot carried the article over to where Joe was silently waiting. Joe's photoreceptors made a record of the top page, then it picked up the article with its hand-like manipulators for deposit into a lost & found bin. Items in the bin would be kept for 30 days, after which they would be dumped in the incinerator.

3 million years later Fulmer's article was long gone and forgotten. On a space station orbiting a distant planet, a council of terraformers gathered to discuss recent developments with some of the colony worlds.

"There's an era of unrest on Ma'adim, with continuous warfare among our children living there." The Council Manager reported.

The Council Manager knew that 'Ma'adim' would eventually be called 'Mars'.

The Council Manager's physical appearance was human, but three thousand millennia of gradual genetic improvement and natural progression resulted in a body exuding light and energy, connecting to enormous amounts of information exchanges. In short, this advanced being had eons ago grown into a state where all the matter in his person had naturally adapted into a computational substrate. He was a living Urim & Thummim.

"This is the unfortunate fate of many of the younger worlds — they destroy themselves as soon as they achieve a bit of technological advancement." Noted the First Councilor, who shared the Manager's blindingly brilliant countenance.

The Manager wished that the day's business would have been less stressful, such as adding asteroid and comet material to a smaller body until it achieved a target gravitational mass or seeding extremophiles in geothermal lakes. Even a populated world with governments operating according to lawful frameworks based on liberty and protecting the inalienable rights of their citizens would have been welcome.

"How long does this era last?" asked the Second Councilor.

Each of the members of the council, also advanced beings of light, turned to face the Manager.

"It's about a hundred local years." The Manager began, "At the end of the hundred years, all humanity will be lost from Ma'adim. We'll need to find as many among them who will listen to us, whom we can lead away from the destruction."

Feeling deep sadness for the loss of so many children, the First Councilor queried, "What will you have us do to make sure the hundred-year era ends most satisfactorily?"

Many solutions would be available to them. On the one hand they could visit the people of Ma'adim in force and take away their weapons. But such a solution would deprive them of their agency, which was not allowed. Unfortunately, those who were determined to trod a path of destruction would find another way to do so. Perhaps the most merciful action the council could do would be to allow natural disasters to take the children first, before they had an opportunity to raise their hand against a neighbor. When the hundred-year era ends, and the bio-mechanical bodies of all those billions of children cease to function, their operating software will be called home to dwell in peace and self-reflection.

The Manager instructed, "Use the medium of Ke-e'ban-raš to visit the beginning of the era, then go back and forth in time as needed to find those who might be willing to listen to our warnings. Find a good location for them to avoid the destruction of Ma'adim. Let us adjourn now, then come back and report your progress."

Going back and forth in time, manipulating events, naturally spawned numerous parallel alternate universes that all needed to be cleaned up and taken care of. The meeting took a short break, while the council members all executed their part of the plan. The hundred-year period on Ma'adim was long ago, over 3,002,348 years previous. Ke-e'ban-raš was a system of wormholes that connected powerful black hole power generation plants, stellar white holes, and even accommodated transportation between distant locations in the universe. The First Councilor used the Ke-e'ban-raš network and expanded an appropriate primordial quantum wormhole that went back 3,002,348 years to go visit Ma'adim.

The First Councilor could not speak to the inhabitants of Ma'adim face-to-face for several reasons. First, the amount of raw energy exuded by the dense computational substrate of his Urim & Thummim body would be too great for the children to withstand — if he were to actually visit them, even the metals and plastics and stone making up their buildings would melt in the fervent heat.

Secondly, he wouldn't be able to filter the energy in order to speak with them via a projection. Though technically possible, such a projection would alert the inhabitants to the existence of technologies beyond their own, and perhaps give them ideas that could lead to the misuse of knowledge without having explored the ethics and consequences of its use. No, projections could only be used in special cases, and only after extensive forward and backward time travel studies where al parallel timelines spawned because of the projection are cross-checked for causal paradoxes.

Instead, the First Councilor would have to contact each person individually, by editing neuron molecular entanglements for cortical stimulation, or regulating levels of dopamine, oxytocin, serotonin, and endorphins. In other words, 'inspiration'.

The 'inspiration' process was time-consuming, but usually yielded positive results with zero causal paradoxical risk. But for a being that had unlimited time and could travel forward or backwards at will, the eternal nature of 'inspiration' could be accomplished easily. One had to monitor the subject through situational awareness obtained by borrowed entanglements in the environment. When the subject makes an observation that forwards the goal of the 'inspirer', artificial remote cortical stimulation and endorphin increases spur the subject onward to make more positive observations, all on their own free will.

One had to begin at a young age, 'inspiring' the child to feel good when they do the right thing or have a euphoric 'aha' moment when they make a breakthrough.

Unfortunately, there were situations that tended to deaden the reception of 'inspiration'. Drugs and substance abuse tended to hijack the pleasure mechanisms built into the biomechanical bodies of the settlers on Ma'adim, so it became more and more difficult to hear the 'inspiration'. And again unfortunately, those who chose to abandon themselves to such abuse, also tended to be less receptive of 'inspiration' and could also exacerbate self-destructive tendencies. Ma'adim had become a world full of such wayward children.

The First Councilor moved forward and backward along the hundred-year timeline but out of billions of children, very few would listen.

A short time later the council met again, and the First Councilor gave his report, "I have found a man named Noah who has a wife and three married sons. The entire family will listen to our council."

The Manager remembered his child Noah and was pleased with the choice. The Manager and other council members had the astounding capacity to know all of their trillions of children on countless planetary colonies.

The Manager was heartbroken and asked, "Is that all? Are there no others?"

The First Councilor looked down in sadness but could not say anymore.

The Manager had hope regarding his child Noah and wondered, "Where can we send Noah's family?"

The First Councilor replied, "There is another planet nearby called Jah-oh-eh that is suitable. We already have small Chinese, Indian, and African outposts there."

The Manager remembered that Jah-oh-eh would eventually have other names, like Terra, or Earth.

The Manager ordered, "Have Noah build a ship that can carry his family from Ma'adim to Jah-oh-eh. The biosphere on Jah-oh-eh is not as complete as Ma'adim, so instruct Noah to gather representative male and female pairs of each phylogenetic animal group, along with cryopreserved embryos. Instruct Noah to collect as many human embryos from the varied races as he can find donors."

The Second Councilor asked, "Is there any direct assistance approved for Noah? Or must we keep ourselves hidden from the family?"

"Construct two Urim & Thummim handheld units that can interface with the Ke-e'ban-raš network to help bring light and power into the ship. Instruct Noah to keep them sacred from his family and others — they should only be seen by Noah and our chosen representative after he dies." The Manager instructed.

Portable Trim & Thummim were small password-protected devices that linked into the Ke-e'ban-raš network, equivalent to modern-day human smartphones, except that they had millions of years of advanced technology built into them.

It was a standing rule that if an Urim & Thummim were to be given to any of the children of men, it should be used properly, carefully guarded, and taboos attached unless the children use it for destructive purposes. For their own protection, the colony children must not know about the council, or the vast interstellar community, or any technology unless it is learned by themselves, lest some one of them misuse the knowledge without understanding the consequences.

The First Councilor worried about how to sustain Noah on the new world, "Jah-oh-eh is without technology. If the family grows and multiplies for several generations and spreads out on the planet, the ship and their technology will not work anymore. There won't be enough time to establish a sufficient manufacturing economy. The ship will eventually decay and go away. The children of Noah will forget us and turn to primitive hunting and farming, spending all their time occupied with finding sustenance."

The Manager replied, "We need to inspire a system of religions, oaths, covenants, and traditions that primitive peoples will understand and tend to remember until they crawl back out of darkness, and we visit them once more."

The council adjourned again, in order to execute the new parts of the plan. That period in the history of Ma'adim and Jah-oh-eh had many asteroids and comets intersecting the planet orbits. Also, the planetary orbits were not as stabilized at that time. The 'crossing star' called ṅgah, which would eventually also carry the name 'Venus', travelled all over the sky. Moving forward and backward in time using the Ke-e'ban-raš network, the First Councilor verified that the vast populations of Ma'adim would destroy themselves from nuclear war but could be saved from the worst parts of it through natural disasters. The council calculated that ṅgah would pass close by both Ma'adim and Jah-oh-eh, causing planet-wide flooding events. Generations of Noah's children having reverted back to primitives, would be confused about the floods on two worlds, with non-technical peoples modifying true accounts into stories and myths of an ocean-going ark rather than a planetary ship.

A while later the council met again. The hundred-year era was watched, and Noah's family relocated, but countless children were lost, and their operating software brought home. The council grieved that so many would choose not to listen to the council's guidance but choose destructive paths instead.

The Manager stood up and asked about the post hundred-year era, "There are only representative phyla in the biosphere of Jah-oh-eh now. Has Noah and his family been active causing in-vitro births among the animals? How long does it take for the humans to use up their embryos to revive the genetic diversity through in-vitro births?"

The First Councilor replied, "Noah's family uses up all the animal and human embryos after fifty years, which is about the time the technology begins to malfunction and break down. After this time, we can freely vary the animal phyla in the biosphere without Noah's children discovering our presence."

The Manager gave one last set of instructions, "Proceed to locate various animal phyla as they multiply and replenish Jah-oh-eh, and cause variations to occur that can fill out all the ecosystems."

The council members used the Ke-e'ban-raš network to expand primordial quantum wormholes that were entangled with molecular machinery in the germ cells of representative animal phyla females on Jah-oh-eh. The council used the network and entanglements to 'fax' instructions that would gradually cause births with the greatest number of allele variations. CRISPR-like technology, already present in the cells, allowed for remote gene editing and engineering. Some organisms, like bacteria or mosquitoes that had hitched a ride to Jah-oh-eh on Noah's ship, were 'faxed' instructions for modifying viruses that could be transferred horizontally and modify germ cells. In this way gene drives could be utilized to modify entire populations according to the council's designs. Insects designed to inoculate genetic updates into germ cell coding could be deployed and Noah's posterity would think it natural. Using the Ke-e'ban-raš network, all this was done in a matter of hours or days according to Council time, because they could quickly move back and forth along the timeline to cause a change, then immediately view the fruits of their labors hundreds of Jah-oh-eh years later.

The council met one last time regarding the troublesome era in Ma'adim's and Jah-oh-eh history.

The First Councilor reported, "Full diversity was achieved in all biosphere ecosystems on Jah-oh-eh. Ma'adim was wiped clean of humanity and may again be colonized when the time is right. We will next work to stabilize the orbits of ngah and the other planets of that era."

The saving of their child Noah and the remnant of the populations of Ma'adim was complete. Other troublesome eras in Jah-oh-eh's history would undoubtedly need to be addressed in later meetings. The Manager excused the council until the next time.

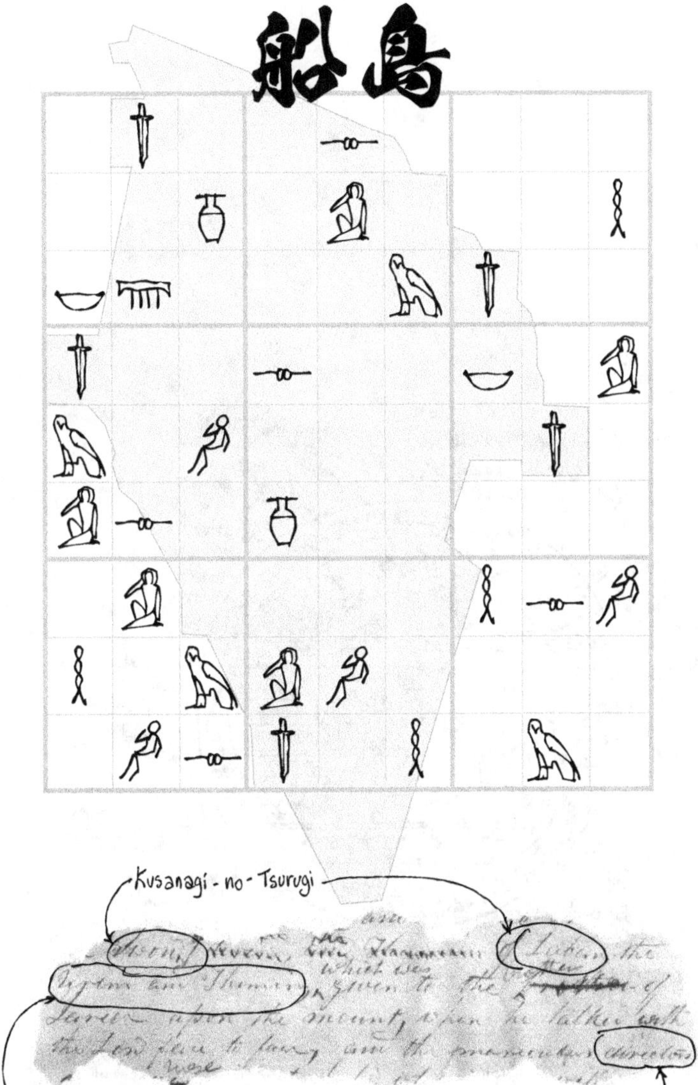

船島

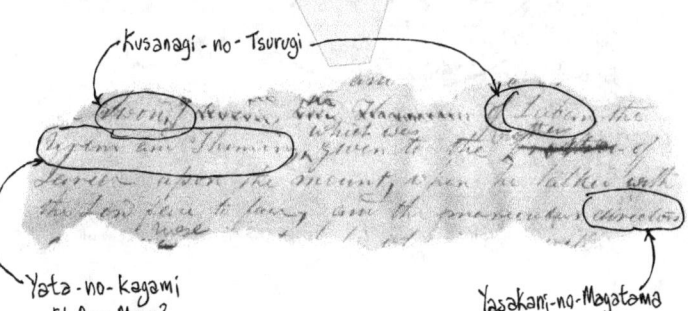

Kusanagi - no - Tsurugi

Yata - no - Kagami
- El Gran Moxo?
- Quantum Holographic Encoding
  (Moon Et Al 2009)
- Computing power of a rock (Kurzweil 2005 p131)

Yasakani - no - Magatama
- Silurian Hypothesis
- Antikythera Mechanism
- Liahona

wi3 n bb (rāgi'ya RAUKEEYANG)
1000 Cubit boat of a million years,
(solar boat) generation ship

wn-nb-n-iśw (Oliblish)
- Stellar White Hole
q3b (Qarob)
CELESTIAL ENGINEER
Eternal Light/life
  - self-replication
  - Code of the lifemaker
  - Advanced automation
    for space missions
- Craig Venter (2010)
  - Life at the speed
    of light
  - genetic code
    'wow' signal
    (Shcherbak 2013)
- Message (Hsu/Zee 2006)

Space-faring Colonizers
  - 50-year window (2016)
THRONE OF THE ENGINEER
ORBITING QAROB

Eternal progression
of humankind

i3ht
(Jah-oh-eh TERRA)
Terraforming four Quarters

wnś-s3 - 'Iwnw - t3ś (Sol)
- Stellar White Hole
  - Holographic Schwinger Effect (Sauter 2013)
  - EPR Pair Temporal Loops
  - Gilbert Fulmer (1983)

3h3h (Hakkokābīm):
q-ri-prw.s-3st (Sagittarius A* Major)
nb-gri (Sagittarius A* Minor)
uses Q3(i)-pn-rś(y) (Ke-'ebau-raś)
exalted Key gateway power source
  - Wormhole Enlargement (Krasnov 2002)

Dear reader: Hirayuki Doei researched the Egyptian hypocephalus, and found various articles and scientific papers that backed up his theories of what it all meant. The list below includes Doei's references and additional material found by the Hughes family. The following references are all real except for a few fictional links that were needed to keep the story flowing well. All fictional references are labeled as 'fictional reference'.

Hirayuki Doei's technical references:

- Sudoku puzzle overlaid on Funajima map
- Manuscript remnant: Revelation, June 1829-E [D&C 17] Page 119. The Joseph Smith Papers. https://www.josephsmithpapers.org/paper-summary/revelation-june-1829-e-dc-17/1
- Japanese Imperial Regalia. https://en.wikipedia.org/wiki/Imperial_Regalia_of_Japan
- Schmidt, Frank (2018). The Silurian Hypothesis: Would it be possible to detect an industrial civilization in the geological record? *International Journal of Astrobiology*, Volume 18, Number 2, pp142-150. https://arxiv.org/abs/1804.03748
- Antikythera Mechanism. https://en.wikipedia.org/wiki/Antikythera_mechanism
- S Csizi (2014). Gran Moxo Világító Gömbje (The Illuminated Sphere of Gran Moxo). *Titkos Történelem: Fejezetek Az Emberiség Elfeledett Évezredeiből* (translated from Hungarian: Secret History: Chapters on the Forgotten Millennium of Humanity), Kategória: Ösi Technológia (Category: Ancient Technology). http://titkostortenelem.org/osi-technologia/30-gran-moxo-vilagito-goembje
- Liahona. https://en.wikipedia.org/wiki/Liahona_(Book_of_Mormon)
- Hieroglyphic hypocephalus imprint: Book of Abraham, Facsimile 2. *Pearl of Great Price.* https://www.churchofjesuschrist.org/study/scriptures/pgp/abr/fac-2?lang=eng

- DR Hurst (2002). Pearl of Great Price: Facsimile 2. *Facsimiles: Book of Abraham*. http://www.freeenglishsite.com/LDS/PofGP/Facsimile2.htm
- J Gee; WJ Hamblin; DC Peterson (2005). Chapter 1: 'And I saw the stars': The book of Abraham and ancient geocentric astronomy. In J Gee & BM Hauglid (eds), *Astronomy, Papyrus, and Covenant*, pp1-16. Provo, Utah, USA: Foundation for Ancient Research and Mormon Studies, Brigham Young University.
- Ke-'eban_raš (grand key of power, gateway power source). *Book of Mormon Onomasticon*. https://onoma.lib.byu.edu/index.php/KAE-E-VANRASH
- Raukeeyang (million-year solar boat). *Book of Mormon Onomasticon*. https://onoma.lib.byu.edu/index.php/RAUKEEYANG
- Hakkōkābīm, Jah-oh-eh, Oliblish, Qarob: all searchable in the *Book of Mormon Onomasticon*. https://onoma.lib.byu.edu/index.php/Main_Page
- J Sonner (2013). Holographic Schwinger Effect and the Geometry of Entanglement. *Physical Review Letters*, Volume 111, 211603. https://arxiv.org/abs/1307.6850
- H Koyama; SA Hayward; SW Kim (2003). Construction and Enlargement of Dilatonic Wormholes by Impulsive Radiation. *Physical Review D*, Volume 67, 084008. doi: 10.1103/PhysRevD.67.084008, https://arxiv.org/abs/gr-qc/0212106
- (author? date?). EPR Pair Temporal Loops: Primordial Closed Timelike Curves? (Note: this is a fictional reference)
- Murakami (date?). Stellar White Holes: Einstein-Rosen Bridges to Galactic Core Singularities. (Note: this is a fictional reference)
- G Fulmer (1983). Chapter 3: Cosmological Implications of Time Travel. In RE Mayers (ed), *The Intersection of Science Fiction and Philosophy: Critical Studies*, pp31-44. Westport, Connecticuit, USA: Greenwood Press.
- RA Freitas; WP Gilbreath (1980). *Advanced automation for space missions*. Proceedings of the 1980 NASA / ASEE summer study (Conference publication 2255). Washington DC: NASA Scientific and Technical Information Branch.
- R Kurzweil (2005). *The Singularity Is Near*. New York, New York, USA: Viking Penguin.

- C Moon; L Matteo's; B Foster; G Zeltzer; H Manoharan (2009). Quantum Holographic Encoding in a Two-dimensional Electron Gas. *Nature Technology*, Vol 4, pp167-172.
- doi: 10.1038/nnano.2008.415
- JP Hogan (1983). *Code of the Lifemaker*. Riverside, New Jersey, USA: Baen Books.
- AS Howe (2015). 50-year Window to Establish a Space Faring Civilization (AIAA-2015-4565). *AIAA Space 2015 Conference & Exhibition*, Pasadena, California, USA, 31 Aug – 2 Sep 2015. Reston, Virginia, USA: American Institute of Aeronautics and Astronautics.
- DG Gibson; JC Venter; et al (2010). Creation of a Bacterial Cell Controlled by a Chemically Synthesized Genome. *Science*, Volume 329, Number 5987, pp52-56. doi: 10.1126/science.1190719
- JC Venter (2013). *Life at the Speed of Light*. New York, New York, USA: Penguin Books.
- S Hsu; A Zee (2006). Message in the Sky. *Modern Physics Letters A*, Volume 21, Number 19, pp1495-1500. doi: 10.1142/S0217732306020834, https://arxiv.org/abs/physics/0510102
- V shCherbak; M Makukov (2013). The 'Wow! signal' of the terrestrial genetic code. *Icarus*, Volume 224, Number 1, pp228-242. doi: 10.1016/j.icarus.2013.02.017, https://arxiv.org/abs/1303.6739

Further references found by Professor Hughes and the Hughes siblings:

- (author? date?) pamphlet on Japanese origins (Note: this is a fictional pamphlet based on actual historical data)
- (author? date?) pamphlet on Ise Shrine (Note: this is a fictional pamphlet based on actual historical data)
- (author? date?) story about Ninigi-no-Mikoto (Note: this is a fictional pamphlet based on actual historical data)
- Yamato People (2019). Imperial Regalia of Japan / Three Treasures / Sanshu no Jingi. https://yamatopeople.blogspot.com/2019/05/imperial-regalia-of-japan-three.html
- Yata-no-kagami: The Mirror of Yata. https://www.boloji.com/articles/14809/yata-no-kagami-the-mirror-of-yata

- Z Oyabe (1929). The Origin of Japan and the Japanese People. Tokyo. As described in Japanese Author Traces Nippon Origin to Hebrew Race. *Jewish Telegraphic Agency*. https://www.jta.org/archive/japanese-author-traces-nippon-origin-to-hebrew-race
- A Murakami (2016). *An Epic Tale of the People of the Covenant.*
- BA Shillony (1992). *The Jews and the Japanese: The Successful Outsiders.* Rutland, Vermont, USA: Charles E Tuttle Publishing Co, Inc.
- AE Smith (1949). *Comparative Study of Judaism and Shinto.* University of the Pacific, Thesis. https://scholarlycommons.pacific.edu/uop_etds/1089
- C Van Dam (1997). *The Urim and Thummim: A Means of Revelation in Ancient Israel.* University Park, Pennsylvania, USA: Penn State University Press.
- S Jacobovici (2014). Japanese Jewish Connection. *The Times of Israel.* https://blogs.timesofisrael.com/japanese-jewish-connection/
- John D (2014). Jewish Connection. *Green Shinto.* https://www.greenshinto.com/wp/2014/08/29/jewish-connection/
- K Thorne (1991). Do the Laws of Physics Permit Closed Timelike Curves? Nonlinear Problems in Relativity and Cosmology: *Proceedings of the 6th Florida Workshop in Nonlinear Astronomy*, Gainesvile, 2-4 Oct 1990. A92-17951 05-90. New York Academy of Sciences, Annals (ISSN 0077-8923), 10 Aug 1991, Vol 631, pp182-193. doi:10.1111/j.1749-6632.1991.tb52642.x
- M Visser (2002). The Quantum Physics of Chronology Protection. *The Future of Theoretical Physics and Cosmology*, conference in honor of Professor Stephen Hawking on the occasion of his 60th birthday. arXiv:gr-qc/0204022
- M Van Raamsdonk (2010). Building up spacetime with quantum entanglement. *International Journal of Modern Physics D*, Volume 19, Number 14, pp2429-2435. doi: 10.1142/S0218271810018529, https://arxiv.org/abs/1005.3035
- P Koiran (2021). Infall time in the Eddington-Finkelstein metric, with application to Einstein-Rosen Bridges. *International Journal of Modern Physics D*. doi: 10.1142/S0218271821501066, https://arxiv.org/pdf/2110.05938.pdf

- JM Diamond (1997). *Guns, Germs, and Steel: The Fates of Human Societies*. New York, New York, USA: WW Norton & Company.
- RA Freitas; RC Merkle (2004). *Kinematic Self-Replicating Machines*. Georgetown, Texas, USA: Landes Bioscience.
- M Beech (2009). *Terraforming: The Creating of Habitable Worlds*. New York, New York, USA: Springer.
- M Fogg (1995). *Terraforming: Engineering Planetary Environments*. Warrendale, Pennsylvania, USA: Society of Automotive Engineers.

Biomechanical 3D metal printers, motors, jet propulsion:

- D Quicke; P Wyeth; J Fawke; H Basibuyuk; J Vincent (1998). Manganese and Zinc in the Ovipositors and Mandibles of Hymenopterous Insects. *Zoological Journal of the Linnean Society*, Volume 124, Issue 4, pp387-396. doi: 10.1111/j.1096-3642.1998.tb00583
- W Wang; S Li; L Mair; S Ahmed; T Huang; T Mallouk; (2014). Acoustic Propulsion of Nanorod Motors Inside Living Cells. *Angewandte Chimie*. doi: 10.1002/ange.201309629
- P Krueger; A Moslemi; J Nichols; I Bartol; W Stewart (2008). Vortex Ring in Bio-inspired and Biological Jet Propulsion. *Advances in Science and Technology*, Volume 58, Sep 2008, pp237-246. doi: 10.4028/www.scientific.net/AST.58.237
- Y Konishi; T Tsukiyama; T Tachimi; N Saitoh; T Nomura; S Nagamine (2007). Microbial Deposition of Gold Nanoparticles by the Metal-reducing Bacterium Shewanella Algae. *Electrochimica Acta*, Volume 53, Issue 1, 20 Nov 2007, pp186-192. doi: 10.1016/j.electacta.2007.02.073
- C Broomell; M Mattoni; F Zok; J Waite (2007). Critical Role of Zinc in Hardening of Nereis Jaws. *Journal of Experimental Biology*, Volume 209, pp3219-3225. doi: 10.1242/jeb.02373

Links:

White holes:
https://www.space.com/white-holes.html
https://en.m.wikipedia.org/wiki/White_hole

Sagittarius A*
https://www.space.com/milky-way-monster-black-hole-cool-disk.html
https://en.m.wikipedia.org/wiki/Sagittarius_A*

Hieroglyphic phonetic alphabet:
https://aegyptonline.weebly.com/hieroglyphics.html
http://www.paleoaliens.com/event/hieroglyphics/translator/index.html

Vimanas ancient spacecraft India:
https://www.crystalinks.com/vimanas.html
http://veda.wikidot.com/ancient-sanskrit-from-india-tell-of-ufo-visit

Granite Mountain Records Vault:
https://www.ldsliving.com/elder-renlund-shares-whats-inside-the-churchs-underground-vault/s/81066
https://mysteryofutahhistory.blogspot.com/2020/04/the-mystery-of-granite-record-facility.html?m=1
https://thirdhour.org/blog/faith/family-history/mountain-records-vault/

ABOUT THE AUTHOR

A. Scott Howe is a retired senior engineer from NASA Jet Propulsion Laboratory and has two PhDs (in architecture and robotic construction systems). He continues to be involved with space industry efforts to build long-duration human habitats for deep space, and permanent outposts for the moon and Mars.

Look for these other science fiction novels by A. Scott Howe:

Waterball (2012)

Blister (2013)

Chronosphere (2014)

Replicycle / Retrocause (2023)